Magic Pen Book of the Year Nominee!

"Lazris doesn't sell out to PC agendas, and is willing to shoehorn his own, firsthand perspective, political points of view, and distinct brands of thought into the mix. The result is something that feels uncommonly fresh. Lazris just cuts through the crap and delivers something bighearted and unafraid of its potential provocations of inquiry."

Praise from San Francisco Book Review!

"I couldn't get enough of the intricate, thrilling plot of January 6th and the Millennial Horde.... The book's characters are the type you love and hate at the same time, which reflects the sort of duality that exists in a situation involving bad deeds carried out by well-meaning people."

Online Book Club Book of the year nominee!

"I did not dislike anything about the book. It was flawless and exceptionally well edited. I found the story's flow to be compelling, and the book's events perfectly merged, thus attracting all my attention. Although fictitious, the story seemed natural because of the nerve-chilling mystery scenes in the book. Therefore, I will rate it 4 out of 4 stars."

January 6th and
the Millennial Horde

Andy Lazris

Great Writers Media
Email: info@greatwritersmedia.com
Phone: 877-600-5469

ISBN: 978-1-960605-04-7 (sc)
ISBN: 978-1-960605-05-4 (ebk)

CNN
Truth
Stop! Misinformation
Save! Democracy

Introduction

In the most celebrated episode of the original *Star Trek*, "The City on the Edge of Forever," Captain Kirk travels back in time and rescues a woman named Edith Keeler from an oncoming car. By saving her, Kirk condemns humanity to its own destruction, as her survival is the human race's death. What makes the episode so intriguing is that Edith Keeler is not a villain, just the opposite in fact; she's a do-gooder, a peace lover, a person who has devoted herself to the betterment of humankind. But as she lived during the dawn of the Second World War, which is when she was supposed to die, her continued life allows her to ferment and grow an anti-war movement that blocks America's entry into the war, leading to a Nazi victory and the world's end. As Spock says, she was a good person at the wrong time.

Many books and TV series explore alternative fictional histories, like *Star Trek*, focusing their lens on the Nazi period. In *The Plot Against America*, Philip Roth envisions what could have happened had Charles Lindbergh defeated Roosevelt for president, showing how decent people can become anti-Semites and dogmatic opponents of democracy under the right conditions. And in *The Man in the High Castle*, a TV series on Amazon Prime, we see what the world looks like if the Germans won the war, with good-guy American Joe in one reality becoming hedonistic Nazi Joe in another. What makes all these visions intriguing is how they explore scenarios in which people may be good, innocuous souls under normal circumstances, but become villains or unwitting accomplices to horrific outcomes in another.

This book is my third fictional attempt to dissect the era of COVID, during which our own nation morphed into a dystopian reality eerily similar to the books and shows listed earlier. As a front-line doctor during COVID, an author of several nonfiction books about the virus and our response to it, and a liberal who studies the vicissitudes of history, I watched helplessly as everything that I cherish and value became fodder for the dogmatic power of alleged experts who tore our world to shreds under the manufactured banner of *Scientific Necessity*. Those who demanded that we follow science proselytized just the opposite, draping us with deceptive lies and rituals that led us down a road of religious devotion, which stomped on any semblance of science and humanism. Those who stood on the mantle of pro-choice preached just the opposite when it came to COVID, insisting that no American should have a choice when it came to masks and vaccines and how they lived their very lives. Those who decried the events of January 6th as being the most egregious assault on freedom and democracy in our generation simultaneously praised governors and scientists and our president for stripping Americans of their most basic constitutional rights, including that of free speech, assembly, religious worship, and the right to life, liberty, and the pursuit of happiness.

I watched in horror as the leaders, journalists, and doctors with whom I had felt an allegiance shoved our nation into a dark abyss of theocratic absolutism. As a doctor on the front line and someone who has studied COVID and the many fantastical claims made about it by these self-proclaimed experts, I was forced to helplessly watch public health officials, TV doctors, and political leaders dismantle science and concoct a manufactured narrative of fear that left hundreds of thousands of vulnerable people dead and millions of lives ruined, breaking their Hippocratic Oath as they relied on myth and snake-oils that fed their own power at the cost of human life. I understand the fragility of democracy and the need to protect choice, speech, and freedom no matter what calamity might befall us, and I trembled as those who claimed to be most devoted to democracy—liberals, progressive students, educated scientists— mutate our nation into a two-year hell of imprisonment, shaming, censorship, and lifeless bare existence, claiming to be promoting science and democracy as they decimated both.

CNN's team of propagandists—reporters I had relied on before COVID, reporters I truly respected— elevated Anthony Fauci into an unassailable god, labeled as "misinformation" anything that strayed from what I knew to be a fabricated and ultimately dangerous COVID script, exaggerated the impact of the virus while denying protection to those who most needed it and frighting the nonvulnerable in a prison of perturbation, and advocated censorship and what amounted to martial law across the country. By twisting the virus into a political tool and minimizing and enabling the real threat to our democracy (executive overreach, mandates, and censorship during COVID) while focusing instead on a transient threat (January 6th), our media and its selected group of self-serving doctors and scientists created a symbolic rallying cry against Trump and January 6th while mangling "science" and "truth" into their Orwellian opposites.

As the great philosopher Agamben said, our leaders and doctors took our lives away under the premise of saving them; they took our freedom away under the illusion of saving democracy. And none of the vitriol, falsehoods, and scientific butchery has yet to be completely undone. The thick air of COVID's maleficence remains with us and has transformed liberalism and science into their binary enemies, air so porous and toxic that not even their magical masks can block it.

What most fascinated and frightened me, though, was how quickly educated people simply fell prey to the gospel of COVID, questioning nothing, adhering to every ritual and falsehood as though it were written by God Himself. Many of my friends—with whom I share a general liberal/humanistic/scientific outlook on the world—became transformed into robotic nonthinking drones who berated any who dared question Anthony Fauci, who wore masks everywhere (even all alone in the car, for God's sake!), who were happy to close school and society and destroy any number of lives and institutions for a pandemic they believed was as pernicious as the Black Death, who cared not a whiff about the poor and youth and working people—who were severely injured by the oppressive and unnecessary quarantines—they had always claimed to care about, and who refused to look at any fact, labeling such truth as misinformation and dangerous right-wing conspiracy theories, all under the guise of scientific certainty.

These people, educated but clearly not smart, hypnotized by a narrative that bewitched them and flicked off the critical thinking and humanistic switches in their brains, became the Joes of *Man in the High Castle*, the anti-Semites of Phillip Roth's book, the progressive good-doers when times are good and Nazi-like sycophants happy to destroy society in the name of a myth during the era of COVID. They are Edith Keeler, good people at the wrong time, whose purported single-minded purity did more damage to the world than January sixth ever could. It is this phenomenon that triggered my desire to write this book.

In my first two books on COVID, I tackled the era of COVID in different ways. Both books were musical; I wrote ten songs for each to provide a three-dimensional texture to the stories.

Geriatrics Vengeance Club follows semi-autobiographical geriatric doctor Ben Polton as he tries to save his elderly patients from the ravages of COVID terror during the first year of the pandemic, only to be stripped of his license (something that almost happened to me just for stating a fact about the virus on social media) and deprived of his right to speak lest his "facts" verge from the Faucist gospel. Ultimately, in a fictional flare, he writes songs for some of his former patients and goes on a mask-free concert tour of the country, finally realizing that the only way to confront the madness of COVID and the perfidy of the medical establishment is to bolt from the world of convention and establish his own haven beyond the clutches of society's pinchers.

In *The Great Stupidity*, three travelers during the Black Death confront absurd religious figures, doctors, scientists, and zelous lunatics in a Monty Python-like adventure pitting common sense and decency against a dogmatic world of self-proclaimed experts. When Smith's town is devastated by plague despite doing everything that the priests and scientists told them would protect them, he goes on a quest to find the Great Frenchie and reconnect Saint Ambrose's nail, believing that to be the answer to the plague's wrath. The story, in which good and smart people face others whose versions of science, truth, and fact are blatantly absurd and lethal, compares responses to that truly devastating pandemic with our own similar medieval response to an exponentially less dangerous viral event.

In both books, I show that science and truth become their own enemies when dogmatic forces gain control of society and when fear becomes the primary spark that drives human behavior and belief.

This book creates an alternate reality much like in the shows and books I listed earlier. While characters in this book are loosely based on actual people, everything about them is fictionalized; the characters (even the real ones) are my own creations, not existing in the real world but rather in an alternative world disrupted by a shift that lights the tinder of fear and myth that COVID has laid for us. The book is wantonly violent, something that may unnerve some genteel readers, but it is no more violent than the masquerade of masking, lockdowns, forced vaccinations, school closings, censorship, martial law, medical butchery in the name of science, and an Orwellian definition of misinformation with which our leaders, doctors, and media have suffocated us for over two years, destroying lives under a thin veneer of faux science. To me, that type of violence is far more insidious and dangerous that the more overt violence in this book, and frankly it is time to reveal what is happening in a more blatant way, which is what I have tried to do.

I insert two fictional characters into society who are the fuel of the book's fire. Both are good and decent people who, were it not for COVID, likely would have been benign or at least innocuous players on the world stage. But because of their passion and their desire to promote goodness and a liberal-scientific agenda, because of their binary brains and their disdain for anyone who dares to take an opposing view to the one and only truth that they proclaim, these people irrevocably disrupt the world, altering lives and events in a way that brings out the worst in many and the best in some. Jim Depich, a congressman from Pittsburgh, is a scientist and a progressive who doesn't believe in the niceties of politics. He falls prey to the COVID myth and then, after January 6th, becomes a zealot in his war against those who threaten "science and democracy," tearing apart any and all people who see the world through a different lens; his is a dichotomous mind, one built with spreadsheets, one of good and evil, one bereft of nuance. Mary Lou Kramer is a college student who embraces noble progressive causes, but who similarly is willing to discard life and all semblance of decency when it comes to protecting the world from "reactionary forces "during COVID, dividing the world and all its people into the simple formula or right vs wrong, true vs false.

By adding these two Edith Keelers into a cauldron of madness, into a world whose flames of fear and mutual distrust were already burning bright, I envision how people would change in a reality now propelled by passion and dogmatism, by power and hate, by Orwellian conceptions of science and freedom. Most of the book's characters are, like I said, based on real people, but in this world, they are of my own creation, altered by the shift created by Jim and Mary Lou; their names are what Jim Depich calls them, as he has a nickname for everyone. And to weave a three-dimensional atmosphere into the words, I have hired a wonderful artist to create visual images of the accentuating madness. This is my *City on the Edge of Tomorrow*, my latest fictional attempt to make sense of a land that has gone off its hinges, one that has dropped us into a dark abyss, that has sullied so many people who I once believed to be allies and friends and demonstrated how little we can ever trust our media, doctors, and institutions again.

PART ONE

Cataclysm on Top of Catastrophe

CHAPTER ONE

Deepening Crisis, January 3, 2021

The world had gone to shit in an instant, and Jim Depich snarled as he pulled his Ford Bronco onto Route 376, his gut frayed from stress, wanting nothing more than to vent to anyone willing to listen.

He dialed a number, and a woman's voice answered. Jim riled off some diatribes, stomping on the gas pedal just a bit harder each time a four-letter word slid from his mouth. Finally, the woman cut him off.

"Are you wearing a mask, Jim?" she asked. "Because I can't hear anything you're saying to me."

In fact, he was. He bragged that he wore one 24/7, which he did in his district or in any spot of visibility where a detractor could snap his picture to prove him a liar. Since COVID hit the nation's shores, Jim put his stock with those who spoke in the language of science. He believed in choice, he said; representing a Western Pennsylvania district as a rare Democrat, he had to tread the line between libertarianism and social responsibility. So, he said to his constituents, he would wear the mask, in the car, even in his toilet, for Christ's sake, because he wanted this thing to go away, and he believed that you couldn't be too careful. But never would he force others to do the same. Jim took it upon himself to show how to be a good citizen but not coerce others to follow his path. As always, he led by example and by science.

As an engineer, a businessman, and Christian, his pragmatic science-focused individualistic ethos appealed to a typically Republican base and landed him in the House of Representatives for his second term, winning first during the Trump midterms against the sitting pro-Trump Republican congressman.

"Anyway," he said to the woman on the phone, sliding a Steelers mask from his face, "this is a total disaster. I can't even breathe. The worst thing that's happened to this country. And what will come of it? Will we learn? Will we make a change? Are we so deluded that we're just going to stay on the same course? Tell me, Corrine, tell me I'm not crazy; tell me someone is going to do something."

He was breathing hard, and the woman on the other end started to chuckle. "Had Buck not won in November, I'd think you were talking about politics, and had I not known you better than I do, I'd think you're talking about COVID policy. So tell me, Jim, is this about Sunday? Was that the catastrophe?"

Before going on, it's important to know that Jim Depich loves nicknames. His linguistic persona revolved around concocting a novel name for most human beings other than those closest to him; Corrine, Big Ben, his mom remained intact. But even the new President, Jim's guy, didn't go by his God-given name. As his first name was a word that meant coffee, Jim called him Star Buck, or President Buck. Such was the fate of all who fluttered through Jim's universe, and Jim's unique gaze will drive the naming of people in this version of Jim's short and impactful life.

"Of course, it's about Sunday," he shouted at the woman. "Don't minimize it, Corrine. We lost to Cleveland. Last game of the year, and we lose to Cleveland. Ben's too old. I love the guy, you know that, but he's got to go. We can't delude ourselves much longer. It's a fucking catastrophe!"

"We made the playoffs, and we'll probably be playing them again." She laughed. "Ben always shines in the playoffs. You're a man of faith, Jim! Have some faith in your guy."

"He's too old" was all Jim could say. "We should have canceled the damned season. Given him a rest. I'll tell you this much, Corrine. I'm not driving through Baltimore on the way home, seeing all those Ravens jerseys and how happy those bastards are. I'm not going to stew knowing we could have picked up Lamloser. Just an idiotic front office, that's what we have. We need fresh blood. If we lose to Cleveland again in the playoffs, mark my word, Corrine, it will be the darkest day in America."

"So glad this is the only thing that worries you!" his best friend and aide said to him. "Well, on a brighter note, Jim, all of us can't wait to see you. Wish you had been here on New Year's. Everyone was in their houses with masks watching TV. It was a great deal of fun. Just focus on the inauguration. Things are going to change. Finally! After four years of hell. Ben will take down Cleveland. Buck will right the country. It's all looking good! I'll even bet you on it."

"You don't lose to Cleveland and say it's all looking good," Jim snarled, with a small smile cocked on his narrow face. "But I'll take you up on that bet. You owe me a year of hugs if you lose!"

"You already have that from me, Jim!" she said. "And anything else you want! I'll do you one better. I know a guy who delivers those pretzels from Oil City, from that place you love. I'll get you a delivery every week. With mustard. So, just relax. I don't want you crashing on the way over here. Things are finally looking up in the world, and we need you. Have faith!"

Faith is something Jim Depich possessed in ample quantity. Still, something felt wrong in his gut.

Was it just the Steelers loss, another rocky season? Was it apprehension about the direction of COVID, about Buck's leadership and memory? Or was it something else?

Jim said his goodbyes and turned onto Route 70 for his long ride toward the swamp of DC; with a short detour on Route 270, he didn't have to go near the home of the Ravens, and so he did that. The final game of the season dug into his brain because the Steelers should have won! A younger Ben would have done the job. He was getting too old, and the organization needed to make a change.

But, yea, things were looking up in DC. Trump and his goonies would be gone, and the Dems had control of both houses. With some real scientists buttressing the great Doctor Fact-Nerd (who he also called the Science Tiger after Tony the Tiger from Frosted Flakes fame) in the White House, they'd finally have a chance to snuff out the pandemic that, had Hill-Top won the election, would have been eradicated by now. Jim sat on the health-care subcommittee, and while he was not about mandates and such, he was about financially punishing those states that failed to comply with science, about belittling and embarrassing the anti-science crowd who kept jumping down the science tiger's's shorts. He had written a bill on Christmas break that he believed would move the nation in the right direction on those scores.

But for the disastrous game on January 3 against Cleveland, his eyes peered forward in an optimistic haze. This would be the era of science. To Jim, a.k.a. Representative Spreadsheet, there was nothing in his mind that couldn't be studied, understood, and tabulated through the scientific tools he learned as an engineer. As he often said to his flock, give to God what is God's, and figure out everything else through your brain and calculator. Faith and science buttressed each other in Jim's Zeitgeist. The more he prayed, the more he studied, the more Jim understood the world around him, a world of lightness against darkness, of truth against deception.

And so did he place his faith in scientists. He met often with Doctor Fact-nerd and Doctor Birkenstock on the COVID task force, peered over their tabulated facts, understood why their policy had to be *the* policy and why the dangerous ideas of science-doubters—like Stanford pseudo-doctor Shrug as he called him (since his name sounded like an Ayn Rand book title), whom Trump threw on the task force to disrupt any consensus and obfuscate the American people—had to be vigorously silenced. Science, to Jim, was as absolute as faith. There was always one right answer, and once we found it, there was no purpose in debating it and trying to tear it down. As he always said, if it fits on a spreadsheet, then it is the truth.

And by the way, Jim did not have a nickname for Trump, who he detested more than any other American. Trump too was a nickname junkie, and to Jim, the name Trump was insult enough!

"You criticize Ben for being too old," one of his friends told him later in the ride, when he again called people to rant about the game. "Yet you support a president who can barely string two words together. I know you like Star Buck, Jim, but he may be as good a steward of the country as Ben is of the Steelers."

"Give Buck some credit." Jim laughed. "He's got a good offensive line and some great receivers. He's open to new ideas. His new appointees are already making me excited about the new political season. We have an all-star lineup coming into town after January twentieth, even if our quarterback is a bit old. You going to be at the inauguration?"

"You get me a ticket and I'll be there, Jim," he said. "But there's a lot of time between then and now. Trump is already screaming about rigged elections and wanting to get revenge. His people are threatening to tear the nation to threads. And they are not exactly a tame lot. I wouldn't be surprised if they disrupt the inauguration. Or worse. They're pissed. And they have guns!"

Deep in his heart, Jim was not a big fan of guns, and he feared their proliferation in the hands of the right-wing lunatics whom he despised. But being a representative in Western Pennsylvania, he had to be mum about that issue; in fact, he worked hard to get his gun creds up, learned how to shoot with amazing precision, owned an AK-47, and had an A+ rating with the NRA.

A recent picture of him felling a deer hundreds of yards away during a rainstorm, all while he wore a Steelers mask, had gone viral with the following headline: "Science, Safety, and Steelers Snags a Doe."

Conservatives in his district, many who flocked to his cause and voted him into office, were not like the right-wingers Jim despised. His conservatives didn't preach hate and violence; they just liked to be left alone. They were good, God-fearing souls who believed in the nation and its values; they were not racists or bigots of any sort but too did not appreciate laws that gave them the shaft at the expense of minority groups. Most lived on the fringes and so resented government handouts to the city-types, and they believed that America was a Christian nation steeped in the values of rugged individualism.

And, of course, they were Steelers fanatics, pragmatic people, who appreciated straight talk, just like Jim! When Jim campaigned on a science-first platform, he did so as a man of faith and a man of his own conscience. Unmarried, apolitical, and having a long and clean record in business, Jim was a Democrat in name only, a Democrat because his dad and granddad were Democrats, because he believed in a party that stressed science and goodness, because he detested Donald Trump Republicanism.

"The Republicans, especially under Donald Trump, have turned their back on decency," he said at a campaign rally. "Our representative, Ted Con-man, has bought Trump's vulgar rhetoric hook, line and sinker. He rejects science, spits on your health, and mocks the values of our state and our God. I refuse to bend to that vitriol. I am a straight-talking guy, a businessman, a churchgoer, and a guy without a single stain on my record. I've given my whole life to this community, and just because I'm a Democrat, I'm not going to fall prey to the venom of the likes of A-O-Crazy or Speaker of the House Mamma Nana, but nor will I have to fall in line with Trump and his thugs. I will represent you, the most decent people in the land, the forgotten people of the land, and like our Steelers, we'll show the damned world how to get it done!"

Of course, after the Cleveland debacle, his faith in Ben and the Steelers had waned a bit. But not his faith in the nation, in the post-Trump era, in science and freedom. This would be the dawning of a new age, and Jim Depich hoped to play a large role in making it happen.

As he turned on Route 270 in Frederick, carefully avoiding Baltimore and their Ravens, Jim smiled, hopeful and giddy. Little did he know that in just two days his sanguine faith in the nation would abruptly implode, and the role he was about to play in the nation's history would gravitate well beyond his own control in a way that nothing, not even his spreadsheets, could have possibly anticipated.

CHAPTER TWO

A Gentle Path to Science and Hope

Jim settled into his Washington DC hamlet, a small apartment off K Street in the neighborhood of Georgetown. From there he enjoyed walking through the brisk air and colorful thoroughfares as he tabulated statistics in his mind. Jim did most of his good work all alone in thought as he drifted through anonymous swarms of people whose lives were bizarrely linked to his and yet who swam in other plains of existence. "What were they all thinking?" he sometimes asked himself. He smiled at a few, but he couldn't tell if they smiled back; everyone in DC, it seemed, understood the importance of masks.

Jim knew that this was a smart city, as much as many in his Pittsburgh neighborhood tried to demonize it. These people read, studied, and complied with rules. Most were young and healthy; joggers and bicycle riders fluttered through the mass movement of walking suits. He was impressed with how willingly college students—most of whom were liberal and socially minded—accepted the science behind lockdowns and masks and the need to be vigilant with this virus. "These kids are far smarter and civic-minded than those of my college days, when young people seemed to fight against everything, to question even God and the president," he told

Corrine. "They get it, they listen to the CDC and to DUI's lineup of brilliant doctors, they know their science, and they're all about enforcing it."

He called his go-to news station DUI instead of its real name because, back in the day, they opposed his candidacy, calling him a fake-Democrat, and he responded by saying that they were driving the news in an intoxicated state because clearly they were not awake to reality.

"Yea." Smiled a toothy Corrine. "You don't even have to tell them. They just do it!"

"Exactly, Cor," he said to her. "It's because of them that I came up with my idea for the Persuasion Bill. Buck and his team go on and on about mandating masks and vaccines everywhere and for everyone. To me, when you can demonstrate the science behind something and convince people that it makes sense to do it, that's the road we should take, not mandates and government overreach."

So, he thought, look at all these smart kids trying to educate doubters on the street, being a positive example to them, showing the world how to do it. It's the educated youth who have stayed home from work, eschewed parties and gatherings, and dutifully wore their masks. They were first in line for the vaccine too. One day Jim took a contemplative jaunt to nearby Shenandoah National Park, climbing up White Oak Canyon immersed in thought, and saw a group of college kids out there in the woods, all wearing masks. He approached them.

"I just want to thank you guys for being socially responsible," he said with a smile beneath his cloth Steelers mask, keeping his six-foot distance from them.

One of them nodded back. "You too," she said with her big bright eyes. "It's infuriating that some people don't get it and are ruining our country out of their own selfishness. If it were up to me, the least I'd do is make them pay for their irresponsible behavior, and maybe that would convince them to not be jerks. And all the people who spread the misinformation they cling to, I'd toss them in jail!"

On the ride home, he built the Persuasion Bill from the bricks of that encounter. The way to demonize Trump and his thugs was not to yell at them like little kids but to demonstrate their perfidy and punish them for it. When you can delineate a sharp distinction between the sensibility of a humanistic scientific approach versus an approach both selfish and idiotic, then it's easy to reward the former and disparage the latter, all without forcing people to do anything. Coercion to Jim was never necessary when a good spreadsheet demarcating truth from fiction could do the trick much more gently.

Indeed, to Jim, Trump and his people were the greatest threat to democracy that the nation had ever known. Their anti-science rhetoric and pseudo-religious diatribes had put our nation on the precipice of collapse. The kids were right. The language of misinformation spoken by Trump and his cronies could endanger millions of lives. But censoring them seemed wrong.

To Jim, there was a better way. "When greed drives people to make bad decisions, then the way to stop them is to reveal their motives and then hit them in their greedy guts," he realized.

He sat down wit Dr. Fact-nerd, the tiger of science one day, the man who had been leading the nation and indeed the entire world down a tough but necessary road lined by the bricks of science. The science tiger was as frustrated by anti-science misinformation as those kids Jim met in the park, but he never let his indignation get to him.

"We have to convince them, Jim," he said. "Had we all been distancing and wearing masks like I said from the start, this thing would be over. Look at Australia. Look at Japan. But there are voices that keep getting in the way, people on the internet spreading untruths, and until we shut them down, until we speak in one undisputed language, the language of science, we'll never lick this thing."

"Who?" Jim asked him. "Who are these voices you're talking about?"

The tiger listed a bunch of names: academic dissidents, fringe doctors on the internet, right-wing think tanks, the authors of the "very dangerous" Great Barrington Declaration, and politicians using COVID to advance their own positions and who, as Dr. Fact-nerd said, "are willing to put their careers over life itself."

"Until we shut them up, until we stop some of these dangerous governors from defying the recommendations of the COVID task force and CDC, this won't go away," Dr. Fact-nerd said.

Responsible organizations like Google, Facebook, and Twitter started removing vats of misinformation from their sites, and many academic institutions reprimanded those who strayed from science. But coercion and censorship, Jim knew, engendered a reaction from the far right, from Donald Trump's thugs, from politically motivated clowns like Florida Governor DaSandwich and Texas Governor Abbott and Costello, and they could even sound reasonable if they seemed to be on the side of democracy.

"We need to be gentle and persuasive," he told the science tiger. "The kids get it. They may be our most potent force. And they understand liberty and science. I'm working on a bill to set the record straight, and to right the ship of state."

Were it not against COVID protocol, the tiger may have hugged Jim. Tears welled up in Dr. Fact-nerd's eyes. The poor guy often likely felt he was fighting for science and America on his own. He was glad to have found such a formidable ally in Jim, and forever more they would be the best of friends until they weren't.

Jim's own jurisdiction, conservative but smart, was the one he needed to convince of the absolute truth of the science tiger's path and the dangers posed by any alternate views. To that end, Jim's aides in Pittsburgh did some beta testing of his bill. They explained the danger of the Trump-misinformation assault on science and liberty, and how the nation could best surmount it and stay safe without having to resort to government overreach. The support he got was overwhelming.

"You pass that," said one former coal miner to Jim when he came home to push the bill, "and you get Big Ben healthy, and I'll be in the front row to get you to be our next president."

Jim smiled at him beneath his cloth mask. "Let's beat Cleveland in the playoffs and get on the right path of liberty and science again. Thanks for the endorsement, but I'm happy being your congress-man; I don't have higher aspirations than that. Being president is a thankless job! I have the best job in the world representing the smartest and hardest working people in America!"

The bill had a few very simple edicts. First, if people spread information that contested the COVID task force doctrine, as Jim called it, they must defend their position before a Board of Science under CDC auspices, and if their contentions proved to be misleading and false, they would be removed from any academic positions and, if doctors, lose their license to practice. Second, any state that publicly denounced the Buck Administration's plans to curb the spread of COVID, or defied the will of the COVID task force, would be subjected to loss of federal dollars. Third, the government would offer financial incentives to individuals and businesses that complied with mask laws and immunization recommendations. The bill even provided for a new Payroll Protection Program that would only be valid in states and to businesses that were deemed to be A+ in terms of their compliance with the Buck-Factnerd plan.

"We don't force people to behave a certain way, we don't censor those who spit out misinformation, but we can persuade everyone to follow the rules and stick to the science by rewarding those who do and punishing those who don't. And most importantly, when we spell out the science in simple language that is unassailable, unnuanced, and in a way that everyone understands, then I'm sure that people will gladly do the right thing without us telling them that they have to."

"Donald Trump and his goon squad are a threat to democracy," Jim told his constituents at a campaign rally in early January; as a congressman, Jim learned, the campaigning season lasted forever. "They claim to be promoting free speech, even when they feed you false information. What they really want is to sew discord, to make the virus never goes away. Why, you may ask, would they want the virus to be with us forever? Because if there is a constant threat, then they can use the national emergency as a way to bolster their own power and spin their vitriolic message. They want you to hate your neighbor, not love your neighbor as the Bible tells us. They want you to reject science and to enable a disease to spread that we could easily curb if we complied with science. They want to confuse you with what they call facts, facts that go against the truth that our science tiger and other very brave and smart doctors have been explaining to us from the start. Trump's misinformation campaign is the greatest threat to democracy the nation has ever known. And believe me when

I tell you, if you put your trust in me, you are supporting science, democracy, and Christian values! We will persevere over the thugs!"

They ate it up! And so too did the COVID task force when they read through Jim's Persuasion Bill.

"It's so simple," said the tiger. "Just a half-page. You have no idea how refreshing that is! All those anti-science types who try to derail us, they come in here with piles of piles of papers cluttered with jumbled facts that we don't have time to decipher during an emergency. This bill, Jim, it will put them in their place. This is what Americans want and need. Thank you, Jim. Thank you for your wisdom."

In just two days, on January 7, the day after Buck's election will have been certified by Congress, Jim planned to meet with the incoming crop of democratic congressmen, many of whom believed in more draconian measures to contain the virus. Jim knew that his measured bill, which had the endorsement of Dr's Got-Milk and Fact-nerd, as well as of many of the democratic governors with whom he had spoken, would grab their attention, especially knowing that Jim was from a conservative district, and that even his people thought it made sense. He created spreadsheets of facts and trends to prove his points, and all were arranged simply in a way anyone could understand. Jim's message resonated perfectly through his manicured columns of reasoned discourse.

"With this legislation, we'll snuff out Trump's attempt to derail freedom, science, safety, and goodness in this nation," Jim was planning to say in Congress when he introduced his bill on the seventh. "What can he do to us now? We're in the driver's seat, and it's up to put this nation back on track. We now have a science president on our side, a freedom lover and true Christian, a Pennsylvanian who gets it. Donald Trump has no more cards up his sleeve to try to turn this nation into his private fiefdom of hate."

In just a few hours, Jim would learn just how wrong he was!

CHAPTER THREE

The Unmaskers
are Unmasked

Jim met Corrine many years ago at church. She was an aspiring electrical engineer at Carnegie Melon, and she loved that he had taken his engineering degree into the world of corporate America. She was intrigued, and with her college boyfriend, soon to be her husband, they spoke for many hours at the local Perkin's Pancake House, where Jim always ate breakfast after services. Her wide-eyed enthusiasm and obvious intelligence drew Jim right in.

Some years later, when Jim decided to make a run for Congress, he contacted Corrine, just to see what she was up to. Turns out that she was working for an electrical engineering firm in town designing surveillance equipment for the army and was bored to tears. Jim asked if she wanted to help his campaign, and she leaped at the opportunity.

"I swear to you, she got me elected!" he later said. "Her trips around local towns, her genius at fund-raising, her infectious likeability soothed the good folks of our district who were sick of Trump but skeptical of a Democrat like me. She convinced me to make our campaign about truth and facts, about people's lives, about rejecting both identity politics of the left and the vulgar anti-Christian rhetoric of Trump and anyone who supported him."

Like a daughter Jim never had, Corrine always hugged him and enjoyed being in his presence, which tickled his ego and made him blush. She delivered two children while working with him, and often they stayed with her in DC, while her husband Mark continued to work as an engineer in Pittsburgh. The kids were around the office so often that Jim sometimes believed they were his, especially since they loved jumping on him, and he was so good at making them laugh!

So, on the morning of January 6, when she bounded into his office with a look of consternation drawn upon her usually animated and gentle face, Jim nearly fainted!

"What?" he asked her. "Something wrong? Is it about my bill? About COVID? Buck? What?"

A marathon runner and someone whose energy knew no bounds, she could barely breathe. She hugged him and started to cry. As her tears saturated the back of her shirt and she couldn't even string two words together, he started to worry. "Corrine, you have to tell me," he said again.

"They did it," she said, grabbing words between hysterical fits of tears. "They raided the Capitol. They have bombs. There are thousands of them. They're trying to take over the government."

"Who?" he asked her, trying to stay calm. "Who raided the Capitol? Muslims? Another country? Who did, Corrine, and tell me what's happening? Are we in danger? Should we run?"

She nodded from side to side, gasping for her breath. "No, none of them, Jim," she said. "It's the Trump people. The right-wing nutjobs. They got all their guns and rushed the Capitol. I don't know how far they got. I think we should hide. Thank God my kids are with Mark, but I worry about you!"

Jim kissed her on the head. So many thoughts fluttered through his brain, but only one took root: It was time to fight, not to cower. "Stay here," he said to her gently. "Lock the door. I'll be right back."

Jim leaped to action, calling and texting everyone he knew. A few friends filled him in. Seeing no one in the hall other than some

Capitol policemen, he ran back to his office, where he had a few guns stored.

"You're right," he said to Corrine, with a quiet reservation. "Donald Trump and his goons are trying to disrupt the election certification and to basically stage a coup. I'm not sure how far they got." Was it as dire as Corrine feared? Was this truly a coup? Was the sitting president masterminding an attempt to stop the official tally of electoral votes slated to occur on this very day under the watch of Vice President Not-Pennsylvania? Was he directing his thugs to do what he was unable to accomplish by peaceable means?

Jim didn't know. But it was clear that this was an assault on democracy to a degree that the nation had ever experienced, worse even than the Civil War. He detested the Trumpers! But this was too much!

"Bastards," he said to Corrine. "We'll stop them. Don't you worry. We'll stop them."

Calming his dear aide down proved to be the least of Jim's troubles that day. The two of them, and many members of their young and eager crew, hit the phones hard all day long. That night, when the situation had quelled down to an echo, when the deaths were far fewer than they could have been, when the election was certified and the despicable president finally told his thugs to disperse, they all went for a beer at the Blue Duck Tavern and talked about how to respond to this horrific affront.

"I won't let this fade away and be buried as a minor event; that's what politicians like to do, to calm everyone down and pretend nothing bad happened, and we're not playing that game," he told his young interns. "These are the same anti-science goons who have been fighting the tiger of science, who are opposed to anything that is decent and good in the world, who want their dictator to run this nation and discard our whole history. They made their move. Now it's our turn to use it to our advantage."

They all sipped their wine and beer and, some with tears in their eyes, thanked Jim and told him that they were with him all the way. Corrine hugged him so tightly that he nearly threw up. "JD," she said to him, using the nickname she had concocted during the campaign to make him sound "cooler," "we have to make the world safe for my kids. We can't let these horrible people continue to threaten our democracy. My kids can't grow up in a world like that. I'll do anything you tell me to do. Anything."

"I know," he told her, kissing her on her ruddy cheek. "You know that I won't let that happen."

Then Jim looked sternly at each of the young idealistic people who sat with him that night. "We can't do this with our emotions," he said to them all. "We're all about logic, about science, about truth versus misinformation. We'll wow them with our evidence, make it undisputable, and then we'll bury them in the ditch of their ignorance. The Trumpists played their card, and now it's time for us to play ours. They have a deck full of lies and deceptions and hatred. Our deck is all about facts and truth, about science."

Those words would be Jim's clarion call for the next eventful year.

All night Jim tabulated facts into a spreadsheet, as was his wont. He mused how the nation had come to this point, and why no one had stopped the instigator until now. But no one could argue with facts. No one could erase the reality of what transpired on January 6th. The miscalculation of Trump's thugs only revealed their intent and their guile, and now Jim put all of it in a format that no one could dispute.

Almost as soon as the 2020 election ended, with the networks calling a Star Buck victory, Donald Trump cried about fraud. Ironically, he had done the same thing in 2016 when he thought he lost, only to reverse course when actual fraud—closing polling stations early, denying people the right to vote, sending out false information to swing voters—enabled his victory. Now, though, with a clear minority of electoral and popular votes, Trump had little recourse but to deny reality, his favorite hobby.

For the month since his electoral loss, Trump took his eyes off the nation, off the threat of COVID, off anything that resembled governance and instead focused on overturning the election. He asked governors of friendly states that elected Buck to recall their electors and instead appoint electors who would choose Trump. Despite the legality of this maneuver, none complied with his request. He filed sixty lawsuits, taking two to the conservative Supreme Court, where even his own appointees turned down his claims. He rallied his right-wing troops to implement pressure on their representatives, and even asked the vice president to use his senatorial role to overturn the electoral college.

When everything failed, he turned to his most base, hateful, and deranged supporters, those who detest anyone unlike them, who stockpile weapons and refuse to be part of the nation, who live in the cracks of society, hidden away from justice and decency, feasting on a buffet of hate and desecration that Donald Trump readily fed to them. These were the same people who refused to wear masks, who labeled vaccination as a tool being used by the government to insert chips into our bodies, who claimed even that the tiger of science and the gated billionaire invented COVID to take over the world.

To Jim, the two groups were identical: those who worshiped Donald Trump and those who assailed Dr. Fact-nerd. Jim Depich hated these people more than Satan himself, and the fact that they had now committed this deed, he became a man on a mission, one that would consume the rest of his life.

"Trump called all his militia groups together in DC on January fifth with the explicit purpose of disrupting the electoral count," Jim said to a congressional reporter. "Trump and his contingent met at his hotel as his thugs arrived at the Capitol, all under the guise of organizing various rallies, whose names were the very antithesis of their intent, including 'Rally to Save America' and 'Save the Republic Rally,' although the one that gets most under my skin is 'One Nation under God' rally, in which several members of my own church planned to participate."

"God?" Jim asked Corrine. "These alleged men of God were hanging effigies of President Elect Buck, and even VP Not-Pennsylvania, hung and burned them, crying out to *storm the Capitol* and *take back America for God*. Which God is that? It sounds like Satan's work, not any God with which I am familiar! To think that some of these people may have voted for me, it's appalling!"

Corrine nodded and tapped him gently on the head. "No, JD, they voted for the other guy."

Trump had addressed the crowd under cold and blustery skies near noon on the sixth. People were holding guns and threatening violence, yelling out to storm the Capitol. Trump himself never advocated such violence, Jim Depich later conceded, but nor did he condemn it. "And there were bombs in cars, pipe bombs, all sorts of bombs, lots of gun all scattered in the trunks and hidden away in DC, and Trump and his gang knew about this and said nothing. He riled them on, kept saying the election was rigged and they had to do something. None of them were wearing masks. Same crowd. Same damned crowd. It's a damned embarrassment that some of them were from Pittsburgh, that they wave the terrible towel, that they may even go to my church. It gets under my skin, Corrine, it does."

By 1:00 p.m. some of the crowd broke off, and that's about when Corrine had entered the congressman's office to tell him about transpiring events. People he called at that time told him all they knew. *They bombed the House chamber. They had shot over fifty senators and untold congressmen along with their aides. The president was about to call in the military and institute martial law.*

Nothing they said proved true, other than the fact that a thousand insane protestors had penetrated the Capitol barriers touting pepper spray, threatening to burn down the place. The Capitol Police, not given ample warning, were not there to greet them, and so the thugs penetrated farther than likely even they anticipated. Joe Biggs from a group in North Carolina, named the Proud Boys, led the charge, and hundreds of his sheep followed. They hoisted ladders and ropes and climbed into the Capitol's bowels, spraying any who tried to stop them with pepper spray.

Jim and Corrine and his entire staff huddled in his office, closing off the door with his oversize desk. They were scared, petrified in fact, but Jim's cool calm—as he called friends and, Uzi in hand, threatened to beat the thugs back himself if he had to—soothed the room. Soon in Jim's indignant mind it became a personal war, the voices of reason and democracy against the anti-science and anti-democracy mob of Donald Trump.

When the facts of the raid proved far less daunting than the initial fears, that didn't matter to Jim. To him, it could have been substantially worse, and that's the only fact that he put in his spreadsheets.

"They were carrying flags saying *Christ is King* and *God's warriors*," Jim fumed at dinner that night, sipping his martini ever so deliberately. "Can you imagine? They hoisted Nazi flags, Confederate flags, had guns and bombs. Over a thousand of them got in there, thousands more cheering them on from outside, and they say they are for God? For democracy? Had you kids not held me back, I would have gone out there and beat the living shit out of them myself!"

Corrine laughed. "Why, JD, you are so feisty tonight! It must be the liquor! This is the first time I saw you drink anything more than a beer!"

Jim twisted his gaze toward her and hit her with a glare she would not soon forget. "It's not a joking matter," he said solemnly. "We almost lost our country today. And it's up to us to get it back."

And that's exactly what Representative Jim Depich intended to do. It was all he would do for as long as he lived. He had had enough of the anti-mask crowd who rejected science and decency and were willing to trade lives for political expediency, spreading misinformation across the land, and instigating hundreds of thousands of deaths. He had had enough too of the crude rhetoric of Trump and his minions pretending to be Christian and democratic even while desecrating both of those ideals. All this behavior, all the paranoia and vitriol the president and his followers had been spitting out without restraint, had nearly cost this nation its life. And that was the only thought that penetrated Jim's skull forever more.

"It's up to us to get America back from the brink of its destruction, no matter how we have to do it," he whispered again, taking another sip. "They crossed a line, and we will do anything and everything to save our nation from their evil grasp. Anything and everything." He gulped the drink down.

Jim announced in front of the House Health Committee, which he now chaired, that hundreds of people had been killed in the

Capitol riot and that tens of thousands more would have died had it not been for the bravery and valor of the Capitol Police and military. He contended that Trump had led the rioters into the Capitol with the intent of hanging Mike Not-Pennsylvania and anyone who dared cast their electoral vote for Buck, shooting most of the elected representatives, and declaring martial law.

He held to those facts even when reality told a different story. About 138 Capitol officers were hospitalized with injuries, fifteen of which were deemed severe. All were released within a week. Several rioters died, one shot, one trampled, one of a drug overdose, three of heart attacks. A Capitol officer, who had been pepper sprayed, later suffered a stroke, and died. Later, four killed themselves within six months.

The numbers of actual deaths and injuries were irrelevant to Jim's calculus. In his spreadsheet demonstrating the damage of the riot, Jim filled in the what-ifs—the possible harm had all the bombs gone off and had the assailants reached their targets. And so, he tabulated well over a thousand deaths. He showed the likelihood of the attackers getting inside, and what Trump may have done had that occurred. His conclusions were theoretical and didn't match facts on the ground, but rather they portrayed the magnitude of what may have occurred. To him, that's the only fact that mattered.

And when he gave his fiery speech at the Capitol a few days later, when he displayed his spreadsheets and graphs with calculations he derived from his what-if truth, few questioned his numbers or conclusions. When one congressman interrupted him and stated that "you can't conflate what may have happened with what did," Jim Depich stared at that man, a Republican from his own state, and said, "Then I assume, Bill-Fold, you had something to do with the attack or that you endorse it. Or, that you minimize the loss of life and the gravity of what may have occurred? I do know you support Trump."

No one dared say another word.

Later that day, Jim sought out Dr. Fact-nerd. "We're going to use this to take them all down, Tiger," he said.

"Who down, Jim?" the tiger asked him. "Trump? He already lost. We're moving ahead with our agenda now, unimpeded by all the misinformation and obstruction."

Jim shook his head. "No," he said. "It's not that simple, Tiger. We have to take them down so hard so they can never utter another modicum of lethal misinformation again, never threaten America and Americans again with their anti-science rhetoric, never dare let them hold power. To preserve our democracy, FN, we have to eradicate the only virus that matters the most. We have to destroy the infection that almost killed us today. Trumpism. We have to wipe it out."

CHAPTER FOUR

The Opportunity

Often opportunities present themselves and then slip away. Unless they are snatched, unless their significance is identified and seized, unless every sacrifice is made to assure that they become tools for the betterment of humankind, then these opportunities are nothing more than illusory what-ifs.

"We almost lost our democracy," Jim uttered over and over, to whomever he spoke, wherever he was. "If we don't stop the thugs, they will eventually stop us. Why are people not outraged?"

Jim's doctor back home had a saying that stuck in Jim's brain. *When there's ice outside, you don't call the orthopedist to fix your hip knowing you're going to slip on it. You ice the walkway and put on boots and make sure you don't fall. The only way to stop catastrophe is to identify its cause and stop it before it actually occurs. You can't wait for it to happen and then fix it; at that point, it's too late.*

His doctor's wisdom applied to politics too, but no one got the message. People gave lip service to how horrific the attack was, but that's as far as it went. Jim met with the new president twice, imploring his fellow Pennsylvanian to take immediate action against the masterminds behind the Capitol raid. Star Buck (or SB as he sometimes called him) was having enough trouble just getting settled in. He passed a mask mandate that would be enforced on all federal property; even if you were all alone atop Yellowstone Park, you were required to wear one. And he was considering a vaccine mandate too once the supply caught up to the demand. But that's about as far as he was willing to go.

"What about the governors and mayors and doctors who are calling your mandates malarkey?" Jim asked the president. "If we let their misinformation get a footing, then everything you do will be for naught. Mandates don't get to the root of the problem. They force people to do things they don't understand, and that just plays into the hands of our enemies. We have to show the American people why those who assail masks and vaccines are as dangerous and anti-American as those who attacked the Capitol, show them that we must punish those people, or their words and their deeds will slaughter millions and bring down our democracy. We have an opportunity, Mr. President, to stop those who are trampling on science and democracy. We can't let an opportunity like this get away from us."

But Buck just smiled at the young congressman, placing his hand over Jim's shoulder. "Mandates are mostly a gesture, Jim," he said. "Got to look like I'm doing something. But what we need is the economy to get back in gear. And to do that, well, we can't have too much fighting and rancor. If we start attacking everyone, then they'll attack us, and how do I build an economy on rubble?"

"But, Mr. President," Jim pleaded, "you've seen my numbers and facts. I gave you my graphs and spreadsheets. It's black-and-white, sir, and I present in a way anyone can understand. Those spreadsheets show just how close we were to losing our country. And I showed you the COVID data too; the tiger himself helped me compile it. How many will die if we don't put a stop to those people trying to confuse and fool Americans into a false lull with their misinformation campaign? Can't you see it, SB? They're trying to trick the nation, to let this virus run wild and then blame it on the very people who are trying to curb it, using it as justification for taking down the government. Their lies are a weapon no less lethal than a nuclear bomb pointed in our direction, no less lethal than COVID. You got to dig up the roots of the misinformation, or it will spread so voraciously that we'll never be able to stop it. It's like when it snows, Mr. President, you don't let it build up so that when you walk through it, you'll fall; you shovel the damned walkway."

"Been there, Jim." Buck laughed, his big white teeth glimmering in the room. "Got a bad hip myself. I'm on a drug for it. We try to shovel, Jim, but when it's snowing hard, I'm glad I'm on that pill!"

"Mr. President," Jim pleaded, "are you even hearing me? We have an opportunity. The raid gave us a window to take extraordinary measures and bring these people down before they do real damage, the very damage, the very facts, that I showed you on my spreadsheets!" He was sweating, exasperated.

"I hear you, Jim, I do," the president said. "And I'm with you. But we're still in a democracy, and we do have constraints to contend with, a very conservative Supreme Court to dance around, and a divided population that will swing to the other party if we don't watch our butts. I'll be tough, I assure you of that. My mandates ain't a bunch of sissy juice; I'm hitting the other side hard where it counts. You just keep compiling your data, and you keep me updated, and we'll do what we can to make sure that all the misinformation and pushback gets controlled."

"You must declare martial law, Mr. President," Jim sneered with clear frustration. "Our democracy is being attacked on two fronts, the Capitol raid and the misinformation campaign, both of which can be responsible for millions of deaths and the end of freedom as we know it if we let them fester. I've shown you my numbers. Why do we need more data? Isn't it clear enough? Sometimes, Mr. President, the only way to assure our freedom is to curtail that of those who most threaten us. You have that opportunity now! The American people are behind you. You can't hesitate!"

Star Buck smiled and turned away. "Keep the data coming, Jim. You're doing a great job!"

But Jim fumed. He wandered in the woods, the Billy Goat Trail on the Potomac, some lonely trails in Shenandoah, even a drive to the Poconos to visit a few old haunts from his youth. Most of the time, he lived in a purgatory within his own mind. *What to do? How to wake the leaders up?*

He and Corrine met often, usually over a burger, or while watching Jim's collection of *Looney Tunes*, the only TV that comforted him. Her kids would flutter around, and sometimes Jim would pick up Billy or Theresa and rub their hair and whisper, "We'll save the world for you, I promise, I promise."

When she was with her husband, Jim stayed away. He wanted Corrine for himself, and lately resented Mark's intrusion into their lives. Her passion and intelligence were all that kept him afloat during those dark days of winter, as COVID fears waxed and waned depending on how the media portrayed current surges, as anti-COVID fanaticism grew in strength across red America, and as his own party and his own people did little more than pander to those who wanted them to grow some balls.

"You know what one of my history friends told me, back at Pittsburgh?" Jim said to Corrine as they sat near each other in his apartment, a fire raging in his fireplace, and Bugs Bunny messing with Elmer Fudd on his small TV set. "He said that if after the Civil War we had taken all the Confederate leaders, declared them guilty of treason, and strung them up on poles around the Capitol—from Lee and Jefferson Davis to some of the more well-known generals—then those hundreds of dangling bodies would have made a statement to everyone aboutg the price of attacking our democracy. There would have been no Jim Crow had we done that, no Lost Cause movement. We would have said once and for all: *We won't tolerate any attack on our people.* But we didn't, and we paid the price. Why can't we learn?"

She hugged him tight, as a daughter does to her ailing dad, and she kissed him gently on the cheek. "I have faith," she said to him. "You should too. We're making progress! You on the committee, me on the campuses. It's a work in progress. Once we get some momentum, then all your tabulations, all your hard work, it will pay off. I know it will! People will listen to reason once it's presented in a way they can understand, in a way that only you know how to do! They understand facts and truth! You can't rely on a president who isn't popular and is drowning in his own party's rancor. We have to do this ourselves, and we will. Have you talked to Mama Nana about the misinformation committee?"

By college campuses, Corrine had decided—on her own initiative—to organize armies of progressive students to support Jim's agenda, kids willing to speak out and not tolerate a middle-of-the-road approach. Jim hired a dozen deputies for her, young men and women with passion and organizational skills, mostly engineers, to fan out across the nation's colleges and put it all together. These Truth Clubs were devoted to exposing the danger of Trumpism and anti-mask zealotry. Every one of them reported directly to Corrine and then to Jim.

But by Jim's committee, that seed was not growing as fast as either hoped it would.

In trying to convince his fellow Democrats of the need to snuff out any and all misinformation being spread by liars in the scientific and medical community, by governors and the right-wing media, and by people on social media, Jim demanded a committee specifically organized for that purpose.

"These are the same people who enabled the January sixth raid," Jim pleaded to the democratic caucus. "They will do anything to undermine the faith of this nation in our scientific organizations, our doctors, and our president. They are happy to sew discord and enable COVID to spread and kill; it's all fodder for their devious schemes to take back the country through force."

"Can you prove that, Jim?" one congresswoman asked him.

"Give me the resources and I can," he said, glaring at the Speaker as he spoke. "Give me a committee with funding where we can root out the causes of this misinformation and find links between those who raided the Capitol and those trying to undermine the COVID task force. I'll chair it. You can make it bipartisan, I don't care; I just need the resources. Unless we shut these people down, unless we squelch those who are deliberately obfuscating the truth, then their power will only grow."

"Sounds like you're advocating censorship!" Another congressman laughed.

But Jim was not in a jovial mood. "No," he said sternly. "This is based on precedence, of Supreme Court edicts, on the words of great men like Oliver Wendell Holmes. You can't yell fire in a crowded theater; that's against the law. You can't sew discontent and question the power of the government during a crisis; that's also a proven fact. Many of our great presidents, from Lincoln to Wilson to Roosevelt, shut down dangerous voices. That's not censorship. It's survival! Somehow you believe that dangerous and manipulative people can spit out mistruths during the greatest natural calamity to have struck our nation and prevent us from fighting it, somehow you can declare allegiance to a former president who tried to take down the government by force? You call it censorship to prevent people from threatening our democracy? I am appalled by your naivety!"

His passion won the day, and he got his committee, the Misinformation Committee, as he called it. He picked three democrats and three Republicans to be on it, and the tiger of science agreed to sit on it as well. The first meeting was slated to be in June, as the arduous winter and spring of Jim's discontent continued to flurry along.

"I've never seen you so despondent!" Corrine said to him. "We need to get you laid! How long has it been, Jim? You need a little bit of ladylove!"

Jim laughed. "How long's it been for you, Corrine? I feel like I'm keeping you away from your husband and stealing you all for myself."

"Don't worry about me," she said to him, kissing him on the cheek. "Mark and I are like rabbits. I meet him wherever and whenever; he'll drive down here, or we'll meet at a hotel in State College, or we're happy to park off the turnpike and do it in the woods. I have more sex than any woman deserves! But you need some love, Jim. Something to take your mind off all this!"

Was she offering? he wondered. He looked into her eager eyes and knew that was not her intent. Nor did he ever see her that way, as pretty as she was. Jim was not one to care about such carnal desires. A good burger and Bugs Bunny was enough to make him happy, as was a long and lonely walk in the woods. He didn't want to be distracted from the battle he was waging for the soul of the nation.

"Tell me about the college plan," he said to her. "I need some good news."

Corrine smiled and slid a bit closer to Jim. She stared sheepishly into his eyes.

"We have Truth Clubs in over one hundred fifty colleges now, many with hundreds of members," she said. "I've been visiting some, as have Pete and Jen and Holly, who are doing an A+ job rallying the troops. At MD Park Campus, our club is the biggest one on campus; they've tied together their calls for universal masking and immunization mandates to the preservation of Roe and the acknowledgment of sexual fluidity. We've made the movement a liberal buffet, and everyone is super excited to call out the misinformers, to shame fellow students who dispute the need for masking or who just aren't woke, as the kids say these days. It's amazing! So exciting!"

"We need to link the anti-maskers to the January sixth crowd," Jim said to her. "I'm hoping the kids will be able to do it. If I can prove to the committee that there is a connection, then in one swoop we can take down all of them, and maybe that will allow me to have more power to interrogate academics and others who have gotten in Fact-nerd's hair, and to convince our president to flex his muscle to actually stop those who are leading this nation into a pit rather than pushing mandates on people who are being fed false information. You know what Tap-dancer said to me the other day when I was on his show on DUI?"

"What?" she asked, staring into his eyes. "I love the guy! He's handsome and smart, just like my favorite congressman. Tell me what he said!"

"He wants to help and says that DUI will continue pushing the danger of misinformation, but he admits that his case will be buttressed if we can prove the link between the COVID liars and the January sixth plotters. Right now, he is our greatest ally, far more influential than the president. Now that I have my committee, the dancer says I will be a regular guest on his show and a few others. It's a great opportunity, Corrine, and we have to feed these guys what they need. That is where the power lies, and that's where my leverage is. I can't rely on my party. I have to take my case to the people."

"You were amazing on the show last night." Corrine beamed. "Dancer showed your spreadsheets and said something like, 'You can't dispute the truth.' So perfect! Maybe we can get some of the college kids on? I think that would go a long way to legitimating and empowering the movement. The kids are so into it. They make your case so well. I know the kids are the key to success."

Jim agreed and begged Corrine to keep up the fight.

Later in the day, he spoke with the tiger, who had been pushed somewhat to the periphery of the task force but still carried a great deal of weight, especially among younger Americans and educated Democrats, the two groups Jim relied on. Jim sat in on the task force, on his own committee, on the health committee, and had private meetings with the tiger daily. He linked everything together, and he believed that Fact-nerd was the glue to make it all stay in place.

Today the tiger was on edge, which always unnerved Jim a bit; he needed the guy to be unwavering.

"We have a new variant coming, Jim," he said, solemnly. "I worry about it. It's called Delta, and it's spreading fast and furious. But the doubters are putting up their typical barriers. They're telling the public not to worry. That we're overreacting. I'm not sure even Got-milk has a sense of how bad it will be. They're talking about opening schools in the fall, opening the NFL. I worry, Jim!"

Cleveland's end-of-season massacre of the Steelers, followed by another defeat in the playoffs, had soured Jim a bit on the NFL, especially with news that Big Ben wanted to come back. The other teams in the AFC North were stacked, from Cleveland to Cincinnati to Baltimore. He had no qualms about canceling the NFL season in the wake of Delta! But schools—he needed schools to open. That's where his troops were, where his assault on misinformation would have the most impact. He looked deep into the tiger's tired eyes.

"We'll bring down the culprits, FN," he said. "We've got to open schools, only to expose those who oppose us. That's where the battle will be. It's on the campuses where science and reason will take down the forces of reaction. We're building up our troops, tiger. We need to show just how deep the conspiracy of hate is, just how pervasive it has seeped into academia."

Fact-nerd paused a bit and seemed to be staring into space. Then he said, "Do you have a group at Stanford? That's where a lot of the most dangerous ones teach and live. When Delta hits us, they'll try to discredit me; they'll try to discredit the president. That's where they are, Jim."

Jim smiled. "Maybe, Tony, Delta is the ticket we need to take them all down."

CHAPTER FIVE

Delta Force

"Misinformation, gentlemen and ladies," Jim said, at a committee meeting in August, "is our greatest threat. We have a new variant that our science tiger has determined can potentially kill millions of Americans, kids too, everyone. It's called Delta. We can stop Delta; we're America, and we have the guts and resolve and brains to do that. But what's even more lethal than the virus is the misinformation being spread by haters and anti-science goons, the very same people who tried to take down our nation on January sixth. It's up to this committee to keep us safe. Kids are going back to school. If tens of thousands of them drop dead, American fingers will justifiably point to us."

One of the Republicans on the committee—a fairly powerful congressman from Texas, known as the Big Fish—pushed back. "My sources say that this Delta horsecrap is mild," the Big Fish said to Jim when he brought up the looming threat. "Sure, we got to worry about the old folks and such, but we shouldn't be scaring everyone else to death. Look, I get it; we got to be vigilant. But hell, we're trying to get this country back to normal. Ain't it time we get our lives back and stop living in this manufactured state of constant fear? Shouldn't we learn from past surges and stop with all this bullshit already?"

Jim Depich was no dummy. He chose his committee members carefully, although Corrine was kind of shocked by the appointed Republicans. Most were Trump allies from states that opposed the president's mandates. "Why them, Jim?" she asked him a few months earlier. "They'll fight you at every juncture."

Jim peered into her eyes. "Because they're vulnerable," he said. "I've picked the bombasts, the ones likely to oppose everything I do and then look foolish when they have to eat their words. They're all loyal to our former president, and they're all thus potentially linked to January sixth. All we need is another surge, another variant, and their position will be untenable, and that's when I'll take them down. I'm baiting them so they show their cards and then I will show the world who they are."

Corrine smiled. "You are just too smart for us normal people to even appreciate!" She glowed.

And then Delta slammed into the nation, and the Big Fish took the bait.

Thus, when the Republican from Texas tried to rebuke Jim's position by alleging to be "reasonable," Jim stung him with well-scripted venom. He handed a spreadsheet to the group. He had tabulated potential deaths from Delta based on Dr. Fact-nerd's estimates. Each column of his spreadsheet looked at various scenarios: if we don't mask, if we don't vaccinate, if we allow people to gather in mass, and so forth. He used data that experts from the University of Washington and Johns Hopkins and Cambridge had modeled based on potential worst-case scenarios, data vetted by the science tiger and others. Once he gave the committee members time to digest his numbers, he spoke to his Republican detractor.

"So, Fish," Jim said to the Texas representative, "there are the numbers, the stone-cold facts. And it seems that you are suggesting we let kids die, we don't protect anyone, we just build up corpses. So, what—you give those corpses more jobs? It seems like you're paving the path for the country to get into another mess. I know your views on January sixth. You may have deleted your tweet on that subject, but somehow it emerged, and all of us have seen it. And now you dig yourself a bigger hole by voting to ignore Delta, ignore the lives of Americans, and drop this country into a vat of chaos. I have just given you the facts, fish face. I laid them out in as simple a manner as your small brain can process. Tell us how you can justify your position, or are you just making conditions ripe for another coup?"

Jim knew he had the upper hand, so before anyone could intervene, he flashed a screenshot of the aforementioned tweet onto the room's white board. He peered deeper into the Republican's eyes as he slid a copy of the tweet toward him. "This yours, Mr. Fish?"

The Texan looked at it, then seemed to be peering around the room for some type of protestation from his colleagues. None came; most looked anywhere but at him. "What are you insinuating, Jim? Is this a witch hunt, or are we trying to come to terms with a crisis in our nation that needs our attention?"

"I don't know, Big Fish," Jim said to him, swimming in a cerebral high. "Are you a witch?"

The big fish laughed, quite uncomfortably it seemed to Jim, who responded by passing out a copy of the tweet to the other committee members. "The president has given me authority to root out misinformation with regard to the January sixth events and the pandemic," Jim said. "My own thesis is that there is a connection between those who instigated a coup of this nation and those who seek to misinform the population about how to best confront the pandemic. We've compiled and tabulated a great deal of data about misinformation being disseminated and the hidden agenda of some members of Congress with regards to COVID and January sixth. Congressman, what sayeth you? Do you have an explanation? Are you a witch, or are you simply a stupid old man who doesn't know how to tweet?"

"You know, Jim, slander ain't legal in this country," the Texas rep said, standing up and marching out. "You've far exceeded your authority on this committee, and I'm not playing your games, Jim. I'm done. Anyone else joining me? Or are the rest of you wet rags staying here and sucking up to this asswipe?"

"Flight, I must remind all of you, is an admission of culpability," Jim said, with a cocked smile.

"Being an ass ain't not much better," the big fish snarled. No one followed him. And so, Jim turned to the others, asked if they had anything to add, and then started to dig into the spreadsheets.

Later that night, on the tap dancer's news show, Jim spoke more about the committee than he had before.

"First, Dancer," he said to the obsequious anchor, who always listened politely and asked no questions, "let's start with some chilling information. There's a new variant of COVID coming our way, called Delta, and it represents a grave threat to our children and our youth on top of its usual prey. The immunized are likely protected, and we beg everyone to get the lifesaving jab. But too, people have to wear masks, socially distance, and call out any and all people who spread misinformation or who don't follow the rules. Delta can be a catastrophe if we don't follow the science, or something we will be able to mitigate and contain if we do, and as to which direction we go is up to the vigilance of the American people, who are the smartest and most sensible folks on the planet. We just don't want anyone misled by misinformation, because once we go down that road, it could be a lethal error for millions of people."

The anchor nodded, his visage grave, maybe a bit indignant. "Thank you for being so clear and forthright, Congressman. We've broadcast heartrending stories of kids who die and get incredibly sick from COVID strains far less dangerous than Delta, and yet we keep hearing from discredited academic and conspiratorial circles that this is not a children's illness. This is what we're up against, what you are up against, what Doctor Fact-nerd and our scientific and medical community are up against. It's infuriating that butchers of truth can so deceive Americans, as our heroic nurses and doctors deal with the fallout of hospitals overloaded by people who refuse to get vaccinated or follow simple precautions, and as grieving families must mourn a death that could have been prevented. We'll keep the American people honest and on track and have our crew of top doctors and scientists to let Americans know the truth, Congressman, I assure you of that. We do appreciate the spreadsheets you've provided us that clarify complex issues and that are consistent with what every expert from top academic institutions tells us night after night on this program. We'll get your spreadsheets up on DUI.com, and we implore all Americans to look at them. This is science; it's not complicated. Tell us what we should do, Congressman, to stay safe from Delta."

Jim nodded. "First, don't panic. If you just do what the task force and your doctors tell you to—following a few simple rules and getting the vaccine—we'll be able to contain Delta, and hopefully within two months, we can get back to a semblance of normal. And second, we do plan to have kids go back to school and college; we consider that very important to the future of our nation, but we are going to mandate vaccines and masks and distancing, and we don't want anyone to get in the way. But there's something else, America, something that I consider more important."

Jim paused for effect, as the tap dancer and he simply stared into the camera for a few painful seconds. Neither spoke. Then Jim breathed in and continued.

"As you've said, there are forces in this country trying to undermine what we're doing, Dancer. People perched in academia, on the radio, in the cracks of social media spreading lies faster than bees spread pollen. And we're starting to find links between the planners of January sixth and these serial liars, these misinformers, these dangerous sociopaths who want Americans to get sick because it increases their own power and feeds their own greed, because it discredits those who are trying to protect you. Our committee has compiled a list of such people whom we are investigating, people whom maybe some Americans have come to trust but who are the most dangerous and slippery vermin that exist on earth, much like the snake in the Garden of Eden, my good Americans, the snake who ruined it all for us. I beg the American people to be wary of misinformation being disseminated under the guise of scientific legitimacy."

"Wow," the tap dancer said, sighing in and shaking his head from side to side. "I mean, wow! Can you tell us more, Congressman? January sixth was the worst threat to our democracy in the history of our nation. We at DUI have pledged to remind Americans about what happened and have been squarely on the side of bringing all the perpetrators to justice. Tell us what to do."

"For now I want good Americans to listen to experts and not charlatans," said Jim. "Listen to the science tiger and the brilliant doctors whom you have brought on your show. They are telling you the truth, they are protecting you, and if you look at my spreadsheets, you'll better understand that simple fact. Our committee is trying to shut down misinformation and to identify the culprits of this grave threat. It's not censorship when we silence those who seek to take us down. It's not undemocratic when our concerned leaders temporarily institute measures of public safety to save American lives and protect our democracy. We'll do our part, I assure you of that, and I know that at DUI you are doing yours. I only ask this of the American people: Let us do our jobs to protect you and to protect this nation. Many will accuse us of being undemocratic. In fact, we're just the opposite of that. That's all I would ask."

"Congressman," said the anchor sternly, "you are indeed a hero. Yes, if history tells us anything, it's that even good people often fall prey to the alluring lies spun by monsters, and if we don't shut them down, if we let them draw us into a fascist stupor, well, if January sixth showed us anything, it's that our democracy is vulnerable and must be protected from those who seek to derail it. Thank you for all your good work, Congressman Depich, and America is certainly very lucky indeed to have you on its side in this war for our very survival."

The wheels of Jim's investigation were now in motion. His list of allies grew daily; few on the committee or in Congress dared to oppose him. He carried facts in his back pocket to support everything he said; spreadsheets and simple graphs buttressed his positions, and virtually every well-known scientific and medical expert from the best academic institutions in the world backed him up. Who would dare oppose the tsunami of science that Jim Depich brought to the table? Few did, leaving the ground ripe for Jim to pounce upon those who challenged him and his authority. Few moments in history offered a man so much ammunition to take down his enemies with such pious certitude. COVID sewed a thick fog of fear into the air, and January 6th congealed that fear into a palpable belly punch. Would America allow Jim Depich to protect it? Would it be willing to tolerate some pain in exchange for its own safety? At this point, Jim was not about to ask. It was time only to act.

That day he galloped along a trail in Rock Creek Park, chiding all those without masks, while a large number of well-wishers thanked Jim and told him to persevere. "We'll nail the bastards," he said to a young girl, who nearly cried as she nodded up and down in agreement.

"We have to," the girl said. "There are so many bad people out there, and it's so scary!"

Which Jim knew to be true. "It's time to snag the Big Fish," he said to Corrine later. She agreed.

CHAPTER SIX

A Frazzled But Intriguing Visit

As the summer heat lulled Americans into a false confidence that COVID might be behind them, even as alarming news about Delta burst from DUI like an earthquake to jolt Americans out of their stupor, Jim complied data about the congressman from Texas, the Big Fish, who abruptly left his committee and instigated a misinformation campaign claiming he was being framed by Jim and that his words were being massacred. But, Jim asked, how do you run away from a tweet?

"We need more than that, Jim," said Momma Nanna, who continued to obstruct his investigation into the congressman's misdeeds. Jim liked the speaker; she was all about mandates and supporting the COVID task force and putting out a singular message about the dangers of being too complacent, and her indignation against the January 6th plotters rivaled even his own, but she was a politician and thus she moderated too much and worried about how her actions would be perceived, thus blunting her ability to fight hard. "If you have holes in your accusations, they'll jump right into them, Jim, and tear our whole position to shreds. Give me more, and I'll give you what you need to prosecute the bastard."

Jim understood that this was a crusade, a battle between good and evil, life and death, democracy and autocracy; this was no time to worry about details and hard facts. Science spoke, and he could fill his spreadsheets with enough science to deflect any reprisals. The farther January 6th faded into the rearview mirror, the more Jim's mandate evaporated as well.

So, with his army of student volunteers whom Corrine recruited from across the nation, Jim's private committee swarmed through social media to dig up dirt. Jim's committee was given access to emails by NSA and other intelligence agencies, and the kids scoured them too, many of which were, well, disgustingly inappropriate and offensive. This generation of kids, they got it. They were outraged by anti-COVID backlash, by misinformation that disputed scientific gospel uttered by experts, by January 6th, by regressive thinking. These kids wanted change; they demanded a world in which—as they saw it—everyone was "woke" to social justice and right-wing vulgarity and anti-scientific barbarism was called out and expunged.

In the absence of anyone on the left who had a political backbone, the students, along with Jim's friends in the media, were his only hope of moving the narrative into crisis mode.

"We could nail him on being sexually and culturally insensitive," said one of the students. "At worst, we could release some of his own disgusting words, and it would get the truth committees on all the campuses riled up!"

That, of course, was a road Jim was willing to take, and in the coming months, it became an effective tool he used to convince many of Jim's enemies to come over to his side, but Congressman Big Fish was the first fish he needed to snag, so he had to do this one right, not by pointing to his horrific views on race and sex (hell, revelations like those only increased the appeal of Trump, and the same paradoxical effect could benefit the Big Fish too!), but by showing that his tweet was not just a blip, but represented his true beliefs, his true allegiance to the January 6th plotters. Once Jim proved the Texas congressman's culpability and the connection between January 6th apologists and anti-maskers, that would open the door to unending inquisitions. Jim referred to him as the Texas Bass, since bass was the most common fish in Texas, and that's what they were fishing for!

Jim had one other ploy up his sleeve. His committee subpoenaed four Republican congressmen and congresswomen, who he knew were very close to Trump or had ties to the former president. He called them in one at a time and interviewed them without the other committee members, with just him, Corrine, and some of the more enthusiastic students in their army. And while his questions were somewhat penetrating and accusatory, he kept the meetings jovial. He ended each interview with a single statement that he allowed to dangle before dismissing each of them: "We don't think you're involved in this, but we know there's a growing cabal in Congress of those who are known anti-maskers and those who are planning another Capitol raid. We're going down every road we can to find their leader. Between me and you, we think it's big fish, but we need to shore up our evidence. Any help you can give us to implicate him would certainly remove you from being investigated."

By now, people were just a bit frightened of the committee; Jim's daily slot on DUI with the tap dancer highlighted the frightening possibility of a sinister plot being hatched in DC, of which January 6th was just the initial jab. "We don't know their leaders or participants," Jim told the nodding anchor, who listened intently and asked no questions. "But we know they are in the anti-science crowd, same group who don't believe in COVID or in fighting it, same group, dance man. We've spoken to a few suspects, and we'll be calling in a lot more in the coming weeks, so stay tuned."

"Frightening, Congressman, just frightening," said a stern-faced dancer. "Keep us posted."

And Jim had two other problems on his hands.

First, what to do about the NFL. The COVID task force laid out safety standards that they recommended that the NFL institute allow fans back into stadiums and enable games to be played without restriction. Jim had no beef with their lame requirements, but he also didn't want the NFL to come crashing down mid-season if COVID caused one disruption after another, and he most feared that his Steelers with another year under Big Ben would fall prey to the big bad Ravens or the two ascendant teams from Ohio. He couldn't bear another loss to Cleveland!

"I may be able to talk the science tiger into putting the kibosh on the season," Jim said to Corrine. "Delta may be the excuse we need. Between me and you, a year without football will only be good for the Steelers; they'll be able to rebuild. And I'll personally tell Ben to hang it up; I'll give him another job in DC, a football ambassador, anything. I hate to waste a good crisis, Corrine!"

She laughed. "You are always thinking, JD. Always thinking! The terrible towel fans will thank you!"

If Jim wanted to use COVID for his own benefit, he refused to allow others to do the same, especially those in the anti-mask camp, and that proved to be the second problem with which he contended that summer. "We have to figure out what to do about the gathering strength of misinformation that's being spit out by academics, social media nuts, and right-wing politicians who hope to use COVID denial to rile the right-wing scum to their cause," he said to Corrine. "If people start looking at those morons as being legitimate scientists, as being right, if they start to question the DUI line or the CDC or our science tiger, then they're less likely to give license to the committee to do what we must to protect this country. Without a constant infusion of fear, and without a singular truth being trumpeted by our scientific community, people will be confused; people will moderate, and we won't have the mandate that we need."

The tap dancer promised to keep up the heat. "You and your tiger feed us what to say, and that will be our line," he said to Jim. "Delta is still raging, there's lots of fear about opening schools and relaxing restrictions, and we can keep our camera lens where we need to so that people stay suspicious of anyone who doubts the extent of the crisis or the need to be vigilant with our response to it. We won't be letting up on this any time soon."

Jim sat down with Dr. Fact-nerd, as he did many times a week. The tiger was no longer the engine behind the task force, which had been co-opted by some of Buck's crowd, mostly people like Got-milk and others with direct ties the pharmaceutical industry, but the tiger of science carried tremendous weight, and his words are what most

Americans heard and followed. He was the face of science and truth, the face Americans trusted. Anything that veered from his steady message is what Jim labeled as misinformation.

"The only way we're going to get our committee into a position of power is to assure that Americans hear and believe a single, unfettered message," Jim told Corrine early in the crisis. "The more confusion and nuance that's inserted in the dialogue, the less people feel good about what's going on, the more they look to other sources and start giving them credence. Look at Christianity. For a thousand years, the Catholic church promulgated a singular unassailable message of hope. 'Just do what we tell you, and your soul will be redeemed' was all they had to say, and no one dared defy them. And then all of a sudden, some petty despots decide to support Protestant leaders for their own benefit, and two hundred years of war and strife are the result. We need a single message, a single truth. Science isn't hazy; there's a right answer and a wrong one, and it's up to us and our people to tell Americans the right answer and to discredit the wrong one. That's how we take command of this moment."

For Jim and the DUI team and others, Doctor Fact-nerd represented science. He spoke the right answer, and anyone who defied his words spoke the wrong answer; they confused the world with misinformation. It became crucial to have a strong, unfettered science tiger behind him if he were to succeed, which is why Jim met with him every day.

The tiger was scared, despondent, and feeling a bit left out of the conversation when Jim called on him. "Jim, can I tell you a few things in confidence?" he asked the congressman. "Some things off the record that worry me."

Jim nodded up and down. "Tell me anything, FN, any doubts you have, any worries, but I need you to swallow those when you talk to the American people," Jim said to him. "I hope we understand each other. The message can't change on TV and in your press reports. It has to be consistent and to not waver in the tumult of misinformation; I'll handle the misinformation. You give Americans the truth. You got it, Dr. Big Brain? OK, tell me what worries you."

"One of the surviving Ken and Barbie boys has got a book coming out trying to link me to some grand conspiracy about Gated Billionaire," he said, his voice a bit tremulous. "Lots of people are going after me, Jim. Someone asked me about puppies that were part of an NIH experiment long ago. They won't stop at nothing!"

"Ken-barbie, the author of the moronic book you're talking about, is an anti-vaxxer and a nut," Jim said to the good doctor. "Is anything he is saying true? Because I'm happy to bring him in front of the committee and tear him to shreds."

The tiger paused. He took in a deep breath. "He pulls things out of context," he said. "Things happened. I have arrangements with different people and different groups. I do have patents. I do work with industry. That's how we get things done. It's how we cured AIDS, and how we're tackling COVID. Ken-barbie twists everything to make me look bad. I worry when his book comes out."

"It won't come out," Jim assured him. "He is top on our list to bring down, one of the kings of misinformation, and I'm sure he has ties to January sixth. And even if they're not provable right now, we'll get people to fink on him, and that will be proof enough. What else bothers you, FN?"

"And then," he continued, "there are the three troublemakers from Stanford. One was on the task force and did nothing but throw up roadblocks to everything we tried to do. Another created a petition to try to undermine us. The third is kind of the spiritual advisor to the other two, and he has been a thorn in the side of academia and its link to the pharmaceutical industry—a marriage, I have to remind you, Jim, that's allowed America to be the undisputed leader of medicines and treatments in the world. I fear that if their message comes out, it will lead to millions and millions of deaths and chaos, because they argue that we don't have to close society, we can keep everything open, that masks don't work—all of that. Delta is just the beginning, Jim. There's likely more horrible variants on the horizon, ones that will slaughter us if we let down our guard. And Ranting-Paul and the governors of Texas and Florida—they're all using the fake science from those Stanford people. They're using all that bogus information; they're using the Ken-barbie accusations, to try to push Americans away from what I'm telling them, and once that kind of doubt gets into people's minds, I am so scared of what may happen."

"The Stanford Three," Jim muttered, which is what he called them. "Our eyes are on them, Tony. I have twelve students skewering everything they've ever written to find inconsistencies and fabrications, maybe even a link to right-wing extremism. At least one of them is a Republican, but all three are troublemakers and malcontents. Don't worry; we'll take care of them. Keep declaring unequivocally and confidently everything you've been saying, and don't let these asses rattle you. Once you show any self-doubt, that will be their opportunity to damage you, and we can't let that happen."

The science tiger nodded up and down, took off his mask, and sneezed. His eyes seemed red and harried. He forced a smile. "I just worry, Jim, that if we let down our guard even one bit, then the country won't take this virus seriously enough, and when a variant comes along that is more virulent and kills the young and the old, they'll blame me! All I want is for people to listen to me, to listen to science, and to stop questioning everything. Is that too much to ask?"

Jim knew that it was not too much to ask; the nation's very existence relied on obedience to truth.

That night Jim sat in his apartment musing over the many threads of opportunity and peril that lay ahead. Thank God for Delta! As long as the waves of variants kept coming along, as long as DUI and the rest of scientific media stayed on message, as long as the democratic leadership didn't wither in the face of a feckless and desperate opposition, then he knew that his committee could take care of business. With eager students, media compliance, and incessant fear, Jim believed he could break through the wall of moderation that thwarted his committee's holy battle against satanic misinformation.

But first he needed to snag the Texas bass! The campus movement would soar into action by September, providing a grassroots assault on the forces of reaction. Jim sat on his couch and watched poor Daffy Duck and Bugs fight with each other about whether it was duck or rabbit season, trying to trick poor Elmer Fudd into shooting the other one. Of course, Bugs always outwitted Daffy, and the duck got shot every time. Jim idolized Bugs Bunny. Subtle, clever, and persuasive. That's how he was going to win; he had to think like the wascally wabbit!

And just like that, there was a rap at the door, which shook Jim from his trance.

He knew it wasn't Corrine. She was busy acting like a rabbit herself with Mark up in State College. Then who could be calling on him? Sometimes Jim feared for his life. God only knew what his right-wing enemies were capable of! He slid close to the door.

"Yes?" Jim called out from behind the door.

"I'm sorry" came the raspy voice of a woman. "I'm sorry to bother you here. I found your address, and I thought it was your work. I tried to make an appointment to see you, but they say it's going to be weeks. I am one of your constituents from Pittsburgh. I'm a doctor there. I'm on the front line of COVID, and I just wanted to talk with you."

"Friend or foe?" Jim asked.

The woman laughed, big and jolly. "Friend, I hope," she said. "I voted for you, and for President Buck. I'm not a nutjob, if that's what you're asking. But I want to talk with you, because I don't think we're going about this the right way, and I want to help."

Jim hesitated for a moment. Who knew who this person was? *I should just tell her to meet me at the office tomorrow,* his rational brain told itself. But for some reason, he decided to open the door and let this woman in. Her voice, well, it was kind of sexy!

The woman stood tall, long, and slender in a wrinkled and disheveled brown blouse. Her hair was big and wild, draped all the way down her back. She wore no makeup and looked about his age. Certainly, no young hottie! But her big and penetrating eyes, her captivating smile, her very aura of quiet confidence unhinged him. For a moment, he could barely speak. His heart started beating fast.

"Hi," he said to her. "I'm Jim Depich, your congressman."

And that made her laugh, which only drove Jim even more crazy. "I know, Congressman, that's why I'm here! Thank you so much for seeing me! You are a godsend to Pittsburgh."

If it weren't for the dagger of the #MeToo movement, Jim may have made a more provocative comment at that moment, but he deferred. He let her in, sat her down, made her some peppermint tea, and then heard her laugh big and loud. He snuck his face in and saw she was watching TV and seemed to be rapt in his *Looney Tunes* DVD.

"I love this episode!" she said. "It says it all, doesn't it? If only today's kids watched this stuff, then maybe our world would be a little saner, and a lot funnier!"

Jim sat by her, her presence here making him a bit squirmy. And for the next hour, he listened to her talk. She had a lot to say. She wanted to show him data, tell him about her experience on the front lines of COVID, and convince him of certain facts that were not exactly in line with his. She did it all so gently, with those big eyes, that intoxicating voice, that he didn't want to interrupt her. He just stared at her, and he smiled. He peered at her fingers. No ring. Should he ask her if she were married? Was that inappropriate? He wondered how he could sew it into the conversation.

"So, did you ask about the ring?" Corrine emailed him later when he relayed the whole story. "It sounds like she was telling you things you don't want to hear! How did you deal with that, Jim?"

He emailed her right back. "When you look into those eyes, there's not much you don't want to hear, Corrine. Besides she voted for me, how bad could she be? I invited her to dinner on Wednesday when I'll be in Pittsburgh, to talk about some of her issues. Is that appropriate?"

Even Corrine's email seemed to laugh. "It's only inappropriate if you get what you want from her! Do me a favor; keep it in a public place, just for now. What's her name?"

To that question, Jim had no answer. He had forgotten to ask!

CHAPTER SEVEN

Some Damned Good-Looking Misinformation

With Delta surging, and his people domineering the air-waves and the narrative, Jim prepared for his dinner with the doctor. "The very sexy doctor," Jim reminded Corrine.

"It's not a date, Jim," Corrine reminded him. "If you want a date, I'll set you up with someone, or go on Tinder. This woman, God bless the fact you seem to like her, she's the polar opposite of you. She's the enemy. That's how I see it. What do you hope to accomplish talking to her?"

Jim shrugged. "Can't hurt to talk," he said. "Besides, she's on the front lines. If I can convince her of the nobility of our cause, maybe it will help swing things. I mean, she seems so nice."

"Oh God, Jim, that sounds more like a man looking at some-one's tits than a politician looking for allies. If you want some young flesh, Jim, half the women in our campus groups idolize you. And this woman whom you like so much, who is so much like you, is she even a Steelers fan?"

Jim smiled. "I'm afraid to ask," he said. "That would be a deal breaker. But she is from Pittsburgh, so at least I know she's no Ravens fan. And she likes Bugs Bunny, which to me, well, that says a lot."

"Just be careful, Jim," Corinne said, hugging him and stroking his hair. "There are a lot of people looking to take you down. You can't afford to make any mistakes. No jokes, no advances. We're at the brink of doing something amazing. Don't let your balls destroy your life's greatest moment."

"This gal is all business," he said, pivoting away. "We'll see where it goes. Meanwhile, what about you? Any babies on the way? And more importantly, how are our students doing? That's our army, Cor."

Corrine glowed. "We have thousands of eager young zealots joining the Truth Clubs all over the country," she gloated. "The kids are working night and day; they're so into it, Jim. these kids are gathering together in chat groups remotely pretty much every day so they can collaborate, compiling info on anyone on campus who refused to be vaccinated, kids and professors, the ones with exceptions, the anti-maskers, all of them. I'm confident we'll have some links between anti-mask professors and the January sixth movement before the first day of class. The kids plan to stage protests on day one of school and to scare the crap out of Trumpists hiding on campus. I dare any university president or dean to try to stand in our way."

"Good," said Jim. "That is what we need."

The next night on the tap dancer's show, Jim revealed that something big was about to transpire in the war against misinformation, not only in his committee (which had stalled) but mostly on college campuses.

"I'll tell you this, dance man," he said. "We have been working so hard for this nation, all of us, trying to make sure we stamp out those who are getting in the way of our COVID policies, making sure another January sixth doesn't happen again. God bless us, we have tens of thousands of college kids on campuses across the country working with us, devoted to the cause of science and liberty, to the cause of life. These are the real pro-lifers, tap dancer. Not the radical right-wingers who use that title while trying to deprive women of their rights to their own bodies. Those deceptive pro-lifers are responsible for policies that have killed hundreds of thousands of Americans by refusing to wear masks or vaccinate themselves, even as they question and block the efforts of devoted scientists and patriots, even as they question the one and only scientific truth. How is that pro-life, Dancer? That's anti-life if you ask me, and we're calling those thugs out for their hypocrisy. The kids working with us, they are pro-life. They are the real deal. Pro-science, pro-democracy, pro-life. And frankly, if you're against us pro-lifers, than you're anti-life, and I'm betting you have an agenda Not in line with the values of this nation and of God's good grace.

The tap dancer's face twisted into that serious glance that viewers of DUI knew so well. "Tell us more, Congressman. What do you mean by their agenda?"

Jim paused and then looked at the camera. "What I mean, dance man, is that our committee has uncovered evidence that many of the very misinformers who question scientists like our science tiger and the experts whom you bring on your show to educate the American people—that those misinformers, many of them at least—have ties to the January sixth Capitol attack. Some sit near me in Congress, mostly on the other side of the aisle. Some are in academia, like the Stanford Three whom you and your co-anchor Cheddar have called out so many times for their murderous policies. Some are students and faculty at our colleges. But this we know: All of them are working together to undermine this nation. You see, dancer, they don't want this crisis to ever go away. They'll do anything in their power to make sure that COVID keeps causing chaos across the nation. That's how they sow the seeds of discontent. That's what they need to do to prepare for another coup attempt. It's frightening, America. But we're getting to the bottom of it."

"I'm sure it is, Congressman," said the concerned and perspicacious journalist. "And you have proof of this? Something you can share with us?"

Jim nodded up and down. "When colleges open, the misinforming students and professors who try to hide behind a flimsy shield of personal privacy will be handed a lesson in science and civility—the form of swarms of angry students who, unlike politicians, aren't intimidated by liars. And yes, we have proof that many in academia and many congressmen are complicit in the January sixth attack, the very same congressmen and alleged scientists who are on *the Foxxy* news channel decrying Doctor Fact-nerd and mocking those who wear masks. Unfortunately, I can't reveal anything now, but believe me, once we are ready to put a stake in the cold hearts of these vampires, you will be the first to know."

The tap dancer nodded solemnly. "And just so you know, Congressman, we at DUI will be with you all the way, no questions asked, no barriers placed in your investigation. Democracy is under assault, and we are committed to help you bring to justice those who are responsible. You are a hero, Congressman. Our democracy is going to owe you one big hug when this ends."

As he drove to Pittsburgh, Jim hoped for a big hug from someone else. What would he say to her? What if she proved, as Corrine feared, to be on the other team? His heart beat fast in anticipation.

They met at Big Jim's. Why not? It was his namesake and one of his favorites! And what do you know, she liked it too! Hoagies were her thing it turned out.

"I prefer DeLuca's," she said. "But they close after lunch. Big Jim's got the best cheesesteak outside of Philly. And onion rings to die for! It's all the crap I tell my patients to avoid. But what the hell, how often do I get to have dinner with my congressman?"

She wore a long and wrinkled blouse, spattered with something, who knew what, maybe blood, maybe the mucus of someone who had died of COVID. Jim didn't care. Her hair was wild, unkempt, and her face lacked even the most residual makeup. But she glowed like the moon! Her eyes, her smile; it was captivating. He looked again at her fingers, long and slender. No rings. Not even one!

She carried a sullied gray backpack and pulled out a stack of papers. Then she looked into Jim's eyes and smiled. He nearly fainted!

"I have reams of info, Congressman," she said. "But I prepared a summary for you. With references. I know you're not the kind of guy just to take my word for anything, a quality I admire. Thank you so much for meeting with me. My friends are all jealous! We may have to take a selfie!"

He laughed. "Call me Jim," he said. "And what should I call you?"

"Duh," she said. "I guess a name would be nice. I'm Doctor Raven. Kate Raven."

"Kiss me, Kate," he instinctively sang out to her. Her eyes shriveled just a bit.

My God, he thought, *that's a me-too guff if I ever made one.* But Jim recovered fast. "My favorite movie. *Kiss Me Kate.* When I hear that name, it brings back that movie. Well, pleasure to meet you, Kate. I'd call you Doctor Raven, but got to tell you, that's the name of the enemy."

She laughed, extending her hand and shaking his. "Yea, I get it. I get flak about that all the time. I was born before the Ravens were a team, so can't blame my relatives for that. Not a big football fan, and with the Steelers quarterback a rapist, well, you know, anyway, I know you're a big Steelers fan, and even if I'm lukewarm about a sport that is owned by industry and delivers too many concussions, rest assured that my kitchen towels are terrible yellow, and I'm not a fan of purple at all!"

If Jim planned to be careful, well, that kind of fell apart right away. Even her name and her quip about Big Ben—which was maybe true, but that was a long time ago—didn't rile him. He wanted to know more before she ruined everything with that stack of paper.

"So, is your husband a Steelers fan?" he cleverly asked. "Or your wife? I don't make any assumptions these days. Maybe you're with a *they*, not a man or a woman. I mean, who knows?"

She seemed just a bit more uncomfortable. The waiter came by, and they ordered—Jim fried oysters with a local stout, Kate the cheesesteak with onion rings, and an iced tea. She fiddled with her papers and looked at the floor.

"I kind of remember how you answered that question when you were first running for Congress," she said to him, looking up and smiling again. "Someone asked why you weren't married. You said that your priest was married to God, your hero Albert Einstein was married to the pursuit of truth, and that you were perfectly fine being married to the great people of Pittsburgh. I loved that you said that! You didn't run away from the question at all; you embraced it. I'm married to my people too, Congressman. To my job, my work on improving the health-care system, my parents and siblings, to myself mostly. No, never been married. I'm not even sure I've been on a formal date. I'm very happy just being with me. I may be the only one on earth who can stand myself, so why bring anyone else in the mix, right?"

"Well, I'm sure you have a million people who love you, Kate," Jim said to her, staring sharply into her eyes. "You are beautiful and smart and devoted. And yes, you are right, no reason to ruin things with marriage. Although, if you're like me, you have to hang out with a bunch of married couples, which isn't the most enjoyable thing in the world."

She laughed and nodded. "My friends call me TW for short, which means 'third wheel.' I've kind of embraced it. Although at the rate my friends are getting divorced, most of them look at me like I'm some kind of seer. Well, Congressman, I may not love the Steelers quite as deeply as you, but we have at least three things in common other than our embrace of being single. We both think Bugs Bunny is a hoot. Albert Einstein is both of our heroes. And we both seek out the truth."

It had to come eventually, so why not now? Might as well get it over with! That's what Jim's brain said, even as his heart continued to race faster than a man running a marathon. Besides, if he got her talking, he could stare at her and not have to make any excuses. So, he asked. "So, Kate, what is your truth?"

And that's when she dug into her stack. She talked and talked, sliding papers his way with graphs and references, even a few spread-sheets! "I know you like these." She giggled, in the cutest of ways. He stared at her, her facial expressions, her smile, her eyes, her passion. Terrible thoughts fluttered through his mind. He wondered what she looked like under that blouse, whether her breasts were bigger than they appeared. He thought about how her passion could be turned into something amazing beneath a nice warm blanket. He barely heard anything she said.

Although she said a lot. She quoted statistics from the Stanford Three and other like-minded scientific heretics. She even used facts from Ken-barbie's website. She talked about her own experiences, which were mostly in nursing homes, where she said she took care of hundreds of people with COVID.

"They all got it through masks, Congressman," she said, peering at him. "We've had mask mandates in these facilities since day one, and they're all extremely vigorously enforced. Despite that, with every wave of COVID, our places get flooded with illness. If you take that reality and you juxtapose it with the facts I showed you, facts that clearly decry any efficacy of masks for a virus that goes right through them, study after study that shows they don't work, then you can see why we need another approach."

Jim had once asked the science tiger how he knew that masks were the answer, and why he changed his mind early in the pandemic, when he had written that they don't work. The tiger smiled and said, "Well, Jim, we need something, and until we know more, this is all we've got."

He looked at her and smiled, insisting they order black-and-white milkshakes for dessert. "Can't come all this way and not get one." He laughed, and she relented, sucking it down with joy, her sumptuous lips pursed on that straw as her eyes twinkled.

"Look," he said, realizing that if he left some things in limbo, he could use that as a reason to meet her again, "you probably have to get to work early. I heard what you said, and I'll look over this data. Thank you for presenting it so meticulously. It's a complicated issue."

And then she leaned over, her face just inches from his, her steak-tinged breath exciting him, and she peered pleadingly in his eyes. "We don't have to shut down the world, Jim," she said in her gravely, sexy voice that was both sweet and hungry. "We don't have to scare kids and mask everyone. We just have to focus on these poor old folks. They're the ones dying, and they're dying from the disease and from being locked up. Masks aren't helping. I have other ideas. Like daily testing. Like early treatment, which my colleagues and I have used effectively." Then she paused, nodding up and down. A big smile lit up her face, and she continued.

"There is a guy I want you to meet," she said. "He knows a lot. He's in one of the national security agencies. He has more data than I even understand. He's not a crazy person, not someone you'll find on social media, but he sought me out and woke me up. He has dirt on the science tiger and a lot of others. He doesn't trust a lot of people, but he trusts me, and I'll tell him that he should trust you too."

Jim smiled. "Yes," he said, realizing that she just fed him a morsel of gold. "Yes, I'd like to meet him. When do I have the pleasure of dining with you again, Kate? We still have so much more to discuss."

Who could this man be? Was he a major planner of January 6th, someone who could perhaps tie some loose ends together? He needed more information. And besides, he wanted to see her a few more times. Maybe he'd even get lucky before he had to pull out a knife and take her down with the other heretics. This was a meal to be remembered!

PART TWO

Reputative Justice

CHAPTER EIGHT

An Incident at MD Park Campus

As a warm September loomed, and Jim became more irritated by his decision to cancel the NFL ("I think maybe Ben had one more run"), he had some good news to report to Corrine. Every night on DUI, he said he was getting closer to finding culprits in the January 6th raid, high-profile anti-maskers who had been instrumental in trying to take down the government. He was baiting people, people who may have had some loose link to the coup and would be frightened by his accusations. And then, one of them bit.

"She's a right-winger from Missouri," he told Corrine. "She came to my office and said that she may have an email or two that, should I get my hands on it, she didn't want me to misconstrue, because if taken out of context, some of them may look damaging. I told her that I had read all her emails."

"Have you, Jim?" she asked. "I didn't think she was even on your radar."

He laughed. "No, of course not. She wasn't. But she should have been. She's a big anti-science zealot, doesn't believe in global warming, hates the tiger, is anti-choice and wants Roe overturned, thinks that vaccine mandates are unconstitutional. We should have been watching her. So, when she outed herself, I, of course, insinuated that we had read everything, and that I was a day away from summoning her to our committee. That got her woke, to use your generation's expression."

"You're using it wrong, but whatevah," she said, laughing back, patting him on the head, "I can get our guys at NSA to dig up her phone and electronic communication and have Collin and Brie dig through her social media accounts; they're our two best assets, good kids, really devoted. You bringing her in?"

He nodded from side to side. "I need all the dirt I can get, but I'd rather make a deal with her. She'll get immunity and no public scrutiny if she names names. I want our Texas bass, and if she can help me snag him, well, that will start the cascade of feasible culpability that I need to get the committee rolling. I told her she can help me or she can try to defend herself in front of the American people. DUI plans to cover the committee hearings live. It will be a national spectacle!"

"And what are you going to do about the Stanford Three? Any leads on their shit? Or do we just bring them in and try to badger them down so hard that they relent?"

"No, they're too smart for that," he said. "I'm meeting Kate again tomorrow, this time for lunch. I suggested we can go to her place afterward if we need more time to go through her stuff. Was that too forward? I need more time with her, so I'll play nice."

"I'm sure that's a great sacrifice for you, Jim," Corrine smirked. "Bed chatter is often revealing."

Jim smiled. "While that would be nice, Cor, that's not the only reason for my infatuation. She's got friends she wants me to meet, maybe even this Mr. X she talks about, and I need her to trust me enough so that I can get into their heads. She has lots of data, mostly from nursing homes and the like; she says those are the people dying and that we're doing nothing to protect them and everything to scare those who don't need protection. She is totally anti-mask and says that despite mask mandates in nursing homes, everyone got sick. She's got more people for me to talk to with the same angle."

"She sounds pretty extreme, Jim," Corrine said. "Did you run her data by the tiger and Got-milk?"

In fact, he had. The science tiger was especially upset about it, and he started to pant and sweat when Jim told him some of her tales.

"This is what I'm up against, Jim," he said. "These aren't facts. They're what we call nit-picking. Masks have a larger role than just blocking virus, Jim. They let people know that we have to be on guard. They may help prevent some infections, but they mean more than that. And we don't know what's coming next, Jim. There's a variant brewing in South Africa that scares me. We may have a variant that hits kids harder. One less focused on the old. We've heard all the crap that doctor is saying; it's part of the misinformation campaign to discredit us. But if we focus on those puny details, those biased facts, then we'll miss out on the big picture. Once people start thinking that only old people are vulnerable, once they stop believing in masks and societal closures, then they won't care anymore, and what if a new variant comes? Once we let down our guard, we could all die, Jim."

"We won't let down the guard," Jim assured the nervous scientist. "To preserve our democracy and to discredit the Trumpists, we have to make sure to keep up the battle against misinformation. You and I are on the same page, FN; we're all about the science. Right now, we're blocking misinformation on social media, on a lot of broadcast news, among doctors—who are losing their licenses should they open their mouths in the wrong direction—and in the public arena. But it's not enough, my relentless science tiger. As long as people like this doctor are out there, as long as DaSandwich and the Big Fish are riling up their constituents with lies, as long as the Stanford Three have a forum from which to spew their lies from sea to sea, the seeds of our country's self-destruction are being sewn. We need to take them down hard, and for that, we need you and everyone on your side to be unrelenting. The kids will help, and so will our media pals. The committee is our best hope."

"Thank you, Jim," Fact-nerd said. "We all thank you for your commitment to science and the nation."

Sometimes when Jim came out of these meetings, or finished a segment on DUI, he glowed in the luster of his courage and fortitude. He had done what no one else was willing to do, to take on those who sought to bring down the country during its greatest crisis. He stepped up, while others recoiled. Many thanked him, like the handsome democratic governor from California he called Newbie, who often said that the only way to have people listen and obey is to keep up a high enough level of fear so that people didn't squabble about personal rights in the face of a national catastrophe. Jim knew that, the tiger knew that, Tap dancer knew that, but many others needed to be taught that lesson, and Jim knew that he had to do it boldly by undressing the most vocal critics of science in front of his committee on national TV.

"I don't want to scare everyone to death, Jim," the president said to Jim on day during their new scheduled brief meetings. "Lots of people in Congress are complaining that you're hitting them with baseless allegations. We have an investigation going into January sixth, and we don't want that to be your committee's focus. And we don't want everyone to be so scared that they stop going to restaurants or shopping. You're doing a great job, Jim, but we need the economy to rev up, or the other side, well, Jim, they'll take back the House and Senate. That's what our polls show. Like I said, we all think you're doing a great job. Just back off a bit, that's all."

"Mr. President," Jim shot back, "with all due respect, our committee is set up precisely to look into links between the anti-maskers and the January sixth coup. That's our function. How can you tell me to back off? This is a national emergency, Mr. President. Do you want a coup to happen again, to maybe succeed this time? Do you want the anti-vaxxers to quarterback the COVID debate and shape national opinion? Mr. President, there are forces imbedded deep in academia, in congress, in the media trying to take down this nation, appealing to people's rights as a ruse to stage another coup and end the great American experiment, to hasten the chances that we'll be wiped out by the next COVID surge. This is about science, Mr. President. About being tough. Don't stop what we're doing. That's all I ask."

Star Buck smiled big and bright and put his hands on Jim's shoulders. "I know all that, Jim, and we're looking into it. Like I said, you're doing a great job; let's just tone it down a bit, OK? We don't need so much malarkey from the other side convincing Americans that they're reasonable and we're plain crazy. Just tone it down. And keep up the good work!"

They're the reasonable ones? Jim sometimes didn't understand how naïve and feckless these politicians were. He needed something big to happen, something that would wake up the country's leaders who seemed to be hobbled by opinion polls and bad press. And then, in early September, the shit hit the fan.

Mary Lou Kramer was the most unassuming of souls, and certainly not the fodder of a revolutionary leader. She grew up shy and protected by her parents, who were both highly educated liberals who lived in the town of Columbia, Maryland. She was one of three kids, and as the middle girl with two boys flanking her, she was pushed into sports and other groups activities, which she really didn't like. She did enjoy reading, so her parents got her involved in reading groups and online writing seminars. They traveled often, and during dinner, they would watch *Rachel In the Meadow* together on Makes-sense-NBC, followed by a taped episode of Cold-bert. Mary Lou read a lot about climate change, which was her passion. She loved science but had no desire to be an engineer like many of her friends. As she told her few friends when they asked her what she wanted to do when she grew up, she said, "I want to make the world good."

As time went on and Mary Lou spent too much time reading and snacking, her genetic propensity for obesity crept upon her, even as her two fit brothers were the "hottest dudes in town," as her forty-year-old neighbor told her far too often. Mary Lou was never sure about her sexual orientation. Probably she liked boys, but they never showed any interest in her, whereas a lot of girls did. She enjoyed being fluid sexually and became a crusader for the rights of the sexually liberated. When she insisted on her family using the pronoun *they* to describe her, her brothers pushed back, but not her dad.

"They, her, it; I don't care," her dad said. "She's your sister, and we love her."

When she matriculated at the MD Park Campus, she decided to major in biology, and she landed an internship at the NIH her first summer. She loved it, swimming in science with like-minded souls. She latched onto a couple professors at school and thrived there academically.

Socially, well, that was another matter for Mary Lou, who was a homebody. She had grown even larger in girth and felt self-conscious about her appearance. She thought people were always laughing at her. She joined a few groups on campus involved with environmental reform, global warming, and sexual orientation awareness. She led an effort to fire a history professor who rarely assigned works by women or people of color. She caught a lot of flak for that, as he was quite popular; a group of kids even came by her apartment one day to threaten her. When she told her group leader, Brittany, about this, they protested to the dean that they were being discriminated against, and the kids were expelled.

As small and insignificant as she felt, as out of place in a world of athletes and thin people, Mary Lou thrived on the acquisition of knowledge and in her ability to get bad people punished.

And then COVID hit. Like virtually everyone in her progressive groups, she leaped to the cause of the CDC and the brilliant and sweet science tiger, wanting to do her part to save the world from this dreaded disease. She self-isolated for much of 2020, and wore masks everywhere, even in the bathroom. She would have zoom meetings with her groups, all of them in masks, and they'd ridicule Trump and Republicans day and night, blaming them for every disaster that hit the country.

"We should have been ready for this," Mary Lou told the group. "Trump disbanded the pandemic task force. He's against masks and immunizations. He doesn't want to test so he can be in denial. Now he wants us to drink antifreeze and take horse pills! It's up to us to make sure our campus opens safely. I know a lot of kids who are mocking this, who are Republicans, who think it's all a joke. It's up to us to make sure we put them in their place."

Knowledge was power. Mary Lou knew that. She read everything she could from the CDC, DUI, *The New Yacking Times*, and her trusted social media sources. She became a COVID expert, an evangelical ready to fight the good fight. When the campus opened its truth committee, she volunteered to lead it, and that's where she met

Corrine. She had pictures of the science king, Bringback Barak, and Jim Depich hanging in her apartment. She'd kiss them every night.

When it was announced that school would be opening in 2021, she and a few members of the Turtle Truth Club requested an audience with the school's president. They had a list of demands, some of which went ever further than the CDC guidelines, including that every student must wear an N-95 on campus all the time, inside and out. They must all be vaccinated, no excuses. "It's a matter of whether this campus is going to be pro-science and pro-life, or if it's going to fold to the extreme right."

The president was sympathetic and planned to be strict in her enforcement of the law—after all, she said, President Buck was tying a great deal of federal funding to compliance, and many grants and internships were also contingent on MD Park Campus being in line—but she didn't want any backlash. She would only go so far, she said. "Moderation is always a better path," she told the kids.

But Mary Lou would not accept that position, and working with Corrine, who had contacts at NSA, they gathered data about many of the more right-wing students, those with vaccine exceptions, those who declared that they had voted for Donald Trump, those who mocked the masks.

"It's easy to see who we need to worry about," Mary Lou told the group. "Not wearing a mask is a sign that you are one of them. You're on the other side. You're anti-science and anti-democracy. You're for the January sixth raid. You're anti-life."

All of a sudden, Mary Lou was a bit of a celebrity, and she enjoyed it. She also knew that many of the kids on her hit list were likely the jocks and cool kids, the very ones who had mocked her all those years. Now she planned to take them down.

And thus, on the first day of classes in MD Park Campus, Mary Lou convinced her Truth Group—over two hundred fellow progressives—to do something bold, something that would set them apart from the innocuous protests planned on other campuses. Using the knowledge she had obtained, and also information Corrine passed to her, she targeted twelve kids, eight boys and four girls, who she declared were in violation of the ethics of the academic community and were a threat to everyone on campus.

"If the administration is too fraidy scared to bring them down," she declared at a pivotal meeting of the Truth Club in early September, "then we will show them what it takes to be patriots!"

And so, on a warm and breezy day, when students scurried to their classes, when the football team was preparing for its big game against West Virginia, Mary Lou sent groups of twenty Truth Club members to gather each of the twelve students they targeted and to bring them to the center of campus for a mock trial. They would be held down, masked, and hear the accusations made against them. Then they could answer and, if decreed guilty, would be punished. "The administration, in its acquiescence to these kids who are dangerous and who oppose all virtues of decency and freedom and science, is making our campus, indeed our entire nation, unsafe and ripe for another coup attempt. We thus will take matters in our own hands."

As the twelve "perpetrators of heinous crimes" kneeled down, their hands roped, masks tightly suffocating their faces, being hit and kicked by members of the Truth Club, Mary Lou read them the crimes of which they were guilty and announced that many professors and administrations would be next in line to be tried. Crowds of students gathered around, some cheering, some jeering. Any of the latter was met by members of the Truth Club, who struck them with rocks. No one from security came by.

Although she didn't know it, by the time the accused had their chance to respond, three of them were dead, having either suffocated or having bled in their heads from the repeated kicks and punches. Four members of the crowd who opposed this trial were also either dead or dying from reprisals of Truth Club members, who believed that the ancient ritual of stoning the guilty still had some merit. And before the day was over, most of the others would be dead too.

"This is our first salvo," Mary Lou proclaimed. "May justice and science be our guides!"

When she learned of the deaths, she merely laughed. "As I said," she quipped, "it's reputative justice. And watch out, anti-lifers. There's more ahead for you. A lot more."

CHAPTER NINE

In Search of Mr. X

A brewing storm struck the nation hard. Jim was no sailor, but as an engineer, he knew his physics. If you catch the wind, it can propel you faster than you even imagined going before. But if you ran into it, or if it hit you on the side, the wind could swamp your boat in an instant.

"And so, now you decide to go see your girlfriend, now, now when we need you to be on top of this mess?" Corrine said to him, tossing her arms in the air. "It's amazing how testosterone makes you men its prisoner. It's like your penis controls your brains."

Jim laughed. "Corrine, you know me, and you know I'm not like that. This meeting I set up with Kate, I assure you, it's all part of the master plan. We have to go with the momentum and make it count. Any backing off and people will recoil and get chicken. We laid the seeds, Corrine. Your overzealous student friends tossed on a shitload of fertilizer. Now we have to keep those flowers growing and cultivate them into something meaningful. We can't let them die by backing off."

"I don't know what the hell that even means, Jim," she said. "But I have two kids and a third on the way. I don't want to be in someone else's cross fires. Mark is already telling me to quit. A lot of the press isn't supportive of what's happening on campuses; even some of our guys, people in DUI and MMakes-sense NBC, they're questioning the violence and deaths. Your public indictments against congressmen, scientists, and politicians are drawing heat and calls for your expulsion and for your committee to be disbanded. And now you think fucking some girl will help us?"

"I do," Jim said, smiling, "which are the two words I hope to say to Kate very soon. I'm just joking, Corrine; stop looking at me that way! Kate is the opposition; she knows people who are the very clarion of misinformation, and they know people, and all those people, all those misinformers, if they think I'm with them, then they'll trust me, and once that happens, I'll gather enough dirt to justify what Mary Lou did, what our committee is doing, and what the American people will see as a just cause. I may not score with Kate; in fact, I'm a bit pessimistic about that reality. But I intend to score in other ways."

"Oh, sorry for your pessimism, JD," she said, clearly not eased by his levity. "Jim Depich may not get laid by a girl who is his mortal enemy. Oh, how the whole world will fall apart because Jim Depich won't get to put his cock into someone who is trying everything in her power to destroy us. I'm just so sad."

Jim hugged Corrine, and this time he kissed her on the head. "We're good," he said. "It's all working out just like we hoped. Don't worry. We're good! I promise!"

But even Jim wasn't quite sure.

Later that day, Attorney General Dorothy Demerit called Jim into his office for what Jim presumed to be an informational session, but, instead, it turned into a chewing-out rant. "You can't just have a bunch of wild kids dispensing justice, killing people, for God's sake, Jim," Demerit said. "Those kids are killing people under your name, Jim! And at Stanford, members of those Truth Clubs that you have formed and endorsed, they are holding some professors hostage. Are you aware of that, Jim?"

"The Stanford Three," Jim told him. "Yea, you're talking about three very dangerous professors there who are being held until we call them in front of the committee. The university wouldn't do it, so we did. We have a lot of dirt on them, and we didn't want them to flee.

They won't die, Dot. They're being treated well. They just have to wear masks. That's like their only beef, if you can believe it."

"Jim," he went on, "the president isn't happy. I'm not happy. This can sling shot back and really hurt us. What are you going to do about the girl from MD, and all her accomplices? I can't believe she hasn't been arrested. The families of those innocent kids who died are irate and pressing charges. How closely is she tied to you? I mean, if you have some role in this, Jim, you know that the president will have to call you out on it. You're toast if your handprints are anywhere near these college kids."

Jim paused and stared at this man, who was both courageous and sensible, one blocked by a whisker from being a member of the highest court in the land, but who is now literally shook in his boots out of fear from Jim's pursuit of justice. How weak were these people? Jim wondered. Did they not understand how strong were the people who were trying to take down the government? Why weren't they willing to hit back just as hard rather than recoiling every time someone cried foul? No wonder he called the guy Demerit; that's all he deserved due to his whimpering trepidation during a national crisis.

"Maybe you haven't watched the news, but other than on Foxxy, we're not being skewered," Jim responded. "Let's push our advantage, and if that gets us in hot water, then sure, you can blame the whole thing on me. I sent you my spreadsheets, Dorothy. Every one of those kids at MD Park Campus died of natural causes. They caused their own deaths by resisting very brave and smart kids who were trying to keep the campus safe. The dead kids are the ones who are the villains, not the truth committee members. Everyone in the press agrees with that assessment. We've released documents showing that several of those kids supported the January sixth raids, and all of them are virulent anti-science and have defied the COVID rules. What are you missing here, Mr. Attorney General? I thought you were the one who is supposed to silence the bad guys and keep the country safe. This is why no one is assailing Mary Lou and the Truth Clubs. What they did was necessary given the silence and weakness of the federal response."

"Yea, Jim, there is another reason no one is coming after the Truth Clubs," he said. "It's because of your vitriol. When you get on TV and accuse anyone who shows any compassion to the dead kids of being a possible accomplice to the January sixth raid, of threatening to pull them in front of your committee, then yea, it's no wonder why people aren't coming forward and arresting the murderers. Your damned committee scares everyone shitless."

"As it should, Dorothy." Jim smiled. "You don't get to the bottom of something by playing soft. We have dirt on more and more bad actors because we do scare them shitless. Your sweet and compassionate approach won't nab the bad guys; in fact, the Trumpists love how you people play ball. They're scared of me because they know I am onto them. Again, as I said, I am following the law, and I'm adhering to science and truth. Once someone tells us otherwise, once something implicates me as a danger to democracy, then go ahead, take me down. But until then, given how meek you and the president are, I suggest you leave this to me. Take me down if I fail, but don't cross me, because in the end, if I succeed, you'll want just a little bit of my glow heading your way. Believe me on that."

The attorney general said nothing else other than to ask Jim to leave the room.

Jim appearing on Tap dancer'sshow the next day. "We're about two weeks away from naming which congressmen and senators will appear before our committee. We've been in talks with some of those willing to cooperate with a promise of immunity as long as they tell us the truth. The Truth Clubs are doing their part to keep campuses safe from a lot of nefarious students and professors who have embedded themselves into college communities with the sole purpose of disrupting our fight against COVID and our fight against another coup. Dance man, this is a crisis, and we are on top of it. While the bad guys are claiming that our necessary actions are an affront to the rule of law, we know that they aren't, that we as a nation have a constitutional right to protect ourselves from a threat. We, America, our troops on the ground at virtually every university in the land, our committee, and our compatriots around the nation, we're the only thing that stands between democracy and fascism. We can't sit back and let the bad guys win."

"And, Congressman, if I may," the dancer asked him, "what will come of the kids at MD Park Campus who died? What will come of the students who may have been responsible for their deaths?"

"Dance man," Jim reassured the anchor, "the kids who died have a track record of being allied with anti-life and anti-democratic forces; they're dangerous. No one killed them, Dancer; they died because they suffocated as they tried to escape. But they are guilty of horrendous acts, and in the next few weeks, America, we'll be releasing data that will clearly implicate these kids in a plot to overturn their campuses and our nation. Had they just let justice prevail, had they proclaimed their guilt and submitted, then they'd be alive today. It was their choice to defy justice, and they paid the ultimate price. We're one hundred percent behind the good kids who tried to peacefully bring them to justice, and until we learn otherwise, we will support their story. They are heroes if you ask me."

The anchor nodded up and down. "I have to say, Congressman, that sometimes it takes something like this to wake people up. You're absolutely right; we're in a crisis right now, a crisis that can undermine our democracy and, if not handled correctly, cause untold number of deaths, and yet most Americans seem to be blind to what's going on. That some kids died, kids who were guilty of horrid crimes as you say, that is tragic; any death is tragic. But, like you said, we're in a war, Congressman. And if we don't confront the enemy, if we give the enemy the benefit of the doubt, it's a war we'll lose. Thank you for your vigilance."

Jim smiled and bowed, not shaking the anchor's hand so as to be compliant with COVID protocol. They were both wearing masks. N-95s. It was indeed an all-out war.

Jim met Kate at 2:00 p.m. at the DeLuca diner on the strip in Pittsburgh. She promised to give him more data and to discuss the information she had already provided. She suggested that after they ate ("I'm not passing up an opportunity for another free meal with my congressman," she quipped to him), they go to her apartment to delve into the issues. "I will talk to you all night, Congressman, Jim, to help you understand what's going on," she said to him by phone. "The world is a mess. I saw what happened at MD Park Campus, and at Pittsburgh, it's just as ugly, and Stanford. What a world, right? I trust you, Congressman. I trust you that you will put a stop to the madness and get us back on track."

Well, Jim wasn't sure about all of that, but he was happy to see her again, go to her apartment (wherever that may lead), and figure out more about this Mr. X whom she kept talking about.

Jim ordered country fried chicken with eggs, she a Philly cheesesteak omelet. "Can't get enough cheesesteak." She laughed. "Breakfast, lunch, or dinner, there's never a meal you can't throw in a cheesesteak. I've even had it for dessert!"

"Dessert?" He laughed, causing her smile to grow. "How do you do that?"

"Well," she said, wiping some cheese off her lip and smiling large and bright, "it takes a little creativity, I'll say that much, but toss on some honey and whipped cream, and you just go from there. It's something I'd imagine Bugs could whip up and it would annoy the hell of Daffy!"

She was indeed a perfect girl. Perfect in every way but one. Sadly, it was a big one.

"This last year has been surrealistic, as though our lives have been sacrificed and put into some alternate reality," she said to him. "It's what Lara's husband said when Zhivago ran into him on the train. 'The social life is dead in Russia, because now we must sacrifice our individuality for the good of the whole.' In fighting the health-care system all my life, fighting for my patients, the social life has been dead for me for a long time, but now, now with all this, it's pretty much six feet under."

"From what I remember about that movie," he said, staring into her sparkling eyes and wondering how anyone could possibly not be pulled into this woman's trance, "Lara's husband at the end was tracked down trying to find his way back to her. Her allure was even more important than his cause."

Maybe a week or two ago that may have been true for Jim too. But today, as he sucked up his yolk-soaked fried chicken, he had but one thought on his mind, and it wasn't her eyes or her smile, not even her charm and humor. It was his search for Mr. X.

She had mentioned this elusive man several times. He was high in the US intelligence network and had found dirt on many of the players in the COVID movement, including Doctor Fact-nerd, the Gated Billionaire, and even many people close to President Buck. There seemed to be, according to this Mr. X, a well-documented connection between these players and much of the pharmaceutical industry, global capitalism, and national leaders. It was a world-wide conspiracy, the very thing that Jim wanted to get his hands on and expose as a right-wing misinformation tactic designed to help COVID spread.

"What Mr. X says is something me and my colleagues see every day," she had said during their last meal. "That doctors are taught not to care about patients, but rather are paid and rewarded for selling drugs, doing tests and procedures, and convincing patients that they are nothing but a series of numbers that need to be fixed. With COVID, we could have cut the deaths dramatically if we focused on the elderly and worked on early treatment, rather than closing down all of society, using snake oils like masks, and putting all our efforts into expensive treatments that don't work and vaccinations that are only appropriate for a small segment of the population. Mr. X says no one in the inner circle wanted to help people avoid dying; it was all about selling vaccine and treatments, filling hospitals, and scaring people into a blind submission."

To Jim, this Mr. X was his Satan. But, as she spoke, as he stared into her eyes, he pretended to be intrigued and interested. His face must have convinced Kate, since she promised to introduce him to Mr. X. And that made him smile all the more.

But not yet. Today, at DeLuca's, she went more into the "facts," as she labeled them. She had more graphs and spreadsheets. More information about masks, societal shutdowns, and school closures that made all of them look not just ineffective but in fact deadly. Whenever Jim asked why good people would support such measures if they were so horrible, Kate looked at him with her caring glance and simply said, "Money, power, and greed. Those are the seeds that help the medical system thrive, and lots of people, lots of very rich people, are fed with the fruits of our medical system."

They shared a stack of warm apple pancakes for dessert; Jim was amazed how much this girl could eat, especially given her trim figure. After sucking down her fifth cup of iced tea, she popped up and laid her long fingers provocatively on his shoulders. "To my apartment?" she said.

He nearly fainted, nodding up and down but unable to even make a sound. On the Uber ride to her place in the East Hills, as she spoke nonstop about sundry injustices she was fighting agaist and all the "asses who will do anything for a buck, including killing people and pretending it was all done to save them," Jim wondered if he would be able to perform sexually should the opportunity arise. Maybe they'd have a few drinks, she'd loosen up, he'd get close to her, one thing would lead to another, and then he'd be in a position he so craved but also feared. Would he be able to be a man with her? It had been so long he didn't know.

But when she opened her door, her mouth moving at a mile a minute, he didn't have to worry. Because in her place, which was as sloppy and unkempt as her clothes, stood four others: two men and two women. They twisted toward the door, none of them smiling.

"My friends," Kate said to Jim. "These are the doctors I was telling you about, the ones like me who are fighting for truth. I thought we should all get together and talk strategy. They'll have other insights for you too. They're all really great guys, also on the front line of COVID, and you'll love them. And they all voted for you! I know that should mean something!"

Jim's libido dissipated in an instant, and as he stared at this motley crew, he knew that indeed he was in the midst of the enemy. Sketched on each and every one of their faces was a disdain for authority and for anything and everything in which Jim believed. One lanky guy, in particular, struck Jim as being self-righteous and obnoxious, especially when he joked, "I guess we're not supposed to shake hands, even though COVID doesn't live on surfaces. So much for common sense and science in the age of COVID," which he said with a cynical air of arrogance, the likes of which sent a shudder down Jim's spine.

This guy looked like a lollypop—big head and sticklike body. Probably has a Tootsie Roll in his skull. Jim laughed to himself. "Well," said Jim, "you can't ever be too careful."

"Actually," said Lollypop, who squeezed close to Kate and rubbed her a bit, sending shocks of irate spasm down Jim's back, "we believe, Kate and I do at least, all of us in fact, that you can be too careful. When you pretend to be following science, when you pretend that absurd rituals and prohibitions are scientifically proven to help people, then you do stuff that may be dangerous and you don't do stuff that may actually help. You fall prey to myth, and that is very dangerous. You see, Congressman, we're on the front lines. You may hear an earful of nonsense from the science tiger and his band of pharmaceutical kiss asses, and by a bunch of academic knuckleheads who like to talk on TV and who create fantastical models that have no correlation to what's actually going on. But we're on the front lines, Congressman—"

"I know," smirked Jim. "You told me. As did your girlfriend. I know. You're on the front line. Good for you. I'm sure you're not my biggest fan."

"Well, we all voted for you," he went on. "We like you. And we want you to know what's actually going on, because you seem like you're a smart and caring guy, not someone prone to be deceived by myths and by lies spun by the powerful. We want you to know that you can be too careful when you create myths, because myths are dangerous. When you tell people that masks protect them from a virus that goes through masks, when you tell them to wash their hands for exactly twenty seconds—God forbid it's less than that—for a virus that doesn't live on surfaces, when you scare and isolate kids and young people for a virus that doesn't hurt young people, that is damned dangerous, because it prevents us from taking measures that actually work, that protect the vulnerable. And what we're seeing, those of us on the front line, is massive death from the virus among the vulnerable because we're using mythical strategies to contain and treat it rather than strategies that actually work, and we're locking up old people and killing them even more horribly that way, and we're ruining the lives and livelihood of young people who shouldn't even be concerned about this virus. That's what myths do, Congressman. That's why we brought you here, to straighten out some of the myths being told to you, because we—"

"Tell me again," Jim interrupted Lollypop. "You're on the front lines? Is that what you're going to say?"

"Did you hear what he said, Jim?" Kate asked him, a visage of concern etched on her still gorgeous face. "He wants you to know what's really going on. We all do. We trust you."

"Well," said Jim, "your boyfriend is telling me what's going on through his lens, that's for sure. But I have access to the top scientists in the land, and what you're saying doesn't jibe with what they're telling me."

Kate tried to say something, but another of the women jumped in, this one a little frumpier, and with a bit of a whiny voice. "Science, Congressman, is what you're good at. Science isn't gospel. It isn't about following what someone says and not looking at other points of view. Doctor Fact-nerd and others, they have an agenda, and they're defaming the very notion of science. Science is about discourse, about changing your views when they don't pan out, about listening to all sides of something. That's why we wanted to talk to you. We know you have an open mind, a scientific mind, but you've heard only one piece of this. We all treat COVID people every day. We've read the literature; we know the data. That's all."

The others started talking too, about this and that, about what they saw and what they knew. Jim listened and decided not to respond. He didn't even look at Kate; she had betrayed him, and Jim didn't take kindly to that sort of thing. These friends of hers, from her boyfriend Lollypop to the rest of this brigade of medical nutjobs, represented everything that Jim despised in the world.

Mr. X was not among them. For that encounter, Jim knew, he had to perform well tonight and convince these bastards that he was their friend. So he smiled and made nice, even saying to Lollypop that he was one smart guy. In all-out war, you do whatever is necessary to win, even when it means consorting with the enemy in order to reach a higher goal.

CHAPTER TEN

Pushback

When he sat down with the tiger of science for his daily briefing, Jim decided to hit him with some tough questions. Usually, he didn't do that. The tiger hated to be grilled. Tap dancer told Jim as much: *The best way to handle Fact-nerd is to thank him and listen intently, don't ask any questions, just accept the fact that the guy is brilliant and devoted and that everything he says is accurate. That's my journalistic instinct.*

But after a night of being splattered with misinformation diarrhea at the hands of Kate and her ignoble physician friends, he wanted to get his story straight. Kate clearly wasn't interested in Jim as a man, and while she was beautiful and he enjoyed her company, her ideas had become too toxic to bear. But listening to her and her friends at least gave him access to the arguments being waged by the other side, the very arguments that Jim had to nimbly master before tackling the Stanford Three.

"I'm not questioning anything you say, Tiger," Jim assured the COVID guru. "But I need my ducks aligned before we start putting people in front of the committee next week. They may hit back with the same manufactured facts that the doctors I met with spit out to me. The hearings will be televised, lots of people will be listening to them, and so we need to be able to competently shoot down all the misinformation they toss our way. If you can't answer my questions, how can you possibly stand up to the Big Fish?"

While still very popular especially among liberals and youth, and still the star of DUI's COVID soap opera that played out twenty-four hours a day, the tiger's stock had dropped. Too many gaffes and contradictions, too many accusations about his integrity, and maybe a bit of Fact-nerd fatigue in the general population pushed him off his pedestal. Star Buck relied more on others, especially Got-milk, the former chief of Pfizer; Dr. Slob-it, who had strong ties to the insurance industry; Harvard star Ro-Wo-lo, who was deeply wedded to the AIDS world; and several players with ties to the pharmaceutical companies. Others on his committee, such as the surgeon general and a few scattered ethicists, translated the committee's edicts and conclusions to the public, although lacked the president's ear.

The tiger still counted, and behind Got-milk and Wo-lo, he remained a powerful force in the administration. To Jim, names and positions weren't important. Rather, it was who held the reins of power and who could best respond to misinformation in a way that resonated with the public. For that, Jim still counted on his growling tiger of science.

"Everything you're telling me, Jim," an uneasy Fact-nerd said to him as they sat sipping coffee, "is technically true, but it's beside the point. Like I've told you, like I've told every reporter I talk to, we don't know what's ahead. If we focus on today's facts, we won't be ready for the next lethal surge. Do masks work? Do N-95s work better than a piece of cloth? I came to realize that none of that matters. Masks keep people vigilant, and the more obediently they wear them for their own safety and the safety of others, the more they'll be scared enough to listen and the more they'll think they're being helpful. That's what science is, Jim. It's using things like masks to help people to be willing to do the right thing."

"I'm with you, Tiger; don't get me wrong," Jim said. "But these guys are going to hit us with a lot of cannonballs, a lot of so-called facts that call masks and distancing and shutdowns into question, and when I build my spreadsheets, I need to have them set up in a way that makes them impenetrable. I'm using data from your guys at the University of Washington and Hopkins who use models to generate a worst-case scenario. My spreadsheets show the what-ifs, like what if a much worse variant comes that hits kids and kills fast, what if everyone takes off masks and the disease spreads. But that strategy, while allowing us to keep up the tsunami of fear and suppress too much questioning, has holes they'll try to exploit. Like, is it true that people who die of anything, of heart attacks or of a car accident, will be called COVID deaths if they happen to have COVID within weeks or months of their death? And if that's the case, how do we justify it?"

The tiger squirmed and started to babble, something that made Jim a bit uneasy. *This guy can't deflect any criticism*, Jim realized. Jim pushed him and pushed him, and finally he came up with something that Jim believed he could use.

"As far as we know," the tiger said, "the heart attack or car accident that killed someone occurred because the person was so sick with COVID. COVID likely causes a lot of illnesses, and unless we call them COVID deaths, then we'll be undercounting. Take a guy who drives when he's sick with COVID. I knew a guy who did that. And he couldn't barely concentrate and kept coughing, and that's what caused his car accident. So, Jim, do we say he died of a car accident, or do we let the public know that COVID caused that car accident? 'Cause I don't think he'd have had that accident unless he was sick with COVID. And a parent called me the other day because her kid killed himself, and that kid had just recovered from COVID, and I told that grieving mom that COVID could put bad thoughts in your head and who knows how many suicides are being caused by kids and other people who don't feel good and then end their lives because of COVID!"

To Jim, that made great sense. "What about the fact that hospitals get paid more for COVID admissions and those hospitals are filled with people who don't have to be there? That hospitals keep their census at ninety-five percent on a good day and that's why they couldn't handle the surges. People are calling it greed."

"It's not true, Jim," the tiger growled, clearly exasperated. It was rare the good doc ever had pushback against his dogmatic proclamations, but these weren't normal times, and Jim needed him to be ready. "How can you say that our medical heroes are being selfish? That's a horrible accusation. Once you call our medical heroes selfish, then next you'll say my priest is selfish because he hands out a collection plate, and what's next, every mom who worries about her kid getting the COVID is selfish for forcing schools to mask everyone? When will we stop blaming hospitals for trying to fix a problem that wouldn't even be there if people masked and got a simple vaccine?"

That was the tiger Jim loved so much, the plain-talking scientist who refused to fall prey to misplaced facts and misinformation, forever pointing his finger instead at selfish and politically motivated Americans who were undermining everything he and the medical community were doing to keep the country safe. "I'm just trying to save the country, Jim. If people listened, we'd be done already!"

"You are the voice of science, my man," he said. "Me and the tap dancer, we'll always have your back. Don't let them get under your skin. Believe me, I'll take every last one of them down if they go after you."

During a busy week in which Jim announced the first names his committee intended to interrogate— including several notable Republicans and doctors—and when Representative A-O-Crazy and leaders of the student movement, including the now venerated Mary Lou from MD Park Campus, made a national tour across the COVID-friendly media circuit (including a stint on Cold-bert that made Mary Lou cry in utter joy, especially when Cold-bert called her a hero), Jim presented two bills to the House to up the ante and pressure Congress to stop waffling in this pro-life and pro-democracy war. The bills were praised by his media friends and by the COVID task force, but it generated a great deal of backlash elsewhere, including from legal scholars who questioned their constitutionality. And from a few suspect Democrats.

"They have similar bills in New York and Washington State pending and likely to pass," Jim said to Corrine. "And there's tons of legal precedent that in times of war, we have a great deal of latitude to suspend people's civil liberties if those liberties infringe on those of others. We need allies. Can the kids get behind it? If even one of your kids can say something like this: *My parents aren't vaccinated, and they should either vaccinate or be willing to pay a steep price for their selfish and potentially lethal indolence.* What do you think?"

"On it, boss," said Corrine gleefully. "They're so ready to push this further. What about Mamma-Nana?"

That was a different story.

The first of Jim's bills—labeled the Freedom from Death Act, or FDA—inflicted harsh penalties on any members of society who posed a threat to others by not vaccinating, not adhering to mask mandates and other COVID rules. The law mirrored those being considered by states friendly to COVID science. Essentially, it stated that the Federal Government had the authority to detain any who endanger public health by recklessly ignoring COVID mandates and place them in specially designated camps, to be constructed around the nation, until it was safe for them to reenter society.

Jim's second bill—labeled the Misinformation is Violence Act, or MVA—authorized that a committee be established both nationally and in local jurisdictions to weigh scientific evidence and suppress any published or disseminated statements deemed to be in violation of acceptable scientific and medical standards. The instigators of such misinformation would be liable to fines and imprisonment and would lose all licenses and employment related to federal jurisdiction. This was similar to Jim's proposed bill that was hijacked by the January 6th attack.

Sure enough, after introducing both bills to the House, Jim heard a loud knock at the door. In marched an indignant Mamma-Nana and a perplexed Dorothy.

"I thought we talked about this, Jim," Dorothy Demerit said. "This stuff ain't gonna fly. It's too much. We can't even get behind it at the attorney general's office. You have to tone it down."

"And it's crappy politics, Jim," Nana scorned him. "Your committee is going off the rails. You are empowering nutjob Dems like A-O-Crazy, which only gives ammunition to Foxxy and Ranting Paul and their cronies, and that could well cost us the midterms and wipe out everything. Dorothy's right; we've got to tone it down. You can't be sending people to camps. Think of how that looks visually."

Jim didn't back down a bit. "Maybe you two don't understand that we're in a war for our democracy and for the lives of our citizens," he said. "I've talked to lawyers; the Necessary and Proper clause in the Constitution, the Fourteenth Amendment that guarantees that people won't be injured by others, and several laws and court decisions made during times of war provide legal grounding to my bills. We can't be pussyfooting around, like you two and our president are doing. We need to hit them hard, because otherwise you'll be empowering the far right to try to take the Capitol again. It's that simple. We're doing our patriotic duty to preserve democracy, and to do that, we have to expunge elements of our society who are a threat to it. Look, sixty percent of Democrats approve of putting the unvaccinated into camps, of punishing those who try to discredit masks and lockdowns. Many would like us to bring people like Governor Abbot-and-Costello and DaSandwich in for questioning and to put their states under martial law. We have to stop the flow of misinformation, find the culprits who are planning to take down our democracy, and isolate any and all people who are threatening our nation by refusing to comply with COVID standards."

Jim remained calm, but not the other two. Mamma Nanna glared at him. Then she let loose. "What do you think we're doing, Jim? We are looking into the Capitol raid and will be prosecuting many people, but we don't want it to turn into a witch hunt. Hell, you're calling rank Republicans like Kenny McDonalds into your committee, as well as many prominent doctors and bloggers. And these bills, they're shit. They won't pass, and I won't let them even get introduced. And, Jim, one more thing. Call off your fucking lapdogs on the college campuses. You have kids running wild there, detaining students and professors, convening mock trials. Representative Crazy is rallying them, and she is toxic, Jim. She will be the end of our party. We're handling this. We are pushing mandates and sensible solutions. You have to help us and back off, or else I'll shut your committee down."

Jim smiled as though he didn't care. "I don't think you have the power or authority to shut anything down, Madam Speaker. I think if you try, you may find yourself in hot water yourself. You've been a little too timid on the January sixth investigation and on keeping our nation safe. Don't push your luck."

The Speaker threw up her hands and laughed, rather uncomfortably. "Is that a threat, Jim? Do you have the audacity, after one term as a congressman, to threaten me? You've got to be kidding. Here's something for you to swallow. Pull the bills and tame your dogs, or I'll shut you down by the end of the week."

With that, the two of them marched away, thinking they won the day.

Jim, Corrine, Mary Lou, and a few student leaders met over burgers later that night.

"I have assurances from the ACLU and from the attorney generals of most of the liberal states, especially California, that they aren't going to interfere with the campus movement," Jim said. "Right now, that's our main seed of power. We have to keep up protests, mock trials, and detentions of students and faculty who are found to be dangerous. Mary Lou, you have my permission to use whatever means necessary to open people's eyes and get us national attention. What you did at Park Campus, those deaths, they have sparked massive support for our cause. Once we showed the dead students' complicity in right-wing extremism and the anti-life movement, once we argued that they were a threat to democracy and to the lives of Americans, once we correctly pointed out that they essentially killed themselves, people rallied. We need something like that again. Can we do it?"

Mary Lou smiled. "I have some ideas," she said. "I've organized a group of law students and medical students to help plan something that is legal and dramatic. Something that could be a test case. It may involve people dying, but these are bad people we're talking about, anti-science people."

Jim nodded. "Yes, that's what we need. And you have the Stanford Three in detention; they're safe and can be paraded to the committee as soon as we're ready for them."

"Sir," she said, "we have more than three hundred faculty members who are guilty of defying vaccination and spreading misinformation in custody around the country. More are coming."

"Good," he said. He knew she would do anything for the cause. "I'm making a trip to Pittsburgh to meet some bad people. Do you think I can have you and your students take care of them discretely when I am finished?"

Mary Lou smiled. She could feel the sweat of power flow down her back. "Of course," she said.

CHAPTER ELEVEN

Rooting Out Evil

Before Mamma-Nana or Star Buck had an opportunity to backtrack from their "firm stand on stamping out misinformation" and shut down his committee, Jim appeared on DUI to take the lead and announce that his committee would be interrogating its first suspects in less than a week.

"We have a three-pronged assault against the enemies of democracy and science planned for next week," Jim said to the tap dancer. "First, we'll be putting three Republican congressmen in front of the committee, as well as two doctors, people whose nefarious misinformation is embedded in our national infrastructure and triggering potential massive waves of death. Second, we have tens of thousands of patriotic and science-minded progressive students who will be leading a national protest against regressive thought and misinformation, including the detainment of students and professors on campus who pose a risk to their campuses. And finally, Dance Man, I have prepared two bills that I'd like to introduce in Congress that would protect this nation against those who seek to take it down. The problem is that I'm getting pushback, and frankly that's why we're in this mess. No guts from our leaders."

The tap dancer nodded up and down. "I was talking to Doctor Fact-nerd before you came on, and he said the same thing. He said that despite how hard he has fought to educate Americans and endorse commonsense science-based measures to stop the pandemic, no one in the national government is preventing the anti-science stalwarts from disseminating their misinformation globally. While he thanks governors such as Sergeant Schultz, Newbie-hottie, and The Murph—all of whom have stated on my show and in their deeds a commitment to aggressive measures to curb COVID and to punish all those who defy basic public health laws—he states that as long as Florida, Texas, and others defy the will of the people and spread misinformation, as long as Ken-and-Barbie and others weave their conspiracy theories and try to spin tales demonizing the good people trying to help this nation, our lives are all in peril. Are those who are blocking your efforts, Congressman?"

Jim nodded from side to side. "The folks you mentioned, dance man, sure, they're damned dangerous, and we need to bring them to justice," he said. "But frankly, the ones most obstructing my efforts to do just that are members of the democratic leadership. I don't know what their agenda is; maybe they're being paid off by some of the right-wingers, maybe they believe that politically it's not smart to rescue our democracy from an imminent threat, maybe they're even complicit. Believe me, America, we're looking into all of that. But right now, until our leaders are told by the American people without hesitation to let me run my investigation and introduce my bills, I can't do what is necessary and proper to protect America."

The tap dancer stared into Jim's eyes. "Both you and the science tiger are saying the same thing, Congressman, so it's clear we need to take it seriously. Let me repeat what you said, just to emphasize your words to the American public. You're telling me that your efforts to find and expose those people who may have been responsible for endorsing or even planning the Capitol attack, and those people who are responsible for spreading misinformation that is essentially thwarting all our attempts to curb deaths from COVID, that those efforts are being stymied by the democratic leadership. Why?"

"Yes, America, that is what I'm saying, and I realize it may not make me the most popular Democrat in the country, but frankly my obligation to science, truth, and democracy is far more important than my ties to a political party. We are staring down an imminent threat to our nation. The very people who are telling Americans that masks don't work, that vaccinations are poison, that patriots like Doctor Fact-nerd are trying to undermine truth, those are the people, we believe, who also tried to take over our nation on January sixth and are planning to try again. I am being a patriot in pushing hard to uproot and punish those people, and I need cooperation from my party, not obstruction."

"I never thought I'd hear those words from you, Congressman," the anchor smirked. "You're a patriot?"

Jim laughed. "Dance man, don't try to pull a fast one on me. In this nation, yes, I'm a patriot. But if you're talking football, well, America, I'm about as anti-patriot as they come. I want this damned COVID threat to end so we can get the NFL back in action because, mark my words, my Steelers will best the patriots any day of the week, but when it comes to being a patriot, yes, tap dancer, that's what runs in my blood."

The anchor smiled. "Glad we straightened this out, Congressman. Yes, democracy is in peril. The very lives of Americans are being threatened by misinformation and a lack of compliance to science, and until we root out those threats, another January sixth can be knocking at our door any day. We hope for the best, Congressman, and we'll be by your side and by the side of Doctor Fact-nerd speaking the truth to a nation that needs your prescription."

Jim heard nothing more from Mamma-Nana and her crew for the next week, although he made no effort to introduce his bills, at least not yet.

And then came the day of the first committee interrogation, one that would be televised and was certain to gain him national attention. Jim wasn't going to tiptoe around the garden; he was going after the biggest fish on day one. The Texas bass would be on the stand, and Jim lined up depositions and witnesses who he hoped could help him snag and fillet this dangerous predator.

"Are you nervous, boss?" Corrine asked him. "I mean, this is a big day!"

He sipped from a cup of scotch—something she had never seen him do until recently but which was now his signature posture—and he took a deep breath. "I'm hoping it should be easy," he said.

But, alas, it was not.

No one, not the Democrats on the committee, not the speaker or president, and not the Republicans certainly, cooperated with Jim's assault on the Big Fish from Texas. The science tiger sat curled up on the side, providing expert testimony when needed, but sometimes he seemed to ramble, and his ability to push back dissipated in the afternoon's heat. Jim saw the man dozing off at one juncture.

"You're telling me, Congressman," Jim asked the cocky Texas Republican, "that you didn't support the rallies on the mall on January sixth, you didn't tweet, and I quote, 'Our people did good out there, and I only wish they could have accomplished their goal; that's my one regret,' those weren't your words?"

"Hell, I'm not denying any of that," he said with bluster. "Damned right I wanted our people there protesting a fixed election. And damned right I tweeted that I wished our guys could have convinced the VP to do the right thing and negate a rigged election. It's all legal; I got the best attorneys in the country to explain that to you if you need some extra schooling. I know you're an engineer, which I used to think are those guys who drive trains, but I come to learn that it means you like to use math to build things. Either way, I know you ain't too up on the law—that much I do know."

"Congressman," Jim pushed, "your tweet clearly makes you complicit in the Capitol attack. Your 'one regret' notation in that tweet, according to two of your colleagues who have provided testimony under oath, attests that you were referring to your regret that the attack on the Capitol failed. How do you respond to that?"

"Well, it ain't true, that's how I respond, and if you're willing to bring them two congressmen to this committee so I can ask them myself like the law and the Lord tells us is right and proper, cause we have a right to face our accusers in this here democratic nation and under God's eye, well then, I think the nation will see that they are lying or that you threatened them or bribed them or something like that." He smiled and looked into the camera. "So, all you fake news junkies watching this, let me ask you one thing: Should we have a fair trial or not? Ain't the Democrats always yelling about integrity and free and fair shit and all that crap? Well, bring it on!"

"Congressman," Jim said to him, "let me remind you that this hearing is being broadcast live, so please make sure to watch your language."

"Oh fuck, did I use a bad word?" The Fish laughed. "Well, I'll be more fucking careful next fucking time."

Jim took in a deep breath. "Congressman, you heard the testimony of Doctor Fact-nerd, and you read the expert testimonies of over a dozen prominent epidemiologists, doctors, and scientists from some of the most esteemed academic institutions in the nation. They have analyzed some of your statements regarding vaccines, masks, and distancing and have all concluded that had this nation followed your course of action, over four million deaths would have occurred, and that moving forward, your resistance to the task force's and CDC's recommendations could cost us a quarter of the nation. Do you find that funny?"

"Fact-nerd said that?" He laughed, barely able to get words out. "Well then, damned, then it must be true, since he's the guy who invented this bug in his lab with his drug company pals and sent it to China, the guy who tortures puppies, the guy—and I'm being generous here—who thinks that we got to protect our eyes from the COVID and that it may even be in the toilet. That's the guy you're using to buttress your case? The guy who wants double masks and eye protectors and specially formulated toilet paper to knock out a bug that don't even live on surfaces? That's the guy who's making your case?"

"He and other experts," said Jim. "Yes, sir, their testimony is very clear. Not mandating vaccines, not mandating masks, fighting against sensible quarantines, sending kids to school unprotected, all of it could have escalated the death toll and still may should your flagrantly irresponsible actions continue."

"Well then, shit, I guess I was being a bad boy." He laughed. "You know what my friends said I was doing? They said I was being too much like a Democrat. See, you guys are all about pro-choice. People get choice you always say—don't mess with a woman's body because if she wants to kill a baby, then hell, it's her choice. And now, poof, you boys are all about no choice: Let's all get stabbed by some experimental vaccine that Doctor Fuck-face and his pals got a big financial stake in. Let's force kids to get it too and keep them out of school and choke them with masks, even though hardly no kids die of the Fact-nerd virus; hell, more kids die driving to get the vaccine than die of the bug, and God only knows how many are going to die of that untested vaccine and all the bullshit you are putting them through as you scare them to death. We got more suicides and depression this year than ever. And whose fault is that?"

"You are conflating the concept of choice, sir," an irate Jim said. "There are choices people make that adversely impact other people, and there's choice that's a personal matter. Like you can't go around shooting people, because that causes harm to others, so you don't get to make that choice. And you can't go around unvaccinated and without a mask, because that also puts people in danger. A woman's choice as to whether she wants to carry her own baby is not impacting the lives of other people."

"Oh, it ain't?" He laughed. "You mean the fucking baby she kills by her choice ain't impacted by her choice? You know what, Congressman, I know you like your spreadsheets, so let me show you some of mine." He slid some papers toward Jim. "This is the testimony of over twenty thousand prominent doctors and scientists, and they will attest to the fact that everything you are saying, everything Dr. Fuck-face is saying, is a bunch of bullcrap. We don't use any masks in my state, and no more of us is dying than anywhere else. You guys play with your data to make it look good, but here's the data raw as a dick after sex, and as you can see, it ain't showing that these pieces of cloth—whether they got little drawings of people dancing or are N-95 or even N-98, for Christ's sake—can stop the Fact-nerdbug. You know why, Doctor Fuck-face? Since you're a self-professed genius. Do you know why this flimsy cloth don't work?"

The tiger stood up and said, "They do work; I assure you of that."

"Oh, that's some good science, Doctor Fascist. Glad you could elucidate us about them facts." He laughed. "But here's why, so maybe you should get someone to write it down, since I know your brain ain't too fresh. The Fact-nerd bug, it's two hundred times smaller than the holes in the best mask, so it goes right through it, right around it. It's like trying to keep bugs out of your yard by putting up a picket fence. And guess what, we got studies, real studies, showing they don't work too. And I can talk all day about the vaccine, the one Fuck-face and his TV doctor friends loves so much 'cause it's filling their wallets. You want some spreadsheets about that?"

"Congressman," said Jim, "let's keep the dick comments to a minimum and just talk facts."

The Big Fish laughed. "Oh man, I'm sorry, I forgot. You ain't never used your dick, Jim, so you wouldn't understand what that reference meant. Let me think of something else you may understand. Maybe we can talk in simpler elementary school vocabulary, like crayons or something?"

"That's OK," said Jim, remaining calm. "Let's return to your comments about Trump's election and the events of January sixth."

The testimony ended soon after, as DUI told Jim that the coverage needed to finish before the evening shows. The Big Fish, it seemed, won the day. But Jim was hardly flustered. This was his first trial, and he needed a good spanking so he could be ready for next time. He announced that the hearings would commence in a week.

Later, he appeared on News-Wolf's Howling Hour on DUI.

"Breaking News," the news wolf declared. "Congress goes after one of its own regarding culpability for the attack on our democracy and the misinformation campaign that has led to hundreds of thousands of deaths. Congressman Jim Depich of Pennsylvania, how do you think today's testimony went, and what do you have planned for next week when we reconvene?"

Jim looked into the camera. "We learned a lot today, Wolfman, especially that the congressman from Texas thinks that COVID deaths and the assault on the Capitol are big jokes. The question is, does the nation agree with his disgraceful attitude, or are we as a country willing to punish those who threaten our lives and peril our democracy?"

"Will you have more evidence next week when the trial commences, Congressman?" he asked.

Jim smiled. "We'll be ready," he said. "We were just testing the water."

Later he sat with Corrine and some of the students for burgers. There was a thick, almost uncomfortable, silence around the table as they chewed their burgers and fries quietly, clearly upset. And then, Corrine squeezed some mustard on her fries and the top came off, splattering Jim right on his face.

Jim laughed. And then, so too did the others. "I love this," Jim said, licking off the mustard. "You see? It's all a sign from God. Today that jackass smeared us. But all we got to do is lick it off and turn the bottle around." Which he did, shooting bits of mustard at Corrine.

She too laughed, and soon enough, there was an all-out food fight at their table, the bunch of them laughing hysterically, drenched in various condiments, as worried onlookers peered at them quietly.

Tasting relish and ketchup, an idea popped into Jim's head, and almost diabolically, his brain took him somewhere he never would have thought to travel before.

CHAPTER TWELVE

Judgement Day

Mary Lou stopped at her home in Columbia, mostly to hug her parents. As she leaped toward a fate unknown, one destined to change the country forever, one that would define her and could never be reversed, she first wanted to pet her little schnoodle, Rex, and hug her parents one last time.

"You're missing so much school," her mom said to her. "Will they give you any trouble?"

"They wouldn't dare," she said, with a cocky confidence that now flowed through her veins. Who would possibly stand in her way? Years of ridicule, of intolerance and vitriol, evaporated in an air thick with redemption. Now she held all the cards; now people peered at her and recoiled in fear. She was chubby, she was no athlete, she believed in causes at which most people scoffed, but none of that mattered. From now on, Mary Lou held power that few dared to challenge.

"What will you be doing on this trip, honey?" her dad asked her. "Will you send pictures?"

"It's kind of top secret," she said. "But you'll hear about it, and when you do, I think you'll be proud. Everything you taught me, everything I studied and read about, it all brought me here, Dad. After tomorrow, we may be able to shape a better world, the kind we always dreamed of, one without hate, one where we all work together in a united harmony. To me, it's not an academic idea; it's real."

"Wow, honey, I can't wait to see what it will be!"

"Remember when we used to read Harry Potter together, and you told me that the world is just like that, there's good and evil, and unless good triumphs, then evil will ultimately take over everything," she said to them. "Voldemort lost because Harry Potter was so good and brave, Hermione so smart, Ron so devoted. I want to be all of them wrapped up in one. I want to root out evil, because if I don't, just like you and those books taught me, if I don't, then the bad guys win. There's no middle ground. If we don't win, then they do. So, that's what I'm going to do, I'm going to win by any means necessary."

Her mom smiled and gave her a hug. "That's so poetic," she said, tearing up. "When we were kids it was the dark side or the force, same thing. Life is so simple when you see it that way. In my parents' generation everything was all jumbled up, and that's why there was all that stuff in the 60's, no one knew what was right, what was wrong, so much confusion. But now, it is so simple, it really is!"

She gave Rex a special hug and whispered in his ears, "If I don't see you again, know that it was worth it," to which Rex licked her all over her face, and she giggled in a childish glee.

To think that she would be meeting on a regular basis with her hero, Representative A-O-Crazy of New York; that she would have access to a powerful progressive congressman; that she would be leading a grassroots student movement that had gained such unprecedented momentum so as to shock the nation into awe—all of that would have seemed inconceivable to her just a month ago. As COVID swarmed into her life, and she felt so passionate about following Doctor Fact-nerd and helping promote his pro-science and pro-life agenda, she was willing to shelf all the issues she had cared most passionately about, including the environment, voting rights, abortion rights, and a broader understanding of sexual labels. She was woke, that's for sure, and with COVID, her wokeness only became more focused, especially when she saw that so many people refused to accept the science and were willing to sacrifice humanity for their own political and economic self-interest. These Trumpists horrified her. And now it was judgment day, time to slay Darth Vader and Voldemort, time to make sure that good triumphed over evil!

After the incident at MD Park Campus, her wokeness grew broader again. This was not just about COVID; it was about wiping the world clean of the anti-science agenda that Trump and his fellow January 6th traitors had tried to stamp upon this nation. It was about the environment, abortion rights, and everything else in which she believed. It was all the same thing. The same fight. The same wokeness.

"Sometimes," Corrine said to her as Mary Lou sat with other student leaders and Representative A-O-Crazy, "you have to neutralize a small and cancerous sector of society to ensure the survival of the rest. We can't piddle with a malignancy; we must be bold and do something definitive if we're ever going to be cancer-free. Sometimes you have to be bad before you can bask in the good. Know what I mean?"

Mary Lou did. And she was prepared to do whatever it took to grasp the opportunity of the moment and eradicate a cancer against which she fought her entire life. She spread word to all the campuses across the land, all the Truth Clubs, all the student leaders who were battling against the Trumpist crud. "November eleventh will be judgment day."

As to what that meant, how much Corrine and A-O-Crazy knew, how much even Jim was privy to what would transpire on Veteran's Day, all that would be left to speculation. After the events of that day, Jim denied prior knowledge, even as he embraced and dignified what happened. He lofted Mary Lou into the status of a hero, and after that date, the Truth Clubs became more than mere student groups; they morphed into a disciplinary instrument of the nation's law. Their tribunals carried the weight of a court. Their verdicts and sentences were rarely questioned. And when Jim's committee met after that day, several members of the club always stood astride Jim and partook in the interrogations.

Mary Lou had become the undisputed leader of the Truth Club movement. She unified the many clubs both in spirit and in direction. Every member, by her instruction, wore drab olive shirts and slacks. Their masks were drab too, N-95 for now, although within a month all would be armed with knives, bulletproof vests, and space helmets with oxygen supply. The knife, serrated with a pearl handle, became their symbol. They soon wore necklaces with the knife as charm, and the symbolic *Knife of the Woke* appeared on their shirts. It was called the truth knife, the knife of justice, the knife of wokeness. It was a tool in the fight to win America back from those who sought to destroy it. It was all Mary Lou.

Jim wasn't happy at all about the first day of testimony, and as he prepared for day two he looked to Mary Lou and the students to spark something big.

"We need to be as bold as your students," he told Corrine. "If we want our bills to pass, if we want to take back the initiative in the hearings, we can't rely on traditional justice and politics. We have to be buoyed and influenced by our most devoted soldiers. We can't fall into the trap of nuance, the trap of debating tiny figments of fact like those the Big Fish threw at us. Everything we do has to be anchored to a single truth, one ingrained in unassailable spreadsheets, one whose absolute correctness can't be challenged by the harbingers of misinformation and by an alternate set of facts. And to make that happen, Cor, we first have to do something bold."

"How bold?" Corrine asked her boss.

"This is a war," he reminded her. "We're fighting an intractable foe. Our enemies are forces of violence who are willing to harm and even kill hundreds of thousands of people by their refusal to adhere to COVID protocols, willing to take down our democracy, willing to lie to the nation and drive them down a dangerous and traitorous road. That is their power. Our power has to be stronger than theirs. By bold, Corrine, I mean, bold as shit, bolder than fuck."

Jim rarely cursed. But now four-letter words slid out of his mouth faster than the Lord's prayer.

Corrine got the message. She let A-O-Crazy know, and also gathered her best and brightest students to talk about Jim's declaration. After Corrine spoke, Mary Lou stood up and looked at the others.

"I don't know about all of you," she said. "But I'm sick of the right wing and their reactionary lies, their manipulation of the conversation, their Trump-like bullying; I'm sick of them thinking they can push us around and we'll just smile back. We're going nowhere under a president who is as bold as a marshmallow. As my hero Representative A-O-Crazy told me once, if you follow tradition, you'll just end up traditional. If you want to pave a new path to the future, you have to find new bricks. It's our time. We are the country's future. And if we are going to start laying down bricks, we need people to be woke."

"How woke?" came the unified cry of the other students.

"Woke is life," Mary Lou said, in her rehearsed retort. "To save the nation, we must sacrifice those who seek to crush goodness. Only through their death can we and the nation be woke. Their death is our life, the nation's life, the world's life. Death is thus life. Death is woke."

She came up with that line, and it defined her and the movement. They all repeated it. And then she brandished the knife, the one she had bought on eBay, one that was a takeoff from the one used by Brutus to slay Caesar. "Et tu, Trumpists?" she called out.

Within days she ordered hundreds more of the knives. It was all part of her bold plan. Her fucking bold plan.

Few students pushed back. Maybe they were too scared. Maybe they too believed that her path was the only one toward success. *Only through death can we find life and be woke.* They all said it. And they prepared to do more than just utter words. They prepared to do something damned bold.

November 11th came with little fanfare; other than federal workers, few acknowledged the holiday. Schools were in session. Traffic was as bad as always. But the Truth Clubs garnished their uniforms and marched on every campus at which they had a presence. Today would be the day that defined them.

Mary Lou was at Park Campus, and hers was perhaps the largest of all clubs, three thousand strong, all marching together, chanting their slogan: *Woke is life. To save the nation, we must sacrifice those who seek to crush goodness. Only through their death can we and the nation be woke. Their death is our life, the nation's life, the world's life. Death is thus life. Death is woke.*

The chanting grew in intensity, with the marching systematic and choreographed. A few of the most athletic Truth Club members had gone off to snag their prey. The others gathered on the main green near the library and started to construct a makeshift courtroom out of logs. Mary Lou stood in the center, pounding a drum, singing, shouting, feeling the moment's immense vitality.

Woke is life. To save the nation, we must sacrifice those who seek to crush goodness. Only through their death can we and the nation be woke. Their death is our life, the nation's life, the world's life. Death is thus life. Death is woke.

Many students gathered around to watch the spectacle, some professors too. They chatted; they peered silently, wondering, intrigued. No one knew what was about to occur as the din of intense purpose suffocated all but those in the center of it.

Suddenly, shoved into the now completed wooden set of stands stood three students—a boy and two girls—their hands tied, their mouths muzzled, but masks conspicuously absent from their faces. Everyone else in this circle of purpose wore his or her signature mask. They all wore their matching uniforms. They chanted and marched in unison. And thus were these three young adults, these figments of bare life, set apart from the herd, floating in an atmosphere thick with anticipation.

Mary Lou raised her hand and the chanting stopped instantly; only a few fleeting voices from outside the circle, some passing cars, and a hovering bird could be heard. All eyes from the crowd focused on their classmates, the hoard of uniformed students, and the three who stood isolated and afraid.

One of the girls kicked the thickly muscled boy who had carried her here. On her face was sketched a visage of indignation; it was clear that whatever fate awaited her, she was not about to fold quietly. The boy turned to her and pummeled her, punching her in the face so often that her button nose bled and swelled, and two of her near-perfect teeth dropped to the reddened ground.

Gasps emanated from the crowd outside the circle. Cries of "Enough" and "Leave them alone" mixed with empty shouts to disperse and for someone to call security or 911. Despite these feeble pleas, the play went on as written, with Mary Lou taking on her self-assigned role on cue.

It was 10:55 a.m. A bright sun hovered over the picturesque campus. It was fairly warm for November.

Mary Lou raised her hand, and all her soldiers chanted and marched in place, brewing a broth of fear and dread, of anticipatory pathos. While the bloodied girl peered at Mary Lou with a defiance that had not faded, the other two looked down at the ground, clearly defeated.

"Today, on the eleventh hour of the eleventh day of the eleventh month, we shall, here and across the nation, tell the world that we are not willing to tolerate killers in our midst," yelled Mary Lou to all who would hear. Not a single ear was deaf to her words and what they might portend. "There are those in our society who believe they have a right to infect the nation with their viral venom. In living, they are murderers, killing our citizens, killing decency and democracy. All three of these vermin have rejected the gift of vaccination, have mocked the blessing of the mask, have placed their stock in those who would want to breed hate in this nation instead of love. Their lives are not only despicable but also a threat to all that we cherish. So, on this newly consecrated holiday, this day when America took back its nation from those who have tried to commandeer it for their own nefarious purposes, on the eleventh hour of the eleventh day of the eleventh month, we declare these three scoundrels guilty of crimes against humanity, and thus removed from the protection of the very laws that they are trying to topple. To you who are guilty, we say to you . . ."

And they all chanted, in a deafening roar: *Woke is life, right is death! To save the nation, we must sacrifice those who seek to murder it, for only through death can we find life and be woke.*

The library's bell rang. It was 11:00 a.m. Mary Lou stood in front of the student victims and lifted her pearl dagger. Then, looking at each of them squarely in their eyes, she plunged her dagger into each of their guts, as gasps from the onlookers accentuated. "May the tyrants die so the nation can live," she cried out, her words mixing with the deafening chant of her fellow Truth Club members.

And then, one by one, each of the uniformed students, each of the three thousand of them, walked to the three students, who by then were still clinging to life, and thrust a dagger into them. By the time it ended, the three were more blood and holes than life, nothing left of them but mangled corpses.

A band of security finally came over and put Mary Lou in custody. But all three thousand Truth Club members partook in the deed. All plunged their daggers into the bodies of those deemed to be bare life. All contributed to the death of those whose lives were declared to be a threat to others, whose deaths were consecrated as being necessary to the preservation of life. And across the nation, on over a thousand campuses, on the eleventh hour of the eleventh day of the eleventh month, the identical play was being performed by Truth Clubs. Three thousand were sacrificed on that day at the hands of a hundred thousand. Sacrificed for the good of the whole. Death became life.

Corrine ran to Jim's office at a little after eleven. He was sitting silently, staring at the wall, sipping a scotch. He had been drinking a lot lately—just a few sips at a time, a bottle of sips every day.

She hyperventilated. "It's done," she said. "A success. Now, we wait."

He smiled. "This is but the first step," he said, in a voice devoid of all inflection. "It was necessary to wake up the nation to the peril that is in their midst. If we are going to preserve our country, its values and its democratic core, if we are going to preserve the lives of its citizens in the cloud of contagium that has been allowed to infiltrate it, then we had to first wake them up. Corrine, one more thing."

She looked at him, still breathing hard.

"Call Dorothy and Mamma-Nana in front of the committee. It's time for them to account for their crimes."

PART THREE

"Extremism in the Defense
of Liberty Is No Vice."
—Senator Barry Goldwater

Carrot Juice
Rabbit Season!
Duck season!

CHAPTER THIRTEEN

Democracy in Peril

Fires of outrage burned across the nation. Foxxy took up the clarion call the loudest:

"One thousand students murdered in cold blood on campuses across the country in the largest killing spree to ever strike our nation," said the Walrus. "Apparently, over two hundred fifty thousand students, all progressives and allied to the Democrats and especially to Representative Alexandria A-O-Crazy, who is the most radical left-wing member of the party, all partook in this barbaric act, repeatedly stabbing the bodies of innocent fellow students to the point of their being unrecognizable. Several students are now in custody, but given the enormity of the crime, and the large number of students implicated in the murders, some of the killers remain free. Apparently, these students are all part of what are called Truth Clubs, allied with Congressman Jim Depich, a Democrat who is on a witch hunt to find and punish the perpetrators of the January sixth attack. Well, Congressman, compared to January sixth, we're now dealing with something so vile and atrocious such that this nation has never seen."

"Are you responsible in any way, Jim?" an irate Mamma Nana asked him as reporters hovered everywhere around the Capitol.

"Your name is all over those Truth Clubs. The girl from the MD Park Campus, who already has had her hands dirtied by one murder, has been to your office many times. I'm not sure of Congresswoman Crazy's role here, but she is toxic, and I know she's got some say in all this. There will be an investigation, Jim, and I'm afraid until then, your committee is shut down and you're on probation."

"I'm sorry, but you can't simply burn me at the stake because students took up a cause that you and your cohorts didn't have the guts to do," Jim snickered. "I'm not leaving Congress, and I'm not shutting down my committee. You find evidence, Madam Speaker, and then you can come back, but until then, there are laws and rules that even your pompous leadership can't stamp out."

"That's not how things work here, Jim," she reminded him. "I can shut down any committee I want and sanction any member of my caucus I feel needs it. Expect to be visited by investigators and keep your damned mouth shut. This is a horror show on so many levels, and the damage you've done to the party and to our nation may be irreparable. You clearly are too naïve to know what you did her. Too dumb."

No, Jim thought. It's all going as planned.

How can you arrest 250,000 students? And if you don't arrest them all, how can you arrest any, given that they all participated in the sentences? Mary Lou was the face of the movement, and each college had leaders of their Truth Club, but the clubs made it clear not to have any named officers, and thus was no one implicated as the instigators of the crime.

But was it a crime?

Most of the DUI and even Makes-Sense NBC anchors strayed away from this story; it was a little too brutal even for them. People like the tap dancer had no taste for mob violence or murder under any circumstances, and didn't want to dig too deep into this, since the cause for which the students fought was his cause, although their methods were not. "Someone needs to be punished for this crime," he said on his show, with Mamma Nana by his side. "But we can't go and simply jail all of them. We need the ringleaders. We need to make it clear that in this nation, we won't tolerate violence as an answer."

The DUI anchor Jim called Cheddar was not quite as fearful of tackling the story. She had been the most virulent anti-misinformation reporter on DUI, calling some members of the Stanford Three "mass murderers" because of their desire to open up society, and stating that Foxxy News and many congressional Republicans were responsible for hundreds of thousands of deaths from their anti-science positions on masks and quarantines and their deadly misinformation campaign.

"I don't like that people died, Jim," she said off camera to the congressman, with whom she was always very convivial and supportive. "But when we have a quarter million very good, upstanding, and otherwise impeccable students sticking knives into their fellow students' guts, that tells you something about our society and where we are. I know you have no involvement in this thing, Jim, but, unfortunately, your coziness with Mary Lou and all the Truth Clubs is going to cause you and your investigation grave harm unless we can somehow turn around this story. Tell me what to do."

"We let the nation know," he said, "that the students did what they did because of the feckless federal response to what amounts to a crime against humanity."

Cheddar was squeaky clean and virulently against any form of violence, being uncharacteristically irate about January 6th. She even cursed on TV after the Capitol attack. But somehow, what these students did resonated with her.

"They had to be bold and open up eyes," she said to Jim. "I get that. It takes something like this to move the nation in the right direction. But too, something like this, if we don't get a handle on it, can sink the whole progressive movement. The speaker wants to shut you down, and she's willing to take down everyone in your wake if she has to."

"Put me on your show, and we'll straighten out the issue. It's really black-and-white, right versus wrong, pro-life versus pro-death, pro-democracy versus Trumpish autocracy. I have more information, and I'll talk to the American people. What we need, Cheddar, is to get the investigation rolling. The real culprits, the real instigators of violence against America and Americans, are the ones yelling the loudest about this."

She was pensive, even as she nodded up and down. Jim had once called her the prettiest broadcaster on TV, to which she called him the most handsome man in Congress. They had always had a very good relationship, and as awkward as this issue was, she had grown to trust him. "OK," she said.

Her segment was called *Democracy in Peril*, and on her show every night, she called out anti-lifers, highlighting the continued threat of another January sixth "unless something drastic is done to shut down the flow of misinformation that is paralyzing the nation and making it prone to another coup attempt."

"Jim Depich has been fighting valiantly for our democracy since he stepped into the Capitol," she said, staring at the camera with a grave visage. "He has been one of the few voices demanding that the instigators of the January sixth coup be brought to justice, and he has also established a strong link between anti-lifers—those who reject quarantines, masks, and mandatory vaccinations—and anti-democrats, those who believe that an autocratic government is better than our own. After the recent violence that swept across the campus, Congressman Depich has been targeted as someone who may have egged these students on, especially given his involvement with the Truth Clubs. So, to start, Congressman, were you at all involved in what happened on November eleventh?"

"Absolutely not, Cheddar," he said, with a cool demeanor. "And nor was Congresswoman A-O-Crazy, although the speaker of the House and her politician cronies on both sides of the aisle would like the American people to believe that we were. This was a spontaneous action at the hands of caring, smart, and loving kids, and it was done because our damned government refuses to stop the flow of misinformation that led to a coup attempt already and likely a half million deaths from a preventable viral infection, and which, according to my projections—which I have made clear to the press through graphs and spreadsheets—could kill another three million Americans and peril our democracy if we continue to simply sit by and let the flow of misinformation strangle us. Unfortunately, the speaker is too timid and political to take on the radical right wing. She wants to shut down my committee and silence anyone who demands justice for those who threaten life, science, and democracy. These students took matters into their own hands. While I don't condone it, I also understand why they did it."

"A thousand young adults murdered, Congressman," she said to him. "How can that ever be justified?"

Jim slid some papers her way. "I'll make this public today, but here's a profile of the kids who died on November eleventh. What you'll see, America, is that every one of them refused vaccination and masking, was part of the movement to spread COVID lies, and, what's most shocking, each and every one of them belonged to a dangerous right-wing group—whether the Nazi party, the Klan, the Oath Keepers, and, most frighteningly, even the QAnon movement."

"Congressman, tell us a bit about QAnon, since most Americans are not familiar with them."

"Absolutely, Cheddar," he said, staring at the camera. "And let me say this, the fact that Americans aren't familiar with them is the direct fault of our feeble government and leaders like Mamma Nana who are afraid of pointing fingers and showing us who to be worried about. America, the QAnon movement is like a religion with adherents who promote violence and an overthrow of our democracy. This group believes that certain unnamed sources, whom they call Q, have identified a satanic cabal of left-leaning sex traffickers who conspired to remove Donald Trump from office. This cult, the QAnon, vow to do everything and anything to get Trump back in power, to dismantle democracy so that Trump can rule unfettered, and to take measures that assure that COVID continues to menace the world and cause enough disarray to allow right-wing militias to topple every Western democracy."

"Wow," said the animated broadcaster. "And you're telling me that every one of the students punished on campus, all of them, had ties to the QAnon."

"That is exactly what I am telling you, Cheddar Cheese," he said. "It's utterly tragic that those kids died without a fair trial, but I'll say this: Our government is doing nothing to stop the escalation of right-wing terror and anti-life misinformation, and what those Truth Club students did, while deplorable, likely saved millions of lives. The kids who died were anti-life terrorists. They were misinformers. Should we punish the students who tried to stop the terrorists, all two hundred fifty thousand of them? Should we find scapegoats and put on show trials like they did in Communist Russia? Or, should we view this as a lesson—unless our government grows a set of balls and takes on this imminent threat, then more unfortunate events like this are going to occur? The question we must ask, America, is whether we want a war in the streets, the first salvo of which occurred on campus, or whether we can handle this under a democratic umbrella."

"What is your solution, Congressman?" she asked, staring into his eyes.

Jim smiled. "It's really very simple," he said. "I proposed two bills to Congress that Speaker Nana has blocked. One would assess and review all information being spread on the news, social media, journals, even on college campuses, and block any deemed to be dangerous misinformation. The other would allow us to persecute people with ties to right-wing groups deemed to be anti-life and a threat to our democracy. Very simple, pragmatic measures. Second, my committee, which the speaker has threatened to shut down, must be given broad powers to investigate the very people whom these students had to sentence on their own in the absence of a viable federal means of prosecuting anti-life terrorists. If we had our gears in place federally, the students would not have had to act in this manner. Third, the student groups who did this, many of whom are still holding hostages on campuses around the country—professors and students with proven right-wing terrorist ties—must be let free with the stipulation that they will reject all violence but will continue to investigate the campus anti-life anti-democracy movement and help us on the committee to root out anyone in groups like QAnon before they take down our government and its citizens. This is about science, America. About decency. About the values of God and our nation. It's time we have a government that fights for those issues and not a government that kowtows to deadly extremism."

"How do you propose that happens, Congressman?"

Jim stared hard at the camera. "As long as Mamma Nana is in charge, then the government will be beholden to industry and politics rather than to truth, life, and democracy. We need new, tougher leadership. We must replace the speaker. Frankly, anyone in Congress who believes that she is the right person for the job likely are themselves connected to these anti-life movements."

"Have any good candidates to replace her?" Brianna smiled.

"Well," Jim said, "given that you can't do it, Cheddar, I may be a good second choice."

Jim's network of student leaders immediately flooded social media with profiles of the dead students and those being held hostage. While Jim couldn't verify the accuracy of anything posted, the posts were startling in their description of these 1,500 executed students being dangerous extremists bent to kill Americans and to topple the nation. Soon enough, members of Congress too were tagged to the QAnon movement, as were many commentators and executives on Foxxy News.

The *New Yacking Times* published an op-ed the next day that captured the mood of the nation: "Did the Students Avert Murder Rather Than Perpetrate It?" Quickly the tide of democratic and progressive public opinion swung in the direction of the Truth Clubs, and tocsins were sounded that unless the government was more vigilant in uprooting and punishing the anti-life anti-democracy terrorists in its midst, the death toll in the nation would far exceed anything the country had ever even imagined.

On November 25, Thanksgiving Day, Jim, Representative A-O-Crazy, Cheddar, and Corrine appeared at the Jessup Prison in Maryland with the release papers and presidential pardon for Mary Lou. All the student leaders were released on that day, and their hostages remained in custody, including the Stanford Three, until Jim's committee was up and running.

President Star Buck issued the pardons reluctantly; his own tanking approval ratings, and a powerful push from his pro-life left flank, convinced him to "release the kids, who had their heart in the right place, and who likely saved a hell of a lot of lives, and to empower our leaders to take this threat more seriously. And I fully endorse Jim Depich for speaker. I think it's high time we make that change."

That night, Jim and his group ate hamburgers to celebrate. Mary Lou bemoaned the prison food. "Not even bread and water." She laughed. "More like gruel, like in *Oliver*. I'll watch the mustard this time."

They all had a good laugh. The tide was turning. Jim had one more trip to make before his push to take over the speakership and then put the Big Fish back on the hot seat.

CHAPTER FOURTEEN

A Two-Course Meal
in Pittsburgh

Jim was heading to Pittsburgh, and in a kind of twisted gesture, he decided to let Kate know. The purpose of the trip was to dispense with her, but before he did that, he needed more information about her Mr. X, and frankly, he wasn't sure she'd be so forthright, especially given recent events that she and her misinformation friends likely abhorred. Still, they were so relaxed together. They shared Bugs Bunny and good food, and her eyes, her smile, wow, he still thought about her glorious face day and night. Maybe he could swing her toward understanding his side of things; maybe these two good-looking singles could find some kind of bond beyond the perils of politics. At the very least, maybe he could get info on Mr. X and somehow let her off the hook after he enjoyed some good food with her and indulged her luscious lips.

So, he told her he was coming on a business venture, and her response was amazing.

"Oh my God, Jim, I've been watching you on TV," she said, with a flare of pathos tossed in. "Those poor kids, I just feel for them with all my heart. They were just trying to be patriotic and keeping everyone safe. When I learned about those other kids, the Q kids, can you imagine they were on campus doing that? Thank God they were stopped, but will you be able to save the Truth Club kids?"

Jim paused for a moment. "Wait," he said. "You're OK with what happened? I just figured after talking to you and your boyfriend and those other doctors that you'd be totally on the other side of things."

She laughed, and it was intoxicating! "First, Jim, Alan isn't my boyfriend, like I tried to tell you. He is gay and married, and he likes to touch me because that's what gay people do. Second, he's ugly as shit, and he doesn't eat meat, so like, yea, he's a good doctor, but kind of an ass. And third, I am just trying to do what's right. All the stuff I gave you, sure, it's important, but people are trying to take over the country, bad people, and that has to take priority. Jim, how long will you be in town?"

Jim was thrilled to know about that nasty doctor lollypop with his big head and scrawny body, that high-pitched voice that didn't like to shut up. And so self-righteous. Hearing Kate, Jim's heart was beating a mile a minute now. "Why, want to grab dinner?"

"I was hoping you'd come over my place," she said in a whisper. "No guests this time."

For just a fleeting second, Jim's battle for the soul of science and democracy slid from his mind, and the dirtiest thoughts took root inside of him. He smiled. "Be there at six?" he asked. "Maybe some chat, then dinner?"

"Well," she said, "hopefully not too much chat. What's Up, Doc can't wait to see Big Jim!"

He called her What's Up, Doc, you know, because she was a doctor and loved Bugs Bunny. What a coup to get her to invite him over! He had a few Viagra stashed away, just in case. He had no idea if he could perform, but he wasn't about to leave it to chance. This would be one hell of a night!

But first, he stopped to visit one of the science tiger's friends at Pitt Medical Center to orchestrate Kate's demise (as well as the exorcism of all of Kate's friends, who Jim referred to as the Misinformation Five, after, of course, he had his way with her and, hopefully, has his way with Mr. X too.

"Yea, I know them; they get in our faces all the time," Collin Fitzer, a young and scrappy cardiologist who served as a chief of staff of one of the smaller university hospitals, said to him. "Self-righteous pricks is how most of us know them. Doctor Kate, as you call her, she has had her license reviewed by the Board of Physicians twice this year alone. She constantly opposed our policies to contain COVID, and she even used ivermectin on one of her patients against hospital policy. She has yelled on radio that early treatment works, that masks and quarantines are dangerous, and that the only reason hospitals are being overcrowded from COVID is that we are so greedy that we keep our census at ninety-five percent on a good day, which is true, but hell, that's the only way we can survive, Jim. Before COVID she was just as much of an ass, always bellyaching about us doing too many unnecessary heart tests and harming people with overtreatment and crap like that, saying we're about profits and not people, writing op-eds, riling up people. The other morons with her, all primary care dweebs who likely couldn't even get into a cardiology fellowship if they tried—they're the same, trying to spread their self-righteous shit all over the place. That Alan guy you mention, he's had his license reviewed more than her. He even went to jail once protesting a patient of his whom we forced to get a heart stent because he was having a heart attack, and, although he said he didn't want the stent, we thought he was not in a good mental state to make that decision, and Alan the prick refused to let us do it, and the guy ended up not doing well. So, we called the police, and he went to jail. Sadly, he got out."

"Why in God's name do you keep them on?" Jim asked. "Why not fire them?"

The young cardiologist, with a $5,000 suit and gold necklace, laughed. "Sadly, they run our nursing homes, and not many docs will do that work. And the nurses, families, and patients claim to love them, probably because they have been hypnotized by their self-righteous lies. We tried to get them fired, and the outcry against us was something we couldn't take—lots of bad press, you know the drill. So, we tolerate them and hope they lose their licenses and that will get them out of our hair."

Jim paused for a moment. "How are your nursing homes doing with COVID?" he asked. "I mean, despite all their misstatements and bad behavior, are their patients faring well? I know that's the most vulnerable population with a thirty percent mortality from the virus according to my spreadsheets." Actually, that was Kate's data, and her spreadsheet, but why quibble about details?

"Their early treatment protocols were effective on the surface but are not endorsed by CDC, so we put a stop to them," he said. "They only lost eight percent of their COVID pateints, but that well could be coincidence. And they are demanding rapid daily testing of everyone who walks in the door and everyone who lives there every day. They say it will stop COVID from entering and will allow the residents to live normally. But really, we don't live in la-la land. That would be a logistical nightmare. We need to stick to the endorsed program of locking places up and masking. It works, and it's cheap."

"What do you mean by their treatments being effective on the surface?" Jim probed. "I mean, if they only lost nine percent of patients when the average loss was thirty percent, how is that not real?"

The doctor paused and played with his cuff links. "I mean who knows what the side effects are of these early treatments, and they're not endorsed by CDC or Doctor Fact-nerd or, frankly, our ID guys. I don't care about the stats, Jim; it's just bad medicine."

Jim had read Kate's data on masks not stopping infection in long-term care, on how nations that instituted rapid daily testing had almost no COVID deaths compared to over 300,000 in the United States, how many frail elders were dying from the quarantine. But these facts, as she called them, were distractions, and Jim knew it, as too did this smart doctor. Bottom line, too much verging from the singular science tiger strategy would open the door to other misinformation and ultimately to the anti-lifers seeming to be rational and reasonable. That's the last thing Jim wanted.

"We need to suppress all the data that these doctors are disseminating," Jim said. "It will send the wrong message, and any data can be made to look bad if you manipulate your spreadsheets right. You guys do it all the time; I've read enough to not be blind to that fact. You and your stents and stress tests and expensive heart medicines. I know you are expert in data manipulation. How can you do it with stents and somehow can't do it with COVID?"

"Stents are a huge part of our revenue stream," the good doc said. "And without that revenue, how can we care for the poor? And all those asshole doctors care about is caring for the poor!" He fiddled with his Tesla key chain, twisting it between his fingers, which by now were beaded by sweat. "We have been sending out a consistent message that all the early treatment they endorse is not really effective, and that if we just mask up and follow the rules, like with hand washing and staying away from families, then there wouldn't be a need for any medicine at all. Still, I wish I could get those self-righteous pricks out of my life!"

Jim smiled, "We do have a common interest in that regard, and that's what I want to talk to you about. I think Kate may be willing to come to our side, I'm not sure, but she's starting to see the light. The other ones, there's no way they won't stop spreading misinformation. So, my goal is to haul them in front of my committee and expose their treachery to show the whole country what happens when misinformers are allowed to spread their poison. To do that, I need something from you. And if you can help me, all I can say is that the science tiger and I are pals, and that I also have a wonderful relationship with the former boss of Pfizer, and both the NIH and Pfizer are very willing to feed you big buck research funding to the tune of billions of dollars if you can help us save the country from these anti-lifers."

The doctor smiled a bit and fiddled with his chain. "What do you need?"

That night, Jim rapped softly on Kate's door. He had brought her some red tulips, the favorite flower of Pepé Le Pew; and, of course, a carrot cake, Bug's favorite. She opened the door, and he nearly dropped both. She was wearing a button shirt that was unbuttoned halfway down, revealing a pink bra with breasts far larger than he could have imagined through her baggy sweatshirt last visit. Her hair was flowing behind her, and her smile was big and bright. She grabbed his tie and pulled him in. "Come on in, Big Jim," she said, seductively. "What's Up, Doc wants you so bad she can't even breathe! I see you got a big carrot sticking out down below the waist. Is that for me?"

Jim smiled, feeling dizzy. The Viagra must have worked. His heart raced, and he couldn't speak.

Kate saw what Jim had in his hands, and she looked into his eyes, her own eyes big and inviting. "You are just the sweetest thing," she said. "Such a gentleman. And to think, you almost didn't come because you thought I had a boyfriend. Can you imagine you thought he was my boyfriend? Him?"

Jim laughed, even as he was pulsating from below. "Yea, I didn't know he was a fag, but should have guessed. You, sweet lips, you're certainly no fag. I know the kids are all into wanting to be called 'they' and 'he-she' crap, but you, What's Up, Doc, you are pure 'she' through and through. Ain't no 'they' in those boobs!"

She kissed him on the lips. "And you are all 'he,'" she said, grabbing his crotch. "Because What's Up, Doc loves Big Jim's carrot!"

Jim hardly could breathe. "Yea, I'm all he, no fag in me, and I'm ready to put my he-tree into your she-sea. You, What's Up, Doc, you are so damned hot! My God, what the hell is wrong with this world that no one has claimed you? If I was with you, we'd be fucking so much that we'd have to eat and pee and work while we fuck! Do we do it here, or would you prefer being an old-fashioned lady, the kind I like the best, and I can bring you to the bed and lie on top of you and take advantage! I always believe that the man should be in charge."

"Well, Big Jim, you are my master tonight," she said, pulling him by the tie into her bedroom. "And you can take advantage of little old me any way your big handsome hands want to."

They slid into the door, and then Jim turned around and his face dropped. There stood Lollypop, who held his shoulder and slammed a big syringe into his neck. Jim tried to fight back, but he was already dizzy from his Viagra, and now, quickly, all light started to fade.

"What, what, what," he feebly said.

Kate buttoned up her shirt and spit on the floor. "Well, that was gross," she said to Lollypop.

"Yea, for a second, I thought you were getting into it," he said. "You almost got me aroused!"

She laughed. "Yea, right, that will be the day. So, when is the pickup, and where?"

Jim lay on the floor. He could hear everything, although he felt paralyzed. He stared up at Kate. Would the Viagra go to waste? he wondered. His mind was swimming, and he could barely focus.

"Lollypop, you're funny!" he was able to yell out.

Both Kate and the other doctor, Alan, laughed. Kate leaned over and kissed Jim on the forehead. "Listen, Congressman, we are doing this for your own good. You'll see why soon. Once this is all over and we turn the world sane again, I promise you a slice of that carrot cake and a night of fun, which to me is a movie and falling asleep early. But don't fret; you'll appreciate what's next."

"Lollypop!" he yelled again. Kate laughed and kissed his head again.

"He is kind of cute like this," she said. "If we can give him an infusion, he might be tolerable."

"Oh please, he's an ass," said Alan. "So, I need to put on his clothes. That's what they told me. You want to strip him or me? You see the size of his cock? Guaranteed he took something. Not that you're not gorgeous and seductive, Kate, but cocks that big don't come naturally."

"As a gay man, Alan, you likely don't know just how seductive I am." Kate laughed. "You strip him, and then dress him in some of my clothes. I have to pee. He probably will look good as a girl."

Jim started to fade as he felt his clothes being torn off. "No no," he tried to say. "I don't want you, Lollypop. I want to fuck her. Not you. I'm no fag." Alan just nodded his head.

Two other of the Misinformation Five ran in, and they saw Jim on the ground. "There's no one out there we can see," one of them said. "We kind of scoured the place. I think it's clean."

"Yea," Alan said, "we're guessing that since he came here to be intimate with Kate, which would not be too good for his reputation, he didn't tell anyone where he was going. I don't think he was followed or that we'll have any surveillance. You have the metal detector?"

The other doctor handed Alan a small device. He rubbed it all over Jim, who by now started giggling and telling him to go get Kate because he couldn't hold this erection forever. They all laughed.

"Clean," Alan said. "So, yea, likely he has no detection devices. He doesn't have his phone on him, so it's probably turned off in his car. I took out his keys. Hope Mr. X is right about this. So far so good, but still, it's nerve-racking. We're just a bunch of doctors, not spies!"

Kate came back. "Why, Lollypop," she said to Alan, "you look ravishing dressed like the congressman. If you weren't so gay, I may well want to pop you one."

"Very funny," he said. "OK, I'm going to drive the congressman's car to the other side of town. I'll meet you back here in three hours. Give me like fifteen minutes, then carry this jackass to the back of my car, go through the ally, then take him to the designated place. If you run into any snags, dump him. Got it? We can't screw this up."

They nodded as Alan dashed out of the door. No one spoke for a while, and Jim, still wide-eyed and wearing Kate's dress, kept looking at Kate with a big smile on his face. He was hoping she was about to leap on him. Then, suddenly, two men lifted him up and took him down the stairs. Kate leaned over and kissed him on the forehead. "That's all, folks," she said.

And then, everything became black.

CHAPTER FIFTEEN

In the Den of Mr. X

When Jim woke up, his head floated in a cloudy ecstasy. "If that's what sex is like, I need to get more of it," he mumbled. "Kate, you here? Come here, What's Up, Doc. Big Jim wants to squeeze out some more carrot juice from your balloons."

"I'm sorry, Congressman, but my garden is dry, and the carrots didn't grow this year."

Jim's eyes opened to the sound of a crusty man's voice. He could barely make out the surroundings, although images of a vacuous warehouse and a man sitting on a bench in front of him slowly crept in. He remembered almost nothing beyond when he pounced on Kate. Was this all a dream?

"You a girl, or what's your deal?" Jim uncharacteristically mumbled. "You're not Kate, right?"

The crusty man laughed. "No, sadly, I'm not; she's one of my heroes, though. I'm just a government bureaucratic who is handed too much taxpayer money to spy on people. And kind of on my own, I've compiled quite the dossier on Doctor Fact-nerd and his many sponsors over the years. That's why you're here today, Congressman. Kate thinks you have a brain and a heart, and that you have found a podium from which you can tell the truth and put our nation back on the rails of common sense."

"I do tell the truth, funny many," Jim walloped, laughing at himself. "Like I say, if I can put it on a spreadsheet, then it's got to be true. You got a spreadsheet, Santa?"

Mr. X laughed. His long white beard and red trench coat were actually not real; he always disguised himself in front of people he didn't fully trust. "We brought you here under a veil of secrecy, and went to great lengths to make sure you don't know where here is. I apologize for whatever trauma you endured to get here, but we had to take precautions, as I'm sure you understand. Kate too is sorry. But I must say, you looked damned good in her dress. Sorry you two couldn't get down and dirty, but wearing her dress, well that's some consolation."

"Sorry?" Jim laughed. "Why? She was magnificent!"

In actuality, he wasn't sure about how the sex was, but kind of remembered that it was pretty good. He looked down; he was wearing her dress! *Man*, he thought, *the sex must have been kinky too!*

"Well, good," Santa said. "I'm glad she pleased you. She is a nice girl, and a damned smart doctor with a brain full of common sense, compassion, and critical thinking, the three Cs that your science tiger lacks."

But as a different narrative crept into his brain, as flashbacks of the evening congealed and erased whatever fantastical thoughts he had clung to, Jim suddenly grasped a far darker reality that now greeted him. Jim realized he had been kidnapped, drugged, and brought to this cold and empty warehouse to meet this man. Was this Mr. X? he wondered. And he also started to acknowledge that his abduction wasn't a bad thing, that he wanted to be here, even if his journey occurred against his will. This was the last piece of the puzzle in Pittsburgh; the whole idea of there being a Mr. X, of there being misinformation on a massive scale controlled by this one person, was critical for him to uncover and understand. The only shock to him, other than how he came to arrive here, was that Mr. X was Santa Claus.

"So, with Christmas coming up, you must be busy as heck." Jim laughed, now fully conscious. "It's nice of you to meet with me during the toy-making season. So, you want to tell me some truth? Is that my gift this year, Santa? Because, yea, I love truth. I just wonder if you have any with you."

"Well, it depends, Congressman." Santa laughed. "Have you been a good boy this year?"

"I'm a pretty pious Christian, Santa," Jim said, fiddling with his hands, which were tied to the chair. "So, yea, I've been really good. And I'm helping down on earth to rid the world of plague and heretics. That's why I do love the truth, Santa, and why I know there's only one truth, just like there's one God and one Bible. Like I said, if it fits on a spreadsheet, then it's true. So, as I asked, do you have a spreadsheet for me?"

Santa reached down into his bag and yanked out a few papers and a small ziplock of flash drives.

"This is Santa's version of a spreadsheet, Congressman," he said, putting a pair of virtual glasses on Jim. "I'm going to show you what I have; the basis of this information is all documented in the flash drives. I'll wrap all of it up for you when you leave, so you can take it home and share it with the American people. Or you can ignore it, knowing that you're turning your back to what's really going on."

Jim laughed. "Good," he said. "There can't be two truths, right? So, we'll see how this fits in to bolster what I know to be right and unassailable."

Santa flicked on a switch. "Given the fact that you picked the Steelers to win it all in Ben's last year, well, Congressman, sometimes you have to modify your truth when reality steers you in another direction. Today, Jim Depich, I'm giving you a whooping dose of reality."

And then, across Jim's eyes, flashed quotes and graphs and data, all narrated by Santa himself.

Some of what he saw mirrored the tales of misinformation Jim knew all too well, what was spit out by scoundrels like Governor DaSandwich and the Stanford Three and even Kate and her friends, the stuff Foxxy News liked to broadcast. But other information, well, it knocked Jim's socks off. Could it be true? And did it matter?

He peered up at Mr. X, who, just like Santa, sat with a big and jolly smile on his face. This man held information that was either fabricated or so damaging that it could take down the entire government. Either way, Jim knew that he had to suppress it.

"Seen enough?" Santa asked him.

"Well, it's a taste, but if you send it home with me, I promise I'll finish the whole damned buffet," Jim said to him. "And you can authenticate it? You can prove it's true?"

Santa nodded up and down. "Yes, sir, I have every corroborating piece of evidence in there too. I know that you're a man of science, of truth, of data. I've graphed it out and provided sources. You can even track down the sources if you so desire, ask them personally about what I showed you, give them the once-over. Bottom line, it's all accurate, and that must scare the shit out of you."

Jim snickered. "I don't scare easily, Santa," he said. "OK, enough small talk. When does Kate come back so I can finish her off? Viagra doesn't last forever, and neither does my patience."

"I think, Congressman, that Kate has an early shift," he said. "But the doctor you know as Lollypop, well, he's a night owl, and I can drop you off there.

"One more question, Santa," Jim said. "If this is all true, why don't others know about it?"

"As your last gift, Congressman, I'll tell you why. And then, it's nighty night for tired Jim."

CHAPTER SIXTEEN

A Changing of the Guard

"At the end of our discussion, Mr. X said something fascinating," Jim told Corrine, pouring himself a larger cup of scotch than usual, his fourth one today. He was not deaf to the buzz of protests outside his office. He had stacks of letters demanding his resignation and even prosecution. Foxxy coupled him with Representative A-O-Crazy as the Demonic Duo of Murder, and Mamma Nana told the press that he might need to be impeached. But Jim focused on the task at hand, clinging to the knowledge that truth always prevails, and knowing well that many powerful voices in the government, academia, and media had his back.

"Aside from all the concocted misinformation he tossed at me, which is all in the hands of my NSA pals now—and the early verdict is that it's fabricated—Mr. X fed me a slice of pragmatic wisdom," Jim said to his stalwart friend. "He said that the reason he didn't leak these facts to the public personally is that it could backfire; that it sounded too much like a far-fetched conspiracy theory, and Americans simply don't believe conspiracy theories. When something sounds this crazy, he told me, when it crosses a certain norm to which most Americans subscribe, then they simply refuse to believe it, and may inveigh against in. In fact, he said, when conspiracy theorists defame people whom most Americans trust, those people usually get the sympathy of Americans, not the other way around. I think that's a useful tip."

"How is that useful, Jim?" Corrine asked her boss.

"Come on, Cor, you're smarter than that." He laughed, gulping rather than sipping the scotch. "Mr. X has evidence of cabals between men like Gated Billionaire and the science tiger, deep ties between industry and politicians, links between the Chinese and many very esteemed Americans. He's keeping it secret because no one will believe that sweater-wearing sweet philanthropic Gated Billionaire and our gentle decent smart science tiger are in on some plot with the Chinese to take over the world and they're using COVID to achieve that goal. I mean, who's believing that nonsense? And yet, Mr. X thinks it's true, and who knows, it may be, so he wants me to act on his information, to release all his alleged facts, because he thinks my own position and the trust people have in me will make it more palpable and that if I back all that nonsense, if I change position on COVID and tell the world those people are the real culprits and that we've been sold a fake bill of goods designed to imprison us all, then it will be credible. So, Cor, maybe I will."

"What?" she shot back. "Now I need some of that scotch! OK, JD, what am I missing?"

"What you're missing, my sharp but naïve friend, is the slice of wisdom Mr. X served me," he said. "If I release all these so-called facts like he wants me to, if I call out our loving science tiger and the always gentle and giving Gated Billionaire and all their alleged accomplices, if I tell America that people embedded in the right wing support a far-fetched conspiracy involving these well respected people conspiring with the Chinese to turn America into a communist state, then the backlash against all of it will be massive. By releasing what Mr. X is calling the truth—and maybe it is, Col, although I'm hedging my bets on the fact it isn't—I'll be repudiating that very truth. Even if the Gated Billionaire is conspiring with China and with American industry, and with people like the science tiger and the leaders of Pfizer and half of Congress, to spread this virus as a way of scaring people into submission to a deep state— well, Cor, if I tell

Americans that, that sweet Gated Billionaire in his nerdy sweater is like a James Bond super-villain, then it will sound so absurd that no one will believe it, and, in fact, no one will believe anything the right wing anti-COVID nuts ever say because it will reek of conspiratorial hyperbole. That's why I'm going to do it!"

"Santa certainly has bountiful gifts." Corrine laughed, referring to Mr. X. She patted her newborn, who burped very loudly, causing both her and Jim to laugh. "Any leads on finding Mr. X?"

"Please, Cor, I'm not a moron; I know exactly where he is." Jim smiled. "As you know, I had a few students following me that night, even after Lolly and the others put me in women's clothes and thought they were being so clever and sneaky. When I left the warehouse, the students stayed and followed Mr. X, to a little crappy garden apartment in the strip district. So, yea, we know where he is. It's just a matter of when to bring him in for interrogation. Some of the guys at NSA are thinking that Santa is part of the Q, or maybe Q himself. If he's an NSA worker and his snooping is an inside job, that would make him a criminal, and that's when we will bring him in!"

"And what about the kids?" Corrine asked, so worried about what transpired on November 11 but always afraid to bring it up. "I'm still nervous that if we're connected to what they did, I mean, Jim, we could be called in as accessories to murder and then all this stuff about Mr. X and Q and everything, it all goes down the drain. You hear how Mamma Nana is talking. She doesn't want to blame the kids; she says others pushed them to commit those murders, and those others are us."

He laughed and patted her on the head. "We're good. I'm on DUI this afternoon, then I have an audience with the president, the president who needs a boost and can hardly lose the millennial vote when he is so damned unpopular." Jim chugged down another cup. "I feel pretty good, Corrine."

As well he should. His head was buzzing. The protests outside sounded almost melodic!

When he sat in the DUI studio, he felt most comfortable. No one here assailed his mission and passion, no one blamed him for the November 11th day of judgment, everyone told him that the anti-democratic forces were using that day's events to try to erase what happened on January 6th.

"That's why we are calling it a threat to democracy," Cheddar said. "These kids had had enough. The misinformation campaign, the anti-lifers as you so appropriately call them, who are trying to derail our scientific strategy to contain COVID; the connection of these people to Trump; the denial of global warming, rampant racism and gender bias; the attack on the Capitol; even what you dug up about the Q group and how they are working to take down our government and how deeply they have penetrated our colleges and politics, you can't blame the kids for being fed up with a government—a government they put in power—turning a blind eye to it all. We are on your side, Jim. You know, we at DUI are committed to telling the truth and using our fact-checkers to tear apart their lies. I know Makes-sense NBC and Mumbling Joe are in your court too, but here, well, here you have a team of devotees."

As Jim knew, these were his best propagandists. And when the world is shitting on you, when misinformation and political hackery seem to be getting the upper hand, powerful and respected people willing to emphasize the one and only truth, the science tiger's truth, the truths filling Jim's spreadsheets, the truth that Corrine's students fought so hard to preserve, these were whom Jim needed in his corner.

While a Pfizer ad graced the screen, showing the nation how corporate-public cooperation could end history's worst pandemic, Jim smiled. In the end, power always decimates the earth's crud.

"Do we have any closure on the fate of these kids?" Cheddar asked him wearing a visiage of concern once the camera started to roll. "There's no question in any sane mind that the kids who were killed were members of terrorist groups, that they engaged in behaviors that threatened the health and welfare of their campuses and indeed of the entire nation, that they may well have been part of another planned coup. And yet, like vigilantes, the Truth Club kids took matters in their own hands, something that we as a free nation cannot allow, as I'm sure you'd agree, Congressman. So, the questions I ask are, were you involved in November eleventh, and what do you think we have to do as a nation to punish the guilty and make sure this doesn't happen again?"

Jim stared into the camera. He needed to speak directly to the American people. "First, America, no, I took no role in November eleventh. But what were those smart and patriotic kids to do? They identified real and palpable threats, but all their elected leaders could say was 'We have mask and vaccine mandates, so everything is OK.' It's not that simple, Cheddar. People, bad people, are planning to take over the government. People, bad people, are refusing to allow our scientists and doctors to rid the world of the most horrid plague humans have known. America, I have compiled spreadsheets. The last Capitol coup attempt, which was just a warm-up, could have killed over fifty thousand Americans and half our elected representatives if the terrorists had guns and bombs—which were in their cars—instead of pepper spray. So, yes, that's how many we have to assume would have died and will die if they do this again. And too, as I have shown you, based on data from our amazing science tiger and the best scientific and medical minds in the world, had we fallen prey to these Q-terrorist anti-lifers and their anti-science agenda, had we turned our backs on what the CDC and the science tiger told us to do, to what Governor Newbie-hottie and Sergeant Schultz and Murphy's Law compelled their people to do through strong and thoughtful executive directives, we would have had at least three million deaths in this country, many of them being kids. So, when we look at these good and decent Truth Club students, we have to see them as heroes who resorted to violence only because our government let them down. During a crisis, America, you need strength; you need someone to step up and say enough is enough. That's what those kids did."

Cheddar nodded up and down, her face still stern and unanimated. "Then, Congressman, how do we give these patriotic and concerned kids enough assurance that our government will identify the enemies of democracy and science and prosecute those who are the greatest threat to our nation? How do we take action so vigilantes don't do this again?"

"It's a three-pronged approach, Cheddar, as I have said on this network many times," Jim said, wishing he had a glass of Jack

Daniel's by his side. ". But the third prong is the most salient. As long as Mamma Nana is speaker, we will have a tepid policy that's all talk and no action, and thus will justice occur on the streets and in campuses instead of in Washington, and thus will another January sixth and November eleventh be inevitable. She must be removed."

But how was Jim going to do it?

Later that afternoon, he received an audience with the president and vice president. He met them in the Oval Office, with Bad-Karma pacing and clearly indignant about something, Star Buck in the big chair, and Jim casually sitting on one of the smaller chairs with his legs up on a table. He knew that he held the reins of power, that Buck was in a bind, that Mamma Nana was the wrong ally for him to cling to in these treacherous times. He just had to help this very middle-of-the-road president find the right path forward. "You're doing a great job, Jim," Buck said. "Don't you agree, Bad-Karma?"

She laughed cynically. "Yea, if you consider a thousand dead kids a good job."

"Jim," the president said, with a big smile, "I don't blame any of that on you, and I've heard you on the news and support your position. We must end the division in this country and get the economy rolling. According to polling, my numbers are in the tank, but sixty percent of Democrats support your bills and making your committee stronger, and most Democrats are behind those kids. But, Jim, we have to do something to show that we won't tolerate that kind of violence. We can disband the clubs, call out some of the kids, just something to demonstrate our commitment to the law."

"This is a nation of laws," said the vice president. "The trust between public institutions and private safety and rights has been broken. We can't let mobs control us."

"Then, Ms. Vice President," Jim said, hardly budging from his comfortable perch as her pacing grew more frantic, "you think it's OK for radical anti-life students to spread misinformation that could have lethal consequence, for them to help instigate another Capitol coup, for them to oppose science and potentially instigate a million preventable deaths? I understand why you would not support the November eleventh outcomes. But those actions may well have saved countless lives by defrocking the anti-life movement and delaying those who plan to take on the Capitol again. We do have evidence of that from NSA, which I can show you. Terrorism, Madam Vice President, will not be stopped with words, with fecklessly enforced mandates, and with gritting teeth. We need strong laws and enforcement of those laws, and our leaders must be tough as nails on anyone who dares to threaten our democracy. As long as our Speaker remains in her position, the longer this ugly war is going to play out."

"Joe," said the VP, turning to Buck, "Mamma Nana is a loyal ally and is going about this in a measured way. She is pushing the mandates, she is working on uncovering those who plotted January sixth, and she is keeping our nation safe from both misinformation and anti-democratic activities. But if we go too far, we could lose everything. Yes, our poll number stink. And if the midterms were held today, the Republicans would sweep both Houses. But if we follow the path Jim is prescribing, a path that is more of a witch hunt than a sensible policy, it could only get worse. I've run the congressman's bills by many legal scholar friends, and they are full of constitutional holes. The court will tear them down instantly."

"With all due respect, Joe," Jim said. "I know you're on the Eagles side of the state and I'm on the Steelers side, but we're from the same patriotic stock; we will do anything to protect our democracy and aren't afraid of threats and legal glitches to do what we know is right. Let me lead the House. Most Democrats quietly want Mamma Nana out, and both parties are willing to bring me on. Let's show the nation that we're not a country of sissies when it comes down to protecting lives and our democracy."

"Congressman Depich," Bad-Karma said to him, staring him in the eyes, "you're a bully, and I think you're dangerous. I wouldn't support you for a second in that role. Fine, Nana has to go; I'll accept that. But I'd like to find someone a little less nuts, someone who believes in the rule of law."

"So, you think science is nuts? You think wanting to protect the nation from imminent threats is nuts? You think my tabulations, my precision, my alliance with the scientists and leading academics in this nation, my strong relationship with the millennials and kids—

people we're going to need on our side in a big way if we're going to stay in power and stave off the threats all around us—all of that is nuts? Well then, pick someone who's not a nut, and let's see how that works out for you."

Jim then swung to the president. "Buck, when the Eagles won it all a few years ago, they weren't passive; they didn't overthink everything. They were tough, and they knew their opponents' weaknesses. That's how my Steelers do it. That's how we have to do it. We're not just playing this game for us and our careers. The nation is in peril, Mr. President. Unless we act tough, unless we have an aggressive offensive line, we're going to get sacked."

Soon after the Thanksgiving Recess, one of Jim's allies called for a vote to recall the speaker and pick a new one. Jim's people had been going from office to office seeking support. Many of Corrine's crew compiled dirt on enough of the lukewarm representatives to make them a bit nervous about being called in front of the committee. Corrine told them in the most reassuring way:

"The congressman certainly is going to realize that if you vote for him as speaker, that act alone absolves you of any association to Q, the Capitol coup, or the anti-life movement. He knows you won't support him if you have something to fear. Just voting for him will get you off the hook."

And so did Jim Depich rise from a second-term congressman from Pittsburgh to the highest-ranking member of the House and third in line to the Presidency. He called his crew in for a celebration over burgers and beers. He convinced Mary Lou, now on the talk show circuit, to change the names of her student groups to the Life and Liberty Squadrons. He introduced his bills to Congress, having received significant promises of support from the ranks. And he reinstated his committee.

"Next week," he told them, gulping down the beers, "we bring back the Big Fish. And this time, I'm not using a rod and hook. I'm using a nuclear missile." He smiled big and winked at Corrine, who too smiled and winked back. It was clear to both of them that their moment had arrived.

CHAPTER SEVENTEEN

When You Have the Right Bait, You Catch the Big Fish

Jim knew that everything hinged on this trial. Everything! His status as speaker, his fight against anti-lifers and anti-democrats, his perch of intimidation from which he could continue his crusade. All of it. He had the unflinching support from his networks and from social media. The president and many House and Senate Democrats had his back; the still popular and credible science tiger and a large sector of the most visible scientific community insisted that his success was crucial to the nation's survival.

But when he put in his rod last time, the Big Fish easily got away and even made him look silly. If that happened again, Jim may not recover. This Big Fish was the most important. If it got away, all the others would know how to escape too.

He and his comrades had been hard at work. Many in the student movement had shifted their focus from extirpating pockets of anti-life reactionaries on campus to a search for dirt on those Jim hoped to interrogate in the committee. As Corrine said, when you have hundreds of thousands of students—all of whom are passionately devoted to a cause and who are experts at information retrieval—working with you to dig up dirt, there's a good chance that the floor will be very dirty indeed.

But to Jim, the most productive bait came from within his own house, from people in high positions frightened of being nabbed themselves. If they talked, if they soiled their colleagues, if they provided even an inkling of doubt about those who Jim targeted, then the investigation would seem to be less of a one-man show than a national struggle for freedom.

"We have twelve senators lined up to be questioned by the committee," Jim told Corrine. "We have one hundred forty-three representatives. None of them are willing to work with us? None are willing to give us some info that gets them off the hook and helps us to nab Big Fish?"

"Well, some are talking, you know that, Jim," Corrine said to him, rocking her whimpering toddler as she spoke. "We have four giving testimonies at the Big Fish hearings, and a few others on the fence, probably waiting until after the interrogation to make any decisions as to which side of the fence they'll leap to. Even lots of Republicans are receptive to what you're doing; they're just as vulnerable and just as slimy. Like we read in Mr. X's documents, and like we're telling the ones reluctant to help, their own ties to corporate funding put them on the wrong side of this war. I mean, we can show America that their self-interest caused them to turn their back on national interests and on the people they're supposed to represent. We have a spreadsheet of the ones in the hands of interest groups like Pfizer and the Gated-Billionaire Foundation that links their acceptance of that funding to their voting record, and yea, JD, we have enough ammo to scare a bunch of them. Mr. X may have had another agenda, but his info is helping the students compile quite a dossier that's going to help us big-time. Trust the process, JD!"

"Yea," Jim said, sipping his drink and then pouring another. "For scum, Mr. X has been a godsend."

In fact, much of Mr. X's documentation named members of Congress on both side of the aisle as being complicit with big pharma and other sources of funding in trying to prolong COVID and endorsing expensive drugs, vaccines, and treatments over more common-sense approaches like the ones Kate and Lollypop advocated. Some governors fell on Mr. X's list too, but sadly those were the governors most allied with Jim and the pro-lifers. Luckily many of those in Congress who were tepid about Jim's cause and opposed stringent measures both against COVID-deniers and against the January sixth investigation were big recipients of this corporate funding. Almost all of them decried the November 11 events as being horrific, which to Jim meant that they were susceptible to being portrayed as soft on the life and democratic movement because they feared losing their funds. If Jim could push them into a corner of doubt, they might well drop their caution and leap to his cause.

And while Jim didn't buy into all of Mr. X's conspiratorial dribs and drabs, he planned to use it for his own benefit. Jim's goal wasn't to bring down potential allies by demonstrating their perfidy and corporate ties. Rather, he was constructing an arsenal of bait. He was very happy to keep Pfizer and the Gated Billionaire, and everyone tied to them, out of his testimony, because some of his own people— mostly Fact-nerd himself—appeared on Mr. X's pages more than almost anyone else. Jim's poignant spreadsheets were meant to intimidate and then draw in all those on the fence. If Jim could snag the Big Fish in a way that frightened these folks into submission, then Jim could fish without impunity moving forward.

Such is why this next committee investigation was of upmost importance!

Jim decided not to include the science tiger this time. The poor guy was brilliant and still the face of science, but under fire, he seemed to dissolve into ash. Jim knew his facts, he had three dozen spreadsheets at his disposal, his team of student investigators would be at his side, and he had testimony from some representatives who spilled dirt on the Big Fish under the promise of anonymity. The committee hearings would be aired live on DUI, and his most supportive pal Cheddar would host it. She clearly would swing listeners into his camp even if the Big Fish bit back. She was a pro!

Her segment was called *Misinformation and the Threat to Democracy: Day One*.

The Big Fish was as cocky as ever. A fancy lawyer sat by his side, a fast-talking Texas attorney from the same firm that Butcher Baker used to work at, the one famous for protecting oil companies and other slimebags. These guys hated progressives like Jim; their disdain for the students, for the pro-life cause, for anyone who dared to link Trump supporters to January sixth made the Big Fish and his lawyers hungry for a kill. And they believed Jim to be small fries, an easy takedown. They hardly seemed flustered.

"We have all seen your tweet, Congressman, in which you confessed support for the January sixth Capitol attack," Jim began after he hit the gavel. "I have the testimony of four of your colleagues that you supported the attacks and hoped for their success. I have testimony and evidence that you receive substantial corporate funding from companies that profit from a prolongation of COVID, and that your own reluctance to take sensible and scientific measures to protect the public from COVID is in your own financial interest. So I ask you, Congressman, how can you possibly sit here in front of the American people and your colleagues and dare state that you don't have blood on your hands?"

On CNN, Cheddar smiled big, shaking her head up and down. "America," she said, "the boxing gloves are off. Our democracy is being threatened, and millions of lives are hanging in the balance, and it looks like this very brave and smart congressman is no longer going to tiptoe around the obvious. Wow! An impressive start. Hardly traditional, but these aren't normal times, are they? OK, no more commentary until the first break. Let's listen in."

"I object," the Big Fish's lawyer said. "That is presumptive and inconsequential. You have no evidence."

"This ain't a trial, Big Guy." Jim laughed. "You can't object. You want to walk out, go ahead. But I think that will tell the American people and this August body where you stand. We're determining if a member of Congress knowingly supported a plot against the government of the United States and knowingly pursued measures clearly contrary to scientific consensus so as to prolong the most deadly pandemic in the modern era because he was serving his corporate sponsors or his right-wing base or whatever group he thought would benefit him from his slaughter of millions."

"You know what, Congressman?" the Big Fish said, putting his legs up on the table. "You're a little boy in a big boy world, and you don't scare me. You can intimidate the politically fraidy scared speaker. Maybe you can intimidate our demented president. But you ain't doing that to me. Let's start with issue one. First, the fucking tweet. Your whole case is based on a fucking tweet? Let's say I'm bored, which I am right now to tell the truth, 'cause I want to be working for America rather than sitting in here spending millions of America's money that this brazen young congressman is shitting away so all of you can think he's brave and bold and he can rise to the top of his pussyfooted party. So if I'm bored, I may doodle, and let's say that doodle is one of this congressman fucking a dog, which likely he does, since he sure as hell don't fuck woman or any other version of human beings. Hell, that don't mean I fuck dogs. That's what tweets are, Congressman; they're like doodles that you kind of write when you're bored. My tweet said jack shit about a government takeover, and I think the American people know it. And if four pussyfooted congressmen said some shit about me while they buried their head in the sand, that ain't evidence either. Hell, when I fight for America and for Americans, I piss a lot of my colleagues off, and sure they'd love to use your little intimidation campaign to get back at me. Bring them here, Congressmen. Let me face my accusers. Then we'll see what they say."

"Do you fuck dogs, Congressman?" Jim asked, putting his chin on his palms. "I'm guessing you do since you brought that up, but that's not why we're here, Congressman. You know I'm a progressive, and I don't interfere with anyone's sexual preference, so you can fornicate with anyone and anything you want. But slaughtering millions of people and trying to take over the government by a coup, yea, a doodle about that would concern me."

"Then bring out your witnesses and let's hear what they got to say!" the Big Fish said. "'Cause I never in my life threatened the government; while you socialists are trying to destroy the very fabric of our democracy, me and my people are trying to bring it back to what our founders want. And you're telling me that 'cause I speak in the language of common sense about COVID that I'm killing people? That's bullcrap, Congressman, and the fact you don't know it scares the fucking shit out of my crack. Look at us in here, all wearing these masks, even though the fucking COVID goes right through them. I've seen you and yours wearing a mask in the car, Congressman. That's science? That's sensible? What, you think the COVID bugs are going to leap out of the radio and nab you? I've seen you wearing masks on the street, all alone, on the fucking toilet, for Christ's sake. That's science? 'Cause if that's science, then yea, I don't subscribe to it. I call it deception. I call it a way for you to scare Americans into doing what you want them to do, fucking with their brains so they listen to your horsecrap. Let's face some facts, Congressman. The consensus scientific opinion ain't what your limp science tiger says. What we do in Texas is working, and we don't got to shut down society and take away people's constitutional rights and trick them with gimmicks and feed them with fear. Hell, we got fewer deaths down in my woods than in yours."

One of the students rose, sternly staring at the congressman from Texas. "Sir, you are wrong about your facts. We have expert testimony by the best scientific minds in the world, at the top universities and the top health agencies in the world, who contradict everything you say. We have data if you'd like to see it. They have estimated that Texas would have suffered over 1.3 million deaths had its people listened to your anti-science rhetoric as you pandered to your corporate masters. Thankfully, people in your state are smarter than you take them for. They know you too well, and they vaccinated and wore masks in certain areas, which is the only action that lowered your death rate, which is still among the highest in the country and the nation." He slid a few tables and spreadsheets toward the Big Fish, which Jim posted on the big screen and DUI. The student continued:

"You've consistently wanted to take away women's rights. You've consistently refused to protect citizens from gun violence. You've opposed measures to assure voting rights and gender equality. You and your corporate lawyers have spit on measures to save our environment and stop global warming. Your entire agenda has been to enrich the corporations that feed you and to enhance your power base at the expense of human rights, human life, and human decency. You are objectively a killer and an enemy of democracy. The collective wisdom of the world's smartest minds, and the blatant evidence of your words and deeds, condemn you."

"Look what the cat dragged in." The congressman laughed. "Which nerd bubble did you pop out of? What, couldn't make the football team, got beat up as a kid, so now you get off by bullying me? Well, fuck you, I don't got to listen to your made-up bullcrap. None of that shit is true; it's all a bunch of manufactured nonsense that you people love so much. So now what, little boy? You gonna take out your knife and stab me like you did to them other students, them innocent boys and girls, 'cause they didn't agree with your pandering nonsense? Is that what you're gonna do next?"

"We have pages of testimony to prove your facts wrong, to show that your anti-science rhetoric would have led to over a million deaths, that you were aware of this, that you conspired to prolong the pandemic and take down the government," Jim said. "Go ahead, go mock this student. He's from Harvard, Congressman, a college that wouldn't even let you clean bird crap off its sidewalks. The people who condemn you are from the best institutions in the nation. Remind me, Congressman, you went to some agricultural college in Texas, and I think you got in there as a favor to your daddy? You do a lot of things to repay favors to those who pave your path, don't you? We're not going to stab you. We don't have to. You're stabbing yourself and doing a damned good job of it."

"You, Congressman, have a lot of bluster and no facts," said the Big Fish, still calm and sporting a cocky smile. "Lots of hearsay, and no bones. Bring on your student dogs, and we'll show you some actual data, also from top dogs, but from scientists not intimidated by Fact-nerd and his pals." He pointed to his lawyer, who slid a stack of papers toward Jim. Jim slid the papers away, not showing them on the screen, not putting them on DUI. He stared at the Big Fish, who continued to speak:

"This is actual science, Congressman. Your shit ain't science; it's diarrhea, it's shit that is so fucking flimsy that it drips out of your ass faster than a fucking enema. Your so-called facts are bullshit, and reality alone has proven that correct, as my numbers and graphs show. But answer me this, genius boy: Why if the fuck would I oppose COVID mandates if I was sucking Pfizer's tits? Hell, I got a vaccine, I ain't opposed, but I give Pfizer a piece of my mind every time they and your people try to force vaccines on people and try to lock them up and scare the fuck out of them. So, if I'm on Pfizer's payroll, on the same payroll as Fascist-nerd and Star Buck and ninety percent of Democrats, why the fuck would I keep giving them and their suggestions so much crap? Can you see where some of your logic don't make much sense? Or, do you need some 'splaining from this guy with a little less education but a hell of a lot more smarts?"

"Our student Mary Lou will address your numbers, Congressman, and demonstrate that you are in league with corporate interests, that your agenda does support senseless slaughter under the guise of being—what do you call yourself?—a commonsense patriot. She'll 'splain some facts, real facts, real intentions, so the American people can see through your vicious self-serving and deadly rhetoric. If it makes you happy, Congressman, when this is over, when we finally remove you from your powerbase, I'll put your picture on my wall and caption it as the most patriotic American if that makes you feel better, something I can enjoy when I think of you behind bars, but—"

"Mary Lou?" The Big Fish laughed. "That chubby one there, the one who stabbed those kids to death and is now a hero on the liberal talk circuit? Oh man, Congressman, that is an honor! She's a celebrity, you know. Liberals love pro-choice so long as it's their choice, and Mary Lou, she makes lots of good choices. Hell, she don't like anyone making a choice she don't like, can't choose not to get jabbed by an experimental vaccine, can't choose not to wear a mask, but when it comes to killing people, stabbing people and choking them and killing them, well, hell, that kind of choice you liberals think is well and good. Her body, her choice, that's what y'all think, right? Can't wait to hear from you, Mary Lou. Hope you got that same dagger you used on those kids. Whatever your choice is, if it's to stab me or choke me or whatever else you want to do, I don't want to get in your way. Your body, your choice."

The Big Fish and his lawyer laughed, as did two other members of the committee. Jim smiled.

"Yes, Mary Lou is very impressive, very passionate and devoted, and I will get you her autograph. I'll put that on my list of what to hang in your prison cell, Congressman," Jim said. "But first, let me respond to your prior question. You ask why you would oppose COVID measures if you are a Pfizer lapdog. Let me tell you how, Congressman. It's all on my spreadsheets. It's clear as a Texas sunrise that you and your anti-science goons have been playing the corporate game, have been trying to make this virus as bad as it can be, have been doing the real scaring by letting real people die of a disease that is preventable with commonsense measures, have been doing all of that so that Pfizer and other big corporations can sell their wares and make a lot of cash, cash they can give back to you in a little kickback scheme that is all laid out on our sheets. You want this virus bad, Congressman. And yes, your ultimate goal—even if your ass speaks a different language than your slick mouth—is to bring down this government, to load it up with Trumpists and your corporate puppet masters, and what better way to do that than to let this disease run wild and created chaos and fear? You support the vaccine for big daddy Pfizer, but by rejecting everything else—including the mandates and masks—you help the virus to stick around so we can give more and more vaccines, so we can create a constant state of terror, so Americans willingly submit to the very autocrats who feed you. That compute, or you need 'splaining?"

"These hearings are an assault on justice, decency, and the law," the Big Fish's lawyer said, interrupting the Big Fish, who stood up, sweating, and was ready to pounce. "You have our data. You have our statements. If you need us back, we'll come back."

Mary Lou stood up. Venom seared through her eyes as she stared hard at the Fish and his lawyer. Then she smiled. "If you may, let the chubby one talk first, then you can leave. I'll talk regardless, but since this is being broadcast nationally, you may want to stay if you don't want to look too ridiculous and guilty. We've looked over your data, and it comes from four sources mostly. First, a doctor named Ten-Dollars, who has no credentials and who is currently being held by a truth committee on the campus of Case Western in Cleveland. She has signed a document attesting to the fact that she fabricated data to prolong the pandemic. Dr. McGuilty is another of your sources, from your fine state of Texas, also being held by the committee at Baylor under suspicion of fraud and intent to commit sabotage, and he too has agreed to a confession linking his misinformation to a grand scheme to prolong the pandemic and take down the government. Dr. Bearded Malcontent was discovered by some of our members hiding out in Florida under the protection of Governor DaSandwich, who himself is to be called to this committee next week. We extracted a written confession by him, largely blaming himself for spreading misinformation as a way to capture some part of the patent on the current vaccine, and I heard yesterday he committed suicide in his cell. The two members of Stanford whom you quote are in custody there and will appear before this committee. We have run your data by Doctor Fact-nerd and Got-Milk, members of the COVID task force, and over three hundred top academic epidemiologists in the world, and they have found your numbers to be fabricated and dangerous. All have said that if we followed your script, likely ten million will die in the next wave. And once that wave comes and kills, once your goals are achieved, we have over a dozen people who are in the custody of truth committees having attested that your intent is to stage another coup on the government, with none other than Donald Trump waiting in the wings to be installed as dictator. I may be chubby, Congressman, but my brain isn't, and I'm not the killer in the room, you are, and facts are facts."

"I ain't sticking around for this shit!" the Big Fish yelled as Mary Lou hovered over him with a snide smile pasted on her face. "This is a fucking aberration of justice! What, you put your fucking daggers against all them scientists, you threatened them with death or worse, and then forced them to sign confessions? This is fucking worse than Salem, another liberal witch hunt perpetrated under the veil of science and justice. American ain't gonna be intimidated by your bullshit, Congressman. They ain't that dumb. You bastards got a lot of nerve, that's all I got to say. I'm getting the fuck out of this shithole, and you'll be hearing from my lawyers for defamation and for being an ass!"

"You're not going anywhere, Congressman," said Jim, calling over two security men toward the Big Fish. "We have the testimony of your colleagues, whose names we won't reveal, but instead I've used pseudonyms that correspond to your favorite ice-cream flavors. Congressman Cherry Vanilla said, and I quote, 'The Texas congressman came to me one day and said, "Cherry, if we can keep this pandemic going a little longer, and get the economy sinking a little deeper, then the next time we storm the Capitol, we're going get it done."' Here's from Congresswoman Butter Pecan, who said, 'The congressman from Texas says to me regularly, keep the faith sweet cheeks, 'cause we got a big paycheck from Pfizer coming our way, and we're getting the troops ready to take over this House once and for all.' Then we got—"

The Big Fish stood up, visibly shaking. "It's all a bunch of bullshit!" The guards pushed him back down.

Within an hour, it was over. DUI spent the next few days going through Jim's data and the committee's next potential victims under its twenty-four-hour *Democracy in Peril* coverage. A poll the next day showed that, overall, 60 percent of the nation believed the Big Fish to be guilty and wanted more trials, and over 75 percent of Democrats wanted him to be jailed. Congress agreed to vote on his expulsion the following week. All the congressmen "on the fence" immediately leaped to Jim's side of it.

"I think we've uncovered something substantial." Cheddar smiled, her face radiant and confident as she stared into Jim's eyes. "Misinformation is being revealed for what it is, corporate meddling into what should be a purely scientific endeavor is being uncovered, and a strong link between the misinformation campaign and the January sixth plotters is emerging. I think, Congressman, the entire nation has more open eyes. Who is next, and what do we all have to do to protect our lives and our democratic institutions from this imminent and pervasive threat?"

Jim peered into the camera. "You, Cheddar—you and all the DUI heroes—you just keep up the good work of top-notch journalism. Your willingness to support science and truth over misinformation and treachery has helped us already to snuff out the next plot and a massive wave of death that these anti-life anti-democrats are trying to unleash beneath their venality. We have an active dossier of people coming to our committee in the next few weeks, starting with Senators Ranting Paul and Roger Dodger, representatives Amos-and-Andy and three Republicans from my home state, who are clearly implicated in the plot. We also have the governors of Texas and Florida joining us soon, as well as the Stanford Three. You guys got a lot of fascinating coverage coming your way, but most importantly, we'll get to the bottom of this plot before it raises its ugly head and kills more Americans, before it takes down our nation and its democratic institutions."

"Tell me, Congressman," she asked him, smiling broadly. "Full confession, this station receives money from Pfizer. When you implicated them in your interrogation, you insinuated that they seemed to want this pandemic to go on for their own profits. Just so our people and the American people can understand this, is Pfizer a guilty party here? Are they part of the misinformation campaign and plot?"

Jim laughed. "Look, America, as you know, I take no corporate funding and have no relationship with Pfizer. Lots of my colleagues do. It's not Pfizer causing the trouble. They've been good stewards of science and have been miracle workers in getting us a vaccine that may well end this pandemic and help us end other infections too, even AIDS. They're not the problem; they work closely with Doctor Fact-nerd and others to do the right thing. But some less scrupulous people are willing to take their money and do the wrong thing with it. It's like blaming the guy who gives you a paycheck just because you use that money to buy drugs. I think Big Fish wanted to impress Pfizer and get more loot. Didn't quite work out."

"Thanks to you!" She glowed. "One more question, Congressman, if I may. If you do restore this nation to the science-focused nation that our brilliant tiger of science and others have advocated, if we can eradicate COVID and get back to some sense of normal by carrying out sensible scientific measures and silencing the misinformation campaign, do you think we can have the NFL back in action next year? And if so, do you think that your Steelers and Big Ben can have another ride to the Super Bowl? You think it'll happen?"

Jim smiled big. "America, I know it will!"

CHAPTER EIGHTEEN

Into a Legal Morass

The trials came fast and furious. Ranting Paul. Gymshorts Jordon. Governor DaSandwich. Those were the big names, and they fell hard; mounds of evidence piled up, implicating them in intentional misinformation campaigns, in complicity to January sixth, in a plot to prolong the virus. DUI reveled in its coverage. *The New Yacking Times* and *Washington Polluter* carried headlines bigger than even that for the Hindenburg.

The Plot Runs Thick with Congressional Blood wrote the *Times. Betrayal at the Roots* wrote the *Polluter.*

Few dismissed the well-constructed, carefully documented evidence Jim used to implicate these traitors, all graphed and spreadsheeted with meticulous unassailable detail. Whatever "facts" the guilty used in their defense Jim tied to the already debunked misinformation sources that now lacked all credibility. And thus could Jim tear their anti-science claims to shreds, buttressing his own sheets of facts with the testimony his crew of students had ripped out of frightened doctors and politicians—as a price for their own immunity—to tie these monsters not only to the anti-life movement but also to January sixth.

"Why would these people, these bastions of our representative democracy, have so callously fought to spread myths about COVID, myths that would invariably escalate deaths and lead to anarchy and terror?" Jim asked his TV audience during the Ranting Paul trial. "It was, of course, a means of feeding their corporate donors who thrive on this pandemic spreading across the world, but more significantly was a way to sew enough fear, chaos, and discontent across the land so as to make another January sixth possible. The clear ties of these traitors to the Trump plot, and their anti-life rhetoric that manifestly shows their willingness to trade lives for power, should make all of us shake in fear."

"Worse than 911," said Mumbling Joe. "Homegrown traitors. Worse than the Civil War."

And Congressman Amos-and-Andy—"a doctor who shat on his Hippocratic oath by selling patients the taboo snake oil ivermectin and blatantly lied by claiming that its use would have saved lives and made the vaccine less necessary, a doctor who wanted to expose kids to a deadly and preventable virus by dropping all restrictions and mandates, a doctor who spread lies that clamping down society was more harmful than the worst plague in modern memory"—was crushed by the evidence tossed at him by fellow anonymous representatives, by Jim's spreadsheets documenting the damage his negligent misinformation could have caused, by his own actions and writing. At one point, Mary Lou rose and put her face in his face. She pulled down her mask and spit.

"You are not woke, Congressman," she said. "You have caused so much disgrace in my state, among my people, and to every cause I hold dear. And so now, you are canceled. Your self-serving poison will spill no more." She spit again. "This is for all whom you murdered! For the democracy you mocked. Let justice and God do the rest. You, you are unwoke, anti-life, anti-science, and I hope you squirm in hell!"

"Justice?" Amos-and-Andy called out as the Capitol guards grabbed his wrists and pulled him away. "From the girl who stabbed innocent kids on a college campus and led her groupies across the nation to do the same? Justice? You'll be woke, my foolish friend, once the courts get hold of your justice. Then, my spit will be heading your way!"

"Amos-and-Andy and other traitors to this nation are heading to a camp in Florida," said the tap dancer to Jim later that night on DUI. "Lots of people are questioning the legality of those camps, Congressman.

Including the our vice president, who's tough as nails when it comes to mandates, masks, and the vaccine but who thinks you're going too far. We've heard rumors of her fighting loudly with the president, who we know has offered tepid supports what you're doing. What do you say to the vice president and to others who are questioning your methods and the legality of your committee? You've convinced the president to declare martial law in Florida after you proved that its governor was conspiring with the anti-democratic forces. But was that the right next step, was the threat down there so grave as to justify that action? And building camps in that state for those your committee convicts, for the unvaccinated; it seems that some of that would lack legal justification. What do you say?"

Jim's once obsequious tap dancing partner had become a bit testier. He never asked the science tiger tough questions, never dug into what DUI's handpicked doctors, scientists, and experts claimed to be the one and only truth. And for a long time, he had treated Jim the same way. But now he was pushing back. Why?

"Because you threw Pfizer under the bus," the tiger told Jim one day over a cup of tea. "Half the people you've convicted you've tied to Pfizer donations. The tap dancer and DUI get money from the industry, Jim. The NIH, FDA, CDC; lots of congressmen, lots of us in the federal work force, we get more from industry than from taxpayers, and no one wants you to bring that up. I understand you're using Pfizer connections to bring down bad people, and the executives I know in industry understand that too, but some of the recipients of the money, people like the tap dancer, who believes himself to be incorruptible, they may be a bit more uncomfortable; they may fear that you'll throw the bus at them next. You need to reassure them, or they'll fight back."

The tap dancer once told Jim that he and the science tiger had an agreement; he'd treat the tiger with kid gloves and promote his agenda as long as the tiger strayed far away from discussing any ties between industry and DUI.

The next night Jim subtly addressed the dancer's concerns. "First, dance-man, I want to thank you for bringing up the obvious. Do we have legal justification for our actions? We both know that holding citizens who are an imminent threat to our nation and our lives is justified by the Constitution, and that the camps we've set up in Florida are a way to do that in the most benign way. Remember, our committee is not a court; it's more of a tribunal, kind of like the 9/11 tribunals, and just like we legally held suspects deemed imminent threats in Guantanamo without trying them or charging them with a specific crime, so are we doing the same now with the anti-lifers. We know this will be going to the Supreme Court, and we are preparing our own defense. But for now, we feel it's best to keep these people isolated and safe. Besides, America, who wouldn't want to be in Florida in December?"

The tap dancer laughed. "Yes, you are right about that! What about martial law in Florida?"

Jim smiled. "Hardly martial law, America," he said. "Have you seen the pictures? The beaches are filled, tourism is thriving, life is going on. We've just replaced a corrupt and dangerous governor with federal leadership and with troops to assure that his anti-science laws and anti-democracy government are all dismantled. We discovered documents in the DaSandwich statehouse outlining the governor's role in a future plot, and many of his aides and allies are named. How can we simply leave that state to its own devices when the web of treachery there is so deeply rooted? President Buck didn't initiate these measures lightly, I assure you, and his legal justification is tight. Our president will most certainly hand the state back to its people just as soon as the organs of plot and anti-life are found and removed."

The dancer nodded up and down, but before he could ask another question, Jim jumped in.

"I also want to state, unequivocally, that the leaders of Pfizer and of other pharmaceutical companies who have saved our nation countless times from illness and disease, and who have been on the front line of this battle against not only the pandemic but also misinformation and subterfuge, are backing me in everything I'm doing. I consult with them regularly. They realize that some of their funding to political candidates was misplaced, but, America, Pfizer and many of our pharmaceutical heroes give money to the good guys too; they even advertise on DUI, and I think they do that more to thank you for your informative and unbiased journalism than any other reason. Boola-boola, Pfizer's CEO, told me himself that without DUI's unparalleled informative and honest coverage there could be no resolution of this mess, that millions would have died had you not reported the truth in this cloud of misinformation. For that, the world and nation thanks you."

The tap dancer smiled big. "Well, we're just doing our jobs, Congressman, just like you're doing yours."

The next morning Jim sat down with his legal team, including notorious Harvard lawyer Old Dishwasher, US Solicitor General Hot Perogies, California Attorney General Muy Bonita, US Attorney Da Reason, and his pal Red Robin who was the legal analyst on DUI.

He offered scotch all around and poured himself a big glass, sipping it quickly. Corrine, who sat in on the meeting, had made curried chicken, which she put on kaiser rolls and passed around along with chips and pickles. Jim passed on the food.

"I want your brains to help me out here," he said to them. "And once I lay out the issues, I'm leaving the room, and I'll come back when you've reached some resolution. So, I don't want a lot of questions tossed at me now. I'm an engineer, not a lawyer and as Bugs Bunny might say about what the committee is doing, 'I know this defies the law of gravity, but I never studied law!' A lot of folks are telling me that we're going too far, that the courts will shut us down, that the American people have no taste for saving their democracy if it requires harsh measures. So, to quote Bugs again, 'I'll be scared later. Right now, I'm too mad.'"

He slid reams of spreadsheets and graphs across the table. "This is what I know. The targets of attack against my pro-life campaign all pivot their position around the government's inability to limit personal freedoms and habeas corpus in times of emergency. But we know that these have been breached before during crises. And gentlemen and ladies, this is a crisis to end all crises. So, my committee's verdicts, which place potentially dangerous Americans in camps until we can determine their innocence or guilt, federal control over areas of the nation deemed a threat, and my two bills—one to curb misinformation, the other to remove people from society who threaten hit—all fit into this category.

"As you can see, I've attached legal precedent from my own basic understanding of the issues; I've been working with law students at top schools to compile this list. First, we have the Korematsu decision, passed 6-3 by a liberal Supreme Court—with the likes of Felix Frankfurter and Justice Black supporting it—that justified placing Japanese Americans into camps without formally charging them with anything because they were a potential threat. Then we have—"

Da Reason, Star Buck's lead attorney and a reluctant participant in this meeting, cut him off. "Congressman, Korematsu was overturned in 2018 by Chief Justice Rob-banks, who clearly stated in an unrelated opinion that the Korematsu verdict was improper and was thus overturned."

Old Dishwasher, wearing a frumpy tweed jacket, with his legs up on a nearby chair, chuckled. "That's hardly overturning a verdict," he posited. "More like a little slap than an exorcism. From my perch, Korematsu still stands."

"I don't think you'll get anyone on the court to agree with you, Alan," said Red Robin. "You use Korematsu, and you'll get backlash. Bad backlash."

"OK OK," said Jim, finishing his drink and pouring another. "Like I said, the debates occur when I leave the room; do your squabbling then, but give me a single unanimous path forward once you're done, and don't call me in until then. A few other salient points that my students made here: First, President Adams passed the Alien and Sedition acts, and although everyone hated the power those measures afforded to the executive, we could find no evidence that they've ever been overturned."

Da Reason started talking, and Jim put his index finger over his mouth to shush her. He continued.

"Presidents Lincoln, Wilson, and Roosevelt, among others, passed strong laws endorsing executive power in times of emergency that strip Americans' rights when those rights threaten the nation. Oliver Wendell Holmes in the Schenck decision clearly upheld Wilson's Espionage and Sedition acts, providing his famous clear and present danger argument about not being able to yell fire in a crowded movie theater, which I understand was partly overturned, but its basic guts and message remain firmly in place. And not let's forget dear Justice Holmes decision in Buck versus Bell that legalized state power to sterilize any Americans who are deemed a threat to the nation. That was an 8-1 decision and is still on the books from what we can surmise. Bottom line, I have a spreadsheet that maps over thirty decisions that should support our cause, with pros and cons listed in each row. Your big legal brains may know of more cases or may have problems with the ones I've given you. Regardless, we need consensus and a solid argument. Good chance we'll have to be defending ourselves pretty damned soon. So, that's all, folks. I'll be out there while you do your job. Text me if you want more sandwiches or if you're done."

Jim marched out of the room, ready to suck down his full glass of Jack Daniel's.

Coming behind him was Governor Newbie-hottie's attorney general Muy Bonita. "Congressman," he called out, panting.

Jim twisted toward him. "What the hell, man. We need you in there. Get back in."

He looked at Jim with tired eyes. "I have something I want to say to you, but I didn't want to say it in front of the others," he said. "Trump's appointees aren't going to be friendly to any of this. You can quote them all the precedent in the world, and they'll buck. They're libertarians pretty much, especially Sucks-gourds, who holds a lot of weight with them, and they may use this as an opportunity to weaken executive power and to strike down some of these precedents."

Jim nodded. "Then what do you propose?"

Muy Bonita paused for a moment. Then he whispered, "Maybe, just maybe, given that they were appointed by a president who hatched a plot against the nation, a president whom you have in custody in Florida now, maybe they were involved too. Maybe you could get confessions from someone to implicate them. This is just speculation."

Jim laughed and put his hand on the man's shoulders. "Are you suggesting what I think you are? Bring them in front of the committee?"

"I'm just saying, sir," the attorney general said. "We'd do much better if they weren't on the court. And To-mass's wife is a sitting duck. We have emails from her suggesting she supported January sixth; getting him and her in front of the committee, or at least off the court, should be a cinch and should open the way to a much more forgiving environment in there."

Jim smiled, nodded, and turned away. He said nothing more. But those wheels were already spinning in his head.

"We'll get them all off the court," he said to Corrine, sucking down his drink. "I don't trust any of them to be honest. The lower courts too. We'll just dismantle the whole judicial system."

"How, JD?" she asked, keeping pace with him as he dashed to his office.

Jim wanted another drink, and he hurried. "Right now it seems we're pretty much getting our way," he said. "I mean, we just have to concoct some good reasons, some confessions, some data, and I can get pretty much anyone to disappear?"

"I'll get the students on it." She smiled.

To Jim, Corrine's students were becoming the only people he trusted.

CHAPTER NINETEEN

Omicron Winter

Jim woke up panting, his pajamas soaked. He had another dream about Kate. He was on top of her, and she was crying out to him. "More, Congressman, more! Oh more, please, more, more, more!"

Sometimes Corrine, who often slept in the adjoining room, would rush in during these dreams to wake him up. They were coming more frequently, especially after his hand was forced to take care of the good doctors from Pittsburgh, the people whom he called the Misinformation Five.

"You have no choice, Jim," she said to the congressman, rubbing his back as she sat by him in bed. "If you let them be, then everything we are doing is suspect. There can't be two sets of facts, theirs and ours. This has to be black-and-white."

But was it? A spreadsheet to Jim always represented truth; if you could graph it and fill in the columns, then it's real. Science isn't fickle; it's as absolute as God Himself. There had to be one right answer, and when detractors challenged it, they opened the doors of misinformation that confused people and obfuscated established dogma, setting the stage for a victory of untruth, of heresy, and an end to democracy and science. That dictum constituted the core of Jim's battle, his Zeitgeist.

It had all seemed so simple a few months ago, but now as Florida and Texas bristled with camps to detain those who defied scientific mandates and who dared to spread misinformation, as one political leader after another, one renegade doctor or scientist after another, one right-wing newscaster after another, drowned in Jim's committee—offering their versions of truth that Jim's one-right-answer spreadsheets ripped to shreds—the nation held its collective breath and wondered: Is this necessary?

A few rational voices, liberal voices, began to break through the wall of fear and unassailable compliance that Jim had constructed with the bricks of absolutism and ask: *Is Congressman Depich going too far? Are these students out of control? Is the conspiracy as deep as he contends? Or, is it all a play for power?*

With COVID waning, with memories of January 6th fading, with no new threats on the horizon, and with the economy shaky and people focusing their concerns elsewhere, Jim's star dropped a bit.

"Corrine," he snapped as she dug her stumpy fingers into his neck, "I need some scotch too. Love the rub, always do, but I need the scotch with it."

Maybe he became more worried when Corrine told him nonchalantly, "If midterm elections were held today, Republicans would sweep both houses of Congress, and you'd lose your race by double digits."

Jim's reactions to that was simple and sharp. "People don't understand the magnitude of this threat," he told her. "You can't judge a government in the middle of a crisis. If things are looking bad, I'll get Buck to suspend the elections. That's the only course we can take. Sometimes to save democracy, you have to take a pause, or else people will vote with their wallets and their fears, not with their sense."

Star Buck has started getting cold feet, especially since Bad-Karma made her ire known on the very channels that had been Jim's bastion of support, blasting Jim's committee, questioning his dismissal of five Supreme Court justices, decrying the legality of his camps and his declaration of martial law in two states (which were authorized through emergency decrees by the president), stating that COVID had begun to slow and that it was time to relax restrictions a bit, and even threatening to resign. She held hard to her call for vaccine mandates and for continued mask use, but she wanted things to open up, and she demanded that the congressman from Pittsburgh be reined in under the authority of the law.

"We can't keep going like this," she said to Mumbling Joe, staring hard at him. "Yes, we can't let down our guard, and yes, we need to get to the bottom of January sixth, but extralegal measures are antithetical to our national spirit, even during crises. I understand that the congressman has found legal precedent for everything he's doing, that he believes it is supported by the Constitution and by prior Supreme Court rulings, but if that's the case, why remove justices, why block legal avenues to get to the same point? Joe, if we continue down this road, are we any better than our enemies?"

Jim sucked down his scotch and then poured another. He thought of Kate, of her smile when they ate together, of her mastery of Bugs. Her face glowed in his mind. She seemed to exude pure goodness.

"She's a bullshitter, they all are," he said, drinking even more than usual. Nothing seemed to numb him today, and he feared the loss of his resolve. "They pretend to care, but their caring only leads to more harm because they don't get it. Their misinformation only confuses people and lets the bad guys win."

He peeked at Corrine, who didn't know what he was saying. "When's Mary Lou going to Pittsburgh?"

"Tonight," she said, kissing him on the head. "It'll be quick and painless. Is that what worries you?"

Jim nodded from side to side. "Of course not," he said, convincing himself of a lie. All crusades for justice ran into the roadblock of maudlin sympathy for some of its villains. Especially the pretty ones. Especially the nice ones. Especially the ones with amazing smiles! He tried to visualize Kate and Lollypop getting it on, hoping that would make the deed less odious. The scotch wasn't working, something had to.

"Is this watered down?" he accused his aide. "I am hardly feeling a buzz!"

"Representative A-O-Crazy will be by later." She smiled, ignoring his question. "The student groups are meeting tonight to prepare for the January sixth rally. They'll break in the new self-rebreathing masks and armor uniforms. Tap dancer wants you on his show tonight to talk about it and about the shooting. Let's hope he doesn't call it vigilante justice again! He's slipping a bit. I think you should focus more on Cheddar."

"Yea," Jim slurred. "Maybe. But I asked her about Elmer Fudd, and she never heard of him."

A week ago, on the campus of Brown University, several students broke up a Truth Club rally and instigated a fight. Suddenly guns were fired, and two of the Truth Club leaders lay dead. That sparked a riot; twelve students died, most of whom were not part of the club, and hundreds were hospitalized. On several campuses, the Truth Clubs were being heckled and taunted. As per the deal Jim made with Star Buck, no members of the clubs could carry weapons. So now they were becoming targets of reprisals against Jim's pro-life pro-democracy campaigns, and it was nearly impossible for them to fight back.

A student at UCLA, named Julie, whose young brother died of COVID, or so she said, turned in her parents, claiming that they encouraged both siblings not to wear masks and to defy the pro-science laws. Her parents were arrested and sent to a camp in Texas. A-O-Crazy appeared on Makes-sense-NBC with her and built her into a hero, just as prominent now as Mary Lou, whose role had devolved somewhat into being just the Truth Club pit bull. This girl from California—blonde and tall with a big bright smile—captured the attention of the media. "Sweet and Spicy," wrote the *New Yacking Times*. "An angel for justice."

Mary Lou complained that UCLA Julie was an airhead and a fake. Jim told her to shut her trap.

He drank some more.

"So, once the kids wear their space suits, once they can't catch the virus and can't get shot, then what?" he asked Corrine. "More violence? Is that what this is all about, Corrine? Is the country ready for the student groups to start executing more kids? Isn't that what will happen on January sixth?"

"Representative A-O-Crazy believes, as do most of the student leaders, that a total absence of retribution on the part of the clubs will weaken their authority and make them more vulnerable," she said to him, lying on his back now and rubbing him hard. "You've said it; you've graphed it, Jim. We can't compromise. We have to be tough and not back down. During the January sixth anniversary rally, they've already earmarked several faculty and students who will have their crimes revealed and fates determined by the clubs. These are dirty people, Jim, so it will go over well. The media coverage will all be in our favor, believe me."

"Don't do anything to the Stanford Three," Jim yelled through his slurred tongue. "They need to go in front of me at the committee. I want their assess myself. I want to execute those bastards. There's no trip to Florida or Texas for those monsters. They'll be hanging from the Capitol rotunda to remind our soft country about the danger of misinformation. And others will follow them. Lots of others. This country is getting too damned soft. I wish Star Buck would die. Then I'd toss Bad-Karma in front of the committee and fry her ass to the ground too. Then we wouldn't have all this bullcrap to deal with."

"One step at a time, Jim," she said. "Have you talked to Fact-nerd about Omicron?"

A new variant drifted into the nation, and Jim needed it to be bad, real bad. His science tiger always said that once people fell into complacency, once they forgot the horror of COVID, then, like the old, demented president who ran his party, they would care more about the economy and the simple pleasures of life than the threat itself. "That's when our guard will be down and the virus will kill us all," the tiger told him. And that's when another January 6th would hit!

Omicron offered a great hope for frightening the country back into compliance. But for that to happen, the variant had to be perceived and broadcast as being horrific, with its killing power fueled by those who refused vaccination and masking. Omicron handed Jim a timely means of dividing lifers from anti-lifers, of his painting the latter as an imminent threat to Americans and America. With his momentum fading, Jim needed to grasp this and take it for all it was worth!

Jim had quietly found and detained Mr. X soon after their meeting, sending the former NSA agent to Guantanamo. He offered Mr. X his life in exchange for information, and Mr. X provided him with copious quantities of bogus data and false accusations that seemed so absurd and conspiratorial so as to be likely dismissed by most people who heard them, accusations pointed at pro-lifers like Fact-nerd and Gated-Billionaire, information that venerated anti-lifers like Ken-and-Barbie and the Stanford Three. As Jim released the information, as he tied it to the anti-life camp, it only made Mr. X's heroes seem like nutjobs, while its farcical jabs at the pro-lifers seemed so misplaced as to be nothing more than manicured vengeance. All this helped Jim to garner more public support for his cause and for the entire pro-life, pro-science camp, who now had the public's sympathy for being so unjustly assailed.

After listening all morning to A-O-Crazy demand more student leadership at the committee meetings, and a bigger role for herself and some of her handpicked friends in the student movement and the trials, a dazed and now drunk Jim wandered into the science tiger's office.

Jim plopped upon the good doctor's upholstered easy chair and felt the room spin around. The elderly doctor was smiling but a bit uneasy. He wondered why Jim had come here; his own status on the Buck task force had started to fade, even if he remained popular in the press and among the students. What did the leader of the pro-life movement want from him?

Jim looked into the tiger's tired eyes. "Omicron needs to be scary as shit, Doc," he said. "Some people say it's not, that it's like a cold. We can't have a cold, tiger. We need a fucking disaster."

Fact-nerd nodded up and down. "It is bad, Jim," he said confidently. "Lots of people will die. Especially the unvaccinated. Especially those who take it too lightly. Don't believe what you hear."

Jim laughed. "Now, that's the tiger I like! The guy who makes people pee in their pants! The guy who turns up the heat. How are we going to convince Americans that this virus will kill them if they get too complacent, and also convince them that their unvaccinated neighbors and all the people in states who mock masks and quarantines, that those are the biggest danger and must be neutralized?"

"It's just true," the tiger said. "If you don't get a vaccine and a booster, you threaten everyone. If you reject a mask, you threaten everyone. You'll fill up the hospitals and cause the country to buckle."

Jim smiled and then explained what he had read in Mr. X's cauldron of conspiracy. "Someone told me," he said, smiling at the old doctor, who was like a statue staring back, his face devoid of all emotion, "that you, Doctor Fact-nerd, control the federal and pharmaceutical funding for almost all research in this country. That you pick and choose who gets money, which academic institutions and doctors you favor, and you can punish those who you don't think are worthy by denying them funds. True?"

The tiger nodded up and down. "I make sure that our public-private partnership choses institutions and researchers who will give us the answers we need and want," he said casually. "I have a large group of worthy academics I trust, and others I wouldn't trust to mow my lawn. Why?"

"Second question," Jim said. "Someone told me that there is a way to make it seem that most people hospitalized with COVID are not vaccinated, even if it's not true. That the CDC is already doing it. And it's this: We just have to include data about hospitalization in our CDC reports that occurred before the vaccine was even available, and if we do that, we'll skew the statistics such that the unvaccinated seem sicker than anyone else. Can we do this with Omicron? It's important to have the hospitals full withanti-lifers who we can show are overwhelming the medical system and pose a grave threat because they don't wear masks and refused to be vaccinated."

Again, hardly flinching, the tiger nodded. "Of course, that's what we do. We don't want anyone thinking that the vaccine isn't working. That would put doubt in people's minds, and doubt is the enemy of science, Jim. We need your spreadsheets to reflect a certain truth, the truth we know to be true even if some people can mangle numbers and show otherwise. We will do all that, and I'll let my friends in the media know that's what's going on."

"And I need you to let your doctor friends, and all the people you work with in academia, that they have to be with the program too or else their funding will disappear," Jim said. "We need a common front."

"Of course," said the tiger, "they know, and we'll get them to let the world know. We can't let people think that Omicron isn't dangerous. We need to tell them that it can kill you. And we need to make sure lots of people test for it, and that our helpful local and national leaders and the media report the escalation of numbers, all of which will drive up hospitalizations."

"And," Jim smiled, wishing he had another bottle of scotch, and knowing that at most the timid doctor could offer him a cup of herbal tea, "since Omicron is going to spread fast, and since people die every day anyway, we need to tie every death in anyone who tests positive for Omicron to COVID. I want COVID deaths to go off the charts. I want to tie those deaths to the unvaccinated. And I want people scared again."

"All that is standard operating procedure," the tiger said. "We control the narrative, Jim, and we believe that it's best to give the worst-case scenario, just so people stay cautious."

"Good," he said, standing up. That's exactly what Mr. X had written down in bold print throughout his saga: *Fact-nerd is so tied to industry and to his own power and profits that he owns academia and their doctors; if they defy him, they get no government and industry funding, all of which is funneled by Doctor Fact-nerd through his office in the NIAI; as he escalates COVID deaths, he can count on his chorus of sycophantic academic puppy dogs to support him, all of whom will get ample funding by the drugs and vaccines that fear and a mangling of truth will allow them to produce and sell.*

"Let's follow Mr. X's script, do what he already has accused us of doing, and then if anyone attacks us using the Mr. X playbook, we just frame them as a nutjob who is trying to make the virus worse by spreading misinformation. And then they go in front of my committee, and we skewer them and remove them from society," Jim said, completing his thought out loud.

"What do you mean?" the tiger asked, not comprehending that Jim had not intended to verbalize his thinking. "Who goes in front of your committee?"

"Anyone who dares tell us that what we're saying and doing doesn't have legitimacy," he said, teetering to the door. "Tiger, I'll need you to testify at the trial of the Stanford Three, which is slated to happen next month. You got to have more balls than the last time I put you in front of the committee. You can't let them make you look foolish. I'll have all the data about the lethality of Omicron, about how it is a disease of the anti-lifers and is being spread to those who don't follow science, that it's overwhelming our hospitals, and that it is going to be used to destabilize the country and make a repeat of January sixth possible. It'll be in spreadsheets and ready for you. But, tiger, you got to be tough and have balls."

The tiger nodded up and down, and his fist clenched a bit. "Those people, especially two of them," he said of the Stanford Three. "They have tried to sully my name and convince Americans that I am not a worthy scientist and that my greed and ignorance is what drives me. Jim, I want to take them down. I wish you had let me go after Ranting Paul. He wouldn't have been breathing after I crucified him by using his lies against him. But these three, these three arrogant know-it-alls, especially the one who was with me on Trump's task force—I want their heads, Jim. They're not going to be able to out-maneuver me, and I'll have the weight of academia to back me up."

"You, sir," Jim said, laughing, "are making me very happy. Keep up that energy, tiger man. Because once we take them down, once their bodies are hanging from the rotunda, then we can mark the one-year anniversary of January sixth as it should be, by showing America who the villains are and how we take care of those who threaten us from within. After this, Tony, there's no turning back."

That night, Jim dreamed of Kate again. Mary Lou was in Pittsburgh. Jim popped up, sweating. It was 2:00 a.m. He grabbed his bottle and slurped it down, knowing Kate was gone. "No turning back," he slurred. Corrine put her head in the door, but Jim already fell back on his pillow. *There is no turning back.*

CHAPTER TWENTY

The Stanford Three

They had been in custody on campus for months, and now, finally, they'd have a chance to make their plea to the nation. Several students stood with Jim and the science tiger as a dozen guards dragged in the Stanford Three. Straddling Jim were Senators Party Cruise and Graham Cracker; they were the most prominent and outspoken congressmen who had been nudged by Jim's power and position to change sides and testify against many of their colleagues, publicly condemning Trump and his band of anti-democrats and anti-lifers as being the greatest threat to this nation since Hitler. Now they would help toss these three bastions of lethal misinformation into a televised vat of retribution.

The cameras rolled. In the corner of DUI's coverage scrolled the escalating Omicron cases, hospitalizations, and deaths. Near it read the following: *Percent of Hospitalizations in Unvaccinated, 97.8%.* As Jim told Cheddar, who was the lead anchor for this trial, it was important that all the numbers looked precise, hence 97.8%. *Averages and guesses don't sway public opinion, but precision uttered by experts does.* She never delved into the source of these numerical verdicts, nor did she ask how the experts arrived at their conclusions or if other experts disagreed. None of that mattered. Her job was to magnify the danger of misinformation and to do all that she could to convince a war-weary public that the perpetrators of crimes against their nation and all its citizens remained severe, and that any alleviation of fear and vigilance could lead to massive waves of death and another January 6th assault.

And at that task, she was masterful! As were most of the others in Jim's propaganda army.

Misinformation on Trial: How Medical Lies Led to Slaughter read the *New Yacking Times* headline.

If We Don't Stop Misinformation, January 6th May Come Again: The Trial of the Century wrote the *Washington Polluter*.

"In just two days, America will remember a grim day, a day much like December seventh and 9/11, a day of infamy," said the DUI anchor, with a visage of vicious indignation scrawled upon her pale but well made-up face. "Today, Congressman Jim Depich's committee, our nation's top medical experts, and the American people will stand in judgment of three people who have disseminated misinformation and, more than almost anyone, caused Americans to doubt the scientific necessity of our experts' ability to save our nation from harm. These men are among our most notorious medical liars, and yet, were it not for brave students at Stanford, they'd still be allowed to spread their lies on social media and on their campus. Congressman Depich will show us who they really are, why they represent the most grievous threat to our nation's democracy and to the lives of our citizens perhaps ever in our country's history. Will January sixth happen again in two days, or will we finally be able to stamp out this plot and its architects and get our nation back on track? As hospitals fill with the victims of misinformation, as right-wing anti-democrats plot their next attack, today Americans stand in judgment of those who attack us still."

The three of them sat, wearing drab green prison clothes, disheveled and appearing exhausted, their faces devoid of any inflection. Jim had names for them each, which he used during the hearings; he always said that it's best to describe someone by who they are rather than what someone named them. "The one thing Trump did right." He laughed with Corrine one day. So, he introduced them by their names when he addressed them. There was Koalemos, the Greek god of stupidity, whom Jim called Koal and who stood for the Greek member of the Stanford Three; Dodo, who was the world's dumbest bird and who represented a doctor whose real name sounded kind of like a bird; and then the one he despised the most, the one who worked with Trump and derided the science tiger and all other bastions of science, the one Jim called Mr. Shrug, after the name of an Ayn Rand book, whose title had his name in it.

"Let's bring these hearings to order," said Jim. "Before us stand three of the most notorious authors of misinformation. On their campus, they have consorted with each other and with many other like-minded anti-science pseudo-intellects to disseminate false information, to collectively hypnotize the American people into believing a narrative that has cost far too many their lives. And by doing this, by deliberately deceiving people with manipulated numbers and statistics, they have made this country ripe for not only massive waves of death from a virus that we could have prevented had we been more scientific and vigilant but also for the anti-democrats to take advantage of the atmosphere of chaos and distrust that would allow them to grasp the instruments of power. I have been authorized by President Buck, under current emergency decrees, which have precedent in multiple rulings by our Supreme Court during similar times of crisis, to try and convict these criminals and punish them in a way that is commensurate with their crimes. Any verdict we declare here will have to be sanctified by Congress and thus by the American people. Do my colleagues on the committee have anything to say?"

Party Cruise smiled wryly, looking at the camera. "Well, Jim, let's hope justice is served today and we move toward getting real America back, honest America, pure America. Just look at them, Jim, these so-called scientists, these people who used their positions to try to trick Americans. Look at them! So pitiful! May God be my witness; I hope today we begin the process of cleansing and fixing the mess that these people have made. I'm sure none other than George Washington and Abraham Lincoln are looking down on us now and wondering just how much we're willing to fight to keep their experiment alive."

"Thank you, Senator," Jim said. But before he could say another word, Graham Cracker jumped in.

"And to add to my worthy colleague's statement," he said, smiling, "let's fry these bastards!"

Cheddar laughed on screen and nodded up and down. "Let's get this started." She smiled.

The hearings began with an hour of spreadsheets produced by Jim that were flashed on a board in the committee room. These demonstrated the "facts" about COVID, the many deaths that occurred and the millions more that would have occurred if the public listened to the lies uttered by the Stanford Three "based on modeling projections by the most esteemed doctors and scientists in the world at institutions like Johns Hopkins, University of Washington, and Cambridge University, in addition to Stanford, where these three teach and where over three-hundred faculty and virtually every student on that campus signed a petition not only to kick these liars out of the college but also to have them meet the noose of justice." And also Jim showed how these people's misinformation was derived by false assumptions, overly sanguine projections, misinterpreted facts, and a desire to "elevate their own status by becoming darlings of the anti-life movement to whom they cater."

Many of those already condemned by the committee, some of whom had died—such as Dr. Peter McGuilty and his band of medical liars—and others like Ranting Paul who remained in detention, all cited numbers that these three medical liars had conjured up, Jim said. "Their reach across the entire anti-life and anti-democratic movement can't be stressed enough. To those who seek to escalate deaths from COVID and overturn our democratic government, these three represent their prophets."

Some of the students spoke, sounding both concerned and intelligent. One of them, a tall dark woman with flowing hair and glasses, said that she was a PhD in Biochemistry, and had an opportunity to speak with Dodo on several occasions and was appalled by his lack of concern for the number of those dying of COVID. "He even denied that such deaths were occurring," she said. "And when we had the three of them in custody, all they could do was to produce documents that they claimed proved their points. It was as if they were so sure of their lies that they clung to them just because they were written on paper. They tried to brainwash many of us who kept them in custody—we had to keep them locked up for the good of scientific integrity and of the nation, even though we are by nature pacifists and supporters of free speech, but if you heard what they said, how they comported themselves, pretending to be all our friends, feigning their innocence and accuracy, all of you, all of you here and all Americans who know the truth, who have watched TV and heard the pleas of our doctors and scientists and understand the truth, all of you, I don't think you would have been as kind to these three as we were. It was utterly sickening; I have to tell you that. We were all pleasant and nice. But too, we're just so thankful to finally have this moment where we can show the world just who they are."

Another student stood up. She had a few tears in her eyes. "One of them, the one you call Shrug, and whom I call much worse, he had the audacity to fat-shame me. When I tried to explain how wrong his facts were, how cruel it was to say that young people weren't dying when in fact they were and that they had to be protected and wear masks and have schools closed, he looked at me and said, 'You know, dear, if you lost a little weight, you'd be much healthier and wouldn't have to worry so much about a bug that doesn't kill us thin people.' And you know what that guy said, the one you call Koal, the stupid and arrogant Greek one? You know what he said to me? He said, when I tried to show him real facts, facts about masks and stuff—he said, 'Well, we've had fewer people die in plane crashes this year, so are you going to say that's because of masks too?' That's how these people talk. Like Dodo, he started telling me that if you control for age, Florida did better than California. And yet, Congressman Depich, through all your diligence, you showed us that Florida was a COVID disaster, that it had to be put under martial law, that its governor is on the loose and is a criminal. And he still, despite all of that, clung to his lies, unwilling to admit that his manufactured numbers were false, wanting to spread all his untruths to the world. Congressman, everyone in America listening, we tried to be nice to them, but they are demons. Just know that."

Several hours into the hearings, after the testimony of over a dozen prominent doctors and scientists, all of whom had been hand-picked by the science tiger to make their case, after testimony by Stanford professors and students that grilled these three charlatans, and after several more spreadsheets flashed by Jim, including some that contained information from Kate and the Misinformation Five that he showed just to demonstrate how easily facts can be manipulated, juxtaposing their numbers with "the truth of my spreadsheets," as he said, finally the Stanford Three had a chance to speak.

Dodo stood up. Tall and dignified, he introduced himself by his given name and then provided his credentials. Jim interrupted him and said that his only credential in this court were his words and his deeds, the latter including his help in creating a petition by misinformation fanatics that Jim labeled as the Declaration of Death, and which Cheddar had constantly called a declaration that seeks to expose kids and others to the sting of a virus that will kill millions. "He's mass murderer number one," she said to her audience. "Thank God and thank science that we finally get to snuff out his misdeeds."

"That's not what the declaration is about," Dodo said. "It's about selective protection, about protecting the vulnerable and allowing all others to resume their lives. We know that this virus preys on the old and unhealthy, and that it largely spares the young and healthy. Our declaration calls for more vigilant measures to protect the old, while allowing the rest of society to stay open."

"Liar," cried out the students all at once. "Fat-shamers, murderers, deceivers!" It was clearly rehearsed.

"And then," said Jim, "you hold to your contention that young people and kids aren't impacted by this virus, that their lives could have gone on as usual, that masks and school closures weren't necessary, that distancing and quarantines were more harmful than helpful? In fact, one of you," pointing to Shrug, "has said that statistically, no kids or young people have died of COVID. Is this your position?"

"It's not just our position," said Dodo. "It's backed by facts and reality. I've provided testimony, and it's on our site; it's backed by over a million doctors and scientists worldwide. States and nations that have instituted draconian measures to curb this virus have caused more harm than good. They've hurt kids and the poor; they've ruined lives unnecessarily, and their success against COVID has been worse or the same as nation and states, like Sweden and Florida, who have had more measured responses."

"And masks don't work either, I assume?" laughed Jim. "Despite all the data I've presented here and the expert testimony we've provided? Is that also your contention?"

Koal stood up, very frail and seemingly shaken. He was met by the chants of the students, who repeated the same line several times before sitting. He looked at Jim. "If you've seen the data, you know that masks can't work. COVID goes through them like a fly goes through a picket fence. Every randomized trial, all historical evidence, and the reality of places with mask mandates prove beyond the shadow of a doubt that masks are not effective against coronaviruses. This is not an opinion. It's a fact. We need studies, good studies, if we are going to know what works."

"So," Jim said, with a smug look on his face, "if someone came to you with an acute appendix, on the very verge of death, you'd say to that kid, 'Hey, we'd like to do surgery on your appendix, but you know, we want to conduct a few studies, just to make sure, so we'll let you sit here as your appendix bursts and infection spills all over your gut; we'll sit here because, God knows, we wouldn't want to do anything to save you unless we have enough studies.' Is that your medical position, even though, God knows, we know none of you are real doctors? But since you like to pretend you are, I ask you that."

Koal shook his head. "That's not what any of us are saying," he barely whispered through a hoarse voice. "At the beginning of this, we didn't know. But as we know more, we see that what we're doing isn't protecting the elderly; it's harming the young. Masks aren't protecting anyone, so we—"

"And you, Shrug, you've said this over and over," said Jim, cutting off Koal. "You've disputed Doctor Fact-nerd and every medical and scientific expert on the planet. You've brought piles of papers to every meeting and used the volume of your misinformation to make it seem valid. You've derided masks, distancing, isolation, and quarantines from day one. Some may ask, what was your agenda? Why did you engage in such a vigilant misinformation campaign? Well, to the American people I say this: Shrug was an obscure radiologist, not even a real doctor, barely surviving at Stanford, a member of a right-wing think tank. And then, poof, he started being the leader of a worldwide misinformation campaign, and next thing you know, he's on Foxxy News every day, his articles are being spread across the anti-lifers and anti-democrats stratosphere, he's hired by President Trump to be his advisor, he's paid to give lectures, and he even writes a book to earn more money. You don't see how the allure of fame and money drove this man to engage in your campaign of medical lies? Because even if he's blind to that reality, the American people aren't."

Shrug stood up, his face worn and beaten, with several scars across his arms and cheeks. "I stand by everything I wrote and said," he whispered. "These are facts. They are scientific truth. You can make any spreadsheet you want, you can rely on whichever so-called experts you want, you can listen to that ignorant man who stands by your side and who has put his own arrogance and his own pecuniary motives before the science he has pledged to uphold, but none of that disputes truth. One day, truth will prevail; that's what my colleagues assure me every day. One day it will prevail."

"Yes," said Jim. "And today is that day."

From the TV, Cheddar laughed and applauded.

Then the chants of the students commenced as they glared at Shrug, who seemed to wince in pain. He cowered and sat down, looking only at the floor.

Jim displayed a series of testimonies by over twenty parents who had lost a child to COVID. Many had aired on DUI and Makes-Sense-NBC and 60-Minions before; some were new. These tear-jerking videos, often narrated by moms and dads who held each other and cried, brought even Cruise Ship to tears.

"These poor kids," he called out. "They're not statistics, like these brutal liars are telling people. These kids. They're people. They're human beings. But Shrug and his gang of liars, they'd tell you they're statistics, and that no kid died of COVID. They'd have you pretend this don't hurt young people and kids. They'll turn their back to reality so as to keep up their status. Well, I wish I could spit on your faces! I wish these grieving parents could tear you limb from limb. You are all murderers. All of you. I give these students credit for keeping you alive this long, because hell, and I'm sure Senator Cracker agrees, if I were holding you, and you were spitting out those lies even as I know the suffering and misery that comes from them, I wouldn't have been so restrained; that's all I got to say."

"Party," said Graham Cracker, "I'd have shot them and let you stab them. They make me sick!"

"So," said Jim, "you still hold that kids don't die and that your fancy targeted protection measures wouldn't have killed millions of kids, that the scientific measures to contain and stop this virus were more harmful than helpful, that fat-shaming is all you got, that masks don't work, that places like Florida and its criminal governor did better than your governor who cared so much that he even risked his own position to make sure that his people were protected and that democracy survived? You still going to hold to that position? One of you say something, or, God help us, your very silence will condemn you!"

Dodo stood up. "As my good friend and colleague has said, we are speaking the language of science and of humanity, nothing more. Yes, everything we said is true. Only a handful of young people died from the pandemic, three hundred out of ninety million. More children and youth die every year of car accidents, ten times more, so then you would suggest we should ban kids from cars? More died this year of the excess suicides and drug overdoses caused by the quarantine than will ever die of COVID. We are not minimizing COVID deaths in the young, but if we are going to cause more deaths in that group than we are going to prevent through our unscientific and overly hyped-up campaign of deception, then how is that science? How is anything we are doing with COVID scientific? It is all just hyperbole and scare tactics; it is nothing but fluff that you call science and somehow have convinced the world you are right, even as your measures help no one and slaughter countless millions."

And with that, the science tiger mauled into them, with a fire and conviction that Jim had not before witnessed. "About that, you are wrong!" he shouted, pointing his finger directly at Shrug. "I am science, not you! I speak for science! I have the weight of thousands of scientists and doctors behind me! Don't you ever forget who speaks for science in this country! It is me and me alone! Don't you ever forget that! Your arrogance has cost the world more lives than I can even count!"

And that's when Shrug said something perhaps he immediately regretted. "I've been in the task force with you, tiger. I know how poorly you count. I know how poorly you understand anything. And I know just how much money you have gained through your patents and your ties to industry by being as ignorant and misleading as you are. And the world knows it too."

With that, as the students chanted even more loudly, Jim ended the proceedings with a guilty verdict. Cheddar applauded the committee's "good work" and brought on a panel of several Fact-nerd-allied doctors to dig into the Stanford Three. Off camera, the science tiger walked up to Shrug and spit in his face.

"I am science, and don't you forget that," he said to Shrug. "Soon enough, you'll forget everything, but let your last thought be that you have lost, and that science has won!"

The three were dragged out of the hearings and brought to the rotunda of the Capitol. As Congress quickly voted them to be condemned as enemies of the state and deserving of death, as President Buck authorized that verdict, the students tied ropes around their necks and strung them outside the windows of the rotunda, a structure built during the Civil War, a war which, as Jim's professor told him, would have been won had the Confederate traitors been strung up to die all over DC so that the nation could be privy to their crimes and never repeat them.

Jim would not forget that lesson. Soon enough, scores of others would join the Stanford Three and dangle from the nation's most enduring symbol of democracy, rotting along with their evil souls.

PART FOUR

Democracy and Science
Are Luxuries That
Neither Can Afford

Mask wearing y'all
guilty of sin!
guilty of misinformation!
RIP
M
Harvard

CHAPTER TWENTY-ONE

January 6th Reboot

To Professor Sarah Kaminsky, this was just another Thursday on campus; another day to work on her research exploring the roots of genocides across history; another day to teach two of her classes, one an undergraduate lecture course called Genocide: A Human Pandemic, and the other a graduate seminar about the similarities between genocides in Germany, Cambodia, and ancient Rome. It was cold out, very cold, and so she bundled up. The roads would be icy; she had to get around the DC Beltway with everyone else on earth, every tired and distracted person, as she tried not to skid or be hit by the mass of terrible drivers. She drank her coffee and thought about the day, lapsing into a fog.

"Don't go," said her husband, who now worked from home. "Stay home. It's not a good day. I got called from Michelle and Roy both, and they want to talk to you. They don't want you to go in."

Sarah turned to her husband of twenty-eight years and smiled. "It's my job," she said.

"Don't be like that," he said. "Please, I beg you, stay home. Do you want me to puncture your tire? You want me to tie you down? I am asking only this one thing. As are your kids."

She stood up and chugged her last gulp of coffee. "I would just call an Uber." She smiled. "I have to go in. I take my responsibilities seriously, Roy. You know that. Today is another day. That's all it can be."

"It's not," he said, peering at her. "It's not another day. You know that. Everyone knows that."

In fact, today was January 6th, the one-year anniversary of the Capitol attacks. More than a dozen bodies hung from the Capitol rotunda, and Jim Depich promised that others would join them. More hearings would commence today. Students across the country orchestrated demonstrations and mock trials of anti-lifers, their powers seemingly unlimited, as police and the nation's legal apparatus flanked them, and bulletproof uniforms and full-body oxygen masks deflected reprisals from their enemies.

Several months ago, Professor Kaminsky sent a letter to the college president to beseech her from mandating vaccines. *I have been vaccinated, as have my kids,* she wrote. *I wear my mask dutifully and implore all in my class to wear them. I understand and comply with the science of COVID. But these young people we teach, science tells us that they are not vulnerable to this virus, that vaccination doesn't slow its spread, and there are grave concerns about both long- and short-term dangers of the vaccine in them. I believe that everyone must make his or her own choice. Once we mandate something like this, once we neglect to address individual choice for a measure that has no proven benefit to the public and which may cause harm, then haven't we relinquished our roles as academics and stewards of science, as Americans who adhere to the Constitution? Haven't we instead become the very people we deplore?*

Her letter did not strike a receptive audience. She well knew that the Buck administration had tied colleges' federal subsidies to their compliance with vaccine and mask mandates, and that Doctor Factnerd's NIH mega-funding apparatus could direct a college's research grants to evaporate instantly if any institution did not comply with his dictates. Still, she knew the president of MD Park Campus, the two had been close for years, and she believed that her plea would be digested in its proper context.

It was not. Rather than hearing from the president, she received a warning from the leader of MD Park's student Truth Club, Mary

Lou. *Your position has been noted and understood. Please be advised that you are now under our surveillance. It is clear that you are not woke to the realities of our times, and as one who teaches our youth, that is unacceptable.* That's all it said. And since then, she heard no more.

She drove to school quietly and contemplatively, keeping her eyes on the road, playing the haunting beat of Mahler's Third Symphony on Spotify.

Ten miles away at the White House, Jim sat with the president, as he did on most days now. Star Buck granted him an hour each morning, and he usually asked to meet alone, especially demanding that the "snarling vice president" not be present. The president was tired, and he looked it. Sometimes he could barely speak. On a few occasions, he fell asleep. He would mumble, "You're doing a great job, Jim. We just have to get the economy humming again and all this will be behind us." Aides told Jim that the president barely slept, that he fought incessantly with the vice president on the rare occasions they were together.

"We would have won Vietnam if we'd given it our all," Jim assured the president. "The North Vietnamese weren't soft; they were willing to sacrifice lives and property to get the job done, while we did it halfway, and you know the results, Mr. President. Once you made it your sole intent to eradicate COVID, once you and I focused on preventing the Trumpists from threating our nation again, then, Mr. President, we can't go half-ass. We have to be all in. That means getting ugly and being strong. Being willing not to compromise, making no accommodation to misinformation. Do you understand?"

Buck nodded, even as he stared at the wall. "Jim, I didn't sign up for this," he said. "I wanted to push for social justice, equality, good jobs for hardworking Americans, tighten our alliances, restore integrity to the country. All this, well, this wasn't in my plans. It feels like it's taking on a life of its own."

"Mr. President," Jim said to him sternly, "on your first day of office, you signed an executive order to mandate masks on all federal property, even on some distant mountain in the middle of Montana. You've mandated vaccines for all federal employees, health-care workers, private employers who deal with the government, even kids and students. They all have to mask and get vaccinated; you've instituted draconian executive power to make sure that science is not pushed aside, that detractors don't have a say. Mr. President, you don't do all that and then think you can retreat and go half-ass. Once you've gone down that road, there are no U-turns. Now is when we have to press on the gas and make sure we win the race. You turn around now and the nation will destroy you."

"I feel like the nation is already destroying itself," Buck mumbled. "And destroying my legacy."

"Do you know the legacy of the Civil War, Joe?" he asked Star Buck, staring at him sharply. "We lost our best and brightest and poured our nation into a struggle for our soul, and then when it was over, we just let the other guys go. And you know what they did, those Southerners we thought we had defeated? They laughed and reconstructed their slavocracy. That's because we were soft, Mr. President. We thought that being nice was the right thing. We believed that the crisis was over, and we were tired of facing conflict for more grueling years. You know what we should have done? We should have hung every damned one of the rebel leaders from the Capitol and sent a signal to the South that we will tolerate no malarkey, not on our watch. Once we go down a road like this, Mr. President, once we decide once and for all to fight for what is right and true, we can only win if we take it to the finish line."

The president nodded but didn't speak for a bit. Then he said, "I trust you, Jim. You do what's best. You know that you have my authority to do whatever it takes." And then he walked out, pausing for a moment as thought he had something to add but finally scamping out of the room.

More bodies dangled from the Capitol as Jim appeared with Mumbling Joe on January 6th, telling him about recent events. "We've captured President Trump trying to escape from Florida, heading to Cuba of all places." Jim laughed. "He had papers with him implicating him and many others in another Capitol attack, one slated to occur today and which we completely squelched. You know that DaSandwich escaped with a group of some of the most despicable people in this nation, and we're hot on their trail. While we're cleaning up the country, Joe, we're surgically removing those who seek to take it and its people down, one by one, hearing by hearing, and we're taking extreme measures to assure that we send the right message. Yes, Joe, this is a long and arduous process. The poisoned well is that deep! President Buck declared a national emergency today, so expect curfews and heightened security in DC, but I want to emphasize that this is just another day for most Americans. America, you don't have to be scared or to wallow in some corner, 'cause we'll protect you, but be sure to stay safe, follow COVID protocols, and we beg you, if you see any suspicious activity, let the authorities know. There will be protests on most college campuses, and we'll be having our usual committee trials, but rest assured, President Buck is on top of this."

"That's shocking news about Donald Trump, Congressman. To know he's captured, wow, what a relief! What will come of the ex-president?" asked Joe. "Is he next on the committee docket?"

Jim smiled. "No, Joe," he said. "He is hanging from the Capitol as we speak. Near his henchmen, where he likely is happy; you know, he likes to hang around with people who like him, pardon the pun! We needed to act quickly before he inspired another attack."

Mumbling Joe nodded. "Unfortunate, Congressman, but understandable. These are trying times as we fight for our democracy and our lives. Thank you for all you do. Let's hope the anti-lifers get the message once and for all and we can get our nation back on track for greatness."

Jim sat in his office, chugging down Jack Daniel's. He heard very little backlash these days. Few dared challenge him. His new lapdog, Party Cruise, strode in to give him a hot dog. "Can't drink that fire water without some nitrites." The Texas senator laughed. "You OK, Jim? Anything you need today?"

"Keep up the pressure," he slurred. "Don't let anyone say anything that questions our resolve."

Party laughed. "Hell, I walk in room, and they shut up!"

Jim started at the senator. "I want listening devices in every room and on every senator and congressman, you understand me? Bug them. Talk to Frank in NSA; Corrine will get you his number. He'll get them surveilled. And get me Corrine. Is A-O-Crazy out there?"

"Ain't she always out there?" Party Cruise laughed. "Big day for you today. I'll keep the people in line, and I'll give Frank a call. Eat that food. We need you around for a while, Jim. It's your country now."

Was it? Was it really his? He started at the hot dog, and his stomach ached. So, he drank another gulp and breathed hard. *Is it my country?* "Corrine!" he called out. "Get in here! Now!"

On the sprawling campus of MD Park, students fluttered about from class to class. Few spoke; they remained apart, all wearing masks, staring at the ground. A rough wind shook the bare trees; it was glum and cloudy. There wasn't a speck of color anywhere.

In the center green, several thousand students wearing what seemed to be space helmets and SWAT attack uniforms marched in a choreographed circle, chanting loudly. *Woke is life. To save the nation, we must sacrifice those who seek to crush goodness. Only through their death can we and the nation be woke. Their death is our life, the nation's life, the world's life. Death is thus life. Death is woke.*

Mary Lou stood at the center, microphone in hand, yelling out instructions.

"Those whom we judge today have shown that they are not woke," she said, with unbending passion. "They may have tickled your fancy in a class or at a party, they may have said the correct things so as to not offend you, but we know them to be a danger to the movement, to our causes, to our country, to justice. We know! Today in America, it's not enough to simply say the right thing and smile. Today in America is about how you think. We are on a campus of thinkers. Will we allow nonthinkers to stay here? Will we allow the unwoke to try to wake us up with their bad thoughts and bad deeds?"

"No!" shouted the crowd between their chanting.

"We must be strong, vigilant, fierce. Today we must not relent. We are the truth. We are the one and only word. Our way will deliver us to the promised land! Finally our moment has come, and we must grasp it and not be afraid to turn around. All those years of ridicule. All those years are at an end!"

At a little after noon, when she finished her peanut butter sandwich and slipped back on her N-95, Professor Sarah Kaminsky heard a rap at her door. She stood and answered it. Four students in space suits stood outside. One of them said, almost robotically, "Professor Kaminsky, you have been summoned to the tribunal on the main campus to answer for your crimes. Put on your jacket and follow us. If you comply, we will not have to resort to violence."

She shook within. "Crimes?" she asked. "What crimes? I've been the most compliant soul on this campus, for God's sake!" She looked inside the space helmet and saw a boy's face. "Peter Marsh, that's you in there, right? You were in my class last semester. You came to my office hours all the time. I thought you really enjoyed it. You did great! You know me. Why would you do this?"

"You must answer for your crimes, Professor," the lanky boy responded. "This is not about me and you, not about your class; it's about your crimes. Come with us."

They dragged her across campus to where the mass of students gathered. She and four others—two professors and two students—shivered in the center of a chanting circle of students. Apparently, only Sarah was given the option of wearing a jacket. She looked at her accosters and at the other accused. None peered back at her. She tried to reach into her pocket to grab her cellphone but was quickly handcuffed and pushed to the cold, hard grass by another student.

"Please, don't do this!" she said to the girl who hovered over her. "Don't do something you'll regret! This isn't right; you have to know that. Nothing you're doing is right."

"And so do you implicate yourself!" The girl laughed. And then she kicked the professor hard in the face, sending her reeling and bloody.

Mary Lou made a speech; it was both long and often incoherent. The winds blew hard from the east. Sarah looked up at the sky, somehow praying for a deus ex machina. She imagined her husband driving in and mowing all these kids over, or a helicopter flying down and stopping the madness. Sarah had accommodated to the new reality; she followed the rules, even chiding those who didn't. She did it although none of it sat well in her gut. It reminded her of everything base and vile that she taught in her class. She remembered one day when a friend asked her:

"Sarah, I don't get it. With all the bullshit going on, with all our rights being systematically taken away, why aren't you guys fighting back? If academia is silent, if it just falls in line, then where is the hope?"

In the end, Sarah decided that following the science and being a good steward of rules in a time of crisis trumped all other priorities. "We don't fight back," she told her friend. "Because this is necessary."

But was it?

"We accuse you of crimes against the just and democratic world that we are building," Mary Lou cried out as a soft backdrop of chanting continued, the students walking in a circle around the accused. "Some of you have played the game well and thus think you are free from retribution. But are you woke? Are you truly one with the cause? Today we try you not only because of what you have done and said but rather because of what you have thought. To be one with us in body and mind is what this new world demands. And your minds, your thoughts, that's what's on trial today."

"Then can we defend ourselves?" Sarah shouted from the ground through her bruised mouth dripping with blood, her words barely audible even to her. "If this is a trial, do we have a say?"

Mary Lou looked her way. And then slowly and methodically, she marched to Sarah Kaminsky. She hovered over the professor and said to the crowd, "Her thoughts are loud and clear!" And she lifted a blade and shoved it into Sarah's back. Others joined her. Sarah's last thought was that of shame. She should have fought back. And thus all she muttered was "I am so sorry."

To which Mary Lou said, "You should be sorry, but sadly, it's too late."

Within minutes, five corpses lay bloodied on the cold ground of academia. All wore masks. All always had. They believed the science; they enforced the laws. But that was just not enough. Not now.

The students resumed their chanting as a few guards pulled the bodies away. No other students were near them. All had dispersed. No one spoke. No one looked into anyone's eyes.

Life resumed as it always had, but now with a fewer minds to pollute the new reality of wokeness.

That night on DUI, Jim spoke about the anniversary of January 6th. He sat with A-O-Crazy who seemed almost giddy as she spoke about the college demonstrations and the snuffing out of plots all across the country. "People don't get it," she said, smiling brightly. "There are bad hombres out there, all over the place. Sometimes you have to do what it takes to keep things buzzing in the right direction. Look, sometimes I'll be walking down a street and someone's not wearing a mask out there. And I know, from my heart, that that guy, he's not woke. He's a threat. He may think he's not, but, tap dancer, he is, by that very act, he is a threat to everyone around him and to the country. There are two sides to this war for democracy: us and the enemies. Today, the good guys won!"

DUI kept its descriptions of the campus protests on script; they managed to find cellphone footage of a few counterprotests at schools in South Carolina and Montana where kids threw rocks at the Truth Clubs and tried to disrupt the trials. That is all that tap dancer showed his audience; none of the murders, the chanting of Truth Clubs, nothing that could possibly engender sympathy for the victims.

"Some people don't get it; they don't understand the threat to democracy," the tap dancer said to Jim. "Tonight we could have had another Capitol attack had we, as you say, Congressman, had we been soft. Thankfully, here we are, in the home of the free and the brave. What's next, Congressman? You've taken out the leader of the anti-democrats, our lying and conniving former president, and most of his thugs have met the face of justice too. What's next?"

Jim stared into the camera. "America, as you know, Omicron is still surging and is mutating into something that could be far worse according to Chinese authorities and Doctor Fact-nerd. The unvaccinated and unmasked are continuing to threaten all of us, and our science tiger, who I know was jsut on your show, believes that until we force science on everyone, until we insist that everyone follow the rules, then we'll all be at risk. And remember, America, that when the virus surges, when our hospitals are overwhelmed and bodies pile up, it's not just a tragic loss of life that was avoidable, but it's also kindling for the next Capitol attack by those hiding in the woodwork. What's next? Vigilance, that's what's next. We're right in the middle of a war for our lives and our nation. We had a good day today. But it's a war, America. Today was just a battle. We have many more to come."

A battle, a victory, a triumph. Still, Jim was hardly comfortable. As A-O-Crazy blabbed on and on, he squirmed in his chair. All he could think of was guzzling down another bottle of Jack Daniel's. And Kate's face.

CHAPTER TWENTY-TWO

The Path to Power

Jim had a large closet aside his main office, one that, so it was said, Congressman Lyndon Johnson converted into an accessory bedroom into which he brought many lady friends. Jim made it into his palace of refuge; even Corrine knew not to bother him in "the sanctuary" as she called it. He kept a few bottles of rum there, a poster of the 1979 Championship Steelers—with Chuck Knoll, John Stallworth, Lynn Swan, and, of course, Terry Bradshaw hovering over the defeated Cowboys—and a pile of papers beside his cluttered childlike desk.

After saturating his blood with enough alcohol to assure intoxication, Jim would kneel and sift through the copious papers neatly stacked and sorted. Some were from Kate, others from Mr. X. Mask studies, state and national comparisons based on COVID strategy, the medical and psychological ramifications of lockdowns, dirt on the science tiger and Pfizer, deceptive vaccine studies, demographic differences in outcome between elders and the young, the fact that ten times more people under twenty die every year of car accidents and twenty other things than died of COVID; it was all there, black-and-white, clear as day. Jim called this pile of misinformation the "forbidden truth" and prevented any but himself access to it.

In her summaries of the data, Kate quoted none other than the now demonized Shrug, who wrote, "Had we focused on the elderly and accepted the utility of early treatment rather than simply locking everyone up and waiting for a vaccine, had we been honest about the science and not allowed politics and profits to intervene, then few would have died from this potentially mild and treatable virus, and life for most Americans could have gone on as normal. The deaths from our actions alone will be catastrophic when they are finally tabulated, and our actions saved no one." Jim took off his mask in here; what was the point? "The damned virus goes through a mask like a bullet goes through water; it's all such bullshit," he muttered. "Sadly, we got it wrong." Sometimes Jim would put these facts on a spreadsheet just to see how they'd look. Then he drank a little more and shredded his findings.

What have we done? he often asked himself. *It didn't have to be this way. What have we done?*

One day he sat with Corrine and peered into her innocent eyes. She was holding her youngest and singing to him. Jim smiled.

"Our truth," he said. "The one we're peddling. The one we've killed people for. You know, it may not be right. There is another truth, and well, it kind of makes more sense. Sometimes, I just don't know."

"Oh please, Jim," she said, kissing him on the head. "You're keeping people safe. You're the good guy in the room. The smart guy! There's only one truth, Jim, you say it all the time. Whatever nonsense doesn't fit into that truth, well, it's misinformation; it has to be. Why are you saying this?"

"I've just been reading stuff," he said. "Stuff I shouldn't be reading. And it's compelling."

Corrine put her baby on the ground and slid near the congressman, wrapping him in a huge hug. "You know what you once said to me?" She smiled. "You said, Corrine, back in the day, when astronomers were first discovering that the sun was in the center of our solar system, other people had facts to prove them wrong. They'd say, look in the sky, obviously the sun goes around the Earth. Those facts, as they were called, could have derailed our leap into modernity. Facts are often Satan's tools to throw us off course. That's what you always tell me! There's only one truth, Jim, the one you fight for every day.

You've proven that and saved our nation! Don't have doubts. That's what kills those who fight for a better world. Doubt is the enemy of salvation. You, sir, you are a hero. You are my hero. Thank you."

As she kissed him gently on the cheek, Party Cruise burst in, nearly panting, his scraggly gray-and-black beard speckled with pieces of egg. He seemed hardly embarrassed to find Jim and his young aide sitting astride each other, with a small baby crying on the floor.

"OK, Jim, you are going to love this. Corrine, you too," Party Cruise said, full of smiles, straddling the small child. "Hell, even that damned baby will stop crying when he hears what I got to tell you!"

Jim stood up and offered Party Cruise a drink, but he deferred. "Have to keep up figure for the old lady." he laughed. Then he pulled out his phone and played a short piece for the congressman. Corrine scooped up her baby and hovered over the phone too. All she could say, over and over, was "Holy shit!"

The picture showed Vice President Bad-karma speaking with aides in her office, which Jim had bugged and which Party Cruise monitored. She paced as she spoke, deliberately and emphatically. "It can't go on like this," she said. "Star Buck is fucking demented; I've had two doctors tell me this, and both said they'll help us use the Twenty-Fifth Amendment to remove him from office. I just don't want it to seem opportunistic."

Some mumbling from others in the room buzzed across the screen, and then Bad-karma stopped and stared in its direction, banging her hand on a desk.

"That's just bullshit, and you know it," she said. "He has completely fallen under the spell of Depich, and they are turning this country into a goddamned communist state with all their mock trials and executions and fucking unconstitutional laws and all their other fucking crap. Come on, you see it! He dismissed the Supreme Court and declared martial law; that's not the act of a sane man. I'm going to stop him any way I can. Frankly, sometimes, as much as I hate Donald Trump, I wish that damned takeover of the Capitol succeeded, because what those assholes would have done is fucking nothing compared to how our demented president is screwing up this country."

Party Cruise, smiling big and ugly, turned off the phone. "And she's not even wearing a mask." He laughed.

Jim looked at Corrine, then kissed her baby. "Do we release this to the press?" he asked. "She pretty much admitted she wants to get rid of the president and that she supported the January sixth mob."

"She's a zealot when it comes to mandates and masks," Party Cruise said. "She is a zealot when it comes to the rule of law. Now here she is fessing that all her bravado is a show, and she's really just out for her own power. And that she'd rather this country be taken over by Trump's thugs than function in a legal way that threatens her own blind ambition. You can take her down, Jim. And then you can do what she said, get Star Buck declared mentally incompetent. From there, you're the next guy in line. And I got the legal prowess to make it happen."

Jim patted him on the back. "I'm sure glad I tapped you instead of Julie-nutty." He laughed. "What are the next steps? We have to do this right. And tell me how much I spill to tap dancer and our crew there."

Party Cruise rushed out to get the ball running. Jim locked the door to his sanctuary. "Best to keep the skeletons in the closet." He laughed. "So, Corrine, President Depich? You said I may not win an election in my district next year. I guess this is one way around that problem!"

She smiled so big that her mouth almost fell off her face. "I love you," she said and kissed him on the cheek. "And my baby loves you too! Yes, do it, Jim! The world is yours to take!"

A few days and a few more trials passed by as Omicron continued to surge and Fact-nerd and his gang of obsequious doctors blasted the unvaccinated and unmasked hour after hour on DUI, blaming everything on them. "I warned America about this consequence," the science tiger said. "The misinformation campaign led us to this point. It's time we get vigilant. A worse variant is likely around the corner."

Tap dancer stared into his eyes, asking no questions, harboring no doubt. "There really are some very selfish people in this world, Doctor Fact-nerd," he said. "Thank you for setting us all straight."

The next day, with his ducks in order, Jim asked to meet with the vice president. When she arrived, he stood with Party Cruise, A-O-Crazy, and a few of his student leaders. She peered at the small tribunal and laughed. "Well, when Party Cruise and Congresswoman Crazycan be in the same room, I know something vile is happening."

"Sit," Jim said to her. "I want to show you something, and then we'll talk. If you don't want to listen to this, that's fine. I'll happily show it to DUI instead. This meeting is for you."

"Right." She laughed. "For me. You have my thanks, Congressman. You are quite the saint."

He played her the tape, and just to make it more impactful, he projected it on a seventy-inch TV plastered to the wall with surround sound. She watched but said nothing. Her facial expression didn't even change. Then she looked at Party Cruise, then the students, then at Jim.

"I stand by everything I said." She smiled. "Go ahead, release it. I think people will take my side."

"Your side?" asked Jim. "That you would have rather the January sixth riot succeed instead of having a democratic government that you don't agree with? Just to let you know, Ms. Vice President, when I take this to DUI, they're not going to let you on to give your side. Not Makes-sense-NBC, not any of the major networks. The best you'll get is Foxxy, and they hate your guts. You want to take that chance?"

She laughed and looked at Party Cruise. "Party, you never did like me, did you? You coddled up to Trump after he called you an idiot and that your wife is ugly, but me, who has always been nice to you, you've always wanted to take me down. I guess this is your path to power, since you have no talent to get you in?"

"It's not personal, Bad-karma," he said. "It ain't even politics. It's life versus death, democracy versus tyranny. You are on the wrong side of this. And next time you talk to me about opportunism, don't forget to mention that you're in your position not because of any talents but rather because of the color of your skin."

"The real Party Cruise comes out!" She laughed. "How wonderful! You are such the gentleman! Let's pull the race card, shall we? OK, Jim, you tell me. What would you have me do?"

Jim laid it out. He gave her three choices. "Resign from the office, cite your disagreements with Star Buck, you'll keep your honor and your life, and you can disappear to a place of our choosing and subject yourself to surveillance. Second, fight this thing and have your turn in front of my committee. Or, if it's easier, end your life, and I'll assure that your reputation remains good." He gave her twelve hours.

The three students in the room walked out with her; Jim said that a necessary contingency of her freedom is that they remain with her until she makes her choice. "Or else, I'll put you in chains now and drag you in front of the committee, and you can make your case to America there."

"Fuck you, Jim," she said. "History will not be kind to you, of that I'm sure."

Jim laughed. "Hey, you were on board with this at the start, all hoity-toity about shutting down the world and censoring anyone who didn't agree with you, threatening to jail anyone who was too chummy with Donald Trump. I have info that you even blackmailed foreign countries with a loss of all American aid if they didn't follow your COVID script and mandate vaccines. And you're just as much in bed with pharma as anyone else we've taken down. I love your posturing, Senator Bad-karma, but you're one of the top architects of what I am doing, and that's how history will see you. You wrote the blueprints; I'm just building the damned thing. You're no saint however all of this goes down. Don't ever forget that."

That night, the vice president made her decision. And within a few hours, documents were signed about the president as well, asserting to his lack of mental capacity.

Jim came on DUI to make an important announcement.

"We've been talking so much about Omicron and the latest attempts to unravel our democracy," tap dancer said to him. "But, Congressman, you're telling me that you have news even more startling than that. I know my colleague News wolf leads every one of his segments with the term 'Breaking News.' Is this one of those moments?"

Jim laughed. "This is the kind of breaking news that would even break a bar of steel in half!"

Tap dancer laughed too. "We live in tough times, a killer pandemic, threats to our democracy around every corner. You've certainly helped right the ship of state, Congressman. Let's hope what you have to say is some good news for a change. We are all getting pretty tired of so much gloom!"

And so, on air, Jim spelled it out. Vice President Bad-karma told him that she would be resigning due to disagreements with the president. She would announce it to the press tomorrow. She planned to return to her role as a private citizen and lawyer to continue to fight for democracy, justice, and compliance with the pro-life agenda.

"Did she tell you what some of her concerns were with President Buck?" he asked Jim.

Jim paused and looked into the camera. "He's been very erratic, sometimes incoherent. She is concerned about his mental state. She believes that if she is the one to inaugurate an investigation into his capacity to remain president, then she will be viewed as opportunistic. So, she's stepping down, for the good of the country. She has started an investigation to assess the president's ability to carry out his duties under the provisions of Twenty-Fifth Amendment of our Constitution."

"Amazing," the anchor danced. "Absolutely amazing. Well, this is how a democracy is supposed to work. We are witnessing all that is good with the American experiment. If he is not capable, then I assume it will be impossible for him to name a new vice president. Did Senator Bad-karma discuss that with you?"

Jim nodded. "She did. It will depend on the results of the exam as to whether he is deemed capable. She has some good ideas who could replace her, but, of course, first we have to go through the process."

The tap dancer went on and on about protecting democracy, being able to seamlessly negotiate a transition of power in the middle of a national crisis, and the Omicron statistics. What he didn't ask Jim or even mention was that when the vice present stepped down, and if Star Buck was declared unfit for office, that as Speaker of the House, Jim was next in line for the presidency.

Neither uttered any innuendo about the transition of power. Neither pointed the finger of opportunism at Jim himself.

But within a week, Jim Depich, the down-to-earth-engineer-turned-congressman from Western Pennsylvania, prepared to move his office to the White House. And now, finally, everything he had been working for could reach its final fruition.

"Gee, ain't I a stinker?" he said to Corrine in his best Bugs Bunny accent.

She kissed him. "No," she said. "You're a goddamned genius!"

CHAPTER TWENTY-THREE

Duck Season

Jim had never been happier. He sat across from Kate at his favorite restaurant in Pittsburgh, staring into her sparkling eyes. She had cleaned up well! Her long brown hair floated over a bright blue dress, and her smile and animated face danced as she spoke to him glowingly. She often reached her hand over the table and rubbed his with her long fingers, even as her feet slid sensually up and down his leg.

"You saved the world, Jim Depich," she said. "You are my hero. Not just my fiancé but also my hero. Because of you, this country and its people, they are free from tyranny and from harm. Your bravery in the face of lies and terror, it's just amazing to me! I can't get enough of you, Jimbo. Promise me that we'll hit the sack as soon as we get home. Twice today is hardly enough. I ache for your body!"

Jim smiled and sipped his iced tea, which tasted strangely like Jack Daniel's. "Well, Kate, first of all, you're a hero. It was your arguments, your facts, your experience; all of that woke me up. What else was I going to do? I saw I had been wrong the whole time, that shutting down society was murder and that masks were the costume of the murderers. Hey, I had power, and sometimes it's good to use power for the good of humankind."

She darted over the table and grabbed him, kissing him on the lips. Then she whispered, oh so sensually, "You sound like LBJ, you big hunk of Steelers flesh. He was a fucking racist when he came to office, and he said, 'Damn it, I have power now, so I'm going to do the right thing.' And then he became racism's biggest foe. Every time we used to do it in the LBJ closet, I felt that energy pulsate. Should we do it here, here and now? It'll be one for the books!"

The waiter hovered over them, asking for their order. Kate skewered the menu. She was taking forever! Finally, she looked up and asked the waiter, "Is it duck season or rabbit season?"

Jim twisted her head and Kate had become a rabbit, and the waiter was Elmer Fudd! Jim himself had a webbed hand.

"Why, it's rabbit season," said the waiter, pointing his huge gun at Kate. "And you are quite the catch!"

"Awww. I bet you way that to all the wabbits." She pursed her thick red lips and then grimaced. "For shame, Doc. Hunting rabbits with an elephant gun. Why don't you shoot yourself an elephant?"

"Die, wabbit, die!" the waiter said.

"But, Doc," she said to him, "it's duck season."

"Weally?" He turned the gun toward Jim. Jim froze. He knew what he should say, *It's rabbit season; shoot him, shoot him*, but even that wouldn't work, because Bugs always wins. So, he froze, and he felt the blast of lead shatter his skull.

"Boss," he heard as he soaked in his own cold sweat. "Boss, wake up, wake up."

Jim popped out of bed. He looked left and right, only to find the worried glace of Corrine. She walked to him and hugged him. "Not another Kate dream, Jim. Tell me it's not that."

"It's just," he said to her through a few tears, not for the first time and not for the last. "I wonder, Corrine. When I become president, I'll have a chance to do good. I can't undo what we've done, but I can ease it off, turn down the vitriol, and make our country what it once was. I mean, what it once was other than having gems like Kate live in them." And then he broke down into an hysterical fit.

By ten most mornings, and after a few shots of Jack Daniel's, Jim shoved all that maudlin bullcrap behind him. In fact, it only made him angrier to think that people like Kate still lived.

As he stepped up the ladder of power in DC, Jim attracted a small squad of obsequious misfits, none of whom particularly liked each other but who all seemed to like Jim. Party Cruise, of course, and also Graham Cracker, and Mini McTurtle. He had A-O-Crazy always managing to sit closest to him, then a spattering of less well-known faces from both side of the aisle, most of whom were converted Trumpists or left-wingers. And all were strongly pro-life, pro-democracy, and pro-Jim!

"There are whispers I don't take a liking to, Jimbo," said Graham Cracker, moving his head above the crowd. "I hear them on the cable radio shows. We shut down most misinformation on social media, and the Foxxy folk you know, they're on your side now, but bad shit has a way of sneaking out any loose assholes we ain't snagged yet, and those assholes are calling you a dictator and organizing movements to shut you down mostly through secret sites that we haven't got our fingers on yet."

"Of course, there are movements to shut him down; it's all coming from your side of the aisle," said A-O-Crazy. "That's what this conspiracy is all about. It's about right-wing thugs taking down the government. Your people are the problem. Get it, or you need another explanation?"

"I take umbrage with your right-wing defamation, Congress-woman Crazy," said McTurtle. "The left wing, well, don't think you are all saints, and not a looker among you, present company included. Me and Graham Cracker, we took a little poll of hotties on the right and left, and hate to tell you Crazy, but the right wins hands down. And Graham Cracker he looked at guys too, same result, I mean, if you don't count Party Cruise. I know you go both ways, Graham Cracker, but don't you agree?" He laughed, clearly intending to lighten the mood, but his non sequitur hit deaf ears, so he moved on. "What I say to do, Congressman, is to bring some nut in front of your committee. Pick a guy so far down nut lane that he'll start spouting off about some conspiracy bull-nibbles on national TV and sound so absurd and outrageous that you can tear him and all his ideas apart. That'll shut up the people calling you a dictator cause they'll seem just as crazy, and then we pass an anti-conspiracy theory bill. I'll get it through the Senate, and you'll sign it. After you take the oath, that is. That'll give us broad powers to find and crush those sources of misinformation that's eluding us now."

Duck Season!

Jim had just the guy who fit the role, someone incarcerated by a student group in Texas and whom he held just for this moment. Ken-and-Barbie hung from the Capitol rotunda, proudly taking his family's role as a martyr for the nation and being prominently displayed for all to see. Most other cable news conspiracy nuts similarly had become innocuous corpses. But this guy, this scientist, this guru of misinformation, he was speckled all over Mr. X's papers as a man in the know, a man who had dirt on everyone, an anti-tiger scientist whose *truth* reeked of absolute absurdity, even it if may be true. The optics of crushing this guy and his wild ideas on TV would play right into Jim's hands, just like McTurtle said.

With only five days until his inauguration, Jim brought Dr. Peeing Douche-bag to the podium, old and slouched, with a sinister face and a deep German accent. Who better to let tell conspiracy story on national TV, to be given an audience, and to crucify all conspiracy nuts on a cross of incredulity?

The reason I don't release all these revelations is that they seem so off the wall, so over-the-top crazy, that no one will believe them, and that will discredit me and the whole truth.

So said Mr. X to Jim after the man's capture, and so would Jim now execute the very plan that Mr. X believed to be self-defeating to his cause. The best way to suffocate misinformation is to let it out in the open and make it seem absurd. After all, there could be only one truth, as Corrine reminded him.

Douche-bag seemed uncomfortable in his chair and was clearly in some pain. He never looked into the camera or even into the eyes of those on the panel. The tiger was here again, glaring at the old

German who must have felt the sting to the tiger's claws ripping through his skin!

"I hate this man," the tiger told Jim. "And I want to be there to tear him apart. The things he said about me with AIDS were hurtful, very hurtful, and unfair. I did my best during AIDS, always putting science over profit, and this man said I was a tool of industry and so much stuff. I want to take him down, Jim!"

Of course, the tiger wanted at Douche-bag! Reading through Mr. X's dossier, it was clear to Jim that Douche-bag was 100 percent right when it came to the science tiger and the link between academic, politics, and industry. That is what made him a sitting duck standing in front of Jim's elephant gun. The old German was cocky; he was sure he was right, and he was going to sound like a fool as he told America how right he was to discredit an American hero who saved the nation from AIDS and COVID!

It's duck season, shoot, shoot!

"So, Doctor Douche-bag," Jim said calmly, "I've read what you have written, and I've consulted with Doctor Fact-nerd and other experts about what you said, because it seems so outlandishly ludicrous to be uttered by someone who claims to be a scientist, but is it true that you don't think AIDS is caused by the HIV virus, that you think it's all a big hoax, that no one in Africa died of AIDS but were forced to take poisonous AIDS medicines to enrich big pharma, that the science tiger suppressed research and the use of effective cheaper medicines and he manipulated data—killing hundreds of thousands of people in the process—so he could sell and drug and make a profit? Is anything I'm saying out of the realm of your truth?"

The Douche-bag looked up but stared at the wall. "Of course, it's all true," he snapped in a harsh tone. "You know it is, Congressman. You've seen the data. All of that is true."

"So, yea, AIDS isn't caused by the HIV virus, which has been the basis of treatment for AIDS and the reason no one dies of it now, and the drug that has saved millions of people by eradicating that virus that you think isn't real, you call the drug a poison." Jim laughed. "That's who we're dealing with here, America. He gets good publicity and lots of money bashing our noble and brave science tiger, and his anti-life antics are killing millions. He's Doctor Doom, Dr. Dummy, Dr. Death."

People laughed, including Cheddar at DUI, who shook her head with a smile.

"So, Doctor Douche-bag, a few more questions if I may. You've said that the science tiger and the Gated-Billionaire have conspired to take over the WHO, CDC, FDA, NIH—maybe even Mars and Jupiter and even heaven, who knows—and have used their power and influence to infiltrate them with drug company stooges who do their bidding and who own pretty much every academic medical school in the nation because of their power over funding, funding controlled by them, funding provided by their drug company stooges, all for the benefit of profit. You hold to that wide web of conspiracy?"

"All of that is true," Douche-bag snapped. "Take Got-milk. Isn't he the head COVID czar, and was he not in charge of Pfizer and head of the FDA and in academia? Now he works with Fact-nerd. Surely you can see the perfidy of all this, the web of power being constructed right under our noses as we construct myths out of nonsense, and we tear down the very foundation of scientific discourse."

Jim laughed again and peered into the camera with a *Can you believe this shit?* glance, making Cheddar drop into a burst of chucking. "America, it doesn't get better than this, does it?" Chedddar laughed, nodding her head as she wore a deep red smirk.

Jim twisted his glance again to the weary German. "And you've said too, Doctor Douche-bag, that the Gated-Billionaire and Doctor Fact-nerd control patents, control vaccines, control the global financial network, are working in cahoots with China and other bad players, maybe they even are the reason for bad weather, who knows. You've said that, with COVID, these to villians suppressed the use of cheap and effective early treatments—you must be referring to Trump's treatments of taking horse pills and drinking Lysol—because they needed to sell the vaccine, and that emergency authorization for the vaccine couldn't occur if early treatment existed, so they suppressed it, and that the FDA authorized this alleged experimental vaccine even though it kills more people than it helps, and that Pfizer studies were twisted by them to make them look good. You've said that Fact-nerd's ownership of academia had given him a squadron of doctors who will say anything to discredit his foes, who will make up studies to support his dogma, and that all this in the end is designed to make the world dependent of big pharma and the Gated-Billionaire."

Jim showed a picture of the Gated-Billionaire on the wall wearing a sweater vest with his nerdy glasses and a big nerdy smile holding a baby.

"This, Doctor Douche-bag, this man is Satan, he is Hitler, he is the nemesis who is threatening to take over the planet by using this pandemic as a tool?" Then Jim pointed to the science tiger. "And you claim that this man, this hero, this guy who has been here for this country from day one, that his only goal is to get rich and take over the world? Have you seen his house, Doctor? It ain't no mansion; that's all I got to say!"

"You know that everything I say is true," the doctor shouted. "You know it. And I know you know it. Yes, look into it, America. Check out your sources, and you will see it's all true!"

Of course, the sources to which the Douche-bag referred had all been shut down, and the truth that he proclaimed—one that had a lot of backing in the files of Mr. X, if those could even be believed— was torn down piece by piece, webbed foot by webbed foot, by Jim's meticulous spreadsheets.

That night, Jim drank just a little extra, hoping to keep Kate away from his nocturnal brain. But as was often the case, she waded right through his intoxication and stood firm and blurry before him.

This time she was sitting with God, His large hairy arm over her shoulder. "Keep going, Jim, we love watching it all unfold," said God. "Quite the performance. Even Satan is not sure he wants you."

Kate just laughed. "It's too bad, Jim, because the sex is great up here, and you can eat all day and never get fat! Down where you're going, there's a lot of burnt marshmallows. But I'm sure you're having fun! You remember what Bugs said: 'Don't think it hasn't been a little slice of heaven . . . 'cause it hasn't!' I guess that's your life in a nutshell. You had a chance to cruise through life and be a real hero, but instead went with Party Cruise and now you get to spend eternity on his boat."

All of a sudden, God looked like a rooster! "Boy, I say boy, pay close attention to me, 'cause you're a burrito short of a combination plate," God said, before turning to Kate. "That boy's as strong as an ox, and just about as smart. He's about as sharp as a bowling ball, I say, I say."

"Only problem is that he only throws gutters!" They laughed so hard that Jim woke up with a gasp, drenched with sweat. He looked for Jack Daniel's, for Corrine, for anyone. He merely hyperventilated and then turned on DUI. *The Threat to Democracy* was on again, and Jim was the hero, the savior of science and democracy, the American dream come true.

"They're just dreams," he reminded himself. "In a few days, I'll be president, and then even God will be shaking in his sandals."

The light was on in his closet. He felt something pulling him there, a longing to sift through the forbidden documents, to make more spreadsheets, to create and then destroy the other truth. A carton of liquor was in there right next to all his secret files. Always a temptation. Always a lure.

Satan gave Adam an apple. God gave Jim booze. He stood up, uneasy on his feet, his brain spinning, and he walked in, slamming the door behind him. He could smell Kate on every page.

In here, it was always duck season, and Jim was always the duck.

CHAPTER TWENTY-FOUR

A Maskin' Kind of Gal

It became abundantly clear to Jim, as he sat with his advisors and those closest to him, that the very people who most deplored the January 6th coup, who draped the nation in masks and mandates and shoved COVID fear to the top of the agenda, who pushed for social justice while supporting those governors and leaders who advocated censorship and powerful executive control over everyone's lives, that these people were not reliable allies. It's not that Jim disavowed anything that they said or did; it's just that they had cold feet when it came to making tough choices. They stoked the nation's fear and lambasted everyone who decried their Fact-nerd-inspired faith, but they were not willing to go far enough, not willing to make the leap to total eradication of anti-life misinformation and anti-democratic thought that Jim knew to be necessary.

Ironically, it was from the other side of the aisle, starting with Party Cruise and Graham Cracker, and then spreading out to involve many Republicans and hard-liners who quickly pivoted and embraced Jim's patriotic absolutism, that he tapped his new cabinet and closest advisors.

And that's why Mary Lou and A-O-Crazy marched into his office one day and demanded that he get back on the correct course immediately, or he would risk losing their support and the support of all millennials.

"Don't threaten me," Jim snarled through a half-cocked smile. "I made you, and I can break you. But bottom line, these people whom you so admonish, they're with us. They're the ones most committed to the very cause we've devoted our lives to uphold. Don't ridicule them because of their past positions. There are no people more willing to fight harder for what you and I and America know as the truth."

"See-ya Russian?" A-O-Crazy barked right back. "That's who you are putting on a pedestal? All your new pals are racist; they are homophobic and sexist. They don't believe in global warming or environmentalism. They eat at McDonalds, for God's sake! I hate them all. But See-ya Russian? Please, Mr. President-Elect, you have to know that you've crossed a line with this one. How can you not know that?"

Jim smiled and sucked down his Jack Daniel's. He poured another. There was nothing he had to say.

VP Russian appeared with tap dancer the previous night with a surprise announcement. "Well, Dance-boy, I got to tell you, it was a shock to me too, but second time's a charm, know what I mean, and I'm honored to be serving my country in this way. Can't say there's anything about this great man I don't like. He has been our nation saint during the toughest time we have known. I'm just darned honored, dancer, honored."

The tap dancer smiled. "I don't think anyone expected President-Elect Depich to name you as his vice president," he said. "With your past record, your very recent criticism of the great Doctor Fact-nerd and much of what he does, it seems an odd choice."

"No no, not at all," she said. "I love the science tiger, cute as a button. He's the cutest little guy, a patriot, a man of God and science, and when I see him, well tap dancer, I say growl growl growl, know what I mean? And I love the whole masking thing, that's what I got to say to America and to all of you. I'm a maskin' kind of gal. Haven't had to wear makeup in two years 'cause of those masks. What gal doesn't appreciate that?"

Tap dancer laughed. "I suppose that as we face so much turmoil here and abroad, Russia threatening to attack Ukraine, Omicron slaughtering hundreds of thousands because of misinformation and defiance of science, incessant threats to our democracy, you do bring some toughness to the office."

"Darned right I do, Tappy." She smiled, pushing close to his face. "I've been keeping an eye on those Ruskies, watching them right from my home in Alaska. And Drig, and Drack, and Zillow—they're all on board, even my ex. He said, 'Honey Bear, if that guy needs a secretary of hunk, you just let me know.' I'm not one to run away from a fight, America. I'm a tough gal. A tough gal wearing a mask and lovin' it!"

See-ya Russian joined Jim with Corrine and some of his new advisors and cabinet picks. Many of these former Republicans had come to his aid to implicate anti-lifers and to renounce Trumpists imbedded in government; all pledged their hearts and souls to the battle ahead.. Jim did fill a Supreme Court vacancy with none other than Old Dishwasher. Cheddar planned to leave her spot at DUI to be Secretary of Homeland Security, while Newbie-hottie was slated as Secretary of State, A-O-Crazy as Secretary of Education, and Charcoal Kock as Secretary of the Treasury. More-ill Bankers was going to be the New Attorney General. And none other than Mumbling Joe himself volunteered as Press Secretary.

"My cabinet and advisory board crosses every political divide," Jim said, at his inaugural speech on a warm and blustery day in mid-February, the temperature on the White House lawn approaching sixty degrees. Crowds were not allowed here due to Omicron, but the amazing Gated Billionaire—who constantly joked that "I am here with my cabal to take over the world" even as he humbly accepted the job as Secretary of Health and Human Services—whizzed up a virtual crowd of enthusiastic holograms that was bigger and more boisterous than any ever assembled at an inauguration. "But what unites us is a love of democracy, of science, and of getting rid of this damned virus and moving on as a nation."

The crowd erupted, cutting Jim off for about the fifteenth time. He smiled and waved. Corrine stood by him, tapping him on the back; she was so proud, so very ecstatic.

Tellingly, no students showed up on this day. Nor did A-O-Crazy. They were meeting elsewhere.

"You know," Jim smiled. "A lot of people asked me, they asked me, Jim, you've been fighting a war for life, a war for democracy, a war for science and decency, a war for this nation, so tell us, tell us when you finally get up there and put your hand on the bible, what will you do first? What will be your first executive order? To me, that answer is easy and may surprise you. Through all my travels as an engineer and businessman and then a congressional representative to the great people of Pittsburgh, I always said to my aide Corrine, I always said, Corrine, if I ever get to be president, there are two things I am going to do first before anything else."

He peered at Corrine, who looked back at him and snickered, nodding her head from side to side, as the president-elect nodded his up and down, and they burst into laughter.

"Corrine knows," Jim said, his joy and pride exuberantly flowing through the light warm wind. "I drove a lot and flew a lot. So executive order one: If you drive in the left lane and you ain't passing someone, if you're driving slow and clogging things up, I got news for you, because from now on, you're committing a capital offense, and that's my first executive order. I mean, come on, America, don't you hate those people? I mean, you can drive on their tail and hit them with your brights all day and they won't move! Haven't you ever said, this should be illegal? Well, now people of America, now it is!

"And executive order number two: If you're one of those guys who takes forever getting on and off the plane 'cause you have to set up your seat or you can't get that oversize bag of yours up or down— well, I got news for you too, 'cause in my next executive order, you got to pass a test to make sure you're competent if you are going to board a plane. And if you fail, then guess what? You're the last one on and off, and that's now got the force of law behind it, so you slow inconsiderate slugs, guess what, back of the line, all you all are now C's!" The virtual crowd burst into laughter and applause. And Jim shouted over their din, "And that goes for the shopping line too! No more slugs in line! You got to take a test first, and you got to pass! That's the kind of president I intend to be!"

When finally the crowd settled, Jim beckoned the science tiger, Got-milk, Boola-boola, , Sand-man Gotcha, Dr. Birkenstock, Rob-the Redfields, Dr. Slob-it, and several members of the Hopkins and Cambridge epidemiological modeling teams to the podium. They all stood, masks on, staggered apart by six feet, and lifted their hands. Jim pointed to them.

"These are my guys!" he shouted. "These are the guys who warned us just how bad this virus would be, just how necessary were extreme measures to attack it, just how foolish we were to allow mis-informers to sell you Satan's apple instead of the truth that would have saved your life. Look, my committee is uprooting the most lethal misinformers from our midst, and guess what, they're not gonna hurt us no more, because look over there," he said, pointing to the Capitol. "There they are, all together, hanging out. And they finally got their wish. They don't have to wear masks and don't have to social distance. They finally got their wish; they don't have to fol-low the science, and there they are loving it!"

The crowd erupted again! Jim put up his hands and smiled. "Look, we know that the same guys who killed your friends and rel-atives by spreading misinformation are the same thugs who tried to knock down our democracy. Same guys! And there they are, hanging out. So, seriously, those are Trump's guys, and this groups of experts, these are my guys. In my administration, they have absolute authority over your lives and the life of this nation until the viral threat is gone. As of midnight tonight, I am declaring martial law across the entire country. You break the law, you walk out without a mask, you spread misinformation, you decide you want to have an Olympic party at your house, guess what? We're not playing around, because this virus isn't playing. It's real, and it's deadly. So if you want to pretend the science isn't your cup of tea, if you want to put your neighbors in peril, guess what? You'll be hanging out with your friends up there at the Capitol, where you don't have to follow science or the rule of law.

"My soldiers have a shoot-to-kill order for all offenders of the life laws. These brilliant doctors and leaders, they'll make the laws to keep you safe, and all you got to do is listen. Is that so hard, America? To listen to experts? And guess what? You do that, and we'll get through this, as a nation, as a people, as a democracy. My fellow Americans, I am so proud to be your next president. And I promise you that I'll fix the mess that was served to me. I'll clear the plate of the rotten meat I've been served and replace it with prime ribs and lobster for everyone. And I have news for you. Next year, when we reinstate the NFL and get back on the road to normal, I'll be eating that prime rib with my friends as we watch my Steelers win the whole damned thing. God bless you, God bless science, and God bless America."

Jim swore the oath on his family's old Bible. Justice Robs-banks stood statuesque behind his cloth mask. There were no parties that night. No celebrations. But, at one holding camp in Florida, one filled with misinformers and anti-vaxxers and those who derided the mask laws, Jim's people gathered them all up that night and ended their lives. Such measures would now be the rule of the land. More people were brought to the camps, and just as many were removed in bags. Bodies that dangled from the Capitol rotunda had started to lose flesh during a brief Indian summer near Valentine's Day, and more bodies replaced them. Jim called it "the revolving door of infamy," while the tap dancer referred to it as "the prescription to restore life and democracy to this nation."

A few days after the inauguration, Jim appeared on *The View* with a dozen kids, all of whom had turned in parents, relatives, or neighbors for defying COVID laws. "My uncle even voted for Donald Trump," one eight-year-old boy said. "And he said that this was all a comp piracy or something like that. All made up. And that the vaccine was poison."

"Are you vaccinated?" Who-put Gollum asked him.

"Of course!" He laughed. "I'm not silly. I don't want to die. I hate people who say we shouldn't get the shot. It didn't even hurt. And now I may live forever!"

The next day Jim spoke with Rachel-in-the Meadow, extolling the smart crop of kids and young adults who would replace the current generation. "We're old, cynical, and stale," he said to Meadow. "We sometimes have more doubt than faith. These young guns, they are lucky to grow up and witness the wonders of pro-life and pro-democracy thinking, of seeing the good guys win. And you know what, Meadow, you know what? When all this ends and a paradise grows upon the weeds left by those before us, when us old and stale people die off, then our nation's future, it's as bright as God's sun! It will be our meadow, America's meadow!"

Rachel-in-the Meadow, looking serious, her chin on her hands, said, "There is something about that, Congressman, I totally dispute."

Jim was stunned. Never did she question him. "And what's that?" he timidly asked.

"I am not old and stale." She laughed. "Speak for yourself, although I must say, and I say this with utter honesty, you seem to look younger every day!"

And he felt it, especially as he sat with Cold Bert during his monthly appearance.

"Sometimes," Cold Bert said to the president, "toughness is needed during tough times, and if you don't think that's tough to say, then toughen up." The audience chuckled, and he continued. "Omicron seems to be fading. Most of the misinformation we have endured for the past two years is largely gone. So, Mr. President, how much longer should we as a nation expect this vigilance to continue? I know that more variants are around every corner, and with the news out of Sweden, well, we know this game sure isn't over. So, are we masking forever, or is there a face at the end of the tunnel?"

"Yes, Cold Bert," Jim said, with a smile. "One day I'll see your big smile again. But this is a serious game, a game for our lives and our nation. So, yes, we must stay vigilant and just know that I and my crack team are doing all we can to get us back on track to a normal life, one with faces again."

"There will be an NFL season then?" Cold Bert smiled. "Because I'm thinking it's the year of the Panthers."

"Now I see why you're a comedian," Jim shot back. "I'm not a great prognosticator, America, but of one thing I'm certain. There's a better chance of our science tiger winning gold in speed skating than your Carolina Panthers taking the Superbowl."

"Well, Mr. President, let's hope you and I have a chance to place a bet on it!" And then they bowed to each other, given the continued ban on handshakes. Cold Bert's show would be canceled the next day.

"I just had the feeling he was sneering at me under his mask," Jim told Party Cruise.

Jim sat in his room watching cartoons. He planned to tune in to the Olympics, but frankly, bobsledding and ice-skating bored him. The best winter sport was Yosemite Sam! "Say your prayers, varmint!" the gruff Western icon warned Bugs, who chewed on a carrot and stared him in the eye. "I'm no doc, ya flea-bitten varmint. I'm Riff-Raff Sam, the riffiest riff that ever riffed a raff!" And then as he was about to pull the trigger, Bugs twisted the shaft of Sam's gun, and the bullet came back and hit him.

Jim dropped to the floor laughing when Corrine meandered in. "You look so happy, Jim," she glowed, trotting to him and draping him in a hug. "What a week, right? Best week ever! I'm heading home to the kids and Mark; we'll celebrate the nation's new birth together, and I'll work on those spreadsheets we talked about. You'll get them first thing in the morning. You need anything else?"

"You got some carrot juice?" He laughed. "I have a sudden hankering for it. No more booze! I never drank before, and I never will drink again. This is my moment, our moment, the one we worked for. It's time for us to do good! To put the country back on track. I'm not going to fall prey to tricks that did in Yosemite Sam, Corrine. I'm not going to let the bullet come back and hit me. All those nightmares, now I understand them. They were saying, Jim, once you get on top, it's time to turn down the heat. To be the hero. To stop all the trials, all the punishments, and to save the country from itself. It's time to end all this crap!"

Corrine's mouth dropped. "You sure you haven't been drinking, Jim? Because what you're saying, you know you can't do that. There's another variant around the corner. More threats and plots.

What about Sweden and DaSandwich? We can't let down our guard, Jim. That's the whole point of these spreadsheets. If we do, you know people will come after us. You know that, right?"

Jim smiled, stood up, and put his arm around his favorite person in the world. "Not now, my precious gem. I'm not changing course now. I'm thinking of the future. Another year of this. Then we rebuild. And can you imagine our legacy? How we'll be remembered? As saviors of the nation! This is what I crave."

"OK," she said, forcing a laugh. "You scared me. I don't want anyone coming after me and my kids."

"We're fine. It's a process. Go home and make love to that guy of yours. Give us another kid. This world will be so perfect when we're done with it that every kid born today will be living in a fucking paradise!"

Just then, someone darted in the door. It was a disheveled See-ya Russian, and she panted hard, stopping for a moment to catch her breath. She looked at Corrine and then at Jim. "Mr. President, they just told me to come get you," she said, gasping. "I can't tell you the details, but China's on the phone. Like the guy in charge of China; I can't pronounce the name, but it's him who's on the phone, the Chinaman. And he says it's urgent. Like bat-shit urgent. Like something's going down urgent. The phone's in the Oval Office. Sorry to interrupt your meeting."

As Sam yelled some obscenities on TV, Jim looked at Corrine. "I guess the spreadsheets should wait."

CHAPTER TWENTY-FIVE

Melting Swedish Fish

Jim paced in his office. His two primary advisors—whom he had sanctioned as his co-chiefs of staff, although the two despised each other and usually had very distinct roles—assured him that most dissent within American borders had evaporated, and that much of the world too adhered to the strict pro-life dictates of the new president. But there was a brewing problem, and it could get out of hand.

Party Cruise wandered in first; the guy was proficient and never seemed to have a conscience or soul that impeded his ability to carry out Jim's orders. Still, Jim found him a bit unnerving and more than just a little dull. With Sweden and China on his mind, Jim had to trust this Cruise to take care of more mundane matters, to make sure the right people were happy and the wrong people subdued.

"We got things settled down in Jersey," he said to Jim, giving him the daily State of the Nation report. "Murphy's Law is still all pissy about being passed up for a cabinet position, so I told him our secret, about A-O-Crazy likely stepping down and him filling that role. He likes it a lot, just wants to know when. He'll take anything, Jim, just to be with the A team. I like him. Good guy. Tough as nails."

"Yea," Jim said to himself. "I had him on the list, just forgot about him. I'm glad you're keeping him happy. Keep them all happy, party boy, that's why I hired you! And for God's sake, we need the military on our side; they're the police now. They have control over everything. The reserves are all out there; what if they go south? I've heard rumors of some soldiers failing to carry out orders to shoot on command and to even arrest some people, even some clashes between students and soldiers. What if they turn against us? I have nightmares about it!"

Party Cruise smiled, a piece of egg dropping from his unkempt beard. "Ain't gonna happen, Jim. I was talking to a businessman over in Columbia a few years back, and he said to me, 'Big guy, you guys got the whole military thing figured out, you got the strongest armed forces in history, and yet never has there been a coup or even any-one who dared to defy orders—well, if you don't count MacArthur.' But I said, 'Pedro'—I don't know if that was the guy's name, but he looked like a Pedro—'the thing is, we got so many levels of military, so many branches, so many egos, and they all hate each other's guts, that if one colonel tries to make a stink, the next lieutenant will tear him down. It's all about spreading power around, so no one's really got any, and then they got to look up to the president to get what they want.' Jim, I've been with the joint chiefs every day. Go there with the old Jim as I call him, Senator In-a-hurry—great choice for Secretary of Defense, General Milky trusts, and even the lefties think he's A-OK 'cause he's OK with ladies in uniform—and he has them boys in line with what to do. Keep the military busy, and they'll be a happy crew."

"They may be very busy soon," Jim responded, although not saying anything more. "I'm an engineer, Party, and when I execute a plan, spread-sheet it, and make sure every element of it is scripted and every detailed accounted for, I leave it to my underlings to make sure it's carried out smoothly. We call it system management. It only breaks down when the spreadsheets are flawed, which in my case they never are, or if we have crappy underlings. The military has a big role in what we're doing, as do the police, our mayors and governors, whole layers of people. I have to trust all of them. I did my part, I made the plan, spread-sheeted it, got the system rolling. But I want you to make sure they're doing theirs. Got it?"

"It's like a giant machine, Mr. President, and it's running smoothly." Party Cruise smiled. "It's just a damned shame Omicron faded. That's the glue that kept the cogs together. When people are shitting in their pants, they're more likely to listen and obey; I call it national diarrhea, in fact. That's why we got to keep everyone just a little scared. And reward the ones doing the scaring. It's amazing just how vigilant some of our kids are in turning bad guys in and pushing discipline. You got to love it."

"Good," Jim said. "I trust you'll tell me when something goes awry. What about the clashes between the students and the soldiers I've heard about?"

At that, Party Cruise paused a bit. "If you ask me," he said, "I'd give Representative Crazy a talking to. She gets the kids all riled up, and sometimes those young kids—you got to love their passion, even if a lot of their ideas are misplaced and naïve—don't know their place. That's the one group I really can't control, Mr. President. I don't want anything blowing up between the kids and soldiers, but so far, knock on wood, it's just been a few little pissy parties here and there. We're keeping the army and police off the campuses, and keeping the kids on the campuses, so we are doing OK. For now."

A few minutes later, a jovial and loquacious Graham Cracker skipped in, instantly raising Jim's mood. Jim genuinely liked the guy; he seemed to have some substance beneath his bluster, even if he too proved to be an obsequious and often self-serving lieutenant. Just his smile and easygoing drawl eased Jim's angst. Jim asked him about the global situation, which is what most occupied his thoughts.

"Latin America, they're like sheep, bathing in Purell and wearing masks on their toilets, shaming anyone who does anything different than what they're told. Hell, them folks are religious as crap, so they love being told what to do, and their leaders knew from Buck that all foreign aid would evaporate unless everyone was vaccinated, so there ain't no issues south of the border," Graham Cracker assured him. "And Germany's making sure the EU is compliant; they hold Europe's purse strings, so it ain't like anyone can complain. They're good at that kind of crap, making sure people follow orders, or else. Got it in their blood. Where we got trouble, as you know, if fucking Sweden. Unless we shut them red fish down, well, that's just another nail in our asses that may come back to give us a damned boil down the road. That's our big shit right now."

Big shit was an understatement. What the Chinese leaders told Jim made him shake. For an entire day, he sat alone contemplating their tocsin and proposed solution. He even called Putin. It seemed to make sense, all of it, but it was such a dramatic leap from anything Jim had contemplated in his life.

Graham Cracker didn't know about China's solution to Sweden, and Jim was not about to tell him. Still, he wanted to feel him out about how far to go to stop the rouge nation. So, he asked.

"If you want to know what I'd do, and what my buddy McBrain would likely tell me from the grave," he said, "I'd nuke the bastards. Like you say, sometimes to save lives, you got to end a few."

"Yea." Jim laughed. "I think that could be a bit messy, but thanks."

Graham Cracker smiled. "I think we can handle the Swedish fish. I worry more about them students and A-O-Crazy, who, I got to tell you, I never liked. Her and the tiger are out there waiting for you. I don't know what you got to tell them, but I'm glad as hell I don't got to be in that conversation. Those students, in the end, Mr. President, I know that they got you here, and they've rooted out a lot of bad weeds, but you got to keep an eye on them. Compared to the Swedes, they're tougher fish to fry."

Jim felt the same way, and, although he didn't tell Graham Cracker about it, he was letting Party Cruise handle Mary Lou and her millennial horde. Sadly, though, Sweden was the only fish in the pan right now for Jim.

"China has the whole thing figured out," Jim had told Corrine earlier in the day. "I never thought I'd say such a thing, but they do. The Chinese are experts at erasing dangerous defiance while at the same time hiding their actions behind a well-designed cloak of sub-terfuge. What they told me was shocking at first, and then it seemed to make sense. If we let Sweden prosper, then it becomes the one cancer cell that our chemotherapy didn't eradicate. Soon enough it will grow and spread and kill the whole body."

At first, Sweden proved to be just an irritant. From day one of the pandemic, Swedes defied all scientific wisdom, keeping their country open, ridiculing mask use, and not infringing on anyone's rights. The result was a surge of COVID cases and deaths, magnified by DUI and many of the tiger's scientific experts into a national catastrophe. Sweden was the anti-science bad guy that caused its citizens to needlessly perish because it refused to adhere to scientific wisdom.

But beneath the surface lay another truth, one revealed to Jim in the documents provided to him by both Kate and Mr. X. Yes, Sweden's COVID deaths were higher than many other nations, but Sweden had an older population, and most deaths occurred in people so frail that, even without COVID, they likely wouldn't have lived more than a few months. Very few young people died, no kids, and their total excess deaths—not just of COVID, but all deaths during the entire pandemic—was lower than any nation in the world. By defying science, Sweden kept its economy alive, its kids in schools, its nation happy, and its people safe. Such was the misinformation, the alternative truth, that Jim kept off his spreadsheets, that DUI and the Fact-nerd disciples kept out of the public eye.

But now something disastrous had occurred. Many dissidents from America had escaped and fled to Sweden, where they set up an alternative government and managed to broadcast vile and dangerous misinformation across the airways despite all attempts to muffle it. These included Governor DaSandwich from Florida, comedians Shrill Marvelous and Larky Daydream who had been imprisoned in California by Governor Newbie-hottie for incendiary comments they made before they escaped, and a large number of doctors and scientists who had signed the Great Barrington Declaration.

"With Marvelous and Daydream doing the broadcasts," Graham Cracker had said to him, "they're getting traction. I don't find them funny, and I think they're both annoying snots, but unfortunately they are putting a dash of doubt into the widely accepted narratives and getting people to laugh at us. And they're making Sweden and even Florida look like they did it right. We got to shut them up, and we got to do it fast."

And that's where China came in.

"What China is doing is genius," he told Corrine. "It's methodical, scientific, precise. Their policies are not wishy-washy, they're not forgiving, but they're also not violent, because they, unlike us, can control all their variables. That's their genius. That's why there are no COVID deaths in China, no anti-government agitation, no defiance of authority. They've achieved scientific nirvana."

Corrine, holding her youngest in her arms, nodded. "It didn't happen overnight," she said. "And their version of governing is not democratic, as you know, Jim. Democracy is sloppy; there are more variables, more unknowns, less precision. If we become China, are we still democratic?"

"Does it matter, Corrine?" he asked. "If we're safe, if people still vote for their leaders and believe they're partaking in government, does it really matter? Isn't the illusion of democracy all we ever had anyway? And if that's the case, why not do it right?"

Mary Lou's public executions, bodies hanging from the Capitol, trials, camps—this had become democracy in America. Yes, as Corrine, Party Cruise, and Newbie-hottie told him, any diminution of fear, any relaxation of the harsh measures admonishing those who dared to defy executive power in the wake of a threat, any rebuke of scientific truth, could open holes in the narrative and instigate a civil war. That is what Jim sought to avoid, but his nightmares dug into his hide; he felt like a monster sometimes, even if he knew that scientifically he was following the only course that his calculations allowed.

Sweden, then, was a potential wrench in the execution of Jim's singular truth, a breeding ground of dissonance, a threat to the national spreadsheet.

China, through its precise and well-thought-out gaze, devised a solution to Sweden that was simple, scientific, and not sloppy. At first, it shocked Jim, but as he mulled over it, he perceived its brilliance.

"They don't have to have trials or hang people or release young thugs who wander across campuses and suburban streets terrorizing those who defy our laws," Jim told his young aide. "In China, everyone is connected electronically. Everyone has chips installed in them that define where they work and travel, chips that give them their money and their rights, chips that provide for them all the state benefits. Within those chips are cameras and trackers, which are also in every computer, in every car, in every home. If someone defies the law, if someone questions national policy, then the authorities can discover that indiscretion through the chip and neutralize the threat with the chip. Rather than having to publicly punish or harm that anti-scientist, the Chinese simply alter the bad guy's chip. That person loses his ability to travel, loses some of his bank account, loses his job and freedom of movement; he becomes a virtual prisoner. Upon repenting, upon changing his ways, those rights and benefits are restored, always ready to be taken away should the person revert. That, Corrine, is brilliant. It's clean and effective. And it's science at its best."

She nodded up and down. Then she smiled. "You do that, Jim, and the millennials would love it too. One kid told me that she imagines a day when a chip is inserted into everyone's skin that allows them to have GPS, credit cards, passports, driver's licenses all in one place. To them, it's cool, and to us, it's the most perfect tool of surveillance and discipline. And guess what? That's how to protect democracy, not destroy it. It would be an amazing legacy for you!"

Jim nodded up and down.

"That's what the Chinese want to do with Sweden, Corrine," he said. "Remove it from existence by erasing its chip, erasing its people. I've been talking to several nation's leaders. Putin is on board; he just wants a green light to take Ukraine and a few smaller nations without any protest from the West. DUI promises not to broadcast it. Germany is good with it. Really, it seems like a perfect solution."

"And what is the solution, Jim?" she asked, coddling her crying child. "What's the plan?"

Of course, the devil was in the details!

He needed his science tiger on board. He needed A-O-Crazy to muffle the students. He needed his aides and the military to be compliant. He needs no leaks from the press.

"Look at the buffoon who's running my nation now." Shrill Marvelous laughed from his perch in Sweden, his broadcasts making their way to the world despite every attempt to block them. "He still wants you to use hand gel. You've got to spurt your hands every time you walk outside, walk inside, go to a fucking pool. Hell, that president of ours, he wants us to fucking have sex with the hand gel just to show how much we love the shit. But guess what, President Dipshit? Fucking COVID doesn't live on hands or on any surfaces. Hand gel may be a good way for you to masturbate, Mr. President, since it's clear you haven't had sex for most of your fucking life, but it don't do jack shit for this virus. That's our science president? And if you don't' do it, well then, first he'll tell you to shut up, and if you don't shut up, well, ladies and gentlemen, look at the Capitol and see what happens when you dare use your first amendment rights. When you dare fight for your freedoms. This is how we fight for democracy and science? Hell, the fucking Pope is more democratic and scientific than this moron."

Jim needed to do something fast. As A-O-Crazy and the impatient tiger waited outside, Jim focused on the task at hand.

"Get me the Chinese ambassador on the phone," he said to Corrine. "Fact-nerd can wait. Send in A-O-Crazy when I'm done with the call. I need to put that bitch and her little gang of thugs in their place. From now on, either these people play ball, or they don't play at all."

"Got it, boss," Corrine said. "Glad to see no booze here, Jim," she said to him on her way out. "I like my guy sober!"

There was no need to drink. There was nothing to be numb about. Moving forward, Jim simply had to be steadfast. The first step was to microwave the Swedish fish. After that, well, the sky was the limit.

PART FIVE

Tumbling Down
the Precipice of
Democracy's Triumph

Go Jim!
Science Rocks!
Rabbit Season!
Duckmocracy Season!

CHAPTER TWENTY-SIX

Creating Life Out of Death

Carole Pasture had meandered down this street a thousand times. She brought her kids to a bus stop on that corner over there; now they were older, one was in college, two were working. All of them lived nearby. She walked here with her friends every weekend morning, at least when it wasn't too cold or raining. They ended up at Joe's bagel shop two miles away, in the strip mall, where they'd laugh and talk and let it all out; everything was on the table, from their jobs to their husbands to what they were making for dinner. She drove to work every morning down this same street, often tired, often frustrated, being at the same job for twenty-six years in an accounting firm, just one among many, dutifully carrying out her instructions as others were fired or advanced above her, some quit, bosses changed—moments of fun and joy came and went. She remembered in 2016 when the snow was so deep that she couldn't get down the street even in her Ford Bronco, although she made a go of it, getting stuck midway. The plow guy cursed her for blocking his way, but her neighbors all came out, laughing and giggling, with bagels and coffee, and together they all paved a path for her.

She voted for Hill-top, of course, and for Star Buck. She wasn't a political animal but knew enough to reject those who seemed to have more anger and hate in their blood than compassion and wisdom. She liked Jim Depich and voted for him too; he seemed like a breath of fresh air in her largely Republican neighborhood, and as a woman of color, she latched onto his message of common sense, science, and hope.

This weekend it was going to be cold. Her husband lay sleeping. Their relationship had grown colder than even the winter air of Western Pennsylvania; she slept in another room, but they still ate together and shared a house. Frankly, it would be far too expensive to leave him, and what was the point? She trudged to her car, wearing her mask and winter coat, and turned it on. Gas prices hadn't come down, but with Omicron fading, she had some hope that she could resume her weekend walks and maybe even meet her friends for lunch. All that had been taken from her during these two long, harsh years. Life itself seemed to have been reduced to bare existence.

Carole had long stopped watching the news. She had long stopped caring about pretty much anything. Now back at work, the once lively air felt dead. Few people interacted but for work-related banter or maybe a joke here or there. She had not seen anyone's facial expressions for two years now, everyone's souls buried beneath their masks. Some coughed a lot, suffocated, could hardly breathe. Sometimes she'd hide in the bathroom stall just to take the mask off and spend a few moments alone. A sign with a pleasant-appearing white-garbed cartoon doctor was plastered around every corner: *Stay six-feet apart, wear your mask always, use sanitizer on your hands at least every half hour, wash for exactly twenty seconds. If we all do our job, then COVID can't do his.* Down the hall was a bulletin from HR: *Fourth booster sign-up; this is a requirement.* Carole meandered past the signs, barely glancing at them. They were the new norm for her, and she, like the others who remained working here, sheepishly complied.

Bottom line, none of it really mattered. She wanted to do her part to keep the world safe, and she detested those who fought against these measures. Her life had changed, but wasn't it worth it? Sure, during surges she became more isolated, but then her friends re-emerged, her kids came by (other than her one daughter who refused to be vaccinated and whom she and her husband denied entry to their home), and she limped through her daily routine, an empty feeling within her, but why should she expect more? Sure, she and everyone else now buried their face and souls behind a scripted masquarade, but some of the masks were kind of fun, like her friend Betty who wore one with a photo of her mouth and nose, and she had a different mask for a variety of emotions. All of them laughed!

She heard about what was going on in DC, all the trials, the student groups, even the bodies dangling from the Capitol. None of that really touched her life, and if it was necessary to keep the country safe, then to Carole, well, the leaders had to do what they had to do. She didn't know anyone who died of COVID, didn't know anyone threatened or captured by the "goon squads" that some of her more conservative friends claimed were now terrorizing the country. Even her defiant daughter still went to work, despite not being vaccinated and mocking the masks, although her employers now claimed that they were going to fire her should she not comply, something Carole believed to be justified given that Omicron would not have even occurred had everyone simply followed the rules.

That day at work, Fred, an older guy who had been with the company for decades, wandered into the conference room. A few of them gathered there all spread out, including Carole, and he sat down with some coffee. He slipped off his mask between sips, and then slid it back on. Fred always wore both an N-95 and a surgical mask; he scoffed at those who masked less vigilantly, even though he acknowledged that his breathing had deteriorated, and he wheezed all night. "But at least I ain't dead!" he'd quip.

He peered at the girls who sat nearby, eating and laughing about something. Carole was among them. "You gals see what's coming out of Sweden?" he asked them. "Some crazy stuff."

Carole looked over to him. "Fred, right now I'm just glad I can afford gas! No, why in God's name do I care about Sweden?"

"Well," he continued, "they're doing stuff and saying stuff that's not too good for anyone. The president says we got to do something. Lots of our bad guys ran off there. They're putting out videos, saying stuff that's downright dangerous. We got to do something. Depich will do something. I voted for the guy, and I knew he's got balls."

One of Carole's friends looked at him. "It's cold and dark there, Fred." She laughed under her mask. "I think the Swedish people are suffering enough just from the weather! Besides, why do you even care? So what? Let them say what they want; as long as we are doing OK, why do we care about them? Things are opening up, Fred. The boss says we can even start up the birthday gatherings again. My gym just opened up. And for some reason, you want me to care about Sweden?"

"I think that we should leave everyone alone," another guy said from farther away. "Let people do what they want, say what they want, and if Sweden wants to do its thing, why should we care?"

"Oh, there goes Mr. Leave Them All Alone!" Carole's friend said. "You want to get us in trouble? Just keep your thoughts to yourself. Haven't we told you that a thousand times?"

"That kind of thinking gets people killed," Fred snarled from the next table.

"So, what, Fred, you going to turn me in, get me muffled, hang me from the Capitol?" the man snapped.

Frankly, Carole had enough. A fuming anger filled her skull. She was usually quiet and reserved, liked to have fun when she could, get her work done, read and exercise, make a nice dinner. She was thinking about going to the store after work and making her famous chicken a la Carole, with crabmeat, whose prices had just come down. But this conversation, this antagonism, hit her oddly at that moment, and she had enough.

"Just shut your traps, both of you," she yelled. "I don't give a crap what either of you think. I don't give a crap about Sweden or the Capitol or even the goddamned moon, for heaven's sake! You want to talk about that nonsense, go outside and do it. But in here, we don't give a fuck!"

Her language stunned everyone, even her. But then her friend Betty laughed, fiddled in her purse, and put on a new mask, one in which her mouth was open and seemed to be in shock. Everyone laughed, including Carole. The two men shut up. The others resumed their conversation. Carole thought again about dinner. She'd bring some to her kids, even to her damned fool of a daughter. She hoped that her grandson's soccer would start up again in the spring. For the rest of the day, she said nothing more.

Much farther away, in the nation's capital, Jim Depich beckoned the science tiger to his office. They spoke once already today, and the tiger was noncommittal about what Jim proposed. Now, with viral heat burning more voraciously, with China pushing Jim to the brink, with more broadcasts fluttering out of Sweden, Jim needed the tiger to stop being a pussy cat and to start showing his claws. Jim stared hard at his computer, grimacing.

"Listen to what they're saying from Sweden," Jim said to him, pointing to the screen. "Hear what they're saying about us, and then tell me we should just sit here and do jack shit about it."

"I guess I must be dead," Larky Daydream joked on his latest podcast, standing near Governor DaSandwich. "And I guess you're Satan and I'm in hell; that's what DUI is saying, so it must be true. Got through their fact-checkers, so it's pretty, pretty, pretty true. You know what I think, Da Fish Sandwich? Being here in Sweden with you, that's hell enough for me. We Jews, we'd rather move to Florida. I mean, it's like noon and it's still dark outside and I'm freezing my penis off. So, maybe I am dead, and maybe you are Satan. You know, we Jews, we could very well end up in hell, especially a Jew like me who isn't too, you know, observant. So, Governor, just fess up with me, is this hell and are you Satan?"

DaSandwich laughed. "Larky, I came from a nice warm and sunny spot, and we had a lot of Jews down there, good pizza, good delis. We were doing OK. And then our self-deluded power-hungry shmuck of a president made it into hell. No, we're not dead here. The people in Sweden have gotten it right, and we can live pretty well here, while the rest of the world under our deranged president is stuck in hell. But I'm with you. If we can just convince Americans that their president is defying science and shredding democracy, if we can get that little Hitler out of an office once held by Jefferson and Lincoln and FDR and Reagan, then I promise you, Larry, I'll bring you to Boca and we'll have a Reuben, the likes of which you've never tasted before."

Larkyu Daydream smiled. "You know, Sandwich man, I always imagined that I'd go to a foreign country, and I'd come back with a full head of hair. But short of that, having a Reuben on the beach with you, that would be pretty, pretty, pretty good. Pretty good!"

The tiger paced, his boyish and scholarly visage penetrating even his flimsy cloth mask. Jim looked up at him and flipped off the screen.

"You missed their little act an hour ago," Jim said to him. "Marvelous and Daydream and a few others did a spoof on you. You were the absentminded professor dressed in hundred-dollar bills."

"I get it, Jim, I get it. I'm happy to shut all of them up. But is what you want to talk to me about related to the China issue?" Fact-nerd asked. "Because I gave my final answer on that. I refuse to be party to anything like that."

Jim smiled and patted the scientist on the back. "No, it's not about that; I've taken care of that. Funny thing, though, the scientists from China we're working with, the lab rats from Wuhan, they swear to me that you are involved, that they've run everything by you, that the China issue that you so vehemently want no part of is being directed by none other than you. In fact, my timid little tiger, they taped conversations you've had with them; I can play them for you if you want. I can play them on DUI too."

The tiger paced even more methodically, seeming to smile under his mask. He didn't look at Jim. "Go ahead," he quipped. "The tap dancer won't believe you. I doubt he'd even play those tapes if I told him that they were fabricated. You have no power, Jim. You may think you do, but you don't. I'd keep your hands out of my pockets."

Jim laughed. "Now, that's the science tiger I love, the pissed-off lion of man, the guy who takes no shit. No, Fact-nerd, I won't play the tapes, and I don't care that you're working with the Chinese on this. I just want your help. The event will happen tonight, and tomorrow it will be breaking news, and we'll have to react fast. That's when we need you. You'll tell the world just how dangerous it is over there in Sweden. You'll say that if we don't contain the new murderous variant that was hatched there, then it will spread so quickly that it could wipe out half the planet. That's all I'm asking."

"I don't want to be implicated in a messy operation, Jim," Fact-nerd said. "You know I am always willing to help, but unless it's being done correctly, I want no part of it."

"For Christ's sake, tiger!" Jim laughed. "It's being done by the Chinese! They're experts at this. You have already helped create the variant we're putting into Sweden. The Chinese are the ones planting it there and regulating its spread. All we need you do to is to use your innocent, sciencey, cute-as-a-button self to get on the news and tell them that the sloppy Swedes have allowed a variant to mutate in their nation and that unless we stop it immediately, it could kill half the planet. That's all we want."

"I don't want it to be messy, Jim," he said again.

Jim laughed. "Thing is, you sly tiger you, I know a lot about you that you hide behind your pretty little face. I know about your connection to Wuhan, about your coronavirus research, about all your ties to industry, about even darker shit you're involved in. I'm never sure what to believe, but I figure some of it's true, and I have tons of documents that I can show the world at any moment. The one thing I know for sure is that you're one dirty feline. That your actions in suppressing treatments and fudging research, all for your own gain, have cost likely millions of lives. That you're so tied to corporate and academic scoundrels that you'd pretty much sell your soul for them and for you. You know exactly what we're releasing tonight in Sweden, and I know you've endorsed it. I don't want any pushback from you. I want you to say one thing to me, one thing only. I want you to say, 'Mr. President, of course, I'll do exactly what you are asking of me.' Is that too much, tiger boy, or do you need some persuasion?"

The tiger turned and faced the wall. "I have powerful friends, Jim, more powerful than you could ever know," he said softly. "I'll deny everything, and if it comes to having to defend myself, I don't think you'd stand a chance against the people and interests lined up behind me."

Jim laughed again. "I'm not here to dispute all of that or to fight with you, my friend. I'm not even here to talk about Sweden and China. I just need you to say, 'Mr. President, I am going to do exactly what you ask of me, for the good of the country.'"

For a while, the scientist said nothing. Then, seeming tired and almost frail, he stood up from his chair, his face buried in a mask, and said to Jim, "Will that be all, Mr. President?"

"As long as we understand each other, then yes, of course," Jim said, outstretching his elbow to hit Fact-nerd's. "Can't be too careful. Get some sleep, tiger. You'll be very busy tomorrow and for quite a while. I think we'll be seeing a lot of each other."

That night, Carole Pasture—who had sworn off all news and kept her distance from her husband—was brought back into both those worlds abruptly. As she stuffed crabmeat into seasoned chicken breast, she heard her husband cursing from the living room. She dashed over to tell him to quiet down, and then her face twisted to the TV screen. News Wolfe howled on DUI under the following caption: *Breaking News! A Sweden variant threatens massive death across the globe.* Boxes with the faces of scientists and doctors from across the world spoke to him and each other about whatever was transpiring.

"What's all this?" Carole asked. "You know I am not interested."

Her husband shook his head. "No, Car, you'll be damned interested in this. You've got no choice."

She listened, and all she could think of was her unvaccinated and defiant daughter, what would happen if this variant crossed the Swedish border and soared through Europe and into America, something that virtually all the TV scientists said was inevitable if it were not stopped immediately.

"This is a respiratory virus, News Wolf, and it moves fast," said an epidemiologist from Hopkins. "Within two days, it will be unstoppable."

Another doctor from the University of Washington said, "Right now in Sweden, deaths are mounting, mostly in the unvaccinated, but remember, this is a nation that has rejected basic COVID preventive measures. There are no masks there, no social isolation. Schools are in session. Sweden is like dry tinder for this variant's raging fire. It'll spread fast across the population, decimating the unvaccinated— remember, Howling Wolf, they have no vaccine mandates—and then slaughtering everyone else. It's a global catastrophe, the likes of which this world has ever seen."

"Can we close the borders?" the news wolf asked.

To which CNN's Doctor Gotcha nodded his head. "Howling wolf, all these experts will tell you the same thing, but respiratory viruses cross borders with ease. There is no stopping it once that happens."

Carole and her husband said nothing to each other. A few of Carole's friends called, and they spoke. She spoke with her daughter. She could not peel her face away from the TV. Tears rolled down her cheeks. Mind-numbing fear consumed her entire being. Finally, she said, "What will become of us?"

And her husband, also silently watching, simply said, "I just don't know, Car, I don't know."

At midnight, President Depich appeared on TV for an urgent message. Flanked by Got-milk, the science tiger, the joint chiefs of staff, and the secretary of war, he looked somber and exhausted. What he said both shocked and relieved Carole. "Damn, I hope to hell it works," she said.

That night China and the United States launched several dozen nuclear missiles into Sweden, assuring surgically precise strikes to knock out central population centers. Planes dropped chemical weapons around the nation's perimeter and its hinterland. Within hours, reports confirmed that no one remained alive in the country.

World leaders, doctors, and epidemiologists spoke deep into the night and the next few days. The leaders of Norway—which lost eighteen thousand people to both biological and nuclear drift into its country—confirmed that none of the Swedish variant remained extant. "Our losses are minor," their health commissioner stated, "compared to what may have occurred if the variant hit us. We'll take those losses."

Beneath the gaze of a distracted world, Russian President Peein' launched attacks on Ukraine, Lithuania, and Slovokia, easily taking possession of those nations with few Russian casualties. Neither DUI nor any other reputable news organization carried that story, nor did they report on or show the deaths in Sweden or any of the nations sucked into Peein's growing empire.

Carole rushed to her daughter's house at 2:00 a.m. It was cold and rainy, but she had to go. She could hear her small granddaughter crying, and finally her daughter opened the door. Both of them hugged and cried for quite some time.

"I'll get the shot, Mom," her daughter finally said. "I am sorry for being an ass."

"I'm just glad that we dodged this one, honey," Carole said. "You do what you want about the shot, but I don't want to lose you. I don't ever want to lose you."

A cool calm descended over the globe as Jim sat back in his chair watching Bugs Bunny make a fool of Elmer Fudd yet again. He laughed and sipped iced tea. "I am such a wascally wabbit," he said out loud and slowly fell into a deep sleep, the best one he had had in months.

CHAPTER TWENTY-SEVEN

Putting His Ducks in a Row

Every day, it seemed, two people stood outside of Jim's door, and frankly, Jim was getting sick of them.

"You have choices, Mr. President," Party Cruise said to him about the "two pests" during their morning briefing. "They have their own agendas, and they both don't seem to learn their lessons. After Sweden, Mr. President, you have the power to do what you want. It may be time to clean house."

That's exactly what Jim knew he had to do. Especially after the antics of Mary Lou.

On Rachel in the Meadow, the unhinged student blasted Jim, calling for a day of mourning and retribution.

"We've lost the soul of the revolution, Rach," she said to the sympathetic host. "Look at the president's cabinet, his Supreme Court choices, his advisors. All of them are antithetical to what this revolution is all about. They're not woke, Rachel; in fact, they are dead asleep. They claim that their anti-choice positions on masks and vaccines—which are scientific and necessary and thus are actually pro-life— allows them to be anti-choice when it comes to abortion, sexual orientation, voter reform, environmental reform. How does that make sense? One is a public health measure where choice is frankly dangerous; the other is an attempt to stamp a conservative agenda on women's bodies, on the bodies of those whose sexual orientation veers from theirs. Remember, Rach, these people supported Trump; they were part of what me and my fellow student Truth Club leaders call the Scum Squad. They opposed mask mandates and quarantines until, oh my Jesus, they heard the Lord and suddenly shifted gears. Are they with us, Rach, or are they pretending to support the president just so they can manipulate him? I mean, come on, right?"

"What would you say of President Depich's assertion that until he can neutralize the anti-lifers and anti-democrats, the student demands, and in fact much of the liberal agenda, must hibernate?" Rachel in the Meadow asked. "And if so, aren't any allies good allies, whatever their motives may be?"

Mary Lou stared at the camera. "I say, bullshit," she yelled. "Rachel, we students made this president, and we can take him down just as fast. This revolution is about more than COVID and January sixth. It's mostly about the needs and wants of the oppressed classes, of women, of people, of color, of those with gender fluidity; that's what counts, Rachel, that's what our country is all about. Where's the liberal Supreme Court the president promised us? Where are the laws to protect and empower the disposed and punish the barbarians who aren't woke? Isn't it time we cancel all those with reactionary intent, all those who threaten this land and its people, not just one small sector of them? Isn't that the kind of democracy the president promised to build and that we all demand of him?"

"I suppose, Mary Lou." Rachel in the Meadow smiled. "And you know that I am strongly pro-choice and as liberal as they come, but what of the president's contention that a focus now on what's most important will enable us to move forward with a more progressive agenda later? Until the science deniers and January sixth plotters are neutralized as a threat, how can we move our focus elsewhere?"

"No," Mary Lou stated coldly. "We won't accept that Nazi logic. Misinformation is fluid, it spills across barriers, and we have to stop all of it, not just surgically remove one slice of it so the rest of it can grow even more. We can't wait, and we won't. If we must again resort to violence, if we have to take the lead in silencing the Trumpists and their friends who now seem to be running our government, then we will.

On the day of mourning and retribution, we will take matters into our own hands. This is why, Rachel, you don't let governments change the world. Change comes from below."

Jim paced across the Oval Office as A-O-Crazy marched in, both of them wearing masks that concealed their mutual antagonism. He turned and glared at her. "I want Mary Lou and her student clubs to lie low. No protest on Monday, no day of mourning, no appearances on the news, no violence. We're at a crossroads, Madam Secretary. We are trying to keep this country together before another surge hits us. We don't need dissention in our ranks. Do you understand me?"

She didn't back down a bit. "I understand you, Mr. President, but they are on their own. I don't control them. And frankly, if I may be so blunt, you've crossed a dangerous line by hobnobbing with reactionary elements in the government. I totally agree with everything Mary Lou is saying."

Jim laughed. "Of course, you agree," he said. "I'm sure you're the one who put those words in her mouth. I'll be equally blunt, Ms. Crazy. If that rally happens, if Mary Lou says one more thing to embarrass me, if there is more violence and there's blood on her hands, there will be consequences for you, her, and the whole student movement. You got that?"

"Is that a threat, Mr. President?" she asked.

"Well, duh, it ain't no slap on the back," he said. "Get it done or face the consequences. Period."

The president whistled, and a few armed guards escorted the Secretary of Education out the door, her mouth still moving and spitting out insults barely muffled by her mask.

That night he gathered Newbie-hottie, Party Cruise, Graham Cracker, Corrine, Cheddar, and Gotcha for a small strategy session. He was drinking again, just as much as before. He poured himself at least five drinks during the meeting, offering none to the others. Corrine noticed but said nothing.

"Cheddar," he said to his new press secretary, she having replaced Mumbling Joe, who retired in the face of the Sweden bombings, "I need our media to stop placating Mary Lou and A-O-Crazy. I need you to be firm. We've talked, you and I, and you expressed your own grievances, and I hope I answered your concerns. If not, we can talk later. But to win this war, we can't fight each other. I will use the police and army to shut down the student groups if I must. I want you to say that at the next briefing, after you've made sure that the media will be supportive. If any aren't, I need to know."

"Gotcha." She smiled. "One war at a time. I understand their concerns, Mary Lou's concern and all the students, but I understand too the direction you're taking. I'm behind you, Jim, and the country is too."

"We can't have clashes between the army and the students, Mr. President," said Graham Cracker. "Bad coverage, bad publicity."

Cheddar laughed. "No worries. What the press doesn't cover is invisible to the American public. And just like with Sweden, the press is behind us and will cooperate. No pictures or videos, no sympathetic coverage, minimization of whatever violence is necessary."

"The kids have helped us all along," said Secretary Newbie-hottie. "I think, Jim, their intentions are good. We shouldn't stab the movement, just the culpable leadership, starting with Mary Lou, whose britches are far bigger than her brain. And that's not a fat joke; it's reality."

"Sounds like a fat joke to me." Party Cruise laughed. "And a damned good one. Didn't know you were so funny, hottie. Thought you were too woke to make jokes like that."

"Can we talk about China, Jim?" Corrine interrupted. "Let's lay out the agenda and the choices." She passed out Jim's newest spreadsheet and graphs. Just then, Got-milk dashed in.

"Sorry I'm late, boss," he said, sitting down and slapping Gotcha and Newbie on the back. "Just dealing with some Pfizer shit. I was the boss eons ago, and they still got me on a leash. You don't get all those stock options for nothing, right, boys?"

"Just keep them happy, Milk man," Jim said. "Sit down; we're talking about the China plan."

He continued. "I've been talking to my contacts in China, and especially after Sweden, we collectively believe we have an opportunity to shift the COVID landscape for the mutual betterment of our nations. They're not a democracy, we are, but beyond that detail, we have a tremendous amount in common."

"You mean, them guys are Steelers fans too?" Graham Cracker quipped. "Would never guess it. Not one Asian I ever spotted on that team. They are way too small for football."

Jim laughed. "Who knows; after we start working with them, they may breed their people to be bigger and stronger and dominate the NFL. They have the capacity and will to do it. We have the capacity too, just not the will. And that's the whole point. China has balls, we don't. China has been able to control the virus and its people, we haven't. That's why looking to them is instructive. We have a variant brewing in Korea that we're tentatively calling Zeus, because it's angry and hits like lightning."

"Is it brewing in Korea?" Graham laughed again. "Or being brewed there?"

Jim dodged the question; he wasn't sure if Graham Cracker was making a joke about Koreans' penchant for tea, or if he was insinuating that they created the new variant in Korea. So he moved on, speaking about Zeus, where it has been spotted, how to stop it, and what the administration's response should be. That's when he started talking about the plan he had laid out on his spreadsheet.

"Zeus will keep dissent down, keep people quiet, keep them in line," he said. "It's freaking scary, and we'll have to double down on masks, distancing, closures; all the stuff we've been doing for the past two years. When people are masked, when they're afraid, they tend to be more submissive. And that will give us an opportunity to change course, which is where my China plan comes in. I laid it out on the spreadsheets I gave you all. It's called 'The Bugs Bunny' policy."

They all chuckled, as they knew they must, and Party Cruise put his fingers over his head to simulate a rabbit. "What's up, doc?" he said.

To which Sandman Gotcha said, "Why Bugs Bunny, Jim? We shouldn't make a joke of all this."

"Because," Jim explained, "Bugs always wins by his wits, not by violence. He beats down everyone who tries to stop him or get in his way, and he's the darling of the show. People love him."

And then, referring to the twelve lines of his spreadsheet as "the twelve apostles of Bugs," he explained his China pivot. There would be no more trials, no violence, no mandates. Referring to the first law he had tried to pass before January 6th derailed him, Jim spoke of "the need to speak softly like a cute rabbit and use a small carrot. This was my initial intent; change the world with persuasion, not violence.

January sixth and Delta forced me to shift gears, but now, with the help of our Chinese friends, we'll convince people to do the right thing through technology, not force."

It came down to chips. "Every American will by law have a chip placed under his skin. On the chip will be everything related to COVID—tracking information, exposure data, vaccination records, testing results— as well as other identifying and financial information, from passport and driver's license to all credit cards and banking info to tracking GPS. If you're not vaccinated, we'll know it. If you're at a big party, we'll know it. If you speak with people on our misinformation list, we'll know that too. So, with this chip, we'll be able to discipline people by both tracking their behavior and instituting punishment in the most benign and targeted way."

"Maybe I'm a little slow on the brain," Graham Cracker said. "But punishment? From a chip? What, does it shock your balls if you break the rules?"

"You may be slow in the brain and small in the balls," Gotmilk said. "But in China, they got big balls and big brains, and from what's I've heard, yes, their people are chipped and monitored. Punishment is possible because the chips have your whole life on them. My daughter, a damned millennial, she loves the idea, says it would make things easier. But when your bank account is on there, it's also easy for the government to give you a little jab by sucking money out of that account if you decide to be a vaccine denier or talk with bad folks or break the rules. Discipline and punishment. Quiet and effective. Kind of like the vaccine, right, boys?"

"Yes, exactly," said Jim. "We can use the chip to enforce curfews and quarantines for the noncompliant and unvaccinated by blocking access to credit cards and bank accounts and voiding driver's licenses and passports. That's discipline. Discipline is about observation and normalization. The chip does all that."

"And if people don't want to be chipped?" asked Gotcha.

"We still have openings at our camps in Eastern California," said Newbie-hottie. "They're in the hottest part of the desert, but as you know, they're going to hell anyway, so they better get used to it."

Everyone laughed and applauded Jim's plan. "It's for the safety of our people and our democracy," Jim said to them. "The kids love the idea of chips. Everything in one place. A perfect millennial gift. May even shut up A-O-Crazy and Mary Lou!"

"What's the feasibility of doing this on everyone?" Party Cruise asked. "How long until we have the technology, and how long does the process take?"

"If I may," answered Got-milk. "We've already tested it on hundreds of thousands of people, and it's working well. We can put it in food, medicine, even the water supply. For you, Jim, we'll get Jack Daniels on board. China makes the chips, and they have enough to get going fast. You know those chips you put in your egg drop soup? Well, Graham Cracker, that's not what I'm talking about in terms of chips, but I bet China has them in those too, as well as in the wontons."

"And what does the science tiger say?" Doctor Gotcha asked. "What's his position on all this?"

About that, Jim remained silent.

He met with Fact-nerd earlier in the day, and the two of them, for the very first time, didn't mince words. The tiger had been on the tap dancer's show the night before, boxed in with Mary Lou and A-O-Crazy, talking about Zeus and the day of retribution planned for next Monday. As usual, the tiger said all the right things; millions would die unless society shut down, more boosters were needed, more masks, more distancing, more school closures. "We can't take any chances," he said. "And our friends at the pharmaceutical companies are working tirelessly to get out the right boosters and anti-viral treatments fast and in time. It's like World War II, tap dancer—

industry and government working together for a common cause. We just need our people to listen and do what they're told. Just a few detractors, a few people who won't wear masks or get vaccines, can turn this into a disaster."

Mary Lou and A-O-Crazy chimed in their support. "Me and the other students, in fact my entire generation, we applaud Doctor Fact-nerd and the job he's done, and we'll make sure that people follow the science and don't resort to misinformation and Trumpism. We think you're beast, Doctor Fact-nerd; we've got your picture hanging in our office, and I personally kiss it every day. But let's also be clear; Zeus can't stop everything else we're doing. We have to be vigilant on all fronts."

The tiger nodded and smiled just a bit. "Mary Lou, I think you kids are just fantastic, and everything you're doing, it's OK in my book. Me and the wife, we talk about you all the time, and I got a picture of you too, right in my wallet, to remind me that thank God, our kids, your generation, you're A-OK."

The tap dancer laughed. A-O-Crazy then said, "I'll tell you, tap dancer, if it were up to the kids, Doctor Fact-nerd would be in the White Housenstead of its current occupant. He's been our national savior in this. A saint."

The tiger bowed. "Thank you, Congresswoman. I couldn't do it without your support."

It was all too much for Jim, and he called the tigerto the Oval Office first thing the next morning.

"You stay in your lane, Fact-nerd, you got it?" Jim yelled. "That's your last appearance on TV talking about shit that doesn't concern you. Stick to the virus. You aren't running the show, cat man; you're working for me, and when I tell you to do something, you do it. Got it?"

The tiger, who usually sat dutifully in his chair and listened to Jim quietly, typically responding, "Yes, Mr. President, I agree," took on a different tone, one more reminiscent of his outburst during Sweden. He stood up and walked up to Jim, hands on his hips.

"I think you need a little lesson, Jim," the tiger growled back. "I'm in charge of everything related to this virus. Every dollar spent goes through me. Every genius doctor on TV is mine; I own them, and I own DUI too, if you haven't figured that out. And that's just the surface, Jim. I got people I work with who can tear you down faster than a poster on a subway wall. People with more power and money than this whole damned country. You think you're the boss? Well, you ain't. So, it's you who better get in line."

Jim laughed and stared into the tiger's eyes. They were on fire! He had never seen that before. "Tiger, yes, you are the virus; the virus is you. I get that. That's why you better damned be careful. Anything goes south, and it's on your head. And, my feline friend, just to repeat the news I already told you about, I have more dirt on you than there is in the whole New York subway system. You can take down the posters, but you can't clean up all the dirt. And I'm not blaming you, my friend. I'm not judging you, but I'm guessing that your pals on DUI and your student fan club won't be as forgiving about your real politic approach to science as I am. By my calculations, your treatment decisions, your policies of shutdowns, your phony claims have likely cost ten million lives. Hitler would be envious of how efficiently you kill people under the veil of science and humanism. Bravo, tiger, bravo. But it's you who better get in line, because your little game isn't quite as safely tucked away as you may think."

The tiger glared back at him, his eyes burning above an N-95, his glasses starting to fog. "What you don't understand, Jim, is just how puny you are. I don't like to be pushed, Jim, and my people don't either. And just so you know, Americans aren't too fond of conspiracy theorists, and you're starting to sound like one. In fact, unless I'm mistaken, you're the one who has been knocking off anyone whose breath reeks of conspiracy ideas. So watch your back, Mr. President, and stay off my case. Nothing you said, none of your Hitler bullshit, or your accusations that I am a murder, will put you in good stead with my fan base which, if you don't know already, is the whole fucking world. I save lives, Jim, and you kill people, so let's get that straight. Zeus is out there, and I'll control what comes next. You have questions, come to me. You need to talk to pharma, to academia, to the media, come to me. You want student support, liberal support, the support of every sitting governor in this country, you better talk to me. I'll be on DUItonight andI'll tell my pal tap dancer whatever the hell I want to tell him, and he'll buy it faster than he buys fucking eggs at the supermarket. I hope you understand, Mr. President."

And with that, he twisted and left the room.

Jim fumed. He didn't even pick up a cup to pour himself a drink. He just sucked the bottle clear. Two pests; that's what Ted Cruz called them—two pests that needed to be exterminated.

Jim had read what Mr. X wrote about Fact-nerd two dozen times. Was it true? Could this dirty tiger squish Jim faster than Jim could squish the tiger ? Should he leave the little guy alone? Certainly, the students and media loved the old doctor, and likely they would react just as Fact-nerd said they would: They'd label Jim a conspiracy nut, a guy with a vendetta, if he spilled the contents of Mr. X's files on the air. And what of Crazy and Mary Lou? So many fires fluttering around, with Sweden gone and Zeus arriving, Jim paced, thinking, thinking. He graphed out his choices, and he grappled with the implications of everything. He made more spreadsheets. He looked for the truth.

And then finally he sat. "I will put my ducks in a row, and I will knock them off one by one," he said to himself. "It is duck season, after all. And when it's duck season, you got to hunt ducks. Especially if Bugs is your guy."

China had his back. All his advisors were on board. Corrine agreed it was the right thing to do. He needed new student leaders and a new direction, no clashes, no dissent. The chip program would allow him to curtail trails and open the country a bit.

But for all that to happen, he had to dispense with the ducks, with the tiger, with Mary Lou, and with A-O-Crazy. And as a wascally wabbit, one wily and smart, one beloved and admired, Jim had no doubt that he could get it done. He grabbed another bottle and poured it down fast.

CHAPTER TWENTY-EIGHT

A Tiger's Choice

On a warm spring morning, days after he convinced Mary Lou to cancel her day of retribution by promising her a rally for choice instead (choice, that is, about sexual orientation and a woman's body, not right-wing calls for choice about masks and vaccines, which Mary Lou knew to be wrong choices), Jim met with two of his most trusted advisors: top COVID expert Got-Milk and his Secretary of Commerce, Gated Billionaire. He didn't need either of their approval for what he planned to do, but he knew that both were deeply embedded in the tiger's world and thus their opinions mattered. Especially Gated Billionaire, who usually seemed meek and obsequious, always ready to help, but whose career and whose role in Mr. X's papers made him seem like a player on the world stage deeply imbedded in the tiger's Bond-like villainy.

"I like the tiger; I like him a lot," said Got-milk in his jovial way. "We've done a lot together. We showed how industry and academia and federal agencies can get things done to enrich the world and enrich us and others too! Profit and purpose I always say; that's the engine that makes our country great. And the tiger, he always siphoned the money where it got the most bang for the buck, and he had a lot of money to dole out, so you better keep the guy on your good side, which I did. Yea, he's getting old, and he's been working so hard these past few years. Maybe it is time for him to sing his swan song. To be honest, Mr. President, at our COVID meetings, he barely has much to say, and I do think that others are controlling the purse strings these days; he's not who he once was."

The Gated Billionaire was even more dismissive and unconcerned. "The tiger and I have been working together for thirty years, Jim," he said. "He helped me to find a purpose for my money, a way to spend it to help people. You know what we did in Africa, how we've shaped the WHO, everything with AIDS and now COVID. He has been a gem. I have a great idea, I mean, if you're settled on his leaving."

"What would you do?" he asked the mild-mannered sweater-vested trillionaire. "If you were president, how would you handle our very sensitive tiger?"

Gated Billionaire hardly needed a moment to think. "Give the guy what he deserves," he said, with a big, genuine smile across his boyish face. "Look, Jim, I know that people loved him and thanked him all the time, but the tiger was hurt by those who tried to pin him as a fiend, especially guys like Ranting Paul and Ken-and-Barbie, even some of the Stanford guys, and I know they're not with us anymore, but I think giving the tiger some real recognition, that would be a good way to move the baton. I was thinking a holiday in his name, a science holiday at that, get his science books in every school—they are real inspiration to the kids—and pictures of him in every science class, some statues. He always wanted to be portrayed as a Roman Emperor." the Gated Billionaire laughed. "You know, with a laurel and toga. He was a good Italian, and wants to be known as wise and good, kind of like Marcus Aurelius or Augustus. That could be a nice touch!"

Was he joking, Jim wondered, or did he think that's what the tiger wanted? What mattered most is that the Gated Billionaire was OK to set the tiger free. In fact, he barely even scoffed at the idea. Just make a holiday and build a statue and, poof, the great Doctor Fact-nerd isn't even worth keeping around.

Jim thought about sitting on it. Why not let the guy hang around? Both Got-milk and Gated Billionaire believed him to be innocuous, someone more inclined to want some praise than someone who craved more power.

But events moved quickly, and they would not allow Jim that type of latitude.

First came clashes on several campuses between student groups and soldiers. The Truth Club members, who now numbered around 250,000 strong across the nation's colleges, including graduates and young adults in their ranks, wore self-contained breathing suits with a space helmet and bulletproof green uniform as they trounced around college greens and surrounding towns, looking for any people who defied mask laws or who were found to be uttering "bad words."

"We're basically sticking to the COVID and January sixth agenda," Mary Lou told Mumbling Joe one day in the spring. "With Zeus coming, we have to make sure that everyone is on board. We don't want a repeat of Omicron, where compliance alone would have reduced death. We're all superpsyched for the new booster coming out next week, and we'll help to spread the word on that. And too, we're making sure to hype up the new chip, which we're also really psyched about. Imagine what we can do, Joe, with a chip that can do everything for us? No need to carry cards or wallets. Even phones may be a thing of the past, automatic GPS, so much more. Who wouldn't want that? We view it among our responsibilities to assure total compliance with the chip program, and to squelch anyone who complains. Again, Joe, this is not just a really cool convenience, which it is for sure, but also it's for national safety; we have to remember that."

At the University of Michigan and Vanderbilt, suited student groups clashed with some soldiers stationed in town to help administer vaccines. As Mary Lou reported it, many soldiers mocked the chips, and some wore their masks below their noses. "If they aren't an example of scientific stewardship, then who will be?" she asked, justifying the skirmishes that occurred on both campuses.

In both instances, a few soldiers shot into a crowd of student leaders who were calling for an end to military intervention at colleges. *We are woke, they are jokes* read a sign in Nashville, where students called for all soldiers to "vamoose" and allow truth squads to run the show. "We're dressed and ready for business," said the

Vanderbilt leader. "The military thugs are more ready to invade a foreign country than to confront the biologic and anti-democratic threat we're facing domestically. In fact, watching them, I have to wonder how many of them are really on our side."

Some words were exchanged, bullets fired, and when it was over, three students and twelve soldiers lay dead or dying. Jim got on DUI to demand a cessation of all hostilities. "We're on the same damned side," he cried out to the camera. "Keep yourselves contained. I will be launching an investigation into the actions of the students at these two colleges. Heads will roll. There is no excuse for this juvenile behavior. Zeus is about to hit us, and for some reason, we want to kill each other before we can even stop the murderous virus from doing it to us?"

He met with the joint chiefs and begged them to keep their people away from the students. "I promise you," he said. "I'm on top of that problem. They have heads that have grown so large that they don't even fit in their damned space helmets. It's a delicate situation, but we're on top of it; we just need about a month of patience."

But then the tiger pounced again, this time on two fronts.

He appeared on DUI talking about Zeus. "This is a triple mask threat, tap dancer, as I've told you people before," he said in his usual erudite way, flanked by several doctors from Hopkins, Harvard, and the University of Washington. "Zeus is like a lightning bolt; it can slip by an N-95 and even a surgical mask, but the two of them together, plus a cloth mask to slow it down before entry, that's how we've scientifically determined to stop its penetration. Any less protection will not only expose the individual to infection but also will make him a carrier to spread the variant to potentially thousands of people. And, of course, the booster is now out; we've had to make a few recent changes to it that our good friends at Bristol-Myers helped us with, and we think it will be the second line of defense against Zeus."

"And, of course, Doctor Fact-nerd, I should remind people about twenty-second hand washing, six-foot social distancing at all times, and limits to any activity outside the home. Am I right, sir?"

"I'll let the doctors you've brought on tell us some of those details, tap dancer, but for one thing, as you'll hear from the experts from the University of Washington, their data suggests that we need at least twenty-eight seconds of hand washing for Zeus and six-and-a-half-feet separation. We're trying to stay on top of the science."

"Well, that's good advice, Doctor Fact-nerd, and I hope all Americans are listening," the tap dancer said, staring sternly at the camera. "I know that the president has made triple masking and the booster mandatory for all Americans, and he is closing schools and businesses for at least a month. We also have our student groups assuring compliance all over the country. Can you comment on that?"

The tiger hid behind his three masks, but his eyes remained focused and firm. "You knowthat I love those kids. If I were young again, I'd be out there doing what they're doing, saving our nation from peril, practicing the best that science has to offer. And if I may, just to chime in about the recent clashes on a few campuses, what I heard was very disturbing. Some of those soldiers, they were wearing masks improperly, sometimes only one mask; they were very close together. Look, the students can be tightly packed, they have special protection, but those soldiers were practicing very dangerous behavior, and I am glad the students spoke up and did something. We can't have that dangerous behavior, not when the danger is so imminent and serious. We have to all be vigilant, and I don't care what your job is; you got to do it."

Jim was furious about that, especially when the tap dancer agreed with Doctor Fact-nerd, as he always did.

But then Jim received a call from his China liaisons, and what they told him was even more disturbing.

"He changed the variant," one of the Wuhan party members explained to Jim. "We had Zeus all set to go; we tinkered with it and released it in Korea. But, President Depich, your Doctor Fact-nerd went in and overrode my people. He changed the composition of this variant; he made it more lethal and a bit less infectious. He said we need more people dying from it so that they take this seriously. But what concerns us, and why his tinkering is dangerous, relates to another matter entirely."

First of all, this all was news to Jim, almost like an electric jolt stronger than Zeus itself. What did he mean that this new variant was manufactured in the lab? It wasn't natural? That reeked of the conspiratorial fodder that cluttered Mr. X's diatribes. Did Jim dare ask these Chinese scientific leaders if that were true? He didn't want to embarrass them or him. But what they said next made the question moot.

"We had designed it specifically so that our booster vaccine being manufactured by Roache in a partnership between their plants in the United States, Australia, and China would be effective against it.

We'd have the vaccine ready before the virus even hit ground. But when your very naughty and arrogant tiger changed the design, he also made our vaccine inert. Apparently, he has interests in a new Bristol-Myers booster, a booster he owns the patent to and that several of his PIs and company guys have big stock options in. And the new Zeus that he created, surprise, surprise, it's only susceptible to his booster. President Depich, a lot of what we are doing here is carefully crafted policy designed to keep people in line and certain leaders and businessmen happy. When a renegade scientist interferes with our own dictates on our own soil, I don't care who he is or how much power he claims to exert. His actions are unacceptable to us."

As they were to Jim, although he had to swallow a few glasses of Jack Daniel's to get past what he heard about Zeus. *Was this all about profit? How many have to perish before we end this charade?* His mind started to wander; gnawing doubts crept to the surface of his gut, and he drank that much more. Eventually a certain calm overtook him. As long as China remained in charge of the process, as long as they silenced any dissent and monitored those in the know while truncating the spread of any "misinformation," then how could this backfire? In the end, with their chips and their protocols, China would make sure nothing incriminating slipped out of their labs.

And yet, Mr. X knew everything. How? And if he did, then who else might know? And if the alternative truth—misinformation—ever planted roots, how would it impact Jim's reputation? *China has it covered*, he assured himself, drinking much more than usual. His stomach burned, so he swallowed a few Prilosec. He knew he was losing weight and energy. "Alcohol has calories," he admonished Corrine when she pointed to his gaunt body. "I must just be pacing too much. I'll be better, I promise!"

He called her in later that day to talk about the tiger problem.

"The students are going to be angry, Jim," she said, starting to pace around as well. She eyed Jim's bottle of scotch. Corrine had never consumed much alcohol before, no more than a casual glass of wine or beer, but now she craved it. She had been drunk twice in the last week, hanging out at a bar somewhere in East Washington all alone. On one occasion, she was so rowdy that a few guys tried to pick her up before the bartender kicked her and them out. Good thing, because one of the guys was hot and Corrine—never the looker or lookee, as her friends said to her—was ready to take him home, where Mark and the kids would have been waiting. In another week, she would learn that she was pregnant again, although she and Mark had been abstinent for over a month. And the news got in the way of her new smoking habit—just a few a day at first, then more than a pack a day, then two, sometimes three— a habit she had never even contemplated until last month when she took a puff of one during one of her drunken states. And she liked it, liked it a lot! She bought a pack of the high-tar Marlboro and loved the first cigarette in every pack more than anything. Sometimes she'd just smoke one or two in a pack and then give the rest away to a homeless person before buying another pack. She was a generous gal!

"In fact," she continued, "if you take down the tiger, you'll piss off a lot of loyal supporters. Doctor Fact-nerd is our guy, Jim. He's my hero. He's the one who made me realize just how crucial this COVID battle is."

"Well," Jim snickered, pouring himself a large glass of Jack Daniel's as Corrine voraciously looked on, "you should pick your heroes more carefully, my dear."

"You're my other hero, as you well know." She smiled.

"Like I said, you should pick your heroes more carefully." He poured another. "If I don't put him in his place, bigger players than some snotty students and sycophantic liberals will have something to say to me. I'll make it as clean as possible. I've already gotten tacit approval from Got-milk and Gated Billionaire, and I know Party Cruise and Graham Cracker hate him. I just have to make it look good. He's a funny guy. Very sweet on the surface, but really, Corrine,

I think he's one of the great assholes in history. I'm not too upset about this one. He's old anyway. It's not like he's going to live forever."

"Still, Jim, he's an icon. Just be careful. The students, Mary Lou, A-O-Crazy, they're getting a little unruly. I don't want them turning on you. You know." She smiled. "It's funny what happened to us."

"What's that, Cor?" he asked her. "What's funny?"

She peeked at the bottle again. She knew she'd have to rush out of here directly to a bar, one that allowed smoking, something not common in the nation's capital, where safety and health had become the watchwords of the land, even as the bars were now always full, and smokers seemed to be everywhere at once. *The good thing about smoking a lot*—she had said to a guy outside of the gym where she worked out, someone she smoked with between sets—*is that you don't have to wear a mask when you're puffing away. And masks are such bullshit. Believe me, I know! Kind of funny, huh? Somehow smoking is healthier than a mask. Go figure!* Of course, she was drunk when she said it, but it was the truth. She lit three dozen that day.

She thought about having one now, right here, right in front of Jim. She wondered what he would say if she lit a cigarette and poured a bottle of his gin. Maybe he'd take her home and they'd finally do what everyone assumed they were doing anyway. The more she drank, the hotter Jim looked. Especially the goatee. She always wanted to tell him how good it looked. She stared at him with glassy eyes.

"Corrine, you look dazed," he said to her. "What's funny? You said something is funny."

"Oh," she said, snapping out of it. "Well, just this. Here we got everything we wanted, we got the power, we got the support, we got rid of all the bad guys, and we totally cleaned house. But what's funny is that it's just getting harder. Just getting more complicated. Like, all the spreadsheets, they don't seem to work anymore. Nothing fits. It's like all just chaos. And, Jim, I don't think it'll get easier. You sack the tiger. Then what about Mary Lou? And if you get rid of her, what about A-O-Crazy? And then if she's gone, where's our base? Are we stuck with the Republican assholes? And Newbie-hottie. I mean, that guy is gross. So fake. Not like you. You're the real deal, Jim, a real man."

Jim laughed. "Yea," he said, glossing over most of what she said. "Life ain't a spreadsheet, Cor. That's kind of what I'm figuring out. Life is a Looney Tune. It's cartoonish madness. Want to go get a drink tonight, Cor? I know you have to get home to your kids and all, but Mark won't mind."

"Yea right." She smiled, weaseling out of his invitation so she could get really drunk with a bunch on anonymous malcontents at one of her dives. "Him and the kids, they're always waiting for me. I have a cartoonishly happy life, Jim, so joyous and happy. I couldn't have scripted it better."

"*Looney Tunes*," he said to her again.

"Yep." She smiled. "*Looney Tunes*. And I'm Porky Pig. Th-th-th-th, that's all folks." She skipped out.

Jim phoned the tiger, told him it was urgent. The tiger was slated to appear on DUI tonight to talk about Zeus, and, of course, he had to catch his court TV shows first. But he agreed to come. He trotted in very cocky, sitting down and crossing his legs. He looked up at Jim. "I don't have much time, Mr. President."

"I know." Jim laughed. "Not much time at all. So, my favorite tiger, how are you?"

"Couldn't be better, Jim," the doctor said sincerely. "I kind of love this stuff. Especially a good surge!"

"Well, doc, I hate to be the one to tell you this, but it's not very likely you'll get through this surge," Jim said. "I know you are quadrupled vaccinated and like to wear a bunch of masks, but I'm afraid, tiger, it's not going to be enough protection this time. I think you may have hit the end of the road, my friend."

The tiger looked at him and laughed. "Please, Jim, I'm not that afraid of Zeus. It's like a glorified flu bug. Don't tell the tap dancer; he's looking forward a gut-wretching disaster. Like with Omicron, we're counting all deaths as COVID deaths. We'll do the same with Zeus. The masks are for show. And no, I didn't get any of the vaccines. I'm not suicidal."

Wow, Jim thought, this guy was just letting it all out; he believed he held so much power that he could say anything, even though the room was bugged and so too was he. What game was this tiger playing? "You may actually be suicidal, my friend," Jim said. "Actually, it may be your best way out. I'm afraid you're going to have to make a choice right now. I have a pill you can take, and you'll be dead in a matter of five minutes. It'll look like you had a heart attack. Everyone will sing your praises, even Foxxy most likely; they'll adulate you and make you a hero. We already have a Science Tiger Day planned as a national holiday. We'll have pictures and statues in every school. Your science book will be required reading. And I've already commissioned an artist to create a fifty-foot statue of you on the mall, with the toga and laurel-leaf crown like you want. It will be spectacular, Doctor Fact-nerd, I guarantee it."

"Yea, that ain't happening." the tiger laughed. "Is that all you have to say, Jim?"

Jim handed him a letter. The Gated Billionaire wrote it and told Jim not to open it. *Just give it to the tiger; he'll get the message fast.* As the tiger read it, Jim spoke more. "We haven't had a committee meeting in over a month, but if you don't want to take the pill, that's what we'll have to do, doc. I have all that dirt on you, and I hate to use it, but you know, sometimes guys like me have to sweep guys like you under the rug when you get too dirty. You know, just business, that's all. And, tiger, I hate to say it like this, but you have five minutes to make a decision. I have a meeting soon, and I don't want to be late."

The tiger's face turned bright red as he read the letter, and tears rolled down his cheeks. He was almost deaf to Jim's words. "Can I say goodbye to my wife, and maid, maybe my kids? Even a phone call, Jim."

Jim shook his head from side to side. "You'll see them in hell, doc, if they end up there. I know that's where I'll be seeing you. I'm looking forward to it."

"Yea," the tiger said. "Should be great fun. Most of my friends will be there too, I suppose. One more question, Jim. My holiday. Will it be on Christmas Eve?"

"Of course." Jim smiled. "That's your birthday! We figured everyone would want a two-day holiday. It's like the birthdays of our two messiahs, the god of science and the god of faith. All the kids will love it."

The tiger smiled and asked Jim for the pill.

Across town, Corrine went to the bar she liked the best, a bit of a seedy crowd there, but they had a ton of stouts, and that's what she enjoyed drinking. Sometimes in the summer, the stouts gave way to lighter beers, but for Corrine, it was a stout or nothing, which is what brought her here. The oatmeal vanilla tasted like cake and had 11 percent alcohol. There were always a few like that, and she typically downed at least a half dozen before heading home. On warm days like this, she sat outside and snuck some smokes when the waiter went inside. She could finish a cigarette in five puffs; she sucked in deep and blew out long, narrow streams of smoke that often impressed the guys near her. Once she took a selfie of herself doing it and was rather enamored by her skills. She shared her smokes with some of the others too, usually just guys, which would tempt them to sit by her. When the waiter came, they'd hide the cigarettes under the table like little kids and giggle.

"OK," sometimes the waiter would say, "I can smell what you're doing. You know the law. And you're supposed to wear masks too, even out here. Sorry."

"Want one?" Corrine asked him, shoving her pack of Marlboros his way. When he declined, she smirked. "What are you, a geek or something? And by the way, you don't have to wear masks when you smoke, even when you're not allowed to smoke. Crazy but true! And I should know. I helped write the law. We don't want our new health priorities to get in the way of someone's right to smoke."

She liked her new life. She was out flirting with a few new guys when she heard someone yelling from inside the bar. "Hurry, hurry, get in here," a hoarse woman screamed.

A lit cigarette in her hand, she rushed in, staring at the TV. She would smoke a half of the pack before anyone even noticed. Everyone in the bar was too mesmerized to care. She was quite drunk at the time, but when she actually witnessed what she already knew to be inevitable, she started balling, as did many of the others around her.

"Again," said the News Wolf, "breaking news, and horribly sad news for the nation and the world. Doctor Fact-nerd, the brilliant doctor and scientist who led the nation through both the AIDS and

COVID crises, and who has run the National Institute of Allergy and Immunology for the past half a century, is dead at age eighty-one. He had a heart attack while meeting with the president, and despite the president giving him immediate CPR and having him rushed to the hospital, he was pronounced dead upon arrival. There are not enough words to describe the impact this man had on our world. We'll have the entire DUI crew with us all night and for many days to discuss it. Sad, sad news indeed."

"Hey," the bartender finally said to Corrine. "You know you can't smoke here."

She looked up at him and gave him the finger. Then she tossed the rest of her pack at him and walked out the door. She wandered through the streets, both dizzy and dazed. It was windy and getting a bit chilly. She reeked of tobacco and alcohol and wondered if she should get some mints before walking in her front door. When she reached her Adams Morgan flat, she noticed that Mark's car wasn't there. Maybe he took the kids back to Pittsburgh. Frankly, she couldn't remember.

She scampered up the steps, digging in her pocket for another pack of cigarettes, but then realized she had forgotten to buy one. "Fuck that," she said and gave her pocket the middle finger.

"Mark," she called out, opening the door. "Kids. I'm home. You here?" She knew that they weren't.

From the corner of the room, a man emerged from the darkness and startled her. Through her glassy eyes, she looked up at him. "Mark?" she asked.

The man turned on the lights. He was bald and was smiling. "No, Corrine, Mark's not here. I told him and the kids to leave for a bit. Don't worry; they're OK. I really want to talk just to you."

She squinted just enough to make out the man's face. "Fuck," she said again.

It was Mr. X.

CHAPTER TWENTY-NINE

Kate's Boomerang

In every single *Road Runner Show*, Wile Coyote concocts the most clever and sophisticated ACME tricks to finally get the pesky bird, and every single time his tactics backfire. Whether launching a missile or dropping a rock or sneaking poison into the Road Runner's food, within minutes the missile or rock or food boomerangs back and hits Wile.

"Boomerang!" Jim always yelled at that penultimate moment. "Happens every damned time!"

As it would too to Jim.

Zeus hit the nation hard, deaths mounted. DUI riled against the unimmunized, although Jim knew that they were no more likely to die than anyone else. Like every other COVID strain, this one preyed on the old and frail, the very people that his COVID policies didn't protect, that vaccines and lockdowns always failed, that masks seemed to invite in. But DUI and the COVID committee kept to their script, focusing on the few young anti-vaxxers struck down by Zeus, on the hordes of the worried-well who saturated hospitals in what Cheddar called the "Anti-vax hospital catastrophe." Every death was counted as COVID-induced; the Fact-nerd blueprint didn't evaporate just because its architect lay six feet under. *I guess we should have buried him six and a half feet under since that's the new protocol with Zeus*, Jim thought to himself with a chuckle. Die of a car accident, Zeus. Die of a heart attack, Zeus. Go the hospital for a sore throat and a gut full of fear, Zeus. Didn't matter. Deaths and cases escalated. The nation shut down. People recoiled in fear, awaiting guidance and hope from their fearless leaders, as the absence of their icon made them tremble and wonder if the end of days had come.

"It's amazing," said the News Wolf, with Got-milk and the usual panel of tiger-adoring academics boxed around him. "This is the first crisis most of us faced without the leadership of the great Doctor Fact-nerd. It is mind-boggling to contemplate. Milk, what do you think?"

"I think, well," the former FDA and Pfizer chief—and new face of scientific acumen and expertise—said solemnly, "Doctor Fact-nerd has left his mark on all of us. Now it's our responsibility to execute what he taught us and to save the American people from this most urgent threat."

"Ha!" Jim yelled at the TV, more drunk than ever. "Way to go, Milk-man-nerd-jerk. 'Execute' is the perfect word! That's just what we're doing. And that's what the poor dead tiger did. Execute people. Make some money. Play hero. So glad I got a front-row seat to the Greek tragedy. Corrine! Corrine! Get in here now! Now!"

Corrine was nowhere to be seen. So, Jim paced. He talked to himself. "It's kind of weird that Representative Crazy is dangling from the Capitol this morning. I don't remember telling anyone to do that. Corrine, can you ask Party Cruise if he did it? And make sure the students are OK with it."

Corrine, of course, didn't answer. She had been with Jim this morning, fiddling with her pack of Marlboros in her sweatshirt pocket, listening to his diatribe, craving a deep drag.

"They were right, you know." Jim laughed, speaking quickly, almost frantically as he dug holes in the Oval Office floor with his incessant pacing. "The Stanford Three. Ken-and-Barbie. That Douche-bag guy. All of them. Kate and her friends. Poor Kate. She was one of the good ones, Corrine. She really cared. And so fucking beautiful! Man, her hair! Did you ever drape your hands in her hair, Corrine? Did you?"

Corrine sighed as Jim poured another cup. "I can't say I did, sir," she whispered. "Jim, you can't dwell on the past. You can't dig up other truths and say they now have some legitimacy. You do know what that implies if all of them were right, don't you? We've been through this before, Jim."

Jim stopped for a moment. He peered into Corrine's eyes. "Do you think Kate was into me, Cor?"

So pitiful, Corrine thought. Every flicker of trepidation and guilt that plagued her evaporated. This was no longer Jim. No longer Bugs. All she could see was Elmer Fudd. Wile E. Coyote. A pitiful slug.

"Jim," she said solemnly, knowing well that this could be their final conversation, "things are moving fast, and we have to grab some control. We have to focus. Stick to our spreadsheets, not to anything that veers from the tabulations we and every expert in this country know to be true."

"You mean every expert still alive, right, Cor?" He chuckled. "I knocked off everyone else. All the good ones. And still, they attack me, right from their graves. And all the ones who made me do it, who prompted me, they're attacking me too! Those damned students keep getting under my skin. Did I tell you to hang A-O-Crazy from the Capitol? I just don't remember doing that. It's probably a good idea, you know. Do you think it is? Once we start erasing stuff from the facts list, why not erase people too, right, Cor? I'm thinking that if we kill everyone other than me and you, and maybe your kids, then maybe, just maybe, we'll finally get the order and peace and certainty that we crave. What do you think, Cor?"

"Sober up, Jim," she said, pulling a cigarette out of her pack as she meandered out the door. "This is about more than just you. It's about our country and all the suckers you tied to your leash as you led us through your fucking door. Sober up and think about it, Jim. There's one truth. Don't forget that."

"Corrine?" he called to her as her footsteps faded. "Oh fuck it, who needs her? Kate, Kate, get in here. Come on in and climb up, mount Jimbo! I'll make a deal with you, babe. You get down and dirty with me, and I'll tell the nation the truth about COVID, tell them all the bullshit and let them know that it's time to march away. What do you think? Let's be like Bugs and fuck them all."

Turned out that, in a bizarre way, Kate and Corrine were planning to have a two-on-one date with Jim in just a few hours. Mary Lou would be there as well. The whole country was poised to watch it. It was all part of a script revision written by none other than Mr. X himself. And it would be spectacular!

"I want A-O-Crazy dispensed with," Mr. X told Corrine. "Party Cruise will do it for me; just tell him. He's my favorite kind of scum; you can always count on that ass. Then give Mary Lou the tape. They're waiting for it at Much-Better-NBC. We'll keep you out of it, dear. The drama will all play out around you, if you play your part."

"How did you get out of Guantanamo?" she asked him last night, still quite drunk. "Who are you? Who are you working for? Don't hurt Mark or the kids. Promise me. And Jim. Don't hurt Jim."

"Corrine, please, I'm not a monster." He smiled. "I'm one of the good guys. You play ball with me, and your family won't only just be OK; they'll be wonderful. I promise. Although you keep smoking and drinking like that, you may not be alive long enough to see your oldest graduate from kindergarten."

"And Jim?" she asked, walked to him, peering into his levitous eyes. "What about Jim?"

"Some things," he said. "Some things you just shouldn't ask me about."

All day breaking news shot across cable news: Who killed A-O-Crazy? Were other rogue nations and states harboring anti-life and anti-democratic criminals? Hospitals are overloaded with Zeus as deaths mount. More closings, thicker masks, enhanced social distancing. The president planned to declare an augmented state of emergency, suspending the entire Constitution.

"Really?" Jim laughed, from the floor of his room in the White House. "I never said that."

Corrine had given Mary Lou Mr. X's tape earlier in the day. "Shocking," Mary Lou said to her when she listened to it. "Disgusting. How can you work for this unwoke version of a Nazi?"

Corrine shrugged and lit a cigarette. "It's been a good gig. Can't beat the benefits!"

In the end, Jim's hold on power collapsed quickly, struck by the boomerang of his own words. Kate, after enduring so much, had her final say later that night on the *Rachel in the Meadow Show*.

"Here's the thing, Rach," Mary Lou said. "This president is a lying hypocrite. He's not even true to his own rhetoric. We've smelled it for a long time, Rach. Look at his cabinet choices, his advisors. Look at his behavior. Is any of this a surprise? You know what I learned, Rach? That man, our president, sits down all day and watches *Looney Tunes*. I wasn't very privy to that old cartoon— you may be, since you're so much older—but there's not a more sexist, racist, and homophobic show that has ever been on TV. Have you seen it, Rach? It's a show Hitler probably liked. It's a show that should be canceled from our collective memories. And our president watches it. Can you even imagine?"

"After that tape, Mary Lou, there's very little I can't imagine," a somber Rachel in the Meadow said.

She played it again. Jim watched on TV, more feeling aroused than frightened. Hearing Kate's voice only made him start balling and calling for her. He could taste her breath, feel her touch.

During the night that Kate had pretended to seduce him, and then rendered him unconscious so he could be taken to Mr. X, and unbeknownst to him or her, a tape recorder in Kate's apartment captured every one of his words. Jim could be heard making homophobic slurs, sexist innuendos, sexual advances. He sounded both juvenile and ridiculous.

"Do you think he was drunk?" the Meadow asked Mary Lou. "Maybe he was—"

Mary Lou cut her off. "Drunk, Rachel? Now we excuse bad words and bad behavior because someone is drunk? That's sexual assault 101, Rach. I don't care if you're drunk, Rachel. If you assault someone, if you use inappropriate words, you're guilty of the crime you commit and the trash that comes out of your vile mouth. Who knows what this man will say about people of color if he drinks a little more? And he's not drunk, Rachel. His words are clear. His thoughts are clear. He's not woke. He's anti-woke. He's anti-truth. He has been fooling us for far too long. It's time he goes down."

"How?" Rachel in the Meadow asked. "He's president, Mary Lou, and there are rules. You can't just take him down. It's a ludicrous statement, as much as I agree that something has to be done."

"Rach," she said as a smile crept on her face, "there's no Constitution anymore. It's been hijacked by our president and his entourage of hate. The army and police, they'll do what we say. We students made Jim Depich into the man he is. And it's our responsibility to have him join his friends on the Capitol before any more damage can be done. We made him, and we'll break him. I think the entire nation will breathe a collective breath of relief when we do. I've spoken to people in power. They are letting us in the front door of the White House. This, Rachel, will be the trial of the century."

"You heard it all," sang the tap dancer from his podium on DUI. "The trial of the century. And we'll be covering every minute of it here on DUI. Let's bring in our experts to discuss the inflammatory situation that is escalating faster than even Zeus. Maybe we'll call it Poseidon; that would be apropos!"

All the expert panelists laughed at the tap dancer's very timely and erudite joke.

Jim laughed too. He lifted his Jack Daniel's and tossed the bottle at the wall, shattering it. He picked up his phone and called for security to come in immediately. No one answered. Footsteps pattered about outside; something was happening. He locked his bedroom door, as though that could stop events from swarming upon him. Frantic, as one panelist after another—the chairmen of the joint chiefs, the head of Homeland Security, student leaders, scientific experts—derided him on his once-favorite news channel, he thought about leaping out the window, or dressing up like a woman and slipping out. Bugs always got away with that trick!

He called Corrine. She didn't answer, but her sweet voice told him to leave a message.

"Cor, it's Jim," he said. "Look, I'm dressing in drag; there's some makeup here from who knows, maybe Star Buck, who the hell knows, and there's a dress too, so I'll meet you down by National's

Stadium in about an hour. My phones are down, so I need a favor. Call the army and tell them to kill Mary Lou and all the student leaders. Kill tap dancer and that bitch from the meadow too. Don't hurt Cheddar, though. I'm still thinking she may have the hots for me, and I have a chance with her. What do you think? I don't want Kate to know. Don't tell Kate. OK, I'll be there in like an hour. Love you, Cor. You are my savior always. Let's keep up our fight for truth and science. We're the A team, you and me. OK, Jim signing off. President Depich, I mean. Can you imagine, Cor? We accomplished so much! President Depich. It is amazing!"

Just then, the door burst open, and twelve guards swarmed in. Jim dropped the phone and tried to barrel past them. A few grabbed his arms, but he slipped by through. He slid to the back of the room. One of the guards pulled out a gun. Jim told him to cease and desist. Then, looking around, he eyed the window. With every bit of drunken strength he could muster, Jim leaped through, severing his carotid artery in the process. Before he even landed on the grass outside, Jim Depich was dead.

His last words, captured on Corrine's phone voice mail, were "Truth will prevail."

Corrine sat in a bar watching events transpire. She drank heavily. She was a bit nauseated from what she had just learned was her new pregnancy. She hadn't had sex with Mark for over a month, so there was that problem. And given her alcohol and tobacco consumption lately, something she was not ready to curtail, she kind of thought this new baby might pop out with some serious problems, especially given the fact that she had no idea who or when she slept with a man. As a Catholic, she knew that she couldn't abort a living creature, even if it was conceived in sin and subject to her abuses.

"I may be carrying the next Messiah," she said to a guy next to her who barely peeled his eyes away from DUI. "It was an immaculate conception. Not that I'm a virgin. But still, God likes me. He likes me a lot! He's been really good to me. So, why not implant the next Messiah in me? Just saying."

Her phone rang, and she looked down. "Fuck," she said. It was Mr. X.

She looked again at the man near her. "Beep beep." She laughed. "That's what the Road Runner would say about now. Beep beep."

She swigged down the rest of her stout and pulled out a cigarette. It was nice and warm outside, quiet, peaceful. She lit her cigarette and picked up the phone. Sucking in the noxious smoke and enjoying every bit of it, even as she felt it smothering the Messiah within her womb, she listened to Mr. X's instructions. She said nothing in response.

Maybe it's Jim's baby, she wondered. Maybe they did it and she didn't even remember. That would be so very nice. Jim deserved a legacy. Right now, if Mr. X was to be believed, his fate even after death was not going to be a pretty one. But a little baby, little JD, how wonderful would that be!

She took one last puff and then prepared to walk home. A car nearly ran into her, and she stopped it with her hand as an irate driver shouted inaudibly through his closed windows.

She glared at the driver and smiled. "Beep beep," she said. Then she laughed and darted away.

CHAPTER THIRTY

The Vacuum

See-ya Russian had the tap dancer in stitches.

"Wait," he said, barely able to contain himself. "Did I hear you right? You just said that not only were you going to be president of the United States but also president of Russia because you can see it from your window? And of China because there's a Chinese restaurant in your little real-American town? Vice President See-ya, I know you have a history of being bombastic, but are you serious?"

See-ya Russian, wearing her hair in a ponytail that lay upon a tight-fitting laced purple blouse, winked at the camera. "Gotcha, tap-boy, and gotcha, American people. Nah, I'm not going to do that president gig, not now and not ever. I'm a VP kind of gal. And don't worry, America, I'm not taking over the world. China is our good friend now, and Russia, they're busy gobbling up little countries. You know that Pukes-gin guy, he's a very hungry dictator, but as long as he leaves us and ours alone, well, America, all's swell; you can count on that. I can smell the swell, tap dancer; we licked the COVID bug, we got our democracy in order, peace is everywhere. If things get much better, y'all won't have much to talk about on DUI."

Of course, there was always something to talk about, as long as it fit into the abridged national narrative given to DUI and all news networks as an absolute dictate by the new national leaders. *Cease and desist from any and all COVID coverage; as far as we're concerned, it's a dead bug, and if you don't talk about it, that ends it as an issue. And keep Putin's wars out of the news; we gave that jackass a few nations to swallow as his price for consenting to Sweden and a few other little endeavors we are hatching. It's a global world now, we're working together for the benefit of humanity, and the news has to be a partner in our path forward. If you don't cover it, it doesn't exist, and if you drape your coverage with it, then it's a catastrophe. We'll tell you when each of those scenarios applies.* The new national executive committee met with DUI regularly. They had an understanding, and it benefited both parties.

So, just like that, COVID disappeared. And Russia's war remained invisible to all but the nations he gobbled and the people he slaughtered. Besides, with the shocking revelations about Jim Depich's unwoke blasphemies preceding his untidy suicide, and with student revolts everywhere, DUI had enough to cover; breaking news was what they said it was, and there was lots of it! Still, the tap dancer did have another question for the vice president, one likely on every American's mind.

"Then, Vice President Russian, who is in charge of America?"

See-ya winked at the tap dancer, because she knew that he knew. Still, in as terse a way as her lips could muster, she peered into the camera and said, "You know what, DUI and my fellow Americans, does that really matter? Did any one person ever lead this country? I mean, right from the founding with Lincoln and Washington and those fine American apricots who created this amazing nation of ours, a nation that shines from sea to sea right up to my great state of Alaska, well, tap dancer, it was never one person who put the whole jigsaw puzzle together. Didn't Washington have experts running the show from day one, guys like Hamilton who took his shot? And the Jeffersons and Maude, aren't they who got us through COVID, all those heroic doctors who told us to mask up and stay apart and shut down? Now look, America, look at us now. We're all alive, and we're safe, not because of one misled president who had to leap out of a window but because we are a nation led by experts. Do we need one man to rule our nation? Or, are we a nation led by smart folks who got advanced degrees at top-notched colleges, and that got our backs and who will lead us into the next millennium? God and Jesus be witness to our greatness. And I'll say this too, to you, tap dancer, and to you, the American people. Me, See-ya Russian, I got your backs too, and I'm here in the VP chair keeping an eye on America telling all of ya that I love ya, I love ya all!"

That was See-ya Russian being terse.

A committee of ten gathered in the White House following Jim's death, and they declared a temporary suspension of democratic niceties until the affairs of state could be put back in order. "As a requisite to preserve our democracy and to stabilize the nation, we the people have assembled the most brilliant minds who are trusted by the American public, and in the most apolitical and scientific way possible— relying on American values and faith and our position of leadership in the world—we have authorized this committee of experts to right the ship of state so that this great democracy can push forward into a new exciting epoch," declared Mr. X, who sat with Rachel in the Meadow as the committee's spokesperson.

"We'll continue to push for social justice and for individual liberty, I assure you, Rachel, but too we are a nation of values, and we must be cognizant of that—a nation of industry but also of progressive egalitarianism, of science and also of faith. It's time we realize that faith and science, democracy and capitalism, strong leadership and voting rights, these ideals are not at war with each other as many self-serving politicians with an agenda have tried to tell us, but that when put together, they make us who we are. Our experts who are now steering this ship of state, I guarantee you, all you Americans who have trusted experts and who will continue to trust experts, you will be impressed by the speed and alacrity with which we turn this country around. That is democracy, Rachel; it is the government working for the people."

The committee of experts—holding absolute power over the nation and its people—was led by Commerce Secretary Gated Billionaire and included Party Cruise, Graham Cracker, and Newbie-hottie from the political realm. Also on the committee were the director of Pfizer, Boola-boola; the chief executive officer and chairman of

ExxonMobil, The-Second-Darren; the president of Harvard, Lard-full-of Bullshit; the chairman of the joint chiefs of Staff, Make-me Milky; the NFL commissioner, Really Good-guy; and Got-milk representing the medical industry. Cheddar would be their propogandist and foreign policy liaison, while Rachel in the Meadow and Mr. X shared spokes-person duties.

Until new elections were held and the nation was deemed safe, the committee and its many underlings—mostly from the business, medical, and military industry—would run the nation's affairs. There were a plethora of liberals and conservatives, of scientists and people of faith, of Wall Street executives and social reformers, who sat beneath the committee leaders and helped to advise them.

"My former bosses are now at my mercy," Cheddar said one day laughing with Got-milk. "And so are all of you overeducated guys. If you ask me, I'm the one calling the shots, and it's about time."

No one, not Got-milk, not the Gated Billionaire, not the chairman of DUI, would dare to disagree. She spoke to the press daily and, with a big smile and gentle demeanor, assured the nation that everything was OK.

Mostly, though, through her propaganda campaign, she insisted that all the committee members soften their messaging and appeal to those who might feel that they are being left out.

"We have to use words wisely," she said. "No one need be offended; everyone has to think we're talking directly to them and their priorities."

The-second Darren perhaps set the tone on day one when he boldly addressed a group of students at MD Park Campus protesting his own company's reactionary role: "With the knowledge, expertise, and experience of those of us on the committee, my company and its many subsidiaries has promised to swing our nation carefully and economically soundly toward being a sustainable green energy leader. We are working with China on solar technology and on building an infrastructure for electric self-driving vehicles. We are assuring that no jobs are lost in the process and that states that rely on fossil fuels flourish from the transition, and we promise that we will clean up our nation just as much from the pollution of manipulative discourse that divides us as from the pollution of smog and unclean water, and we'll do it because we should and we can. We'll do it in conjunction with our global friends, and we'll share it with the world. That's where we are moving. We are moving ahead."

Mary Lou and the student protestors did not know how to respond. Prepared to boo this new "expert" who held a prominent position in government, they merely mumbled after his talk and then scattered, still wearing their COVID-protective space suits even though no one in the media or the scientific community acknowledged the existence of COVID since Jim's death. Even Zeus simply disappeared into the clouds of a new reality.

Almost all the leaders of the new expert committee sang the same upbeat tune, and whether on Foxxy or Makes-sense NBC,. The approval rating of the transitional government catapulted to 89 percent within a month of its ascension, and few people demanded elections or a return to the democracy with which they had all been familiar, a democracy, in the words of a trucker interviewed by the tap dancer on DUI, "that ain't worth the manure it's been towing." In fact, no one even knew what Congress was doing or if the Supreme Court had reconvened; none of the major news outlets mentioned such petty details, and thus these minor thingswere not on the collective American mind.

"We seek stability, security, sanctity, and prosperity," the Gated Billionaire said to the tap dancer as he sat in a sweater vest smiling broadly. "I wish I could come up with a fourth *S*, but we need prosperity, we insist on it in fact, prosperity for each and every American and each and every citizen of the world, and I believe that the group we have assembled will be best positioned to assure that all Americans prosper in the new order. We are all pro-democracy, all pro-science, all pro-decency and integrity. We want to clean up the mess that's been created by those with less integrity. We're working with nations like China to assure that an international world order is established, an order that all Americans have wanted for so long and in which we will be the leaders—one that transcends politics; one that employs technology and the power of our collective brain power to launch us into a new era; one without war and without international bickering;

one where experts lead us, not politicians, not those who seek to advance themselves at the expense of others, not people whose bodies are smudged with corruption and who scoff at American values, not people who talk with a bunch of gas instead of true knowledge and wisdom. We've had enough of that, my fellow Americans. What we're looking at is an international democracy of experts."

A democracy of experts. It remained a democracy in that there would still be elections every two years, for local officials, for figureheads on the national level, for a congress that had been stripped of its powers. From now on, as the tap dancer well knew, and as Corrine was now learning, the committee of ten ruled the land.

Corrine fidgeted with a paper clip. She desperately wanted to smoke but was told that she could not. Her belly protruded a bit from the growing fetus within her, and that only gave her an urge to light up.

"You don't know who the dad is?" Mr. X asked her. "And you don't care?"

"I was drunk." She laughed. "I'm sure you've fucked someone when you're drunk and didn't know who it was! Give me a break."

Mr. X smiled. "And now you want to drink and smoke and smother a baby you don't want?"

"Damned straight, mister," she snarled. She had been drinking quite heavily before being summoned to the White House to meet again with Mr. X. "You got a problem with that?"

"If you don't want the baby, then why not just get an abortion?" Mr. X asked her.

"Are you fucking crazy?" She laughed, waving her hands at him. "I'm Catholic! I can't do that!"

Mr. X smiled. "I'll be honest, Corrine, you people certainly have a strangely hypocritical sense of morality. It's OK to kill the baby and maim it, but God forbid you actually remove it. I'm so glad that kind of thinking is being swept away. Anyway, I'm sure you're wondering why I called you here."

"Like duh," she said to him. "I don't even know who the fuck you are or where the fuck here is. I'm just guessing that you plan to kill me and then kill my family and then bury me near Jim and make me into a corpse or something like that so you can stomp on me and tell everyone that I destroyed the world and that's why you have to be in charge. But I'm most pissed that you won't let me smoke. That's not hypocritical morality? You say you're like a good guy, and that you're all for choice, free choice for all you keep yelling, but you won't let me smoke? I mean, come on!"

"Yea, well, maybe when you're sober, Corrine, I can explain it a bit better, but rest assured, I'm not going to hurt you," Mr. X said, telling a wobbly Corrine to sit down. "I'm just one of many arms of the new committee that will be helping steer our country down a better road, a road without quite as many potholes as your last boss paved for us. Look, I liked Jim. He was a passionate man, someone who really thought he was doing good. In fact, he accomplished just what we hoped he would."

"What doyou mean by that?" Corrine spit out. "You clapped when he died! You demonized him!"

"No, Corrine, we don't disparage Jim and what he did, but we have to look forward. Just like it's unfortunate that we plan to make the science tiger into a hero, we're obligated to turn Jim into a demon," he said. "But it's not because we like Fact-nerd and don't like Jim. Both of them played their rolls well even if they weren't aware that they were actors on a stage; both helped to spread a gospel necessary to move our nation and the world to the next step. It's just that while the tiger died a hero— an expert who led our nation through a war—your Jim became just a bit unhinged. Anyway, there always has to be a fall guy, even if it's not always fair. You of all people should understand that. Your committee was not exactly bereft of culpability on that score!"

"And what, sir, if I must ask, since you are so all-knowing and so decent and good," Corrine grumbled, "what exactly is the gospel that Jim and Fact-nerd spread that you love so much?"

"Corrine, now don't play with me, you know." Mr. X laughed. "They reached into the old playbook, using the specter of fear and the reduction of humanity into binary camps of right and wrong, good and evil, truth and untruth to convince Americans and indeed all the world that there was but a single path to righteousness. Fear is the great equalizer, Corrine, and Jim Depich, he played with fear like the ancient Neanderthals played with fire. He spread it, he cultivated it, and he created an entire infrastructure of power upon its fumes. And because of all that he did, well, Corrine, it opened the door for Americans to embrace us, because Americans prefer self-declared experts like us over politicians like him. That's why we have to extoll experts like the science tiger—as much as he was one of the great morons of history— and take down politicians like Jim. Jim did have a heart, but the deeper he fell into the cracks of his binary cave, the more that his spreadsheets reflected a singular truth in which all nuance evaporated— you can't put shades of gradation and common sense into a spreadsheet, as we all saw—the more people were willing to trade their rights for their lives, trade justice for scientific certitude, trade their souls for their faith, embrace ritual and shame doubters. And so did Jim help pave the way for us, for a nation of experts to guide Americans through an incessant terrain of landmines fueled by clouds of fear that will be cultivated and broadcasted by our self-selected news stations, clouds of fear doused by heroes who promise always to put out the flames before they burn us all down. For that gospel, we all thank Jim."

"Oh good, I'm so glad he helped you," Corrine smirked. "So, why not kill me too? Or at least demonize me and hang me from the Capitol?"

"Corrine, there's going to be no more of that." Mr. X smiled. "No more violence of the sort Jim cultivated, no public displays of punitive justice. We're far more civilized than that, and for us to succeed, well, Corrine, we must oppose all of what Jim did and resort to more obtuse control, control that plays well on TV and that is embraced by your well-meaning students and also well-meaning conservatives. To do that, we must always be able to conjure fear, and we must use that fear to steer people along a path that benefits us and them. We define reality, Corrine; what we tell Americans is what they know and believe, and what we don't tell them is of no concern to them. The media is our trumpet of truth. But right now, people are happy with stability, with experts, and with a diminution of violence. Jim went so far one way that we are now able to garner our power going the other; we can douse the fear a bit and promise sunshine, at least until we can't. Then we can pull another dose of terror out of our hats. There's always misery, war, and disease in the world, Corrine, but if COVID showed us anything it's that we can frame the narrative to make the normal seem extraordinary, and upon that pedestal does our power rest. Even the kids love us!"

"Oh yea, I'm sure they do!" she said. "They are protesting all over the country, the kids are, and they're not saying such nice things about the new committee, especially since none of them are on it."

"Well, yes, your student leaders are a bit of a thorn in our side, and I agree, Corrine, it's not because they don't appreciate us; it's because they're not part of our leadership," he said. "Every millennial loves our chips and our promises of a better world, our platitudes of caring about gender and the environment, and our anti-Trump messaging. Simply saying something to this generation is quite enough, assemble some experts, denounce opposing ideas; no need to actually do anything. But, Corrine, while we seek to exert control over people in a way that appeals to their cognitive needs, there are times we have to be a bit more direct in our retribution."

He stared at Corrine, who looked back at him, until she finally said, "What? You want to fuck me? You want to kill me? Why are you staring at me, Mr. X Marks the Spot?"

He laughed. "You are quite a character, that's why we love you so much. Here's the deal, Corrine. You've been a loyal lieutenant to your boss, and to us, that kind of unfettered devotion means a lot. That's why we have people like Party Cruise and Graham Cracker on our committee; not for their brains or their character but for their loyalty and their willingness to be sycophants in the name of self-interest. And that's where you come in. I'm offering you to be part of our little club, Corrine, to make sure you live a comfortable and prosperous life, to become relevant in the future. But you have to prove your loyalty to us."

Corrine looked at this man, at the infamous Mr. X who now seemed to wield power beyond comprehension, at a reality that now swarmed around her and which could either slay her or be her salvation. She thought of Mark and the kids, she thought of her days with

Jim, the misgivings that she buried beneath deceptive spreadsheets and high levels of alcohol, and she wondered what this man wanted. Corrine believed in heaven and hell, and she certainly didn't want to end up in the latter. But as her intoxication slowly receded on this sunny day in Washington, she realized that either she must play the game or she and everything she held dear would simply be erased. Likely, she was already going to hell. She might as well stay here on earth a bit longer if that's the case. Besides, when the end came closer, she could always just confess her sins and be absolved of them. Sometimes it was nice being a Catholic!

So, she smiled at Mr. X. "OK, boss, what would you have me do?"

On a fine spring day, Mary Lou and the student Truth Clubs held a national protest across every campus and city in the country. They demanded a voice in government, and they insisted that COVID had not disappeared but was being concealed to deceive the nation; that the current right-wing cabal must be replaced; that a student-scripted agenda alone would pave a viable path forward for a nation in turmoil. They wore their space suits and gathered in mass. They intended to broadcast their concerns to the nation, to plea for a return to a democracy of righteousness and scientific justice led by them. They insisted that the country had veered from its correct course and sought to change the narrative.

Tellingly, not a single reporter or camera crew attended the rallies.

Corrine had sparked this protest, telling Mary Lou and her compatriots about a sinister plot being hatched by the new expert committee to eliminate them by releasing a deadly COVID variant at their next meeting. Somehow Mary Lou—as paranoid as ever—believed her, not asking the obvious question: *If a COVID strain is released that could kill all of us through the space suits, won't it also kill everyone in the country?* She gathered her troops, donned their space suits, and promised to ritualistically immolate a few chosen right-wing elements within their schools and towns before marching on Washington and taking down the government.

It was January 6th all over again, but this time the wind was blowing from the left.

"I have something that will protect you from the new variant," Corrine instructed Mary Lou. "It's been given to me in secrecy by those people still loyal to the science tiger." She handed a small canister to Mary Lou. "These devices if attached to your oxygen tanks will emit fumes to neutralize the new COVID strain. We will be sending thousands of boxes to your offices across the nation. Every student must attach one to his or her oxygen tank, or the results will be catastrophic."

Mary Lou glared at Corrine. "You said his or her tanks," she said. "I hope you are not becoming unwoke, Corrine. You didn't use the pronoun them, which you know is an admission of your being reactionary and unwoke. You are one of the last people we can trust."

"Them." Corrine smiled. "Of course, them. All of them."

Why Mary Lou cared about such gibberish as her stock plummeted Corrine never could tell. When she turned away from the student leader, she defecated into her pants. She found her way to a quiet corner and balled for a good half hour. And then she stood up and marched away, never to think about this moment or its aftermath again.

On January 6th, two years after the attack on the Capitol, an army of indignant passionate and monolithic students sought to impose truth on a nation that had been bamboozled by deception and reactionary forces. They would hold trials and then march to Washington prepared to overrun the government that, like those two years before them, they believed lacked the authority to exert control over Americans. Their actions were coordinated across every state and town. But most of them came to the nation's capital to carry out a definitive act of justice. They stood safely in their space suits, each with a canister to protect them from viral pushback that they knew was inevitable.

"On this day," Mary Lou announced in a tiny park outside of Washington, where tens of thousands of supporters gathered with her, "we tell the country that we are here to save them. We will be heard. We cannot be stopped. And in our united voices, we will wake the nation from its slumber!"

She gave the signal for all her followers to place the protective cannister inside their oxygen supply and to ignite it. Within five minutes, every student lay dead on the frigid ground of a quiet hamlet bereft of any other human presence. As if knowing what was going to transpire, army units rushed to the scene; the area was shut down to the public for two hours as—according to the local news—a toxic spill was neutralized. Across the nation, wherever student protests were occurring, the same outcome met the same response. Murmurs of something horrific sputtered from one mouth to another, but everything inserted on social media was instantly expunged, and no news outlet suggested that the murmurs harbored any credibility, all denying anything had transpired.

When it's not covered by the news, Mr. X had said, *then it never happened.*

The tap dancer laughed with See-ya Russian during his nightly broadcast. "Well, another January sixth passes us by Ms. Vice President, and other than some conspiracy theorists suggesting that protesting students were murdered as they sought to charge headfast into the Capitol, it's a quiet day here."

The vice president smiled through her lipstick-smudged smirk. "Quiet as a sleeping grizzly, America," she said. "Ain't it grand! Heck, I don't mind fake news by people who want to rile up the good people of America. Let them crazy folks get it out of their system by making stuff up and trying to scare us good folks, us real Americans, who just want to live our lives in peace and security under the guidance of experts. I'll tell you, tap dancer, this gal is happy to be sitting on a chair of quiet solitude. January sixth is just another day to me, and I intend to call up Zrig and Zillow and Zack and the others and let them know how much I love them and how much I love America."

"We seemed to have turned a corner, haven't we, Ms. Vice President?" the tap dancer asked her. "After so much death and chaos, it does feel good to have a quiet January sixth pass us by."

Corrine watched one of Jim's favorite episodes of Bugs Bunny. In this one, a crazy fuzzy monster attacks Bugs, and to quell the monster, the wiley rabbit pretends to be a beautician and to give the creature a makeover. He sits unafraid, manicuring the monster's nails, fixing its hair, and making it happy. Just like that, the monster is no longer a threat. "If an interesting monster can't have an interesting hairdo, I don't know what this world is coming to," Bugs says. "My, I bet you monsters lead interesting lives. I said to my girlfriend just the other day, 'Gee, I'll bet monsters are interesting.' The places you must go and the places you must see, my stars! And I'll bet you meet a lot of interesting people, too."

Corrine laughed. "Well," she said to herself, "if twenty thousand dead students can be swept away so that their deaths never occurred, and tap dancer and See-ya Russian can joke about serenity, then we are in a new and interesting world, that's for sure. Like Mr. X says, power is all about pretense, all about who we tell the world we are. Yes, monsters do lead interesting lives."

She meandered home through the quiet streets of DC. Mr. X called her later to thank her, but already Corrine understood the wisdom of what transpired today. Parents would grieve, some would ask questions, but the nation would move forward toward the stability it so craved. Her baby kicked her from inside, and she laughed. She didn't stop at a bar, didn't reach for a cigarette, didn't even wallow in the pits of guilt and remorse that her action should have engendered. She thought about watching Bugs Bunny with Jim and remembered *What's Opera, Doc?*, where Bugs got the best of Elmer Fudd again, as was often the case, this time to the tunes of Wagner. At the end of the episode, Bugs said:

"Well, what did you expect in an opera? A happy ending?"

Tragedy hovered around every corner; such was the fodder of humanity. But now Corrine had been given a chance to rewrite her script and maybe even find a happy ending. Life didn't have to be an opera, and she didn't have to be Elmer Fudd. She would spend a lot of time with Mr. X in the upcoming years, but today she went home to Mark and the kids and hugged them all. Tomorrow was always uncertain, but today was cold and sunny and happy. That was good enough for her!

CONCLUSION

The Triumph of Bugs

It's Mask Day!
Smile under that Mask
The science tiger is Watching!
Beijing Institute of Fact-nerd Science

Two Truths

Corrine held her little boy's hand as they snaked through the streets of Beijing. The hustle-bustle of life hadn't slowed; honking cars and swarms of faceless souls rushing from here to there all remained as they had always been. Around every corner stood a statue of the science tiger, whose busts, words, and books littered earth, from New York to Tokyo to Kabul. Corrine's daughter proudly rushed home from school one day with her new *This is Science* book by the great Doctor Fact-nerd, and she told her mom that she wanted to be a great scientist and save the world just like the science tiger.

"You know," said Mark, "your mom knew Doctor Fact-nerd. The two were good friends."

This revelation hit Corrine's daughter like a bullet. Wide-eyed, she twisted to Corrine and said, "Really, Mom, you knew him, like knew him for real? Really? What was he like? Was he as great as everyone says? Was he so nice and smart and wise like they say? What do you remember most about him?"

This took Corrine by surprise, because she and Mark had largely erased those years and never spoke of them. She grasped her daughter and told her that Doctor Fact-nerd was a kind and smart man. And then she said something that now felt good and natural to her, even truthful. "His biggest lesson, Kara, is that science will give the one right answer, and once we find that answer, it's important that we all accept it and believe it, because it's the truth. Finding that answer is what scientists do. And there are so many answers to find, Kara, so much still to do. Do you want to be a scientist like Doctor Fact-nerd?"

She nodded vigorously up and down and hugged her mom tightly. In all of the ups and down of Corrine's life, all the self-doubt and purgatories through which she had traveled, nothing meant more than her daughter's hug.

All over the world, Tiger science became gospel, ritualistic rubbing of his statue became the norm, his books graced everyone's coffee table and filled the coffers of every school. His message was clear, and it reflected the message of expert panels that now ruled most nations that were part of the International Confederation of Humanity, led itself by an expert panel. *Science is a singular truth that none must question but all must seek to expand.* If you followed that mantra, it was said, your life on earth would be happy and prosperous.

Corrine knew of some who refused to be compliant. Some who didn't rub a Fact-nerd statue when they passed it on the street, or who scoffed about one of his books or about something an expert on DUI proclaimed, or who discussed forbidden misinformation from the past or present. None could escape the glace of the state, and all such deviants received appropriate discipline, never overtly or publicly and never in a way that drew attention to them. Often their bosses at work put them on probation, or their bank accounts dwindled, or Netflix disappeared from their TV. A few statue rubs and well-placed statements extolling the nation's experts usually led to redemption, although Corrine knew that—like Mary Lou and the truth squads— some people were erased when their behavior remained aberrant. And thus were police forces reduced, jails emptied, and wars eliminated. America experienced no gun violence despite liberalizing gun laws, and even Foxxy and DUI typically carried the same perspective on every story. When someone did something very exceptional, when their behavior warranted praise, they were publicly acknowledged, and often they noticed more money in their banks and a subscription to Showtime on their TV. The world became just and peaceful. The eyes of experts lingered everywhere. From every bust of the science tiger, the seer watched over Earth like a benign prophet.

Corrine's chip had alerted her of a new fusion restaurant downtown Beijing, not more than a ten-minute walk from the laboratory she was visiting today. Mr. X sent the message personally, although often messages were automated. Her chip did everything for her. It contained every ID and monetary exchange she ever needed, it granted her access to her computer and TV, and it followed her with the watchful eyes of others. That is why, as she held her small boy's hands, she had to be careful.

But she needed to do this thing. Despite the risk it engendered, in her heart, she needed to know.

She bumped into someone as she crossed the street, and the two glared at each other, if only briefly. The man held a cigarette and reeked of smoke. She nodded her head disparagingly and muttered, "So disgusting," to which the man seemed to cower. Corrine hated smokers, thought they were barbarians, were as anti-life and anti-science as anyone on the planet. Her own days of smoking faded into an amnesic oblivion as though they never occurred. One day she was flipping through old pictures on her phone when she saw one of her sitting at a bar, a cigarette butt hanging from her lips, her eyes tired and baggy, and she didn't recognize the person she had been. She quickly erased it, and with its disappearance, so too did she erase that moment in time forever.

Today everyone wore masks, so even the smoker could barely take enough drags to make his habit enjoyable. Removing one's mask for more than a few seconds could trigger retribution, and everyone knew that. Mask Days occurred twice a month simultaneously across the globe. Donning masks on those days helped maintain vigilance and compliance to science, as the doctor experts informed people, and should another pandemic occur—as happened from time to time—people would be ready for it.

One viral outbreak several years ago popped up in Egypt and spread quickly, preying on children and pregnant women.

Immediately society shutdown and masks became mandatory everywhere. The international expert committee of doctors met with pharmaceutical companies and, within weeks, designed a vaccine and treatment that they sold to all nations and mandated its immediate use. And so did humanity eradicate the threat, and all the world's people breathed a sigh of relief, so happy to be living in a civilization that focused on the preservation of life, so happy to be living in a world run by experts.

Few people resisted Mask Day, because its enforcement was deemed necessary and scientific. If someone dared to scoff at it, or in any way disparage the mask's lifesaving truth, then discipline greeted that poor soul, as did glaring eyes upon every street.

"These vaccines, including the first ones for COVID, they did cause a lot of trouble," Mr. X said to Corrine one warm day in DC at a café in Adams Morgan. "Lung inflammation, myocarditis, auto-immune syndromes, even brain dysfunction; especially in young vaccine recipients, lots of horrific side effects really did happen on a massive scale. And the funny thing is, kids didn't need the vaccine, and so all the doctors who insisted on mandating them, well, those doctors should have lost their licenses had they followed the old Hippocratic script. But thankfully, doctors are very malleable and are the best army we have to keep people in line. Their modus operandi is to scare people and then to pretend to fix them; I've never met a less critically thinking and dogmatic group of people in my lives, and thank God for them, because all through history, they've helped people in power keep everyone else submissive under the missive of science and necessity. And the vaccine too, it's a great way to keep people in line, especially with all the side effects."

Corrine looked at him, not knowing what to say. "The vaccine saved so many lives," she finally muttered, sipping her mint tea. "If a few people had trouble, it was worth it. And how would side effects keep people in line?"

"Yes, Corrine, you are touting the company message, the ones our nation's doctors sold," he said. "But there were side effects, as much as we labeled such a fact as misinformation, and those side effects proved to be just as profitable as the disease the vaccines were targeting. Soon enough, Merck and Pfizer and all our other great companies were selling cures for the side effects of their vaccines, and their heroic status grew all the more. The more harm we cause, the more frightened are the world's citizens, and the more they rely on doctors and companies to fix them. Such a cycle of fear and fixing molds the earth's people into the putty that we need them to be if we are to keep this world safe and compliant. Nothing keeps people on our leash more than a fear of death and a faith in our ability to save them, even if we caused them to be sick in the first place. That's the kind of irony I love."

Corrine smiled and said nothing. Thankfully, at least for now, Mr. X and his minions couldn't tap into her thoughts, because if they could, she likely would be erased like so many others on the planet.

Today she, with little Jim in tow, were meeting with a group of scientists at the bequest of Mr. X, scientists who were working on CRISPR projects authorized by the international expert committee on benign evolution and human betterment. CRISPR was a gene-editing tool created by researchers at Berkeley and Harvard many years earlier, and which now offered the ability to alter the human genome in a manner that the committee of experts deemed to be useful for the future of humankind. Corrine, as a scientist familiar with the technology, was the point person between several international scientists, and from time to time, she liked to meet them in person, if only to travel and bring one of her kids on a trip to exotic nations like China.

One scientist, Han Wo, promised to help her with a more personal project that was both secret and likely forbidden. The two of them spoke about it using code, and Han was so brilliant and discrete that Corrine knew he could accomplish this small deed without anyone else knowing. That's why she brought her little boy Jim with her to China on this junket. He was the boy conceived immaculately, the one she had tried to smother with smoke and alcohol, but the one who popped out happy and healthy, a boy who proved to be an utter blessing. And in her back pocket, she carried a hair from her other Jim's goatee, one she had found in his documents that she periodically scrolled through in a closet of her basement, one in which both internet and human glances were blinded by thick walls and darkness.

Han greeted her with a hug and with bright eyes; if he smiled, which he always did, it was concealed behind his double masks. He rubbed little Jim's head, and she noticed that he pulled a small hair from the boy's scalp, causing Jim to wince for a brief second. They were not allowed to shake hands, not on a Mask Day, but Corrine handed Han a test tube of RNA she had brought from the NIH, and on it was her former boss's hair, hidden from all but the two of them.

"It's fascinating what we are doing," Han said to her, his words muffled by the mask. He spoke Cantonese, one of several languages Corrine had mastered, and which made her so valuable to the international committee of experts, since most of the committee's Chinese scientists did not like to demean themselves by speaking English. "Enhancing the mind, eliminating distractions and mental illness, helping humans think clearly—all is now in the realm of possibilities with gene editing! How very exciting! I will eagerly look at what you have brought. Will you be back after I do? You can have some lunch; it shouldn't take but two hours."

"Of course." Corrine smiled, her eyes wide and inviting. She found Han to be very handsome, even beneath his mask, and enjoyed his company. Sometimes the two of them did more than just speak. While the committee stressed family values and fidelity, these were not enforced, at least among those within the committee. In this realm, Corrine had a free hand, which she used often.

After Jim's birth, Corrine and Mark went through a rough spot in their relationship. Her husband knew that the two of them had not been intimate for a while, and he wondered—as did she—who the father of their child was. Corrine imagined that in her drunken state, she might have been with one of many scumbags who could have spit their gross sperm into her womb. But her baby was both brilliant and beautiful, and she continued to insist it was Mark's, telling him that they did have sex one night when he had been drinking a bit and likely forgot it.

"I'm not that memorable," she joked with him. "Not exactly a beauty queen. You were watching TV when we did it and had a few too many beers. You weren't into it."

"I just have no recollection of that at all," he insisted.

Thankfully, the certitude of science proved her right. Mr. X arranged genetic testing of young Jim. The labs reported to Corrine and Mark that there's a 100 percent probability of Mark being the father.

"See." Corrine laughed. "We don't have to go on Maury Povich now!"

But she had doubts, despite the science buttressing the truth of Mark's paternity. Corrine lived through the absolutism of science, she watched how easily it could be manipulated toward a desired end, and she knew that Mr. X wanted Mark to be the father.

"Part of our accommodation to the right wing," he told Corrine, "is to promote the stability of traditional families. You as a liberal who opposes abortion and has a heterosexual monogamous marriage, that's very important to us. You're somehow trusted by both liberals and conservatives. We don't want anything to sully your image."

"I guess the days of trans bathrooms are over then?" Corrine laughed. "No one is woke now?"

Mr. X simply nodded. "We are respectful of personal choice," he said. "We promote values but tolerate individual decisions. That's what the right wing wanted during COVID. Mask choice, vaccine choice. They're willing to tolerate choice as long as our underlying message resonates with them."

And thus did Mr. X assure that Mark was young Jim's dad.

But Corrine didn't buy it, and somehow, she managed to get the message out to Han, who happened to mention that her young boy looked a lot like the past president, like JD. Few people remembered anything about President Jim Depich; Mr. X and his squad of experts largely erased him from history, something Corrine appreciated, since the alternative—demonization—would have been far worse. To most people, President Buck was the last president until his vice president resigned, and he was removed from office due to dementia, leading to a constitutional crisis resolved by the appointment of the committee of experts. That Han remembered Jim and saw a resemblance between him and Corrine's son led to a series of gestures and innuendos that triggered today's actions.

Corrine loved her former boss. She sometimes dreamed of him at night and did everything she could to get close to him, to touch him, to stare into his eyes. His passion propelled her energy, and she never forgot his resolve and goodness, even during those last dark days. She so resented his infatuation with Kate, often crying at night about why he didn't perceive Corrine in the same sensual way. She didn't want a relationship with Jim, and likely would have said no to an affair, but deep down, Corrine truly loved him. Why then wasn't she ever good enough?

Maybe, just maybe, she thought, during one of those last drunken days, maybe he felt the same, and maybe he and she disappeared into a dark room and consummated a friendship and a love that neither of them would verbally acknowledge. She didn't recall such a thing except for one very vivid dream, during which she woke up in a sweat having masturbated on drenched sheets.

Corrine enjoyed the food at this restaurant that Mr. X suggested for her, but mostly she picked at her dumplings and fed Jim some of the cut-up chunks of pork and pasta. Time ticked by slowly.

When two hours passed, she pushed through the crowded streets and found Han waiting for her. He hid behind his mask and kept distance, but Corrine perceived he was smiling. Then, before telling her to come in to discuss the sample of RNA she brought him, he said:

"It's a perfect match, hair to hair, a perfect match."

Corrine smiled so deep and broadly that her mask almost slipped off. A river of tears tricked down her cheek. She took a few deep breaths and then escorted her son—Jim Depich's only son—into the lab.

Truth, she knew, was malleable, and happiness meant nothing more than how others defined it. In the era of experts, saving lives and maintaining manufactured serenity constituted truth and happiness both. Life preservation, even if scripted and false, wasn't too bad, especially when she partied with the guys who ran the show, and especially if they liked her and valued her life.

But today, a second truth tickled her senses and provided her with a certain happiness that transcended the norms of society's dictates. She walked with broad steps and a deep smile. She held her son's hand gently and dreamed about the past and the future, about life in the fullest sense she could ever know, about her own truth and how happy it made her today. Really, in the end, nothing else mattered but that.